TWO KINDS OF

It was in February that they found the house;
May by the time they got a mortgage, for the
area was denoted 'grey' and due for redevelopment as a council estate one day; and
early June when they moved in. The gas and
electricity men came and flatly refused to
re-connect, on grounds of safety. The building
society laughed at the request for a further
loan: it had had doubts about allowing ten
years on such a property in the first place.
Peter gave up the job at the tax office that he
had endured since meeting Rose, and went to
work nights at the frozen pea factory. Rose,
fresh from final exams at teacher-training
college and her long study on The Importance
of Place in the English Novel (in twelve
thousand words), insisted on doing the same.
'You don't have to,' he told her. This was
before women were fully liberated. 'I don't
want you doing that sort of work.'

'We're in this together,' Rose replied ardently.
'And, otherwise, how could we afford the
rewiring?

About the Author

Jean Dove grew up in the Peak District and now lives in Leeds, after five years in London and ten in a Gloucestershire village. She was a professional actress and later taught English and Drama in a comprehensive school, having begun training once her children, a daughter and a son, were at school. She took a Master's degree while working full-time, and after that returned to writing.

She loves walking, reading, music, acting occasionally with a University group, gardening, cooking for friends, draught bitter, cricket, Rugby League, and water-colours of the English landscape.

Two Kinds of Summer

Jean Dove

NEW ENGLISH LIBRARY
Hodder and Stoughton

First published in Great Britain in 1988 by New English Library hardbacks

First New English Library paperback edition 1989

British Library C.I.P.

Dove, Jean
    Two Kinds of summer.
    I. Title
    823'.914 [F]

    ISBN 0-450-50811-0

Printed and bound in Great Britain for Hodder and Stoughton paperbacks, a division of Hodder and Stoughton Ltd., Mill Road, Dunton Green, Sevenoaks, Kent TN13 2YA (Editorial Office: 47 Bedford Square, London WC1B 3DP) by Cox & Wyman Ltd., Reading.

Contents

1963

Four floor terrace property, central position,
5/7 flats/bedsitters or convert to family home.
Work needed.
Price including furnishings £2500.

1984

4 fl. terr. prop., ideal fam. hse + granny flat.
Conservation area, close Univ. Immaculate
condition; hse of gt charm and character. Gas
CH, pleasant gdn, delightful views.
£52000 o.n.o.

I

First Summer

1963–4

My dear Beth,

   . . . to hear from you at last, so what we really quite urgently need to know is, will you and Gerald be coming back? Because if Gerald isn't going to be running the farm Peter will feel he should be helping his mother and this is the absolute last thing he wants. I know you're in the middle of excitements and discoveries (not the only one!) but please find time to say about this.

   Is New York like the films? I can just picture you there, quite belonging – but is it for *real* life?

   We're committed now, no going back now we've actually got the house. I'm sometimes scared, to be honest, wondering if we haven't taken on too much, but Peter is so sure – I never met anyone so clear about the future – that it is bound to be all right.

   To think that in six months everything has changed! I owe you and Gerald everything. If you hadn't run off together his brother would never have sought me out to find out about you! I hope you're as happy. It is a pity that Peter and Gerald don't seem close, especially compared with you and Ailsa and me, not proper sisters but always sharing . . .

They knew from the beginning that this was the place. Their aims for it were not, in fact, identical; but trusting in love and being very busy they were not conscious of differences.

There was much to be done, but they told everyone, 'There's no hurry. We don't mind roughing it for a bit. And we'd rather do up a place with a past than go into somewhere with no character.'

At first it was all their own. This was agreeable in that they could make love wherever and whenever they felt like it, and the summer warmth freed them to delight. But there was an awful lot of house left over outside their small encampment, and many sounds in the night. Though they were well pleased with each other, it was not a house for two. No: it was to be a base for like-minded friends to come for shelter, companionship, talk of a better world; a centre of ease and excitement – very different, they determined, from their own homes.

Ease was, just now, a long way off. It so happened that while the project had been enthusiastically supported by the like-minded friends, none was available to help with the work. Peter was disappointed and privately deeply hurt, for he staked everything on the notion of shared commitment. How else was anything fundamental to be changed? Rose was secretly not altogether sorry, because she wanted it to be truly theirs, to owe no obligations. It would be safer, she considered, for the others to come as guests rather than partners. The ideal of sharing was one thing, abandonment of proprietorial rights quite another. After all, it was they who had undertaken the mortgage.

Also, there was much to talk about. But Peter was odd – perhaps men were – in not having much to say about his family. It was Gerald that she was curious about. Her theory was that he, like Peter, had been overwhelmed by the compulsion to break away and, like Peter, would never want to return to his roots. It was, after all, up to the young ones to make life better, more free, to break the mould of custom and habit and stifling expectations. Peter dismissed him briskly and not without nervousness. 'He'll go back,' he said. 'Besides, it belongs to him, the farm. He's older than me.'

Acknowledging that he owed a lot to Sheila – 'Not my mother, remember' – he yet resisted totally the concept of obligation. 'Why should we be bound to follow patterns we never set up? We have our own lives to make, our way.'

Rose's mother, telephoned with the change of address, was sceptical. 'Sounds a bit of a slum to me,' she said. 'And why do you want to stay on in Leeds now you're qualified? Can't you find a job somewhere nice, like Harrogate? Still, no doubt you educated people know best. But to put your money into some old ruin . . .'

'It's a – a way of living differently,' Rose attempted.

She thought her father would understand, when it was fit to ask them to stay.

It was 1963 and all changes from now on were going to be for the better.

The house was one hundred and twenty-nine years old, and had been built at a time of quite similar hopes and certainties.

Trying again with her mother, Rose explained kindly, 'Things are different now. We don't want anywhere "nice".'

We want, well, freedom. Love . . . It's a different world.'
Parents were old, could not be expected to understand.

They would make their fortress against crippling narrowness; would let the sunshine in, tearing down the tattered net curtains of out-dated standards.

They thought of the house as a fortress. Indeed, when they first got the key they found the Sleeping Beauty garden virtually impenetrable with thorny tentacles sprawling across the hidden path to snare and defeat them, but Peter, who though slight was strong, pulled out a broken fence post and macheted a way to the door. 'My hero!' breathed Rose, giggling nervously; but they could not achieve entrance, the hall being choked by months of curling brown envelopes and, as it turned out, the fallen door from the front room. When, at a cost to sleeves and skin, they did get in, they found a darkness that might have been similar to that of a medieval castle, but the stench was distinctively twentieth-century, of gas leaks and stale frying. They nearly gave up – but not quite. They peered through dirty windows at trees in the bright day and children playing in the park, and turned back in.

There were twelve rooms, five gas cookers, none usable, four sinks, and a cram of greasy furniture. There was something nasty in the stained bath; and when they gave up the attempt to open the cellar door out to the back and went along the terrace and round to get at it, they found that an enterprising lead thief had removed the fall pipe from the lavatory.

They returned in silence to the front, took the long view, swallowed hard, called upon their vision, and said 'Yes.' It was a mess and a muddle, but it only needed clearing up.

It was in February that they found the house; May by the time they got a mortgage, for the area was denoted 'grey' and due for redevelopment as a council estate one day; and early June when they moved in. The gas and electricity men came and flatly refused to re-connect, on grounds of safety. The building society laughed at the request for a further loan: it had had doubts about allowing ten years on such a property in the first place. Peter gave up the job at the tax office that he had endured since meeting Rose, and went to work nights at the frozen pea factory. Rose, fresh from final exams at teacher-training college and her long study on The Importance

of Place in the English Novel (in twelve thousand words),
insisted on doing the same. 'You don't have to,' he told her.
This was before women were fully liberated. 'I don't want you
doing that sort of work.'

'We're in this together,' Rose replied ardently. 'And,
otherwise, how could we afford the rewiring? Besides, I'd be
frightened on my own there at nights.'

So for six weeks they crawled home in the clean early
mornings, slept leadenly till midday, battled with dirt and
debris all afternoon, and went back to the glaring factory at
night. They made one oasis, their bedroom, on the first floor
overlooking the park. They lifted the filthy layers of cracked
lino and scrubbed the smooth bumpy boards and laid a
many-coloured rug, set up their bed, their wedding present to
themselves, hauled in a massive wardrobe from another room
and washed and polished that and a capacious chest of
drawers, and Peter painted the ceiling purple while Rose
stripped wallpaper in the hall and dreamed of flowers. The
bathroom was made decent if not charming, and the adjoining small room ('Imagine – it must have been a dressing
room!') was equipped with a Primus stove and a washing-up
bowl; and gradually from top to bottom the other rooms were
cleared of rubbish and dirt. Half stupefied as they always
were, they were hardly aware of progress until the glorious
day came in August when they carted in large buckets of
white emulsion paint and made their first bright marks on the
place.

From that point on, it was theirs. The Salvation Army took
away two lorry-loads of rejected furniture, and the council
took one of rubbish. No time always to peel off old wallpaper;
whiteness flowed through room to room and perilously down
the high stairs and landings as Peter balanced, sweating, on
hired ladders while anxious Rose steadied the foot. Jumble
sales yielded up curtains, which sometimes fitted, and some
good pieces of furniture were reclaimed by dint of ammonia
and elbow-grease. Numerous bottles of Windolene came in
full and went out empty, and sunlight spread. A silent man
worked with reels of cable, gouging out brittle old wiring
and threading in new. The gas men came, shook their heads,
went, came and went, a decent second-hand cooker was
bought one Saturday afternoon, the men came again and

when they went this time, lo! there was gas! Peter changed to working days and Rose left the factory altogether to get on with the painting.

The electrician finished, leaving behind a sediment of plaster grit and a small miracle. Rose waited excitedly for Peter to come home. Taking him by the hand she led him to one of the new square switches. 'Look!'

All you had to do was press, and pretty pear-shaped globes instantly emitted golden brilliance. If you pressed again, it was gone. 'What will they think of next?'

They agreed to keep candles in the bedroom; for the trouble with scientific progess is that it shows up flaws. All that had looked so fresh in the benevolent sunshine, and even better in the softly flickering evenings, now glared imperfect. It was good, though, not to have to creep nervously to the bathroom through shadows. The night sounds faded, too. The night house opened up at the touch of a switch and became accessible, less threatening.

But as the size of the house diminished through familiarity, the extent of the undertaking could now be seen as enormous. White paint did not fill cracks or heal rotten window-frames, did not furnish empty rooms or carpet the flights and flights of stairs. The basement remained a lurking challenge. They camped out upstairs and told each other to bear in mind what had been achieved, not what still was raw.

Just as time was coming to seem more enemy than friend – for Rose was to start teaching in September and sometimes started awake in a sweat of apprehension – Jethro appeared, looking brown and haggard. Peter was delighted. Good old Jethro! Ah, student days seemed a long way off already.

'Can I help?' He meant, 'Can I stay?'

They gave him a mug of coffee and a paintbrush and Rose tucked an Indian spread over the least worst of the beds. He had no money until the fare for his first year's research in America came through, but they shared fish and chips later – by candle-light – and Rose and Peter found it salutary to listen to tales of adventure during a two-month hitch-hike across Europe to Greece, and to hear how simply dreadful England was, and most especially English food, compared with absolutely anywhere else. It was clear that they had become inward-looking that weary dusty summer. Insular. How refreshing it was to have a conversation! They were grateful to be redeemed from narrowness. And there was nothing quite as stimulating as indignation, as they rediscovered during an animated midnight discussion in favour of banning the bomb and supporting the US freedom marchers in their fight against injustice.

Then Peter had the floor to himself in propounding theories of the alienation of workers in industrial societies, reduced as they were to making cogs and being cogs in great incomprehensible machines. This was why he had packed in his MA studies. 'As soon as I met Rose I saw plainly what I had known for ages, really, that going on with history was a waste of time. There's so much to be done! And it has to start with the younger generation. That's why I'm going into teaching – no, *not* history! Kids don't need to know about the past, they need equipping for the future. We've had to drag the dead weight of the past behind us, but not the future generations. You're going to do it through computers, I'm going to do it through the hands. *Making* things, Jethro. Giving them the satisfaction of seeing a job through from beginning to end. Being in control. That's what they need. Not to be factory fodder: to be their own man.'

He and Jethro had been students together, but Jethro had done his MA. He was caught already in traditional academic paths but, kindly, they did not point this out to him.

As they lay together afterwards, hearing other feet trek noisily to the bathroom, they felt pleased that Jethro's coming had reminded them of the original plan. To share.

'It will never be the same, of course.' Rose was the merest touch wistful.

'No. But it couldn't go on like this, could it?'

'And when there are others in need . . .'

'That was the idea, after all.'

'Perhaps we were getting self-absorbed.'

'And another pair of hands . . .' Peter was glad to have another man around.

They made love quickly, a reaffirmation – but were aware, for the first time, that the bed squeaked.

Jethro's hands had little to recommend them except their number. Perhaps it had been unreasonable to expect manual dexterity from a first-class Maths graduate. When in a day he

had spilled a full can of gloss paint down the stairs, detached
the toilet-roll holder from the wall and broken a curtain rail,
Rose and Peter conferred hastily and sent him out to the
garden. They figured that nothing anyone could do there could
possibly be other than improvement. He was, after all, their
friend, despite the large cost in TCP and sticking plasters as
he came off worst in encounters with ramblers and broken
milk bottles.

What he had been doing in the largest room was never
plain, but when he knocked a step-ladder through hardboard
panelling and revealed a pretty cast-iron fireplace they
smiled. Peter saw the room as big enough for meetings in aid
of numerous causes. Rose envisaged a distant time when they
might just sit there, graciously.

On one of her rapid forays to the corner shop for Old
Holborn and Mars bars, she tripped over a heap of cases and
lumpy carrier bags surrounding a slim fair girl who was gazing
helplessly at the postcard advertisements in the window. It
was Ailsa. 'Rose!' The blue eyes filled with tears. 'Oh, Rose!'

She had parted once again from Sam. 'We had these quite
nice bed-sits,' (adjoining bed-sits were the nearest people got
to living together) 'and I thought it was all lovely, exams over
and everything, and all the lovely summer ahead of us, and
then . . . Oh, Rose. What am I to do?'

Sam was ambitious. Ambitious for money and success.
Ailsa was holding him back, he had said. He'd gone off to
doss down with some old friends in London – 'Make
contacts!' – when they had planned (she had planned) a quiet
few weeks of tender love and gentle excursions before work
loomed large. 'And I couldn't stay there on my own; the
landlord was, well, bothering me.' Ailsa was very beautiful,
which she found a handicap.

Rose picked up some of the luggage and took her home.

A rivalry developed between Ailsa and Jethro. They took
to following Rose or Peter about with complicated stories of
disappointments, begging for advice and not listening to it,
analysing minutely what it was about themselves that made
them natural victims when other people – 'Like you two!' –
were born winners, everything just falling into their laps. This
was all good practice for the lucky couple in their roles as
benefactors but they also got pretty fed up and one night took

their blistered hands and twingeing muscles out for a drink and an hour of peace. Peter was all for saying 'Pull your weight or go,' but Rose, who up till that moment had shared the same impulse, now found in herself a reservoir of womanly patience and understanding and said they shouldn't judge others by their own standards and should be understanding with those who were less able to make something of their lives.

'Wouldn't it be a relief if they'd just go to bed together and get it all out of their systems?'

But Ailsa thought of no one but Sam.

However, Jethro proved to be creative with spaghetti, and enjoyed nothing more than being sent out with a shopping list, and Ailsa wrote a moving letter to her parents describing the courage of Rose, whom her father had always thought to be very plucky considering her circumstances, and this resulted in a cheque for a new bed, sheets, curtains, and the installation of a telephone.

Rose wondered if these acquisitions, though marvellously useful, might be giving Ailsa too secure a stake in the household, but reflected that before long Sam would be back and Ailsa would go to him, so she decided to be glad about the telephone and not be mean.

Suddenly Rose had worries of her own. Unpacking boxes of clothes as the weather cooled, she saw that she possessed not a rag suitable for her new job. Nor was there anywhere to put the books and notes to which she would need daily access. How snug and convenient it had been in their tiny old flat, how easy to clean; how impossible it would be to manage this great place when she was tired out at weekends. How even more impossible to survive a single week of school! Her brain had atrophied, she had forgotten everything she ever knew; her hair would fall down and the children would laugh at her, she would never be able to keep on top of the marking and preparation, Jethro had overwound the alarm clock, Ailsa kept putting wet knickers on a string over the bath and Peter hadn't once, not *once*, asked her how she felt about the coming ordeal. They used to talk about everything and now he didn't care, he was so wrapped up in Polyfilla and hinges and floorboards that he didn't care about her any more; she was just the mortgage-ticket going out alone into a jeering world in that hideous old skirt without a decent pair of shoes to her name, while he was going to have a lovely time being a student yet again, making beautiful objects and reading inspiring books and writing exciting essays. And playing his guitar. Curious that Jethro hadn't managed to damage that, while even now her best saucepan sat blackly in the sink, burned beyond reclamation. She had *loved* that saucepan! It was all very well for some people who had the luxury of freedom, not to mention intellectual stimulation, whilst she was committed to this petrifying job at which she'd be completely useless and hadn't even a bit of kitchen table in some unwanted corner at which to do her preparation, let alone clean fingernails – and what was going to happen when it snowed?

Peter, astonished, let the last question hang in the air for a moment, then turned and went out of the room. He had stopped work at the factory so they could have her last week together. Rose shook, aghast, and gazed in terror at a broken marriage. She could see herself in respectable jersey and skirt and sensible shoes, coming back to an orderly spinster's flat in the evenings, with an adequate desk at which to work, and an empty bed.

Her first impulse was to run after him and beg forgiveness; her second to run after him and push him downstairs. In all this time they had been partners, and now on the one occasion, the *one* occasion, that she had sent out a cry for help, he had abandoned her.

His poster of Che Guevara beamed knowingly down at her, not the least scrap of help. Rose sobbed, reflecting on the arrogance of men, and pettishly ripped it down. It tore. She crumpled it to her on the bed, and her heart broke.

The house was utterly still. Ailsa and Jethro were out. Where was Peter? Had the gate squeaked? She crawled down the bed to look out. It was him, going down the street without a backward look, his old duffel bag over his shoulder. And oh, he looked so tired.

He had left her. It was all over.

Night came on early, the summer had gone. Sodium lights glowed sinister beyond the ragged privet. Across the park sparkled broken strings of traffic. The house began to give out its furtive sounds from the dark days. Rose huddled a blanket around her; winter seemed imminent. Where would he go? He'd get cold. Empty rooms were above and below, and lower still the basement lurked, not yet claimed. The plan of warmth and welcome had sunk to this uncompleted end. Time, that had seemed limitless and full of hope, had dwindled to failure. Orange light slanted waveringly through the street trees across the foot of the bed.

Then voices came startlingly loud, the gate protesting. Jethro and Ailsa with the bags of washing, and a familiar figure: not Peter. Rattle of the door, then a cheery knock. They had kept forgetting to have spare keys cut. Oh, go away! But they had been kind to offer to go to the launderette . . . Rose let down the rest of her hair as a rapid disguise and ran down without clicking on the magic light.

Such an accumulation of bags and bodies in the hall. 'We ran into Sam! He's home! – Something to celebrate eh? – I'll just slip back to get some glasses, we brought some cider – What's the matter, lights not working? (Click) – Oh, not feeling too good? – Shall I do a big spag bog? – Where's Peter? Haven't seen either of you for months, wait till I tell you about the Beeb – Didn't we tell you the house was huge? – I'm getting out of that crummy little bed-sit, don't know how we stood it there – Rose and Peter wouldn't mind, would you, Rose? Just for – Ah, best thing, to lie down, oh, poor Rose, I've got some aspirin in my – Ah. Well. Well, what if we go back to my dump? Bring the bottles – Sorry about the head, what if you and Peter, er . . . Ssssh – Well, great house, lots of potential – Oh, what about a key, then we shan't have to disturb . . . Tell Peter I'm back – Oh. Right. Hope you'll soon be – Yes.'

Awkward about-turns in the hall and doorway, tactful steps going away down the path. 'Must have been a real bust-up. Thought they were taking on too much . . . Sssssh . . .' Respectful slowed squeal of the gate; Rose alone. Put off the exposing light, creep back to the barren refuge of the bed, the shame of crumpled Che.

She thought. And Ailsa has Sam back again. And I bet Beth is so happy . . .

Much later, Rose came round from an uncomfortable doze to be aware that her period had started, and that quiet footsteps were coming up the stairs. Across the bare landing. To the door of the room. A pause. The door slowly opening; a man's figure in the dark, and she alone, without a protector.

All the stored remorse flooded out in anger at the fright he had given her. Pushing past him to go to the bathroom she felt cold coming off him, and beat him feebly with her fists until his arms went round her and she wept. 'I was so frightened.'

'I'm sorry.'

'And I'm sodden again.'

'Hurry up. Come to bed.'

Desperately clinging to each other, they slept like the dead.

By mid-afternoon Ailsa could stand it no longer. She tapped on the door and brought in mugs of tea, fearing dreadful discoveries. No worse damage was to be seen than the torn poster. 'They're still asleep,' she reported to Jethro. 'It's not like them. They're normally up early.'

He professed common sense. 'The house makes you fanciful. They're just tired out, that's all.' They thought of all the work, fourteen, sixteen hours a day, and of how little they had done to help.

Ailsa had a cheque from Daddy. 'We'll make them a dinner party.'

It was the closing of the front door that brought Rose to the surface, saturated in relief to wake with Peter, and leaking again. She tried to slide out of bed without waking Peter, but he clasped her back to him. 'I thought I'd lost you.'

'Just try. You'll have to get up, I must change the sheets.'

He looked at the stains of her blood. 'It makes me feel very married.'

They were light in heart all afternoon. It was too late to get going on the house, so Peter went to the launderette while Rose had a good sort-out. There was a skirt that really only needed the hem taking up, and a pair of shoes that were quite all right, given a good polish; they hurt only because she'd been wearing flip-flops all summer. In an upstairs room was a capacious table which, with a good scrub and polish and a wedge under one leg would do for her work; and if the books were laid out along the skirting board they'd be at least accessible.

Why on earth had she been worried about the snow?

She noticed montbretia by the garden wall and unpacked a vase for it, which led to the rediscovery of other neglected treasures: a chunk of iron pyrites, two terracotta pots, a heron made of horn, three black elephants, money boxes in the forms of a pink pig and a letter box; a brilliant wall-hanging she had made in her first year at college, and a sampler. The rubber plant had survived wicked neglect. She dusted it, and polished Peter's guitar. Where were their records? And the red and black blanket? They'd need that soon.

She sang.

A brisk knock came at the door. 'Mrs Stead? Washing machine for you.'

'But we haven't ordered a washing machine.'

'Bought and paid for. Reconditioned, do you a lifetime. Where do you want it — '

'This is number 194. There must be another Mrs Stead.'

'Mrs Stead, 194 Park Terrace. In the hall OK?'

Reverently she lifted the two little lids, one tub for washing, one for spinning. Oh, luxury!

Next came Ailsa and Jethro with carrier bags, and Peter balancing long planks. 'Bookshelves,' he panted. 'Got to get back before the drier runs out. Last time at the launderette!'

'You'll never guess who we met? He's gone to get some wine.' It was Merry, discovered at the Indian take-away. 'Sam's coming too. We popped in to tell him you're all right. Oh, it's horrid in that house, it smells.'

'He can come here! There's plenty of room.'

'Funny little chap, that Merry,' Jethro murmured. 'Friend of yours?'

'Oh, yes indeed. It was through him that Peter and I met.' He had introduced them at a folk evening. '*And* Gerald and Beth . . .' But that was another story, with too many complicated elements to explain to Jethro now.

'Mmm. Funny name, too.'

'His mother heard of this writer, George Meredith. She thought he'd have a better chance with a name like that.' She looked sharply at Jethro. If he thought he could patronise her friend, just because he was tall and Merry was small, or because he had a stake in the house . . . 'I love Merry. We owe a lot to him.'

'Oh sure, sure. No offence. Carries a bit of a torch for Ailsa, doesn't he?'

Jethro wasn't as dense as he seemed. 'You could say that.' The truth was that for years Merry had worshipped Ailsa, and suffered with a smile. 'It's a long story.'

It was lovely to see Merry, he made everyone feel good just by being there. If only Ailsa could have loved him back. It was Rose's opinion that she had made a very wrong choice in Sam; but Merry was so funny, too gentle; she hadn't taken his serious adoration seriously.

'We thought you'd emigrated! No one's seen you since exams!'

'You know how it is when fame and fortune beckon.' He had been working at a holiday camp as a children's entertainer. Ailsa was upstairs. 'How's the princess?'

'She and Sam are back together. He's coming round.'

'Is she well, is she happy?'

'I don't know, Merry.'

She seemed all right. A little subdued, perhaps, and at the same time feverish; but like Rose she was nervous about starting work – and with more reason, for despite the glow at Sam's return she looked more slender and delicate than ever.

'And how's the perpetual student?'

'Oh, I'm not doing MA,' said Peter, wrestling with a cork. 'They were dubious about my topic, anyway. It seems that the history of working people isn't academically respectable, so to hell with the ivory towers. There are more important things than the past, anyway. I'm going to work with kids, like Rose.' He talked with passion about injustice, waste, the insensitivity of politicians and the disgrace of 'You never had it so good' when so many were homeless. Peter believed in the perfectibility of mankind.

Sam and Jethro listened with some unease, being committed to The New because it would be more fun for them. Rose, who had reservations about which she did not speak, watched Peter's ardent face with adoration. They could do anything, together. He might even be right.

They brought down the table and used bits of Che as wedges, assembled chairs from here and there, lit candles and the gas fire, and cracked poppadums luxuriously. It was all happening, the comradeship and warmth and the stimulating talk. From here, there would be action to make a better world.

The toast was 'The House'.

'Merry,' Rose begged, when Peter had gone to the loo, 'tell us about Gerald, who Beth ran away with.'

'Yes, do.' Ailsa and Beth and Rose had grown up together.

'It was pretty dramatic.'

'Beth always was.' Ailsa had been in awe of her; rather afraid.

'It'll be a pity if she doesn't sing any more. She had something.'

'Yes, yes.' They knew that. 'But what about Gerald?'

'That was what was so strange. He didn't look as if he belonged in a folk club, so . . . All old tweed and leather patches, cavalry twills, you know the type. Plenty like that at Cambridge. But he stood apart. He wasn't with anyone. Looked like a lord, to be honest. And sort of – resistant. So Beth set out to win him. You know "Whenever I think of You"?' He had written it for Beth to sing, but it was meant for Ailsa. 'She sang it straight to him. He was hypnotised. It was as if — '

'What? What?'

'Never seen anything like it. Sex, I suppose. You could see it happening. As if generations of repression just melted over, like an iceberg in an oven. He burned. Savage, it was.' He put on a Yorkshire accent to make light of it. 'Ay, your naked savage stirring under the gent's natty suiting. Hah! Even Beth was a bit deterred! And you know she could never give over until she'd worked the magic. More than she'd bargained for, this time. How are they doing, have you heard?'

'Fine, as far as I know — '

But Peter came in and Rose was a little ashamed that she had been trying to find out about Gerald in his absence. He avoided talking about him – why? To her, families were sacred.

'Sing for us.'

Merry was of that rare sort who tunes a guitar in seconds and starts without fuss.

'Evening sun and fragrant grass are both sweet things,
Here we live and here we pass and try to sing
If the sun goes down on pain
We know it will rise again
So we do our best,
Yes,
We can try again . . .'

They sat over the remains of the feast feeling sad and wise and content – though some were not – and then Peter got up smartly. 'Time to go to work.'

He had walked to the factory last night and been taken on again. 'Only for a couple of weeks, the season's nearly over.'

'But I don't need a skirt or shoes now, honestly — '

'No, but we can do with a bob or two, specially if you're going to get a taste for mod cons.' He picked up his duffel coat. 'Now stop that, Ailsa's the sob sister in this house.'

Rose clung to him in the hall and thought, as she often did, Poor Mrs Profumo, and sniffed her way happily back to where Jethro had brought in the Dansette, and they twisted to 'Love, Love Me Do' and 'You Were Made For Me'. She hugged Merry and smiled at him with tears for his loss of Ailsa. Alas, he couldn't come and live with them because his widowed mother was ill, but he laughed that off and wouldn't say more. 'It's a good place you've got here, Rose.'

The curry-smelling bedroom, though she was soon alone in it again, had become the heart of everything. It was all possible. A start had been made.

September was a tight month financially, till Rose and Ailsa got their first pay cheques. But six hundred pounds a year! They'd be really well off as soon as Peter's year of training was over and he was teaching too. But meanwhile his grant was delayed, Sam was due to start at the BBC in Leeds but not yet. Ailsa's father sent a small cheque. Jethro got a job washing glasses in a pub but broke a lot and was fired. Then an old lady who had been taking an interest in the house asked Peter to paint her front door, which led to elderly friends needing this and that doing, and so they managed. It was a proud time for him, being paid for working with his hands. 'It's satisfying,' he told Rose. 'That's what I want to help the kids to do: see a job through, using their own ability. Independence. That's power. They don't need facts, they need skills.'

Rose loved her job. She had thirty-nine eight-year-olds to call her own, and though the rest of the small staff, old-timers, were suspicious and unwelcoming, she was too busy to take much notice. She made plenty of mistakes and learned quickly. It was easy to make an initial impact with her fresh ideas. The response of the children was eager and sometimes wild. When a dramatisation of Daniel in the lion's den led to overturned desks and bitten legs she learned about structuring activity. Sometimes she wept, over her own stupidity or the sharpness of a colleague, but not because of the children. She liked them, even – especially – the smelly ones.

The headmaster was a testy self-indulgent man interested only in 11+ successes and football trophies. He drove daily past the end of Park Terrace and never offered Rose a lift, so she had two buses to catch each way. Oh, the dear buses! (When they came.) Tired in the drawing-in evenings, Rose's eyes could fill with tears of joy to see hers coming. No knight on a milk-white palfrey, no rescuer ever more deliciously welcome as the green double-decker rearing into view to take her home, lugging aboard her heavy bags of work and weary legs.

Ailsa, however, immediately succumbed to laryngitis, which recurred throughout the winter. She feared school, that was the problem. She was intimidated by the children and couldn't manage the organisation. 'You have to be a bit bossy,' she admitted weakly, 'and I just want them to love me.'

But in the meantime it was just possible to turn the day's dramas and disappointments into laughter as they all assembled in the bedroom for supper.

Peter, full of Peters and Scheffler and Bloom, was privately amused by Ailsa's complaints about unbiddable children; and Rose in turn smiled to herself – with her six weeks' experience – as he expounded the necessity to put oneself in the child's place. (He had read *The Uses of Literacy* and could see there would be no problem in understanding working-class mores.)

'The trouble with Ailsa,' said Peter in confidence to Rose, 'is that she hasn't the foggiest idea where she wants to go in life; she just vaguely hopes that Sam will take her somewhere happy.' Not like them, full of purposes.

Had that been the case with Gerald? Rose wondered (not aloud), for assuredly Beth had always known what she wanted, even if it did alter quite rapidly. Perhaps that was what drew him to her, a positive woman. But she couldn't ask Peter.

Sam and Ailsa were living together in the top rooms. The matter had been debated. Naturally people who were serious about each other went all the way. It was not quite the custom actually to take up residence like that. Why not commit themselves and get married? But Sam said he intended to support a wife properly or not at all. Ailsa said nothing but looked shy and incongruously defiant. Jethro and Sam were the principal speakers. The conclusions were a) that it had been agreed that each member of the household should find his or her own best way to live, without interference unless others were thereby disturbed, and b) that they should be careful to distinguish between true and imposed morality. That was the rationale, wasn't it? Not to be limited by the older generation's views of what was right and wrong, suitable and not. And sex was for fun, inhibition harmful; it was nobody else's business to judge.

This was the public concordat. In private Rose and Peter declared that they would murder anyone who came between them. But there was no need for the others to know they were thus reactionary. Other people weren't as lucky as they were and that made all the difference.

Rose didn't think Ailsa was a very modern person either, though.

Towards the end of October they were on their own for a weekend. Jethro had gone to California promising to write often and tell them all about it. Was it really like the films? Sam was on a course at Manchester and Ailsa, pale, had gone home to her parents to be spoiled for a couple of days.

'They are our friends.'

'Of course.'

'It's not that we don't want them here.'

'No indeed.'

'But this is super, isn't it?'

'I've got something to show you.' Peter led her into the big room at the back on the ground floor, the former dining room. 'Look.' In front of the window, propped on a rough frame, was a stainless steel sink with two draining boards, and in the middle of the room stood a large solid table with fat sturdy legs.

'Wonders! Where did they come from?'

'I saw an ad for the sink – two pounds ten shillings. Carted it home last week. The table was in the basement under all those old paint tins, covered in gunge. I've been stripping it. Now we can move the cooker down. We can't have everyone eating in our room all the time.'

'It'll be a lovely kitchen. The afternoon sun comes in.'

'And eventually I'll make a door out to the back with steps down to the garden, instead of having to go out through the basement.'

'I can have pots of geraniums on the steps.'

'Put cupboards all round the walls.'

'A clothes-line!'

'Then once the basement is cleared I can keep all my tools and stuff out of the way.'

One day they'd be living in the whole house, instead of just a few rooms!

The second post brought a letter from Rose's mother Pat. 'Now you've had time to get straight we wondered if you could put us up, just for a night as it's a bit far to come there and back in a day. Your father could do with a change; he's getting a bit run-down and he worries how you're managing with your job and a big house to see to . . .'

'Heck.' Where could they sleep? 'We're not ready yet . . .'

'We can hardly refuse, can we?'

'Beds. We haven't enough beds.'

'They can have our room. There's that old Put-U-Up in the front room; we can camp out on that.'

No excuses, then. Rose rang to suggest the following weekend.

'I'll ring the gas board about moving the cooker and try to sort the kitchen out a bit.' Peter was not best pleased; he had a teaching practice coming up and a lot of preparation to do.

But Rose almost began to look forward to showing off the

house. Her mother would be silently critical but her father would see what it was all about, he always had. It would be all right. They had been selfish, seeing parents as duty, friends as pleasure. She would make them very welcome.

But Ailsa was strange when she came back on Saturday night. She didn't go in to school and wouldn't talk; and on the Thursday evening she collapsed. Sam came back in a hurry and a furious temper. 'Contacts mean everything to me at this stage. What's the matter with her?'

Rose rang home and cancelled the visit. Her mother was uncharacteristically upset. 'Your father will be very disappointed. He'd made up his mind he must see where you're living, and meet this Peter. It's been bothering him.'

'What about Christmas? It's only a few weeks.' There'd be longer to get ready, the others would be away, they could make it a real family Christmas. Her father and Peter would get on awfully well, with more time to talk; they both enjoyed debate. 'We'll be straight by then.'

'He's not well, Rose. And you know how the cold weather upsets his breathing.'

'Look, what if I came over?'

'It was the house he wanted to see. He wanted to have a picture in his mind of where you are.'

Rose was frantically worried about Ailsa. 'I don't know what we can do. She needs looking after . . .'

'Well, if you can't have us, you can't. Friends come first, no doubt.'

'It's not your fault,' Peter said. 'It's just not on, not now.'

Ailsa was in a bad way, flesh limp and heavy, eyes hollow and cheeks sunk, moaning and crouching over. Trying to ply her with soup, Rose said suddenly, 'You've done something, haven't you? You had something done.'

Ailsa rocked herself in pain or shame. 'I had to, Rose. You know Sam couldn't have borne . . . and this woman I met outside the doctor's . . . *Oh*!' Forced out of her was a terrible cry, '*Oh*!' She beat on the table edge with white knuckles.

'Come up, love, up to bed. Peter, help.' They supported her to the hall, pausing every step or so while she crouched rigid, then further. On the landing she cried out and fell, oozing blood.

'I'll get an ambulance.'

'No. I think it's over now.' Ailsa gasped and lay still.

They got her to bed and Rose cleaned her up. The bloody lump that had come away was a little stringy mess. Rose dashed out to buy sanitary towels, terribly distressed. The little mess was flushed away and as soon as she could she went to their room and sobbed for it. Peter was angry. 'Stupid woman. I still think she should go to hospital.'

'She might get into trouble.' Rose blew her nose. 'If she gets a temperature we'll call a doctor.'

Sam said accusingly, 'I thought she was taking precautions, for God's sake. Does she know nothing?'

Rose felt guilty. She was a married woman, she ought to have advised her friend.

Sadly, she made omelettes, not yet having the knack; they turned out rubbery. Peter settled to do an essay on motivation. Sam said Ailsa was asleep and he had to go and see someone at the Beeb. 'Might as well do myself some good, if I'm going to have to miss tomorrow at the course.' If he hadn't looked shaken Rose would have killed him. She made a flask of coffee and settled herself in Ailsa's room with some laborious knitting, a sweater for Peter, turning towards the wall the hole melted in the pink plastic lampshade by Jethro. Poor pale Ailsa slept as if innocent still, though shrunk.

She sat by her through the night, whispering savagely to Sam, much later, that he could jolly well find somewhere else to doss down. The house was still and seemed again too big for these small oases of lives.

What was all this about 'He's far from well'? Her father was not robust – asthmatic – but she couldn't recall his ever having been really ill. And now, instead of a visit from her parents, who had asked little enough of her, here was all this trouble. In the small hours Rose felt lonely and grubby, disappointed in herself and in their wonderful project.

At dawn she crept down to make tea in the bare bones of the new kitchen. A chink of bottles marked the arrival of milk at the front door – and then she felt full of capability, a householder with a regular delivery, one who paid the bill on time and managed orders for her friends, a provider of shelter and nourishment. She stood on the top step looking over the park as golden light edged up between black trees. 'Here we all are,' she thought, 'in our house.'

And there was time to make everything tidy by Christmas.

When President Kennedy was shot Peter pointed out that Verwoerd had recovered from an attempted assassination, and he was evil. If there was any justice, the American would survive. They made tea and waited by the radio. Ailsa came in soberly from town, where she had been to apply for a job in an office. Teaching wasn't for her. 'They'll let me know next week. Any news?' She seemed to carry about with her the loss of faith.

Merry came round. 'The old lady's in hospital and I didn't feel like waiting on my own. Has anything come through?' He looked at Ailsa with love and no hope. She'd gone away from all of them. Sam had moved out into his own flat.

They sat round the kitchen table with the radio on. Fish and chips were suggested but no one wanted to go out. 'It's probably not serious,' someone would say from time to time. 'Verwoerd was all right.' At one time a comparison between apartheid and the civil rights movement was taken up with fleeting enthusiasm, but when Peter reminded them that Kennedy had brought in troops to sort out the demonstrations in Alabama this was felt to be a wrong note at the present time. He was no saint, of course. Nor infallible (the Bay of Pigs). But the nuclear test ban treaty had been signed. There had been hope, such hope.

At 7.22 p.m. the announcement came.

They felt personally shaken. If this could happen, what of the small hopes for good in their own lives?

The women wept. Merry and Peter were darkly silent.

Sam had a television set. 'Do you want to come round and see – whatever they're showing?'

The streets were quiet; even the buses seemed to be moving reluctantly, the occasional car furtive as if afraid of showing disrespect.

The film was shown over and over again, the woman rising and throwing herself over him, long cars outside the hospital, the rangy Texan looking grim.

They parted in silence.

Of course the end of one life would not mean an end to all

the good changes. How could it? The sixties had hardly begun. He was only one man. But a shadow had fallen too early, a fresh generous confidence bruised for ever.

The week before Christmas Rose's father died. Peter took the message and tried to prepare her when she came in glowing and exhausted. 'Honestly, when Joseph dropped the baby, and one of the shepherds tried to kick it out of sight behind the manger! Then the black king – Absalom, that I told you about – he picked it up, dusted it off and gave it back to Mary upside down! Dad? No. It's not possible. There's a mistake.'

Her mother said, 'I told you he wasn't well.'

'But you just said "Far from well", you didn't say . . . You know I would have come.'

'There was no warning to speak of, only that he used to get tired. It was heart, over in seconds. No, at the office.'

'Oh, no!' Rose cried out to think of him lying on dark brown institutional lino, typists running in to stare down at him; for the most private of men no privacy at the end, his neat shabby suit rumpled and his face strange. She choked. 'Poor Mum. It must have been an awful shock. I'll come first thing in the morning. Shall we both come? There must be so much to do — '

'It's all taken care of. Mr Shawcross and the senior staff have been very good. The funeral's on Thursday.'

Wooden with shock, Rose kept saying, 'How can I miss school? I've got the presents for the children. They're going to have a party, someone's got to help them make the hats.' Peter tried to make her rest at the weekend but she kept trying to cook, clean, iron, leaving one job unfinished and going to another and forgetting what to do. He didn't know what to say. Her father had been quite old, hadn't he? Sixty-odd? He wasn't even her natural father.

'He was, he was, no one could have been more a father, he was always *there*! And I turned him away, I said there was no room, and he only wanted to be sure we were all right, I even denied him that, he must have known he was going to die and all he wanted was to be sure . . .'

'I'm sorry I never met him.'

No, not even at the wedding, the jokey excited jaunt to

the register office with Sam and Ailsa and Merry. And since then – the shortage of money, of time, the house, so much to do, always the house, always an excuse.

'No, Rose, be fair to yourself. It wasn't selfish to want to have things right before they came. It was — '

'No, it was meanness. I was too busy with my life to have time for him.'

'You don't talk about your mother.'

'That's different. She had me when she didn't want to. He *chose* to have me, he married her knowing I was there, he wanted me properly.'

It had been a bond with them, neither knowing their natural fathers.

'You will come with me, won't you?'

'To the funeral? What did you expect? Rose . . .'

But it felt now that nothing was secure, no one could be relied on.

They hired a car, refusing to worry about the expense.

Ailsa wanted to come; 'I loved your father, he was so gentle and funny.' But Rose said no. Ailsa reminded her too vividly of mistakes they had made, of bad happenings; and he had been a good man. 'It's just family,' she lied, adding hurt to a friend to her catalogue of wrong-doings.

Peter said at one point on the silent journey, 'You didn't kill him, Rose.'

Oh, I did, I did, I disappointed him. But she was too frozen to weep.

There was quite a crowd in the little crematorium chapel. It wasn't their occasion at all. Pat, elegant in black, hair newly done, was in role as hostess, alongside Mr Shawcross, welcoming everyone with brave restraint, including her daughter. There was no privacy. Rose presented Peter. 'I'm glad to meet you at last,' said Pat with a sharp look and a gracious smile. 'Mr Shawcross, this is Rose's husband.' They were ushered to seats on the front row as recorded music keened respectfully.

He was in the coffin. He was there with them, and not.

Eventually as in a well stage-managed play there came on cue a hush and an unknown man in costume read some words quickly and then looked up and said that John Walker had been a good citizen, a devoted husband and father, and a loyal servant to his country in the civil service. He belonged to a generation that held the highest ideals and standards and was a model for the rest of us if we would only hold this in mind. We would not look upon his like again. The coffin moved slowly towards red curtains and the reverential music came on. Rose wanted to run out and stop the inexorable glide towards the flames and she could do nothing. Peter held her hand but she didn't even want him.

Then she found herself in the cold garden outside and people were organising each other into cars. Peter got her into theirs and they took two women from the office as well. They said how sorry they were, meaning it, and Rose's heart broke with emotion.

There was a reception in a hotel with glasses of sherry and a cold buffet. Pat was making sure everyone had something to eat and drink. Rose said to Peter, 'Can we go now?' All the people were coming between her and her father. They were kind but they hadn't loved him.

'You can't go without a word with your mother.'

She had to queue up for Pat's attention. 'You got a car, then? Peter can drive? You ought to take lessons, Rose, now you're a professional woman.'

'Mum. Come – somewhere, just for a minute.'

They went to the Ladies. Two girls, typists perhaps, stopped giggling by the mirror, put away their make-up purses deferentially, and left them alone.

What to say?

Pat checked the set of her hat in the mirror. 'May as well slip inside while we're here.' She went into a cubicle.

'Mum. Will you be all right?'

'What? Just a minute, I can't hear you.' Water flushed, she came out and rinsed her hands. 'Oh, you mean financially? Oh, yes. The pension's not bad, and I shall look around for a little job.'

'Oh. Good.' There ought to be something she could do. 'If you get lonely – I mean, if you want a change, or . . . Well, there's room in the house. I mean, you could have a flat, sort of, although there's only the one bathroom — '

'You mean come and live with you? Oh, Rose, I'm not an old woman yet, I should hope. I've not suddenly become helpless, you know.' No, by no means. 'But thank you for thinking of it.'

'Or – ' Rose had been wondering if she and Peter should move back here. What did people do? She didn't know. But Pat was speaking, looking appraisingly at her daughter. 'At least he's a gentleman. You've done well for yourself, Rose.'

'He?'

She meant Peter, of course. 'You get on with your life, I'll get on with mine. You worry too much. Now I must get back, I haven't had a word with all of them from Planning yet. It's a good turn-out, isn't it? Just shows how well thought of your father was.' She was very pleased.

Rose, dismissed, went back into the room and smiled politely at faces, found Peter and asked to be taken home.

There was a letter waiting from Peter's mother. 'I am very sad for you in your loss. Peter told me you were grieving because you had not seen him for some time. I know how much harder it is to lose someone far away. It feels as if it would have been more bearable if you could have been there to give comfort and say what was in your heart. But you must not wound yourself with guilt. Remember the years of love you gave. We make mistakes but this does not wipe out love. Please try to keep this in mind and mourn without blaming yourself.'

How could she know so much? 'Oh, I do want to meet your mother!'

There was another page evidently added later, the writing hastier.

'Gerald has come home. He is weary from the flight and had a slight accident coming down the steps from the plane, slipping and hurting his back. It appears that his wife is staying on in America.'

Oh, Beth! How *could* you?

They had the house to themselves at Christmas.

Rose, a dutiful letter-writer, began a correspondence with Peter's mother. Sheila's replies were intermittent but friendly, giving news of the farm and of Gerald's condition. At first the trouble seemed to clear up; but as soon as he tried to work normally his back gave pain. Luckily they had help for the heavy work. '. . . and Gerald is developing skills as a manager, which is what is most important. And dear Caroline calls often, which I'm sure cheers him up. There are not many young people in the district.'

'Who's Caroline?'

'Mmm? The one who was reading Economics?'

'No, at the farm.'

'Oh, Caroline. She's the one Gerald was engaged to.'

'You mean, before he met Beth?'

'Long before. It was more or less taken for granted by everyone. They grew up together. Her uncle has the adjoining land.'

And he had gone, left her. But she was loyal, and still saw him. Rose felt badly the shame of Beth's desertion, and her letters of enquiry ('Beth, what *happened*?') went unanswered.

Tentatively she asked, 'When can we go up to see them?'

'Rose, we've enough to do here. They're managing perfectly all right.'

'Yes, but . . .'

Yes, but: are you ashamed of me?

It became a small permanent hurt with her.

Then in May Sam and Ailsa finally decided to marry after all, and this somehow gave Rose strength. They had seen their friends through a bad time – Ailsa had lost prettiness but was calm – and it had come out all right. It was to be a proper wedding in Rose and Ailsa's home town, and it was unthinkable that Rose and Peter should not be there. 'We owe everything to you two,' Ailsa said, tears not far away. 'No arguing, mate,' said Sam. 'Hire a car and make a weekend of it. You never have any fun.'

'Why don't we go up to Stoners Court?' Rose asked. 'It's only another ninety miles or so, isn't it?'

Peter had his guilts too, and could not refuse.

Ailsa wore white and wept throughout the ceremony, but she was happy. Sam and Peter, in full Moss Bros regalia, looked marvellously distinguished. Merry, alas, could not leave his mother after another major operation; but otherwise they all felt confirmed in what they were doing and quite able, generously, to go along with the conventions of the older generation without losing autonomy.

Rose's mother was duly visited after the reception, and was

again impressed by Peter. 'But what does he want to work with his hands for?' she asked Rose in private. 'You can see he's clever.'

'It's a matter of priorities,' Rose explained. 'It's to do with reversing this awful drift towards alienation.'

'Well, I should have thought he could do something more useful than teaching brats to make coffee tables,' Pat responded briskly. 'Teach them how to make money, that'll make them happier.'

But the visit was not too much of a strain, and Peter got them away soon, before the absence of Rose's father could upset her all over again. A wedding day was not a time for thoughts of death.

'She's all right, isn't she?' Rose asked as they drove away.

'She's a survivor, your mother.' He rather liked her vulgar graciousness, but did not say this to Rose.

So they did not have to worry about her.

As they went north, Peter said, 'It's a biggish house. Don't be put off.'

'Why? Should I be?'

'Just don't start getting any different ideas about me. I'm what you know, nothing else.'

'What's your mother like?'

'She's not my — '

'Oh, words. What's the difference?' She was very curious about what made people what they were. What would their children be like? Who would they take after? What influences would form them?

'My adoptive mother, then. She's – admirable. You'll like her. But it's all – up there – out of touch with *now*.'

'It must be peaceful up there.' Rose was rather off 'now'; Ailsa should have been honestly virginal in her white, not shadowed by the murdered bloody lump.

'Peaceful sure. If you don't mind living in the past.'

'Is that bad?'

'It's everything that's wrong with this country. Holding on to what's gone.'

She forbore to remind him that they had preferred to buy an old house. Besides, she did not believe that he was always, in his deepest heart, convinced by all his pronouncements. She hoped not, sometimes.

Stoners Court was an amazement. Lulled by the open quiet drama of hills and turning valleys, empty roads in the spring light, wondering if one or another farmhouse might be the place, she was unprepared when they turned in at a lodge gate, along a short curving drive, and drew up in a wide gravelled courtyard. There was a line of washing, a pair of golden labradors bounding – and from an open door framed in purple clematis a slender fair woman emerged drying her hands.

'How lovely to see you at last! Rose. Peter dear.' She kissed his cheek, held Rose's hand for the duration of a shrewd and kindly look. 'Down, Rufus, Bruno. I hope dogs don't bother you. We'll have some tea.'

The house was Jacobean, surely enormous, gabled and honey-stoned. The kitchen! Oh my goodness, thought Rose, almost better than Badger's, her ideal. Beams and an ingle-nook, blue and white dishes on a massive dresser, a flagged floor.

'Now if you'll excuse me, I must have a word with Mr Todd – the new vet, Peter, you wouldn't know him. He's come to do the AI and I want him to have a look at Daisy; she's torn a teat and she hates men handling her. See to the tea, will you? I won't be more than five minutes.' She filled a zinc bucket from a huge kettle on the Aga and was gone – close to, much tougher than she first appeared – while Rose, bemused, beamed.

'She's lovely! It's lovely! Peter, why did you never tell me? You just said it was a farm.'

'It doesn't belong to me. It's nothing to do with me. Gerald made that clear.'

'It was your home!'

'It was *a* home. Historical accident. I was here by charity, not right.'

'You were here by love!' Oh, he could be such a prig at times. If he hadn't had the grace to look ashamed she would have hit him. Why was gratitude supposed to demean, while resentment could be cultivated as if it were the token of profound integrity?

When presently they sat down to tea, in fine, odd cups and saucers, Mrs Stead smiled at them both. 'You chose well, Peter.'

Rose blushed in delight.

'I'm well pleased,' he said. 'Where's Gerald?'

'He was so disappointed that he'd be away when you came. It's a hospital appointment we've been waiting for. Investigations, you know. Caroline's driven him over to Newcastle. We hoped it wouldn't be too much of a strain for him. He can't drive an ordinary car, or sit comfortably for long.'

'What exactly is the trouble?' Peter was alert, Rose apprehensive.

'It goes back to that silly fall, as he came off the plane. So easily done – he'd had a few whiskies, he hates flying – and to have such consequences . . . The doctor can't be certain what it is. But there's quite a risk of arthritis. So we'll see what this latest specialist says. Caroline's staying on with friends near Newcastle so she can bring him home. They were both sorry to miss you.'

'What is the outlook, can they say?' Would he be able to go on managing the farm? Rose looked sharply at Peter, afraid he was thinking of possible interference with their plans; but he was genuinely troubled.

'No one knows. He could go on for years with only occasional bad times. Or the condition could deteriorate, quickly or slowly.'

'But he's only young!' Rose cried.

'Four years older than Peter: twenty-nine. Yes, young. But his constitution is strong, which must help.'

And Caroline was standing by him. 'But if it goes badly?'

'We'll manage in any event. George is still with us; he refuses to allow the topic of retirement. And his grandson Hugh, he's very capable. Now, enough of that. Tell me about where you live. And you're a teacher, Rose?'

While Rose talked, Peter wandered out with the dogs.

'Couldn't you come and stay with us some time? I know it's the city, but we have a lovely view.' Rose would have valued Sheila's perspective; she felt they were losing grip on theirs.

'My dear, I almost never get away. One of the agricultural shows, if I get the chance. But who knows? All I need is some strong young grandsons to take over!'

Their room was on the other side of the house, overlooking the largest garden Rose had ever seen. 'I've put you in here. Peter's old cubby-hole is far too small for a couple. Now, take your time; we'll eat about eight. The feed delivery lorry is overdue and I want to check as he unloads. We were three bags short last time. It's a new driver and I suspect he's trying it on.'

Rose sat on a low chair before the mullioned window. 'I love it.'

Peter set down the cases. 'There are seven bedrooms, not counting the attics. For two people.'

'If Gerald remarries they'll need the space. And we've got six bedrooms, if you look at it that way. What do you suggest – turning it into a home for convalescent miners?'

'They'd perish from hypothermia. Apart from the kitchen it's freezing three feet away from a fire in winter.'

'So what have you got against it? I don't understand.'

He sighed. 'Being here again, it's hard to say exactly. It's unfair, that's all. When others haven't got a roof.'

'So are lots of things unfair. It's unfair that some people are cleverer than others or can play the violin or run very fast —'

'Yes, yes. But one tries not to add to it. It's a matter of trying to even out the distribution . . .' Even to himself he must have sounded lame; and yet such a statement would have gone down with acclaim in the circles where they had begun.

Rose looked out over the garden, which was harmonious, though far from perfectly kept up, rhythmic in its shapes, and enhanced here and there with clumps of late tulips and polyanthus. A posy was on the dressing table. It all felt natural, uncontrived.

She had enjoyed the prospect of having the house to themselves now that Sam and Ailsa had their own flat, but she knew that when they got back Peter would be pressing to take others in again. That had been the idea . . . and they were lucky, it was true, to have so much room . . .

Lamb was roasting in the oven. Rose picked vegetables from the untidy patch across the yard and prepared them while Sheila washed and sorted eggs and packed them. Although she was the kind of woman who in a headscarf looked as though she was off to a point-to-point rather than to the mill, Rose felt easier with her than she had ever done with her own mother. The dogs lay outside and fan-tailed pigeons strutted idly about.

Peter went to help with the milking and got a dusty reception from old George. 'Still going about trying to stir up trouble, are you?'

Feeling fifteen again, Peter tried to parody himself. 'Come the revolution! Oh yes, all the old hammer and sickle stuff, ban the bomb and down with bloated capitalists.'

George declined to answer his tone. 'For a married man, it's time you did a bit of growing up. And you can save your breath if you're going to start nosying about overtime rates and union hours – and keep off our Hugh, an' all. When I've a complaint I'll make it heard to Missus, not to thee. I'm a free man, I do what I like and I like what I do. With some folks' watching of clocks and counting of pay packets and these demarcation disputes – bloody idiots – I doubt they're happier men. When you've found a better life nor what I've got, then come and tell me and I'll take note of what you've to say. Till then I've work to do, and if you're going to be any use you can wash off them teats and set the cooler going.'

It would be reassuring to think that the old man had an ironic affection for him, but Peter doubted it. He would have valued George's respect. He was on his side, after all; the trouble was that the latter saw himself as on the same side as Sheila. How were workers ever to get better conditions if they refused to accept that there was a conflict of interest?

In the kitchen Rose, chopping new mint, said impulsively (she could trust her impulses here, whereas at home she quite often had to stay silent in order not to attract looks askance), 'I can't understand why Peter ever wanted to leave.'

Sheila slowly re-folded pastry and turned it. 'People are what they are.' She dusted the rolling pin with flour. 'I was more taken aback when Gerald went, it seemed so out of character. With Peter . . . He was, how shall I say, relieved, when he found he was adopted. He didn't want to be like us, from quite early on. I've often wondered if natural children are sometimes the same? Gerald is my nephew, you know.' (Rose hadn't; she'd assumed he was the true son.) 'But apart from that one episode, he's been happy to belong here. As far as I know.' She placed a dish on the pastry and cut the circle round it. 'There was one particular time. We'd been to Newcastle – Peter was about ten – to see a pantomime, and when we came out of the theatre there were some children begging. In 1950. They were very thin, poor little mites, and ragged. I couldn't think where they might have come from, right up to the middle of the city. They were lively enough, and full of cheek. Everybody gave them money, of course. Perhaps they were put up to it by some present-day Fagin, who knows? Peter was stunned. He kept asking, all the way home, "Why are they like that?" Gerald, I remember, was just furious with the parents. We've had families in the village on hard times now and again, but at least, he said, they managed to wield a needle and thread.'

'And everyone would help them?'

'Well of course. But help is there in the cities too, surely?'

'Yes. Institutionalised, if not neighbourly – WVS, National Assistance. Some people don't take it up because they don't like the idea of charity.'

'Charity meant love originally, didn't it? But trying to get into the mind of a child . . . From that time on, Peter seemed to hold me responsible – naturally enough, I suppose. "Why should we have plenty to eat and they were hungry? Why have we got a big house? Why are some people poor?" He would lie awake worrying about it. He was always tender-hearted. But for a child of that age to feel *guilty* . . .'

'Children get very disturbed by injustice. And he feels responsible for everything.'

'I saw then that if he'd known from the first about being adopted, it might have spared him. When I told him, it seemed as if a weight had been shed. "So I might have been poor too? I'm more like them really, aren't I?" What would you have said?'

'Apart from the usual things like "We chose you" and "This is your home" – '

'Quite. I must have muddled it. One makes mistakes, being alone.'

'I can't imagine you making a muddle of anything.'

Sheila smiled a little as she deftly trimmed the pie crust. 'Oh, my dear, I'm anything but infallible. Just fairly competent at tasks I do very often.'

'Weren't you very hurt?'

'Puzzled. He began to make himself more and more separate; but that often happens anyway, doesn't it, as children grow up? He used to spend school holidays, in his teens, with a friend whose father had a poor parish in Sunderland.'

Rose had for a long time been under the impression that this had been Peter's family. 'Yes, he told me about them. I suppose,' she added thoughtfully, 'that in another age he would have been a Christian.'

Sheila looked at her sharply. 'Perhaps he's a Christian in this age,' she said drily, 'under a different banner.'

'Perhaps there isn't much difference. Perhaps it doesn't matter — '

'There's a danger, though. Christians don't imagine they have to be God.'

'I sometimes wonder,' Rose confessed, 'if any of us knows what the problems are. I mean, if we assign troubles to the wrong causes, the solutions might be wrong.' She asked the question that had been worrying her since they arrived and saw Sheila so busy. 'With Peter away every holiday – didn't you need him here, at harvest time and so on?'

'That's what I meant, about tackling tasks one does understand.'

'He must have been a disappointment to you.' She would be desolate if a son of theirs despised all they tried to do for him.

'Goodness, no. One doesn't take children on in order to get a return. As it is, what complications if both boys had wanted the farm!'

'So, will you be all right, if Gerald doesn't get better?'

'This may sound ungracious, Rose, and I don't in the least mean to be unkind: but it isn't your worry. Gerald will probably have sons – and I can keep going for a good while yet. Then I'll retire to the end cottage and learn how to be a dowager. I shall probably interfere dreadfully.'

While Peter, subdued and irritable, soaked in the great cast-iron bath, its enamel almost ochre with age and with a flat Niagara of emerald stain spreading beneath the massive taps, Rose washed in the wide wash-basin. She was trying to piece together Sheila's life. Married in the comfortable thirties (comfortable here, anyway). Then the war, and her young husband gone. Seemingly Peter had no curiosity about this; he could not fill in the gaps. She found this unnatural. 'Wasn't he wounded at some time? Didn't you say he'd been back?'

'Probably. His elder brother was killed in an air-raid. Gerald's father – and mother. That's how the farm came to him, my father, Sheila's husband I mean.'

On her own, then, taking on one small boy, then another. Soon a widow, with no reunion to live for.

Over dinner the talk was of possible changes that membership of the Common Market might bring. Rose, who had thought no further than that it would be nice for people to travel freely without passports, and to buy wine and perfume without duty, was impressed with Peter's knowledge of the economics of farming and the eagerness with which he discussed the merits of Charolais cattle for beef as compared with Friesians for milk. Was this where his heart really lay? She had not seen him so animated for a long time. Perhaps his reserve about Stoners Court masked loss at the fact of Gerald's possession of the land.

Afterwards they took coffee into the drawing room where, while Sheila shut up the hens and Peter had a last look at Daisy, Rose examined the wedding photograph. The thin, dark, clever-looking man didn't seem a stranger. To think they had had so few years together. Pained, Rose yearned to love Peter, hold and appreciate him in thankfulness for their more fortunate timing, but he had become strange to her here. She didn't know him as she had thought; he had been right to fear she would see him differently now, would, yes, respect him less. Without solid grounds, she felt he had somewhere made a great mistake, and that all he proclaimed was defensive merely.

And yet despite this disturbance, she was sure that if they could stay here all confusions would gradually fade.

Next morning she undertook to weed the vegetable beds while Peter went into Hexham for a spare part for the mower. She moved along the rows of tiny feathery carrot tops, all but submerged by rude groundsel, with bees going in and out of thyme and cranes-bill geraniums and the pigeons bawbling. Her prime emotion was of gladness that the groundsel had not yet gone to seed. She had caught it in time. For the rest of the year, if someone kept at it, the beds would remain clear, allowing good things to flourish. She would, just then, have settled as her purpose in life to keep the vegetable beds free of weeds, summoned every few weeks – 'Come at once, you are needed here!' – and she would leap into a car (she would have passed her test) and speed to Northumberland to deal with the threat, a valuable person with a vital task to do. In old age she would have the dignity of one who has done a worthwhile job. 'We must go and work in the garden' had been taken, by her peers, as the ultimate evasion, the creeping back to smallness of one who could not face the harsh urgencies of the real world. Now, it seemed to her the acme of good sense.

'Tell me,' said Sheila, bringing coffee out to the bench, silvered with age, by the back door, 'about the new mood. I'm so out of the world, I find it confusing. Young people having more fun I can well understand, and people generally having more money, that's splendid and long overdue. But I cannot make the connection between all that and what is called "freedom". What has it to do with using the short Anglo-Saxon words in public? I'm sure you can explain.'

An emissary from the enlightened, Rose should have been able to offer insights. But since neither she nor Peter used the four-letter words except in extreme bad temper or tender intimacy, and since they made love only with each other, she was not best-qualified to expound. Furthermore, she had been upset a few evenings ago to glance out and see two young men relieving themselves in her front garden, encouraged by their laughing girls. When they noticed her they gave the peace sign; when they saw her anger, the other one.

It was all part of getting rid of furtiveness and shame, she offered lamely.

Sheila listened with interest. 'I think I see,' she said eventually. 'So do all problems go away if everyone is quite without – inhibition? Is that the word?'

'That's the idea. It's only when people are frustrated, going against their natural feelings, that they go wrong, isn't it?' It wasn't till later that she recalled Sheila's celibate condition, and nearly died of embarrassment. Now she was anxious to explain how clear it had all been when they started off, but now there was Ailsa's trouble to remember, Beth's defection, Merry's burden of a sick mother, Peter's reserve. Oh, it had all seemed so full of promise! She wanted to explain, recapture how beautiful it was all going to be – but from up here it seemed tawdry, misguided. Perhaps Peter could convey the excitement of it all. It was all new still, and at times seemed as much a part of history as the war.

And how could she tell Sheila, childless herself, of Ailsa's abortion, the other side of the possibly counterfeit coin?

Avoiding this, she said, 'You were very kind when my father died. You knew just how I felt.'

'One does, having been through it.' There was more that Sheila seemed about to say; then she got up briskly. 'It was good of Peter to go for that spare part for the tractor. We really are one pair of hands – or four wheels – short. George will be grateful.'

Rose was careful to give Peter and Sheila time on their own. Whether it was this time with her, or the change of rhythm she didn't know, but she had never seen him so relaxed. It was a magical place, she thought.

But there was no question of their staying. His face closed again when on the way back she suggested, very tentatively, that it might be a solution if Peter were there to do the heavier work while Gerald saw to planning and paperwork, if his disability grew.

Peter was aghast. 'You don't know Gerald.'

Later she noted that he hadn't said, 'My work is in the city.'

Before Peter went on his last teaching practice Rose refreshed him on the principle of the self-fulfilling prophecy. 'If you treat them as decent people then that's the way they'll be.' She was appalled by the attitudes of some of her colleagues who assumed that if a child came from a notorious housing estate then it must be a potential troublemaker. Trouble was, naturally, what they got. 'And don't be drawn,' she advised.

'Drawn?'

'If they want to be bloody awkward, don't get into a confrontation.'

'No, ma'am.'

She was apprehensive for him. He would be dealing with teenagers, not children. She was remembering how Ailsa had wanted to be loved, and had gone under.

He didn't talk much about the experience over the next six weeks, from which she deduced that it had not been rewarding. Luckily he was able to blame all the difficulties on poor organisation within the school. When he had a permanent place he would be in a better position to see through the plans he had. And he had got a job, to start in September. Just what he had wanted: in a poor area. 'Then I'll be able to make a mark,' he said.

Ailsa was eager to start a family, and thought she might be pregnant already. At the end of July Rose and Peter went to their flat for supper and listened to Sam expounding on the desirability of private education. 'I shouldn't like it to go to a rough school,' Ailsa conceded gently.

Peter was very angry and they left early. Striding home, he fumed. 'The sheer hypocrisy of it! He was president of the Young Socialists, for crying out! And now it's all property values and private schooling! If that's what the prospect of parenthood does to people . . .'

He was trying to work himself towards irony, but Rose knew he was hurt by what he saw as a betrayal of friendship. For him, to share ideals was like belonging to a devout brotherhood – more, perhaps, to do with unity against outsiders than affection for those within. He hadn't had many friends before university; it had been wonderful to him to belong. Rose found this childlike and touching and risky, and reflected gratefully that she and her friends had little in common except that they liked each other.

'Let's go for a drink,' she said. 'We so rarely get out.'

'Have we got enough?'

'I've got five and ninepence.'

'I've nearly a quid. Plenty. Thank the Lord we'll have two salaries coming in after September. We'll be rolling.'

Going down the hill towards The Crown he went on, 'I've been thinking, Rose, about getting a car.' She let him go on about the savings on bus fares and the possibility of days by the sea. What she had to say needed the right time.

But before they reached the pub he had reverted to the change in Sam. 'It's family influence coming out,' he said bitterly. 'Bourgeois values. You might think someone's grown out of all that, worked out their own priorities. As we're doing, Rose. But scratch the surface and you'll find them lingering.'

'Perhaps it's different when you have children of your

own,' said Rose dubiously. 'I mean, it's natural to want the best for them.'

'Not at the cost of sacrificing others. If the bright kids keep getting creamed off there's no hope of raising standards in the state system.'

To divert, and because she wanted to know, she asked, 'Do you think it's possible to cast off one's background completely? Because if not, why do we spend so much time talking about instilling a proper sense of values into the kids we teach?'

He avoided the main point; the fact was that his optimism about what education could do had taken a knock. 'It depends on what kind of childhood you had, I suppose. If you know it was wrong, then you can build your own standards.'

'Was yours wrong?'

He took a long breath in and held it and then sighed out sharply, in exasperation or hopelessness. 'Let's just say I didn't belong there.'

'But Sheila chose you!'

'Gerald didn't.'

There was nothing she could say about this. But at the entrance to the pub she stopped him briefly. 'Shouldn't you go home – there – for a few weeks in the summer to give them a hand if Gerald's back is still paining him?'

'They can manage. Sheila said so.'

Infrequent visitors to the pub, they knew their place, which was the table in line with the draught from the door. Regulars occupied by right those by the fireplace, handy for dartboard and dominoes.

Tonight a stranger was at their table. They resented this. He didn't fit in. That Rose's long loose hair and Peter's beard were at odds with the resident style had ceased to concern them; they were accepted. This man had longish hair, dirty, tattered flannels and an open shirt not unlike Peter's, but his eyes stared and shifted, on the move and back and away again. They were put out when the landlord, nodding that way, said doubtfully, 'Friend of yours?' They had imagined they conveyed a sense of stability. 'No!' They wanted to say, 'We belong here, he's just passing through, nothing to do with us.' But there was nowhere else to sit.

Smiling at as many familiar faces as possible to emphasise

that they were not new there, they made their way to the table with the one pint of bitter and the Mackeson stout, nodded briefly at the man and turned to each other. There were urgent matters to discuss.

But before they could speak, he started.

The country was done for. Did they know that two per cent of the population owned ninety-eight per cent of the wealth? They did. Learning this had changed Peter's life some years ago. Suez ought to have made an end of the old order, but look at them, the upper classes, as corrupt as ever, look at this lot in here laughing in their troughs while disaster drew ever nearer – nothing but guns in the streets would shake them, only blood would cleanse. Anyone would think we still ruled an empire, the arrogance of the rich was unshaken, the workers only wanted more money, not change, and now these young ones hypnotised out of what little mind they had by pop and drugs, sex-mad the lot of them, about time somebody did set off the bomb if it led to a change of power, use it ruthlessly to get rid of the dross, exterminate sloppy free-thinkers . . . And so on. At intervals he brought round to them his roving unseeing eyes and leaned forward conspiratorially, as if they were comrades.

It was disgusting to them to hear some of their beliefs warped and spat out in hate, not hope.

When he got on to property is theft Rose was furious that Peter felt it necessary to get involved. She foresaw what would come next: 'You've got a spare room, have you?'

Feeling queasy, she shot Peter a warning look that he felt rather than saw, and went to the Ladies.

A stout wife joined her in the lobby as she waited. 'You don't want to get drawn in with the likes of that one,' she advised Rose. 'On the Assistance and never paid a stamp in his life, I'll be bound. Pity they stopped the National Service, they'd have sorted him. Hey up, get a shift on you two, there's others waiting.'

From within the cubicle came giggles. 'Half a tick, Auntie May.'

'Kids,' Auntie May explained. 'Eighteen, just. I don't approve, them coming into Publics, but their mams are that soft. I'm telling this lady here, your mams are too soft with you.'

The girls burst out. 'No, after you,' Rose said to Auntie, who reminded the girls to wash their hands. There was no towel, but they shook water about and then carefully repaired the black eye-liner and near-white lips before going.

'They don't know they're born,' continued Auntie from within, 'young ones nowadays. It's Beatles this and Stones that, if it's not Herman and his Hermits; mind, you can't help taking to him, nice little chap, lovely smile, his mam's nothing to be ashamed of. But as for them mini-skirts, there'll be trouble, that's all I'm saying.' The cistern flushed. 'Still and all,' she said, emerging, 'they're good enough lasses, go from one job to another but never idle, and when all's said you're only young once. But watch that one. Irish, I shouldn't be surprised. You've other things to think about, by the looks. Put yourself first now, you'll have no chance later.' The door swung to behind her.

Rose looked at herself in the tiny glass. Such a change, already? She felt part depressed, part elated. Empowered, certainly.

Returning, she stood by the table. 'I want to go now.'

Auntie May gave her a nod of approval as they went.

Outside, Peter took her hand. 'I thought we were stuck for the evening.'

'It's your own fault,' she said, suddenly irritable. 'You will get drawn in.'

'But he — '

'It's a waste of time trying to reason with someone like that.'

He maintained, 'It's important to try.'

'He made even fair points sound dirty.'

'You can't choose political bedfellows. If there's to be change at all we're all in it together, you can't exclude anyone you just don't like — '

'I can. Imagine the likes of him with power!'

'You're not turning into one of those best that lack conviction, are you?' He was trying to sound light, but uneasiness came through.

It worried Rose. It had seemed the worst of failings, to lack conviction. That was what allowed injustices to flourish; the more-of-the-same syndrome a recipe for decay. Now she saw the dangers of passionate intensity. Once, it had seemed a necessary cleansing flame; now, intrinsically dangerous, more likely to harm the good, or at least the weak, than purge the bad.

Some of this she tried to say. But Peter denied doubt. 'Ideas don't become wrong just because a few unbalanced individuals take them up.'

'Then perhaps the character is more important than the idea.' She would, in short, prefer that Auntie May was in charge.

Home again, the rest of the way having been in silence, Peter tried to make reparation. 'Well, it's just as well we're not going to be put to the test yet,' he said, flinging himself on the bed with a luxurious sigh. 'Like Sam and Ailsa, I mean. We've a few more years on our own before we get bogged down in family matters. Maybe by then it'll be a safer place to bring them into.'

Rose sat by him and said firmly, though quaking within, 'There's something I have to tell you.'

II

The Rosemary Cutting

1965

My dear Beth,

An address at last, and yet another change! I still don't understand how you could have left Gerald, if he's anything at all like Peter – and I simply don't believe you married Wendell just for his money. You were always ambitious, but not *that* hard! I'm sorry that came to an end too, when I've been so lucky in love. And now our baby. Only seven weeks to go. It must have been conceived at Stoners Court, I expect Gerald told you how lovely it is. It will be a fortunate child, with that start. And poor Ailsa keeps having these phantom pregnancies. You will be sad to hear that Gerald is in poor shape. Some of the time he is almost paralysed with pain. Oh Beth, so much hurt! I'm sure he must miss you, even though there is a girl from before. Couldn't you come back, now you're free again?

Then again, there's obviously something to be said for freedom, if my mother is anything to go by – hair blonde and beehive, going in for ballroom dancing, having all the fun she missed when she was young, because of me. Do you ever feel you were young too soon? I do.

Couldn't make out your writing, that book you recommended – did you put Friedan . . . ?

Peter sat on the front steps, the stone cold through his wet trousers. So much for a Saturday morning trip to the country with some of the hard boys he was desperate to win over: all that way to the school in pouring rain, and not one had turned up. There had to be some way he could reach them! He could not be beaten in his passion to be of service to them.

And then to forget his key in the rush to be there in good time, and Rose in town shopping. If there was any consolation to be had from this fiasco it was that the house was pretty nigh impregnable, from amateur burglars at least. – Ah! He recalled with relief a small repair workshop in one of the back streets. They'd be sure to have tools.

Running, for it was almost midday, he got there to find a tough young man with a Teddy-boy hairstyle locking up.

'Crowbar? Yes, I've got one. Want me to come back with you? Make sure you don't nick me equipment. Hang on a tick.' He put a ladder in the back of his pick-up. 'That's OK, wait till you hear me call-out fee; 194 you said? Posh end, that. Used to be, any road.'

They got in at the kitchen window at the modest cost of one pane of glass and one cut to Peter's wrist. 'Minimum force,' the mechanic had advised. 'You learn that in the Army. Didn't do National Service, I'll bet?' Peter had escaped by going to university. 'Get your pane out clean, new bit of putty, no harm done. No nice paintwork to spoil, that's for sure. You want to get them sash cords looked at, could've had your head off if I hadn't of been holding it up. Right then, I'm off for me Saturday pint. Ah, forget it, buy us one at The Carpenters one day. Terry Buckler's the name. Something about these old places, isn't there? Character. All yours? You must be barmy, you'll never have your hand out of your pocket. Nice, though. Spacious. See you around.'

In town the bus queues were very long and the rain set in steadily once more. Rose was amazed how tiring it was, buying things. She had little experience of going to the big stores: it had always been corner shops, the Taj Mahal Emporium for sandpaper and nails, Oxfam for clothes. But the baby was going to have *some* things new: a teddy bear and a cot-cover, nappies and curtains. But, oh, the crowds! Stopping for a cup of tea she encountered a former fellow-student who knew a lot about husbands. 'Keep him waiting, let him know what it's like not to be sure when you'll be back. I had enough of that, with the golf club. Now I make jolly sure I'm the last in. You won't get valued if you let yourself be taken for granted.'

Rose decided to walk home. 'With all those parcels? You should have got them to deliver.'

'I want to show them to Peter.'

The hill had got steeper since she sailed down it on the bus that morning. She did hope Peter and the boys hadn't been drenched. Lucky them, though, getting out of town. He never suggested taking her. Traffic sallied carelessly by, sending out splashes. It would have been nice to have a car.

At three o'clock Peter put the kettle on ready: surely she wouldn't be long now. Alas, it boiled dry when he went out

for more fine glass-paper and ran into the colleague who gave
him a lift to school in the mornings. His car had stalled and
just needed a push to the top of the hill. The car duly fired.
'Jump in and I'll run you back.' The engine died. There was
nothing to be done but push it to the only garage open on
Saturday afternoons, a mile away. Peter trudged back. By
now the specialist ironmonger had shut.

'You should have taken a taxi!' He was cross with relief.
She was draggled and worn out. It had not occurred to her.

The only problem remaining in the world, now they were
both home, was to decide which ecstasy to indulge in first:
good hot tea (water boiled in a pan), thick buttered toast
made before the gas fire as in the olden days, or a deep bath.
They accomplished all three more or less simultaneously and
then went to bed for an hour. It seemed the best thing.

She said, snuggling, 'Do you think we just muddle through?'

'Hardly even that, sometimes.'

'You don't think we should be more – I mean, know where
we're going, more?'

'I know. Turn over.'

On Monday morning Henry Thomas came up brightly to
Peter. 'It fair pissed it down Sat'day, din't it, sir? Cleggy's
Mam got 'im a new anorak special and all 'e could do was
sleep in, dozy bugger. 'Ave a good day, did you? Me Dad says
you must be barmy, lugging snotty kids round on yer day off,
but we telled 'im, 'e likes it, Mr. Stead. Are we going next
Sat'day, sir? Our Ronald's got this old bike cape I can 'ave a
lend of. . . .'

When Churchill died Rose wept. In few respects had he
resembled her father, but she mourned them both for many of
the same reasons: for the passing of unashamed love of
country (for nowadays this was held as contemptible, denoting
jingoism), and belief in the large virtues. Recently – perhaps
it was her condition – she found it wearing to have to be so
constantly aware, taking nothing on trust, on the lookout
always for reversionary tendencies, in order to be correctly
receptive to the new good and suitably contemptuous of the
old; and to tell the truth she didn't understand why England
had to be despised if the vision of a united world was to be
properly received. Of course, pregnancy being an old-

fashioned state, one had to be discreet about mentioning these subversive reflections; but inside she was defiant, and felt out of step.

They went to see if they could watch the funeral on Sam's television. It was awkward, as they had a number of friends there and the consensus was that the ceremony was a waste of public money that could be better spent on council housing. One man was never worth all this. It was recalled that Churchill had said something very offensive to the miners in the 1920s, countered by a shy person who said that he had introduced wages councils even earlier, to set minimum wages, but this was ignored in favour of a debate as to whether there could be such a quality as greatness. The conclusion was, no: it was not intrinsic but conferred, and could therefore be unconferred as soon as general opinion saw that an error had been made. There was no room now for giants, who were by definition élite, leaving everyone else to be un-élite, which was not democratic.

Rose suffered with the straining Guardsmen bearing the coffin down the many steps, imagining her father saying, 'They'll be proud of this moment all their lives.' But to take pride in service was now a sin.

Peter was not watching. He had come only to humour her, and was embarrassed by her tears. She was too spontaneous in her reactions; it didn't do. He joined a group talking about Allan Ginsberg and the refreshing trend to bring poetry out of the academic closet and make it accessible to all. Just occasionally, though, there was a break in the talk and everyone watched, until someone, to rationalise the interest, came out with, 'Well let's face it, it's about the only thing the country's still good at, putting on a show.'

'However anachronistic.'

Into a silence, as the boat disappeared down the river, the great cranes bowing, one girl spoke out clearly. 'He was a good man. You owe it at least partly to him that you are here to mock.'

They were taken aback. She was a clever girl, no one was confident enough to jeer; there were murmurs of 'Well, in his time . . .' Then it was realised that she was Jewish. That explained it.

Quite kindly they made rueful mouths at each other, and

Ailsa brought Hannah a drink. Rose wondered which of them was likely to have made a wiser evaluation of worth. Herself, she supported her father's view, out of love, and Hannah's, out of deference to suffering. And no death should be callously dismissed. The imminence of giving birth made that very plain to her.

Reading enlightened books, attending relaxation classes, Rose pitied women before this time who, superstitious and afraid, resigned to pain, suffered it.

The actual birth was a shock.

As a pale March sun laid itself on the floor of the nursery and she, exhilarated with energy, stretched to hang the apple-green curtains with the appliquéd cherries, the waters broke. It was beginning! She knew exactly what to do. All was prepared. She was not going to be a nuisance to anyone, not one of those silly women who made a fuss.

It wasn't what she expected, though, and they treated her like a silly woman anyway.

They said at the hospital, yes this could be it but nothing would happen for a long time. They parted her from Peter, told her to go here, wait there, did this and that to her, left her alone. It grew dark, and the sounds of activity slowed and faded. This was all it took to reduce her. It wasn't what the books had said. They said the husband could be a great help in the early stages, holding hands, chatting to pass the time, bathing the forehead with cologne. She had put the cologne ready in the bag – which now lay out of reach. Her feet were frozen as she lay on the high trolley, her face hot. All was black outside the white hard light. Voices occasionally went past, far away.

She jumped fearfully when the curtains of the cubicle were swished metallically aside and a large loud man burst in with a nurse. 'Now, Mrs Er, how are we doing? Mm-hmmm. Hm-Hmmm. Pulse. No need to look so worried, nothing to be afraid of. Hm-hmmm.' He muttered something to the nurse, but Rose didn't listen, being too intent on not sounding like one of those fussy women.

'Please may I see my husband? He's waiting, and he's had nothing to eat — '

'Oh, we sent him home hours ago,' the nurse said briskly.

'Nothing's going to happen tonight. He can ring in the morning. Now pull yourself together, it's nothing to get upset about.'

The curtains sliced to and she was alone again. Her nose was running, and she couldn't even get to her handkerchief.

More time passed, never so meanly

Later the trolley was pushed, swerving, through doors, along passages, making her sea-sick. Through more doors into a silent ward with tidy beds in long rows. Now she was disturbing the patients' sleep. She was doing it all wrong.

No sooner had she been packed into the cold smooth bed than the ache in her back became a continuous agony and in her loins deep convulsions surged and retreated. But they knew best; they had said nothing would happen till morning. When was morning?

The ward was still. One nurse sat doing paperwork under a shaded light. At some point another patient was trolleyed in and whispers ran along the beds: 'A girl. A little girl. Eight three.' A satisfied rustle went round. Three nurses gathered by the desk, sipping tea and exchanging magazines. In a surge of pain, Rose cried out involuntarily. The nurses looked up sharply, and she cowered down like an aberrant child. She would be good, would cause no trouble; this *could* be endured. Surely. – AH!

Long after the tea-break the sister went from bed to bed on quiet shoes. Desperately Rose rehearsed her plea: 'I am very sorry to trouble you, but could you possibly have a look? I think something is happening.' But as the sister passed she was suffocated in pain – and then there was an emergency at the far end and all hastened over there, curtains pulled brusquely, doctors appearing.

Everything went far away, in another dimension. She was drowned in thumping scalding waves of agony, no longer aware whether she cried out or not.

Her neighbour shouted the length of the ward, 'Nurse! Nurse! You're wanted.' Sodden with relief, Rose was instantly attended – 'Tut tut, Mrs Stead, why didn't you ring the bell?' (bell?) – and again the shove and swerve of the trolley, bursting now into a night-factory area of personnel going here and there, metal instruments clashing in metal dishes, the hiss of gas, rush of water, orders given, screams. Into an empty room, the waves a near-constant silent roar as Rose heaved and shook, aghast at her own stupidity. She had left it too late. The baby would die. She had done it all wrong.

Efficient operatives in white surrounded her, her legs were hoisted into straps. She was far, far out of her own control, an appendage merely to this massive purpose at the other end where attention was focussed. From the hot drowning she clutched gratefully at a word she remembered from another life: PUSH.

Oh, she did. This was the final stage, she remembered now. Again. Again. This was what had to be done, though her own flesh tore. Long after she thought she could try no more, she tried. Again again again again . . . And it did not come. Finally the coterie down there consulted, relented. 'Rest a minute, Mrs Stead.' Some saint actually came up to *her* and gently wiped her face with a cool cloth. Such kindness, even to one who was doing it all so badly, not making it happen, who was being such a disappointment to them when they were trying so hard, working at night . . . She lay shivering, desolate. But a warm hand took hers. 'Now you'll just feel a little nick.' And even then they had to wait while she was once more convulsed – and they must be so tired, in this long night. She tried feebly to say 'I did try', tears running weakly – and then a knife cut her there! 'You cut me!' Oh, the betrayal! How could they hurt her so, when she had thought that no more pain was possible?

Hurried words, someone reproved and – '*Oh!*' – another cut; then from the torturers a gentle voice: 'Nearly there, Mrs Stead. A moment – now . . . Push.'

A bursting past belief . . . ungentle fingers, but brief . . . 'Yes, good . . . keep panting, the cord's round the neck . . .' and at last, at last an issuing. A thin indignant cry. 'A fine little boy. You have a son, Mrs Stead.'

Floating now, she was aware of reverent concentration. She waited serenely now, queenly, and it came about: a wrapped bundle was put into her quiet arms, now ready to take on the world. A red face and little head smeared with dark curls, the folded tiny face. 'My son.' This moment could not have been known before in the entire course of human history, or the poetry books would have been full of nothing else. Poor men. Poor Peter. They could not know. They could never know more than ordinary love, never this far further miracle of completion.

They told her to do this and that, and she obeyed, with relaxed confidence. They were pleased with her now, but it didn't matter either way. Ben was here. Eventually they took him away, but she did not hesitate to summon them back. 'Just a moment, please.' Yes, the fingers and toes all complete. She thanked them all most warmly for their pains. 'You've been so kind.'

Back in the ward breakfast was going on. The woman in the next bed asked eagerly, 'What did you get?'

'A Ben,' she murmured dreamily.

'First, was it? Ah well, it's never that bad again.'

A cup of tea, nectar. Oh and *sleep*, such sleep as never before, let the trolleys and dishes clatter as they might . . .

Peter!

The rewards were without limit, now she had done it right. Against all the rules they let him come tip-toeing down the ward, oblivious of porridge plates and bedpans. Haggard, so he could whisper 'How was it?' and she could answer truthfully 'Wonderful. It was wonderful . . .'

Peter was again shut out from the women's world, as he had been from Rose's long night and slow dawn. Lamely he went home. It was as empty as if she had never been there. He supposed he ought to do something essential, take in milk, water plants; women were always occupied. He could not think what to do. He left the neutral-smelling kitchen and went up to the nursery. Everything had been done. If he moved any item he would spoil it. He was an intruder here, it was not his world, it was for them, Rose and Ben. Her idea, the name. Illogical, when it was unlikely to be the last, for she had explained to him that an only child did not make a real family. He hated them already. Already his wife had gone, she would always be more theirs than his, at least until youth was long past. Then he could have back the ageing remnants of his Rose. And in the meantime, years and years of demands that must come first, himself never again her primary focus.

And to bring up children in the city! He shuddered to think of them amid the louts at school. In his childhood he had not suffered from bullies, did not know how to prepare them. All children should be brought up in tranquil places, un-threatened. But Gerald would marry Caroline, their children would be raised at Stoners Court; he and his did not belong. He no longer knew whether he had chosen to go, as he thought, or had been driven out by Gerald . . . he knew only that it was no longer his home. It went to him like a blade when Rose talked of going there more often. Didn't she know how it hurt?

They were here, and would stay.

He was hungry.

He knew she had left a steak and kidney pie that only needed heating. That was too much trouble for a martyr. Instead he opened a tin of beans while the kettle boiled. Bed. Had he slept last night? She'd be sleeping deep by now. No such easeful rest for a father, only an empty bed and the privilege of working to keep offspring he hadn't wanted.

By now he disgusted himself. Sleep for a while, get in a better mood, buy flowers, *tell* people!

No one knew yet. He had a son!

Rose stirred that afternoon to sounds of commotion from the next bed. Her saviour had gone home and it now bore a girl with wild bleached hair, in a bad state. She cried a lot, raucously, begged to be put out and given a Caesarean, resisted the drip – a bottle crashed to the floor – and had nurses running up and down. During the rest period Rose heard her sniffling and leaned over – ouch, the stitches! – to whisper, 'Are you all right? Shall I call for someone?'

'I just want it over with. What's it like? I bet it's awful. Everybody says.'

'It's hard but it's worth it. Honestly. As soon as you hold it — '

'Now Mrs Stead, this is quiet time. Mrs Buckler – all right, Alma – settle down, there's a good girl.'

She was a terrible patient, uncooperative, demanding, barracking the doctors, smoking in bed, and the nurses loved her. Almost always there would be one sitting on her bed listening to her going on. 'I never wanted one, nasty snotty little things puking all over.' But you knew she was all heart.

'Go on, you'll love it when it comes. Look at Mrs Stead, nursing her Ben like an old hand.'

'Well I wish it'd get a bloody shift on. Two weeks over! And it's our Lara's twenty-first tonight, me sister, and look at me. My Terry'll be there, don't worry; catch him missing a good booze-up, and there's plenty of lasses won't be sorry I'm out of the way. You can't trust the best of men with a few pints inside 'em, not to mention he hasn't been getting any for bloody weeks. He's a right so-and-so at the best of times, but I can sort him. Give you an example. Last Christmas . . .'

By the time the tea-trolleys jangled in half the ward had been enthralled. 'She's a proper tonic, that one.' When labour began in the middle of the night she shrieked and groaned with abandon, and the disturbed patients smiled and said to each other, 'That Alma, isn't she a case?' and called out, 'Good luck.'

She had a large boy after a short labour and by morning was eating all before her and giving a pang-by-pang account of the event. Rose asked confidentially, 'It is different when you hold them, isn't it?'

'He's an ugly little bugger. Are they all that ugly? Just like his dad, poor little sod, stick-out ears, and hair to cover them – though he's got lovely hair, my Terry, bit of a Ted though he's growing out of it – and that forehead, stick-out forehead, you know the kind? Stubborn. Oh, and temper! Look at that! No, he's lovely, he is. Well, if his mam doesn't love him, who will? Come on, duck, suckle up.'

It turned out that they lived close to each other. Alma's mother had a corner shop and Alma and Terry lived with her. 'Though he's got his own business, qualified motor mechanic, did his training in the army. I'm stuck with our ma, helping out. I like the company, but Terry says we'll have to get us own house now, he's not having her bring our kid up. Look what a mess she made of me, he says!'

At visiting time Terry and Peter recognised each other from the day of the forcible entry. 'I've been to The Carpenters two or three times, to try to buy you that pint – haven't I, Rose? You must have thought, what a loony. Afterwards I couldn't think why you believed me, looking as I did.'

'For a start, you talk posh. Inspires confidence, does that – unless they're talking cars, in which case don't believe a word. Second, what kind of burglar's going to ask a complete stranger to help him break in? You looked such a mess you had to be genuine.'

They were glad to see their wives too, of course.

New fathers were escorted to the nursery to view their offspring through windows. Ben and young Gary were held up side by side. Each father, stern-faced, glowed to see the unmistakable superiority of his son, and each congratulated the other on the handsomer product. But by the time they had returned and praised the mothers, they were suffocated by the close womanness of the ward. 'Time you bought me that pint, then.'

'Long overdue.'

Free men, they breathed deeply of the chill March air, and soon exchanged it for the masculine fug of The Carpenters, where they accepted many offerings.

The women, with babies duly distributed for the night feed, looked at each other ruefully. 'By, isn't it bloody marvellous?' asked Alma. 'Us stuck here, and them being treated right left and centre as if it was them done the work. Still and all, I'm more at ease in my mind, knowing he's off with your Peter. I tell you what, though, one of these days we'll leave them baby-sitting and take us-selves off for a few. If we don't treat us-self, who will? Men. Mind, isn't he lovely, my Terry? Did you notice the corner of his mouth, where he's got this little, like, dimple? Ooh, I could eat him to death. Wait till I get back, catch me waiting six weeks like they say, soon as I stop bleeding, wow! Hey, though, what if he wouldn't touch me? Hey, wouldn't that be nice? The mark of a gentleman, that's what that'd be, even if he was busting for it, but he wouldn't in case it did you some harm. Ooh, I'd think a lot of him for that, even if I was biting me nails meself. I bet your Peter'd be like that. Shall we have a bet on it?'

Rose's only anxiety, she could not say why, was that Terry's political ideas would not accord with Peter's. She hoped they would like each other anyway. That was far more important. Already she was finding in herself a tendency towards pragmatism. Was this a sign of maturity? Or a farewell to principle? It remained to be seen.

At the end of May when the tax rebate came through, Rose insisted that Ben should be taken and presented ceremoniously to his grandmothers. 'It's what I would want,' she told Peter firmly. She had a new sense of continuity. 'And I'm sure they'd be very hurt otherwise.'

'Sheila's too busy to be sentimental,' he mumbled.

'Why don't you want to go? She's so nice.'

'I've broken away, that's all. We never wanted all that family bit.' And, shifting ground somewhat: 'Already we don't see so much of our friends.' Indeed, Sam and Ailsa hadn't been round for ages. Rose thought she knew why.

He gave in, albeit ungraciously, and hired a car for half term – 'Though the money would have come in useful for a power drill' – adding, 'It's not that I'm ungrateful. Sheila didn't have to take me on. But their world isn't mine. It isn't real up there, they're cushioned from the real problems.'

'Why let it matter? Why can't you just say, yes, they have a different kind of life and leave it at that?'

'You wouldn't understand.'

There was no arguing with that. Rose retired hurt but determined. She wrote to her mother, the telephone having rung without response, suggesting they stay over the Tuesday night and go on to Northumberland in the morning.

It was a let-down to find that Pat was not in, after a struggle to change the baby on her lap in the car so she could offer him fresh and sweet, a triumph of good mothering. She was nervous. A neighbour came to the next door. 'Well, fancy you being the little mother. I thought you young ones had better ideas. And that's your hubby, is it?' It was apparent that Rose had not done as well for herself as a college education might have led anyone to expect. 'Oh, you'll find your mother at The Bull at this time. She does dinnertimes and three evenings – at least, that's how it started out. Doesn't always get back at nights. Overtime, no doubt.'

The Bull had the sort of reputation her father would not have cared for. Yet there was no alternative but to go there. Rose reproached herself: was Pat left so badly provided for that she had to endure a demeaning job? It had not occurred to her that widowhood in middle age would bring financial problems. One didn't expect parents to have problems: it was their duty not to be a worry, when the younger generation had so much to see to.

Coarse laughter spilled into the street. 'You go in,' she begged Peter.

'How can I? I hardly know her.' The funeral had not been conducive to intimacy.

Oh dear. 'Hold Ben for me, then.'

Pat was not best pleased. 'Letter? Oh well. I haven't been home for a day or two. Stocktaking.' A burly laughing man leaned over the bar beside her. They had been joking with a group of customers, all men. Pat fidgetted her lips and said, 'Frank, this is Rose.'

He put out a warm red hand. 'Rosie-posie, eh?' He turned to the company. 'Here's a bonny one, eh? Pat's little lass. How about that?' The smiles and welcome were knowing, if friendly enough. This had been a mistake.

She whispered to her mother, 'Peter's outside. And Ben. I brought him for you to see.'

'Well, I don't finish till after three . . .'

'Shall we go back to the house and wait for you?'

'There's no food in. You'd better bring them round to the back, there's a little snug we don't open at lunchtimes.'

It had been absurd to imagine that this visit could in any way atone for her neglect of her father.

They humped round the carry-cot and the large bag of necessities, and Frank switched on an electric fire in the chilly, sour little room and brought them drinks and sandwiches. 'Take twenty minutes,' he told Pat kindly. 'It's not every day you get a family visit.'

Pat carried in a gin and orange and a cigarette that she didn't smoke very naturally. She made no move to take the baby, and Rose held him away from the drift of smoke while he yelled for a feed. 'Will it be all right, in here?' She was shy to expose herself before this cold woman.

Peter ate his sandwich, pondering on the unlikeliness of blood ties.

'Were you planning to stay? I'm sorry if that doesn't sound very inviting, but we've got a licensed victuallers' do tonight, so I shan't be much company.'

'If we could. Just till the morning.' Rose was humiliated. She had wanted to have a long talk about her father; she had hoped her mother would say something to show his last thoughts of her had not been disappointed.

Under the brash defiance, Pat was in some curious way released. She did not really care whether they were here or not; there was a security about her more powerful than the resentment. 'Well, we'll have to make the best of it. I can't leave Frank in the lurch, we've no other help at this time. When you've done feeding him, go back to the house. Here's a key – better pick some milk up, I've stopped having it delivered. I'll get you something in for tea on my way back from the hairdresser.'

'We're going on to Peter's mother in the morning.'

'Frank and I are getting married, you know.'

'Oh.' Rose found it hard to speak. 'He looks – jolly.'

Pat didn't mind what her opinion was. 'Look, there's another lot come in, I'll have to go. I'll be back soon after four.'

The house was unlived in. The letter, with a few others, lay behind the door. The linen chairback where her father had sat was askew, his stack of books tidy and disregarded. The whole house was dead.

While Ben slept, Peter went for a walk. Rose looked around for reminders of childhood. She had considered herself happy. A photograph of herself on the bicycle she had been given for getting into the grammar school. Her father and Pat in evening dress for a civil service dinner, a not undistinguished couple.

But what sort of life had gone on here? She had no memory of laughter, only of quiet pleasure when she and her father had played Scrabble, listened to the Proms, talked of books and schoolwork while Pat was out playing whist. Rarely had a friend been invited for tea, but entertaining was not common in those days. Beth's parents, and Ailsa's had been better off, respectable, respected. Had her own mother always been looked at askance?

Pat came in with scones, butter, a currant loaf. 'As for supper, there's a Chinese opened on the market place; they're very good. Peter could nip up there, since you've got a car. Here's a couple of quid. I'll leave it behind the clock. You haven't told me about the baby. Did you have a bad time? I suppose they can do more for you nowadays.'

Grateful, Rose gave a brief account as Pat carefully filed and varnished her nails.

'Are you going to sell the house?'

'I shan't need it, shall I? There's a nice flat above the pub. And you're settled where you are, it seems. You wouldn't want to come back here, dreary little dump. Frank and I have got plans. We might even sell The Bull and live in Spain. He knows one or two in the Victuallers who've gone out and liked it.'

'Isn't there anything you'd – I mean, wouldn't you miss home at all?' She had no right to reproach, but she had glanced at her father's chair.

The red-tipped brush stopped in mid-stroke. 'Rose, you've a lot to learn and you'd do well not to pass judgment on what you don't understand. You think you're the only ones entitled to freedom' – broken nights and a mortgage? – 'just because you're young. I'm up to here with reading about these new fashion leaders and these silly lads in pop groups. You wait: now you've a child, you'll find out how the years of your life slip away, tied and trapped; it's not just a child growing up, it's you getting older. It all comes so easy to you lot now. There was precious little chance of making your own decisions in the war: no money, no bright lights, no pretty frocks. And me, having to watch my step for your sake, and having it watched for me, a lifetime of penance for one mistake. Doing the right thing day in day out. Marrying a good man to give you a father. I know you thought the world of him, and as a father he couldn't be bettered; you've me to thank for that if nothing else – but as a husband!

'I shouldn't have said that. I'm sorry. But he got all he wanted, ready-made family, he was content. Wasn't he? Comfortable home, lovely daughter. And I was a good wife to him, don't mistake me. But I didn't get all *I* wanted, not one tenth of it. So I'm making up for it, that's all. People can think what they like. I toed the line all those years: now it's my turn.

'We keep hearing about these swinging sixties – well then, let's all have a bit of fun. Frank makes me laugh, I've never met a man who enjoyed life more. I'm not past it yet. And then you turn up and expect me to turn into a doting granny. Well, I'm not ready for that. I wasn't ready for you, but I had to get on with it – not your fault. Ben's a nice little baby and I wish you all the best. But, Rose, I don't want to know.'

She screwed the cap back on the bottle and waved her fingers like water-fronds.

Rose made the tea and was stirred by admiration for her mother, along with relief at the acknowledgment that they had never liked each other much. Perhaps they might, later.

Pat clipped on diamanté earrings, fastened on a matching necklace out of a new case, and wrapped a fur stole round her shoulders. She looked distinctly glamorous, in an old-fashioned way. As she paused by the door Rose called out 'Mum!' and swallowed hard. 'Good luck.'

'Thank you, Rose. And to you too.'

'I admire her,' Rose said defiantly on the way north.

'So do I.' What Peter especially liked about Pat was that she obviously wasn't going to become their responsibility.

'Do you think I'm like her, at all?'

'No.'

'Then that's odd isn't it? How can we be so different? Even in looks.'

'Perhaps your father was dark and cuddly like you.'

'Oh.' As a child she had imagined him tall, distingué, a doomed hero.

'Love, we're all a complex mass of genes. Probably you're like your paternal grandmother. Or some remote aunt.'

'I wish I knew. It worries me, not knowing.' Perhaps Ben might be susceptible to some rare ailment and they wouldn't know what warning signs to look out for.

'What does it matter? They're dead and gone, most likely. We're *now*.'

But Rose saw the past as being full of vital clues, not something gone and irrelevant.

They each had much to think of on the journey. It seemed that Peter drove more slowly as they approached Stoners Court. 'Do you want to stop and change him or anything? He must be hungry.'

'I've learned to let sleeping babies lie.' Rose felt tired and inexplicably dispirited.

'Gerald will be there, I expect.'

'Yes.' Presently she added lightly, 'Do you think he'll like being an uncle?' but she was apprehensive.

Sheila reassured her. 'My dears. So this is Ben.'

'Do you want to hold him?' Rose could think of no greater accolade.

'I'm dirty just now, I've been feeding the dogs. We'll have some coffee and I'll wash. Peter dear, once you've unloaded could you do me a great favour? It won't take long. Could you slip into Stoner and pick up a gasket for the Land Rover? Mr Edwards rang to say it had come just after Gerald and Caroline left. Hugh can fix it later.'

'I'll do it.'

'That will be a help. We've been stuck for two days without it. Caroline's been running Gerald about, but he's not comfortable in a car. They've been into Newcastle to – to arrange something, and then to pick up the groceries. I expect they'll be back soon.'

Sitting with Sheila on the old bench outside the kitchen door, Rose wished there need be no one else there. 'Ben,' said Sheila, smiling at the child. 'I like the name. And he is very like Peter.'

'Yes, isn't he? Even the ears – look. And when he smiles. They do smile, don't they? The books say not yet, but they do.'

'I'm sure you're right.'

'Was Peter a good baby? I mean, sleeping through the night and so on?'

'You must remember he didn't properly come to me until he was older.'

There was so much to ask – though a certain reserve suggested that Sheila might not be ready to answer – but a dark green Alvis came into the yard and drew up carefully.

From it emerged a tall fair girl, at once gawky and graceful, an English grace. Waving briefly she went round to the other door to help out – it took time – a broader, heavier version of Peter (No, silly, they weren't blood brothers), a strong man in whom it was a cruel incongruity to see pain. This was the man whom Beth had run away with. Gerald.

Her friend had treated him badly; this harm was because of her.

But he was smiling determinedly as he slowly straightened himself, paused as if to recover, and steadied his balance before coming over. Rose stood like a guilty child, half behind Sheila.

'So this is Rose.'

She was conscious of power, almost of harshness, although

69

the smile, of great charm, did not flicker. 'We've been looking forward to this, haven't we, Caroline? And the baby. He looks well, or whatever one says about babies. Where's Peter? Skiving off as usual?' Still the smile and her hand held painfully hard, in welcome of course. Oh, it would be a gift, reparation, if he would like her. She wanted to explain, Beth isn't really like that, I don't know how she could have left you, perhaps America went to her head . . . Instead she suggested making more coffee, wondering if she was usurping Caroline by doing so. She gave Ben to Sheila, feeling now an intruder.

Then, defensive: 'Peter's gone to fetch a part for the Land Rover.'

'Splendid. He'll enjoy seeing some of his old haunts. Not that he was fond of village life. Too narrow for him. And how do you like our little patch?'

'I think it's quite beautiful.'

'Yes, so do we.' He took Caroline's hand, and she looked up momentarily, with gratitude. 'Of course, Caroline always was virtually family, weren't you, darling? Every holiday at your uncle's.'

'I must go over and see the horses,' Caroline said eagerly.

'That's right. I bet you didn't know that horses could pine, did you, Rose?' Gerald was confidential, one grown-up to another. 'But Caroline's do. Well, while you're gone Rose and I can have a good talk.'

'And I must go along and see Maggie,' Sheila said, rising, 'George's wife. She isn't too well.'

'Us poor old things.' Gerald got up with difficulty. 'Now, give me a moment to get into motion, and we'll take a stroll. I need to move, after sitting for any length of time.'

'Did you manage to see the specialist?' For the first time Sheila's concern showed.

'Usual waste of time: arthritis of some sort – might respond to heat treatment, might not. I'd rather do without the journeys. The drawbacks of living miles from anywhere,' he smiled at Rose.

'And that was all?'

'One other strange theory. That it's all in the mind.'

'Good gracious me,' Sheila commented briskly, 'as if anyone would bring such a thing on themselves.'

'Quite. These quacks. If they can't find an explanation it

must be the patient's own fault. Meanwhile: keep mobile. Which I do. Come along, Rose. Has Peter shown you the orchard yet?'

'Ben might wake.'

'I'd forgotten. You look far too innocent to have the burdens of motherhood. But of course you're the same age as Beth, aren't you? And she was old enough.' Caroline appeared to take no notice of this mention of her usurper, but it was hard to read her.

Justifying Rose's expertise, Ben stirred.

'We'll take him with us. They like movement, don't they?' So although a change of nappy was required, Rose picked up the child. 'Very bonny. That's the thing to say, isn't it? More robust than Peter was.'

Slowly they made their way the length of the lawn. 'Terrible state this is in. I'm going to have to treat myself to one of those delightful machines one can sit on, rather than push. A toy for the master. Hugh does his best, but he hasn't an eye for the stripes. I do like to see a lawn properly striped, don't you, Rose? Now tell me all about everything. Mother says you bought a big house. I do agree: nothing could be worse than being cramped, especially with a family.'

She told him what a mess it had been and what they had done and what still needed doing. 'Perhaps when the children are at school I might go back to work for a while, so we could afford more.' So then he wanted to know about teaching, and had amusing tales to tell of his own schooldays. He would have been a hard pupil, she was sure, but she did not have to fear him now. He had Sheila's easy manner, and was very interested in all she had to say.

'And do you hear often from your friend Beth?'

'Not very. We tend to write when something is getting us down, or exciting us. Ideas, I mean. Not gossip – nothing too personal.' It would be embarrassing if he thought she knew all about their separation. 'I mean, I don't know anything about the, er, early time in America. She doesn't confide.'

Idly he asked, holding a branch aside for her, 'Has she remarried?'

'Yes.'

'That fellow with the absurd name – Wensley? Wesley?'

'Wendell.'

'Yes, the one with the yacht. That will suit her, for a while. She wanted to be rich. I was a disappointment to her. A mere country landowner.'

'She was always like that. Oh, not mercenary. Romantic.'

'The first one at school to try a cigarette?'

'That's the kind of thing!' He did understand. A lesser man might have been bitter rather than amused. 'I am sorry, that it went wrong for you. It should have been — '

'There it is,' he said flippantly. 'It doesn't do to marry strangers, not for us stolid types. No harm done, that's the main thing. Lucky for me she settled for her rich man and withdrew her claim for a settlement. What complications if the land had had to be divided!'

She hadn't known about this; and he didn't know that the second marriage was already over. The baby was heavy in her arms.

'No,' he went on, 'I wouldn't have missed my brief encounter with your friend Beth. It was the making of me.' Surely an irony? But he was impassive. 'No, really. I'd had a pretty narrow life: home, school, Cambridge. She introduced me to quite different worlds. She had tremendous vigour, of the kind you only get in the working classes.'

But Beth's family had been very comfortably placed! 'Her father owns a big shop! They employ a dozen or more.'

'Really? I'm impressed.'

Again that smile.

'Did you like it, over there?'

'No. No. I ended back where I belong. And she is happy, you say?'

Rose hesitated. 'She has had a – a loss.'

'Oh?'

'She had been going to have a baby.' Better to say no more.

Gerald stumbled and all but fell. She steadied him awkwardly, squashing Ben.

'Silly of me.' It took him some time to straighten fully, leaning against a warped lichened trunk. 'The old war wound.'

They laughed, but she was uneasy.

His breathing troubled, he struck the old tree savagely. 'These will have to come out, the old varieties. They take up valuable space and don't produce.' All around them the blossom was magical. She waited, soothing Ben as best she could.

Presently they went on. 'So you two are making all the right moves, eh? Peter was lucky to get a woman with common sense. I expected him to end up with some fanatic.'

'Oh yes, we're fine. It just feels a bit daunting at times.'

'But when you're sure you've made the right decision . . . ?'

'That's the most important thing.'

'And then you can face whatever comes.'

'Yes.' She was relieved that they could understand each other.

The meeting between the two men was reserved, on Peter's part, cordial on Gerald's. 'I hear you're becoming quite a handyman. We could do with someone like you here from time to time. Lots of little jobs that George and Hugh don't have time for. And me functioning somewhat below par.'

'We could come in the holidays, couldn't we, Peter?' It would restore a balance if they could contribute something to Stoners Court. She could keep the weeds under control. And the children could grow up with roots here too.

'We must see what can be arranged, then.' Gerald smiled down at her, a jovial conspirator, an elder brother.

Now she had a real family.

They went home a day earlier than had been planned. There was no saying how the idyll was changed.

On the drive back Peter was quiet. Rose asked 'Do you miss it all the time? I would.'

'Miss it? I didn't want to stay.'

'I thought I could see why, the way you used to talk, but now I don't. It's not as if you were brought up in luxury and idleness.'

'God, no, there was always work to do.'

'So?'

'What are you asking?'

'Why you were so angry about it all.'

'Not angry, surely.'

'Yes.'

'Perhaps I overreacted.' This was a concession.

'But you so obviously love the place. And working outside.' He had allowed defences to fall, this last couple of days, despite Gerald's presence. Perhaps once you accepted that something was not for you – like Gerald and Beth – it was simple to be interested but not involved.

Several green miles hummed past. 'Do you ever feel that's the way of life you'd truly like? Because, in the future — '

'I don't know how to make you see, if you refuse to. I *couldn't*. Not once I'd known what most people have to put up with. It would be like running away. And don't tell me we have to have farmers, I know that. But not me.'

'Even though you love it.'

'For goodness' sake, Rose, you talk as though I have a choice! The farm is Gerald's! It belonged to his father. And in any case, a fat lot of progress there'd be if everyone refused to do what wasn't their – their preference.'

'There might be more happy people.'

'That's a fatuous remark and you know it.'

It was, of course. Dirty nappies had to be washed, gutters swept, banks and pubs opened on time . . . There were just tasks, though, and times came when they were done with. Going against natural affinities, though, for a lifetime – that was different. Dangerous.

Ben slept until the first traffic lights of the city disturbed the even motion of the car. Cuddling him to her – 'Not long now' – Rose noticed dirty streets, chalked obscenities on a wall, a lurching drunk, some amazingly unkempt women with scruffy children. They had been away for four days, and she felt shock. How had it been for Peter, a country child, to see such ugliness for the first time? She observed with humility that her reaction now was of distaste. His had been compassion. It still was. But hers, momentarily at least, had all vanished – because of the child. Yes: given the choice, she would have him grow up in cleanness, privilege even – and how, then, would he face harsh 'reality'? As well they could not choose.

And here was home.

It too looked unkempt. They hoped to get the outside paintwork done next year, but had forgotten how flaked and faded it was. Even the bold scarlet of the front door looked merely tawdry. Litter was in the garden, blown there or thrown, and it was dull with nothing blooming between spring bulbs and summer roses.

But she had plants from Stoners Court. She was going to

make a herb garden, and learn to cook like Sheila, whose food tasted as French food might. There would be a taste of the farm right here in the city.

It was better indoors. The kitchen was full of afternoon sun, and the indoor plants had come to no harm. The nursery had been left immaculate and it was pretty with colour and good order. By the time she had seen to Ben and put him down, Peter was back from returning the hired car, very cast down by unforeseen extra charges. He had wanted to buy an electric guitar. Nineteen guineas! No chance now. He had wanted to play blues. He blamed his mother – Sheila – for robbing him of the plangent desolation he had had to acquire at second-hand, to learn what should have come naturally, the gift of moving people to feel what it was to be born poor, to be outcast.

'Go and have a drink with Terry. That always cheers you up.' She thought it was time he outgrew these moods. She would prefer an hour on her own, strolling from room to room, imagining how each could be.

'It's too noisy down there.'

'What would you like to do, then, when we've eaten?'

'There's that tap dripping in the bath. And you wanted me to look at the catch on Ben's door; that'll mean taking the whole plate off. And pick up the damn rubbish in the garden. People are filthy.'

'Some people, not all.'

'Well that's some too many. They should be put in the stocks and have garbage thrown at them.'

'You don't have to start work as soon as we get home. None of that is urgent.'

'I don't know what I'd do here if I wasn't working. It'll be a good ten years before I have the chance to find out, that's for sure.'

Normally his tone might have been ironic. And they would have been looking at each other, sharing the wryness. Now, it came out hurtful – or Rose was hurt by it, one or both. She got up and clattered plates and pans resentfully although he had said he would wash up. 'I see. Home is associated with work and nothing else. For most people it's where they go for peace. Pleasure, even; most people actually take pleasure in their homes.'

'Come on, you know I didn't mean it like that. And leave the dishes.'

'It's the least I can do, the routine chores, when you've got this endless list of *men*'s jobs to see to in this comfortless — '

'Hey!' He put an arm round her. 'What's all this?'

That put her firmly in the wrong. 'Oh don't be all wise and forbearing, it makes it worse.'

He moved away. 'Right.'

'Ah, no!' She turned and hugged his back. 'I'm sorry. I don't know what it is. I do. I want us to be happy here.'

'Silly. Go and crochet a dahlia or something and leave me to the skilled male task of doing the dishes. Go on, shoo.'

Instead, she hovered. 'It all looks so unfinished, seeing it afresh.'

'The trouble is, coming back, I can see only what still has to be done.'

'The contrast. At Stoners Court, it's impossible to imagine a time when it wasn't all complete. Furniture, curtains – it all looks as if it grew there. I've never had such a sense of permanence.'

'That's what's worrying me, though: it isn't. Did you notice the plasterwork in the dining room? It's crumbling, above the window. And all the big cupboards in the kitchen, the way the hinges groan? I had a look: all the framework needs replacing. As for decorating, it's never been touched in my time. Gerald's a good manager, but there aren't any fortunes in farming these days.'

This was terrible: the lovely place deteriorating. But, 'It wouldn't look right, all newly done, shabbiness suits it — '

'It's not surface I'm talking about, it's basic maintenance.'

'And you talk about privilege!'

'You've been caught up by the romance of it. I never thought you had a spark of snobbery in you.'

Rose blazed. 'Well, I always did think you were rotten with *inverted* snobbery!'

From nowhere, it was suddenly the most alarmingly dangerous row they had ever had. What was it about? An old house. He thought so. (Did he?) About hard work and trouble gallantly seen through and unvalued? Rose thought so. She did.

Peter stormed off. She planted the cuttings in the pots, until such time as the door and steps out to the back garden were made, firming them in tenderly. 'Thrive!' she enjoined them. They must not wither, so far from home.

She looked up the meanings of the plants in a prized old book. 'Where rosemary thrives, the wife rules the household.' Did she want that? She loved him so much.

'Listen,' she told him when he came in. '"It takes thirty-three years for rosemary to grow to its full stature, after which it grows no more." That's the time that Jesus lived.'

'Oh?'

'And it represents remembrance, and friendship.'

'Good!'

'You can make medicine from it. "It comforts the heart, and makes it merry. Quickens the spirits and makes them more lively."'

'We could do with some.' They smiled tentatively.

'It's too small yet.'

Peter had a rough time in his first year as a teacher. There was no longer any doubt about home being a refuge. It was Rose's belief that he put more energy into bottling up slights and failures and the fracas of the week than it would have cost to come clean and recount his fears. He had too much pride to admit that he found it all but unbearable. And, too, he was now a family man, breadwinner, with no choice but to endure.

At the end of the month when the salary cheque came in he would go to the pub with Terry and listen to lorry drivers complaining about new regulations and senile car drivers, and to mechanics bemoaning the ignorance of car owners, and he bore the jibes about school-teaching being a nine-to-four doddle, and eventually found that not only did he not mind too much but even felt refreshed.

What he couldn't bear was the company of colleagues, for to hear them talk one would imagine that none of them had now or ever had his difficulties.

What kept rankling was news of a friend from university days, just back from marvellous experiences in Afghanistan.

It was lonely for Rose, but she would not leave Ben. She was glad that Alma lived nearby and called in often for a cup of tea and an enjoyable grumble.

Poor Ailsa, in her brand new house on the outskirts of town, suffered a miscarriage. It was understandable that she did not wish to visit them. So the summer, though not a bad one, frittered away in pottering about the house to no very dramatic effect, walking in the park, only rarely seeing friends. They were, in short, tired and very hard-up, and recalled in wonder the feats accomplished only two years ago. It made them feel not young, and worn out. And they were not in tune. He thought her besotted with the child, and she was profoundly disappointed in his apparent lack of enthusiasm about his son.

In the autumn it was better. Most of the worst boys had left, and Peter had learned many valuable lessons, one being that toughness first, pleasantness second, though morally to be regretted, was effective. Once he was more confident the boys could afford to like him more. He abandoned the idea of Saturday excursions and became passionately involved in plans for curriculum reform based on the dubious theory of The Seamless Robe of Learning. He now came home and discoursed at length. Rose, ungratefully, found this tiresome, but she forbore to mention that she had no wish for Ben, who was obviously of very high intelligence, to spend half his school days playing silly buggers when he could be swotting for exams.

Despite this restraint, however, Peter seemed to have got a picture of her as narrow and restricted and as term went on she suffered more than one evening when for no discernible reason she was suddenly the butt of his anger. One such occasion arose when she had merely said that it remained to be seen whether or not the abolition of the death penalty would lead to more murders. A ferocious attack ensued on all who would not march with the times, and because of whom the victims of society (murderers, presumably, not murderees) would never be able to break free from the dead weight of history dominated by the powerful and callous. It was not made clear to which of these groups Rose belonged. She, beginning to think excitedly that she might be pregnant again, and having had some bad nights with Ben's teething, went to bed in tears, bewildered. Perhaps it was true? Perhaps, without even noticing, she was coming to betray the ideals that had bonded them. She was fat and no longer fresh, regressive and wary in spirit; no wonder she had lost the love of her ardent and weary man. Then, as she hauled herself up to go yet again to the whimpering baby, she recast this interpretation. No. She had grown up. She realised that rights and wrongs were complex, very, not amenable to slogans – unlike this retarded utopianist who, like some male Mrs Jellyby, was so preoccupied with the half-understood deserving that he had not a flicker of feeling to spare for his suffering wife and son.

It was as well that because of a weakness in emotional stamina neither was able for long to sustain high indignation of this kind. Some there might be who found conflict aphrodisiac; they, feebler creatures, needed a substantial proportion of normality in order to have energy for living, let alone loving, and after a day or two of coldness would subside into each other's arms and be sorry and wonder how they could have misjudged this best of partners. But it was an exhausting time.

One Friday evening Rose was recovering from a flare-up – something about Rhodesia, had it been? – so tired that she was still sitting by Ben's cot as he slept, unable to rouse herself. She had sent Peter to the pub but he had said he wouldn't be long. He knew he had been unfair to her.

The doorbell rang: it was Merry. Oh, kind providence! 'How lovely to see you! Come in, Merry, come in do.'

She made a pot of coffee and they took it up to the bedroom, still their retreat, partly because she had seen enough of the kitchen that day and partly to be nearer to Ben if he should stir. And that was where they had talked in the old times. 'Honestly, two years? It seems an age.'

'I feel the same, kid. Gone the irresponsible days of youth, heigh-ho. Look, my hair's going thin at the corners.'

Fortunate women, who had only to worry about getting fat. 'It's getting long, though, and so curly; aren't you lucky? Don't you get told off by the head? Peter does.' Merry had – against opposition, because he was a man – been working in an infants' school.

'As it happens, no. The resident clown can get away with any eccentricity. But I'm off, Rose! I'm off to London.'

'Never. Don't tell me you're being lured by the extra money. I know – you're in love.'

'Not money as such, and not love. You know me, Rose, I'm always falling in and out, I'm dead stupid about women. There have even been times, I can tell you alone, when I have even wondered, just for a split second, that even Ailsa is not entirely without flaw. Is she all right?'

Why tell him about the miscarriage? 'As far as I know, yes.'

'Great. That's fine then. So I can go off without a care. The old lady's popped her clogs, so I've no ties.' His mother had had cancer for two years. That was why he had stayed at home. It was a peaceful end, he said. Not for him, Rose thought.

'What are you going to do?'

'I'm going to be on telly. Seriously!'

It was an intriguing scheme. He was to be attached to a nursery school in a poor area to teach as usual, but one day a week cameras would come in, or they would all go to the studios. 'The idea is for parents to watch too. It's like half teaching, but with a bit more fun, and half your singing-dancing-conjuring-coloured-lights and story-telling – guests, as well as me. Good, huh?'

It was very good, and he was perfect for it. 'It's wonderful, and you're the ideal man.'

'The snag is parting with my present lot. You know how they climb all over you. So many of them don't have dads, Rose, it's awful.'

'But you'll reach more, this way. You can be their ideal dad.'

'And what about you? I take credit for you two; I shall keep checking up. You must not ever disillusion me.'

There was no need to tell him about the rows. Every couple had rows. She said that being parents altered things, and tried to come up with some funny examples.

'But it is all all right, Rose?'

'Come and see, then you'll know.' They bent over the sleeping baby, and she had an apprehension that Merry would not know this for himself. That was part of the love he drew out of people, perhaps: a sense that along with the joy and clowning went a deep thread of loneliness.

Peter did come home early and she was very glad, so that Merry could go away happy about them. His news was celebrated to the extent of fried egg butties and a pot of tea, but Peter was noticeably tired and did not try to delay Merry when he proposed going before midnight, whereas Rose felt the time was so precious she wanted to talk for hours. When might they see him again?

She was sad when he went. Before Ben, she and Peter might then have sat up late, discussing Merry's new work and speculating about what other friends were doing or might do, looking ahead into their own lives. But he went straight to sleep.

Poor man, tired out from earning a living for us. It is different for me: I might be up a dozen times in the night, and never know when there might be a free hour to call my own. But there are flexibilities. I am, second to the small tyrant, my own boss, where Peter is bound to the inexorable pattern of his working day.

I am luckier. And lonelier. But that is part of the condition. No wonder women are strong.

And indeed the rosemary was thriving.

III

Everyone Else is Having
a Good Time

1968

My dear Beth,

. . . Yes, I can see all that about self-centredness being bad – but why do you want to leave 'self' behind? I mean, what's left?

Peter just came in and went straight to bed. He does a lot on local issues. Meetings and campaigns, too much; he's getting very thin (lovely, though, I do love him), and not nearly old enough to be the father of two. Imagine, Ben is three and Amy coming up to two! He went to the pub, he said, and held a door open for a girl, and next thing she was standing next to him in the Gents! A girl (I think) gave me a flower in town the other day. That was nice. But there's a lot I don't understand, especially the way that everyone we know who is active in all these demos and protests against the status quo and for the revolution is well off! (Are you still getting money from Wendell, by the way?)

Gerald and Caroline were married last year, very quietly; even we weren't invited. That's very good, for he needs a lot of care. His condition seems to get steadily worse, or perhaps it just takes us by surprise when we go there at long intervals. It will help him enormously when they have a family, bring him out of himself. He is sometimes very depressed, I suspect, when in pain.

He is always interested to have news of you, so he obviously doesn't bear any grudge. I write or ring every month. . . .

Oh, bed. Isn't the pill marvellous? No more messing about. I get awful headaches sometimes but it's a small price to pay.

Beth, be careful. Can't your mind expand enough without drugs? What about music? Or trees?

Alma had much to say about a new family that had moved in further up the road. 'Mother in a long dress and him with his Zapata moustache, pound to a penny he's at the university, has it away with all his girl students. And the kids! Are those hers at playgroup, little lass with a frock long enough to trip her up and no knickers, little lad can't hardly see through his hair and always in the Wendy house? You don't half get some funny people round here. Listen, did I tell you we was going to be rehoused? Then I'll have a bit of garden, a nice drying ground and try growing a few veggies all fresh; I'm looking

forward to that. Course, me Mam's upset. I mean, you don't
want the rats, and the clothes-line across the street; that
worked all right till there was so many cars, but you'd think
they'd do 'em up, wouldn't you? There's talk of a big street
party before we go, like at the Coronation, but who's going to
take it on, when all the women are out at work?'

She was thinking of looking for a little job herself. 'There's
not enough to keep me going in the shop now, trade's
dropped off terrible since they opened that Pricerite. And I
fancy a change.'

There was some advice for Rose. 'You want to get out a bit
more yourself, you're getting old-looking, not bubbly like
you was. How's your Peter doing? That smashing little bed he
made for your Amy, Terry says he ought to put his mind to
that instead of all his time on them homeless. Put your own
family first, Rose, that's what Terry says and I'm bound to
agree – though you're as bad, collecting tins here, petitions
there; you're taking on the sins of the world when everybody
else is having a good time.'

Peter was in the difficult position of being in favour of all
the changes – how could he not be? – and suspicious of those
closer to the front line.

Sam returned from Paris in high excitement. 'The mood
on the streets,' he reported, 'is like nothing you've every
known!' Rose hoped this would always be the case, having
watched scenes of astonishing violence on the small black and
white television set that Terry had passed on to them. She felt
sorry for those who had to clean up. 'Nothing will ever be the
same again! The students are in the forefront – oh, Peter, we
were born too soon! – but they articulate the feelings of the
great mass of people.' Including the street cleaners?

They listened eagerly to the radio and devoured the
Observer, seeking to understand and becoming more confused. What had once seemed simple and desirable was now
complicated and frightening. It was possible to understand
what it was all against: war and race discrimination, and,
more obscurely, technology. Many voices were earnest in
analysis, condemnation, criticism. But what was it *for*?

To leave all to the young?

Rose was only twenty-seven, but clearly ineligible. It was
apparent that the likes of herself and Peter were in some

mysterious way the enemy. They were, for example, property-owners (them and the building society); preferred that there should be no swearing in front of the children; were classic products of a stultifying and repressive social system; and in their naïveté actually assumed that education could be a force for good!

Sam (who had been to public school) tried impatiently to enlighten them. 'This "knowledge" bit. It's just an artificial construct, after all. It was designed by the privileged for the privileged – and don't give me any of that stuff about grammar school and grants, Rose – those with power have always known the technique of letting through just a small proportion of outsiders who are obviously going to conform, to keep the system steady.'

He was ardent for equality: that is, for doing away with everything that everyone did not have access to, and quite kind about her inability to comprehend the new thinking (he used the word 'thinking') because it wasn't her fault. It was hard to take offence as he poured more duty-free wine, and that made Rose's impulse to smack his face the more reprehensible – though he might rather have approved if she had done it, and congratulated her on escaping from her repressive conditioning. Sam was very much in favour of avoiding repression, which meant that Ailsa spent a lot of her time alone, in an expensive suburb.

Rose ploughed through some bits of Marcuse, and having nothing to lose risked a few silly questions. 'If technology is a bad thing because it might lead to unemployment, why is it a good thing because it will do all the hard work and free people from mindless labour? And if war is bad, why is it all right to fight in Paris and Grosvenor Square?'

This exposed the simplicity of her mental processes. 'It's immature, this hunger for consistency. There is no ideal model for society. There has to be perpetual change. You don't deny the need for change, do you? Well, then. This is the time for action: ideologies can develop later. Outgrow this lust for security!'

But children needed security and it was her job to provide it.

A big house up the road was taken over by the council for homeless families. Counter-petitions had favoured a home for the blind as being equally worthy but less likely to lead to trouble; but after *Cathy Come Home*, over which Rose still wept, compassion prevailed and the refuge, for women and children only, was duly opened.

There were disturbing sights, to be sure. Thin women dragged trails of pale children over to the swings, until they all got broken, and older children hung aimlessly over the railing staring at all that grass, not even a proper street to play on. Couples parted reluctantly at night. Sometimes there were violent bangings on the door by excluded husbands. Sometimes the women fought. Social workers were sworn at.

Passing there one day Rose saw a girl hauling a screaming toddler and berating it with misdirected venom. 'Oh, please don't!' Rose called involuntarily.

The girl stared at her and the bonny clean children. 'You try it,' she said flatly. 'See how you'd be.'

Going door-to-door with her flags for Save the Children, Rose often met with a cold reception. Students didn't believe in charity: it was paternalistic. 'Only the officials get anything out of it anyway.' Older residents had had a surfeit of children running wild and being a nuisance, for squatters were moving into the emptied houses near Alma's before they could be pulled down, knowing this would bring them high on the council lists.

She was almost in tears after one such excursion, when Peter came home furious and guilty after being subjected to abuse from a dispossessed husband outside the hostel. 'You long-haired hippy types taking up the houses, you're half the bloody trouble. I know your sort, drugs and all-night parties, living off benefits, but you're not out in the bloody street, are you?'

'We'll have to do something.' They were agreed.

'There is all this space.'

After the children were asleep – it was that delicious period when they went to bed at six and slept till morning, bliss after teething and small-hours feeds – they went to look at the top floor. Ailsa had left behind some clothes, books, pictures. 'I know I shall hate it out there, and Sam's away so much. Please let me keep a stake in your house.' But Sam was doing very well, and needed somewhere fashionable for his burgeoning social life.

They had let things slip. Brown patches stained the ceiling in various places. 'The roof will have to be done.' Sam had put in some kitchen cupboards when they were staying, but a proper draining board was needed. The furniture wasn't up to much, but for anyone desperate for privacy it might be better than the hostel.

'What about that stuff of Ailsa's?'

Telephoned, she dismissed it all. 'There's no shortage of money here, I've got masses of things. Not company, though. I often wish I was back with you, Rose.' She had had yet another phantom pregnancy. They looked hopefully at each other. To have a friend here again, so there would not be 'all this space', guilt-making. But Sam would not hear of it.

The building society refused a further loan for the roof. A brisk young man came to inspect the improvements to date, to see if the value of the house had gone up. He advised them against spending more. 'All this lot is due to come down, council policy. You've got a few years, maybe five, ten, depends how the financing of developments goes; it's all planned in stages. Look on the bright side: you'll get market value and priority for a council house, or you might go for one of those Barratt Wendy houses further out.' He thumped a solid wall. 'Barmy, isn't it? Another hundred years in this, given a bit of loving care.'

Shaken to their foundations, Rose and Peter sat in the kitchen in the warming sun and could have wept. But then: 'No. Damn it, if it ever gets to that stage we'll fight for it. It's *our* house.'

Meanwhile, the roof couldn't stay like that . . . Terry had an idea. 'Mate of mine does roofs. He's got a new house, bob or two to spend, wife wants the kitchen done out, this Scandinavian look. You're pretty handy, see if you can make a deal with him.'

An exchange of skills was duly arranged. It would take most of the summer holidays – so no visit to Stoners Court, oh alas! – but it was the only solution. The roof was made sound, and Ted's wife had the kitchen of her dreams.

Ted had been very taken with the number of books about the house. 'School-teacher, was you?' He didn't think Peter was the reader, since he worked with his hands. 'Tell you what. Our little lass is coming up to the 11+ next year. She's no brain-box but she's not daft, and we don't want her going to the secondary modern with all the riff-raff. What about giving her some lessons? Proper going rate for the job, mind.'

It was exciting, to be found worthy of paid employment. Rose agreed with pleasure.

In the autumn, Renée and her two children moved in. Alma thought they were crazy. 'It's your bloody house, isn't it? You're for ever sweating and slaving and going skint for it. Look at your Peter, working his guts out all summer at Ted's and then coming back and making you that lovely door and steps down to the back, and you decorating night after night. Catch any of them lot up at the hostel putting themselves out to do up a dump – give some of them a palace and it'll be a slum inside six months. You won't be able to call the place your own no more.'

Renée was a victim. She was twenty-four and her children were eight and three. Her father had beaten her mother into an early grave, and her husband beat her. When he wasn't inside for violence he worked on the motorways. Patrick junior was presumably a chip off the old block, thickset and uncertain of temper, contemptuous of his mother and all women. The little girl was Renée again, sparse and colourless, no bigger than two-year-old Amy. At least, thought Rose, ashamed of her doubts, they don't seem the noisy type.

Noise might have been preferable to the damp misery that seeped through the ceiling. Renée hardly ever went out and the boy didn't go to school unless he felt like it, which wasn't often. Usually he took himself out late in the morning, with Renée calling hopelessly after him, 'Wait till I tell your dad.' He would return for food, and if there was nothing that suited him upstairs would hang around Rose until she took pity on him – which didn't take long, for she feared his heavy stare. If she was out he would help himself. Money disappeared, and cigarettes from their joint ration of ten a day. He could play rumbustiously with Ben and Amy, but found them 'feeble'. He could spend an entire afternoon kicking booted heels on the floor above. The little girl did nothing at all. To give Renée a break, and because she worried about the child's development, Rose took her to the playgroup, but she just sat wherever she was put, looking out of the corners of her eyes.

Occasionally Renée would appear and hover till given cups

of tea. She smoked tiny cigarettes continuously and went out only to cash her benefits and to buy tins of food and sliced bread. 'You are clever,' she mourned, when Rose produced shepherd's pie or chocolate blancmange. 'It must be nice to be able to cook.' Rose offered to teach her, or to lend recipe books, but Renée shook her head with sad satisfaction. 'Oh no, I'm no good at anything like that.'

To Peter she said mournfully. 'That tap's dripping again. I didn't get a wink last night with it. I've had to keep Patrick at home again, it's give 'im a headache. He suffers from headaches terrible.' Peter put in a new washer. Then: 'You know that Put-U-Up? It's done my back in. Me back's been delicate, ever since Dawn was born. I wake up with this ache, all down.' And, 'Baby's got another cold. I think it's the draught from that back window. She suffers from her chest, like her Dad. You'd never think it to look at him, a big strong man like that, but he wheezes terrible in winter, specially when he first comes out; can't get used to no central heating like they has inside. I think they put something in the tea, you'd think it'd go to their stomachs but no, it has this like delayed reaction on his chest.'

'He' was the main topic of her conversation. She missed him and was waiting only till he came out again. 'Then the council will have to find us a place. It's not right to split families up.' This was despite the fact that it was against Patrick senior's principles to pay rent for such a basic human right as a roof over his family's heads. 'Yes they've put us out a few times; its not right when there's little ones.'

Luckily her rent was paid direct to Peter by the social services, but even so they were well out of pocket, with the electric fire on all day up there, not to mention the depredations of young Patrick. 'Oh, 'e's awful, I can't do a thing with 'im, 'e was always strong-willed from a baby. I tell 'im 'e'll end up like 'is dad, in and out, but 'e won't listen. I tell him he ought to show respect, living in a posh house with two teachers but it rolls off of 'im. 'E'd gone and ate all that last tin of beans and sausages, there's nothing left for me and baby till me next postal order. At least in the hostel they gave you your meals regular.' But the hostel had been eager to see the back of Patrick.

As the dull weeks dragged on towards Christmas, tempers

frayed downstairs. Alma said, 'Don't take it so seriously; you should hear some of the rows we have. I do it on purpose sometimes, just for the making-up.' They did make up, dutifully – but were becoming cautious even about that, with Patrick on the prowl.

They reminded each other of Renée's sad history. Often.

Patrick never flushed the lavatory, and the house reeked from unwashed nappies in a bucket on the top landing. When Rose braced herself to mention this, offering the use of the twin-tub, Renée put them all in the dustbin and Dawn wet the bed at nights instead. They were all nicely dressed, though. On allowance days she went up to see a friend at the hostel who ran a mail order club, and parcels arrived frequently with new clothes. Once, a van came with a flowered convertible sofa-bed. ('No, Ben, it's not for us.') It had to wait in the hall till Peter came home, and then he had to get Terry to help him up to the top with it. Then the old one had to be brought down. They put it in the empty front room. After this, the men took themselves off for a drink.

Left to herself, Rose sewed, listened to Radio Luxembourg from upstairs, and came to a decision.

At about nine there was a peremptory ring at the door, and she went obediently to let in young Patrick. 'Where have you been? Your mother will be worried.'

'She won't know what time it is, silly moo.' He turned to flick a fag-end into the garden. 'Nobody tells me.'

Rose closed the door carefully. 'Just a minute, Patrick.' Disdainful, hands in the pockets of his leather bomber jacket, he waited.

Taking her time, Rose turned him round, held him firmly by the shoulder, and smacked him several times across the bottom. He yelled, her hand stung, and she glowed with satisfaction. 'Now go upstairs,' she said happily. 'And keep your thieving little paws off our things in future. And' – calling after him as he snivelled his way up – 'pull the chain after you've been to the lavatory. Every single time. Or else.'

Peter brought in two large bottles of Guinness. 'I thought we could do with them,' he said grimly.

"Good idea. I've got a confession to make. Peter, I've gone against our most sacred principles, and it feels wonderful. I've hit a child. I've assaulted a guest under our roof. I've used authoritarian means to deal with one of the under-privileged. And I feel bloody marvellous.'

'You! What have you done – walloped that little tick?'

She told him, and they clutched each other and fell about laughing. 'Rose, you're marvellous, you always know what to do.'

They played 'Satisfaction', quite loudly, and fell asleep after making exuberant love like selfish pigs in clover.

Guilt would be back, inevitably. But first they would have a party.

It was time that the big room was used for more than a playroom on wet days. If the lighting was kept low the bare floor and plain walls would not look too bleak, and lack of furniture was surely an advantage where many people were gathered. The Put-U-Up was draped with the Indian bed-spread and they brought in a few chairs, not many, and all the cushions. The wallpapering trestle was covered with red crêpe paper and more of this ballooned round the overhead light. They put candles all about, in meat paste jars donated by Renée, who was excited, almost. With 'A Whiter Shade of Pale' playing, the atmosphere was definitely stylish.

What a disappointment that Merry couldn't come. He was working all week and spent his Saturdays at the International Children's Village; they had read of this. On the morning of the party, though, came a massive bouquet of flowers, chrysanthemums bronze and lemon and white, and a card with his love, saying, 'Don't ever go away from there.'

Ailsa and Sam came early. Ailsa, very beautiful in a new haunted way, all floating hair and huge eyes, sat about watching while Rose bathed the children and put them to bed, and sliced French loaves and finally put on her long skirt and brushed her hair loose. Rose was getting rather tired of being watched – shades of Renée – and didn't take too much notice as Ailsa told her how wonderful it was to come here. Such a sense of permanence! 'I don't see that anywhere else, out of the couples we know; only you and Peter. And Ben and Amy, oh Rose . . .'

Her eyes filled with tears. Rose put an arm round her, so thin. 'Try not to, love. There must be masses of good times to come, if only you knew.'

Sam, distinguished in a silver brocade jacket, flared

trousers and a huge gold coin on a chain round his neck, was telling Peter how much he stood to make now that commercial television was taking off. 'Advertising, that's where the money is. But, believe it or not, that isn't what I want. It's documentaries. I've done my stint on reporting, now I want to be more in control. I've got ideas. There's someone in OB who sees what I'm after. The Beeb's taught me well but there's too much aunty-ing, telling the viewers, "This is going to do you good." What we're after is information, sure, but packaged like entertainment. What's wrong with fun in learning? You used to go on and on about it: get 'em to identify, then you can teach 'em what you like.'

Peter, with sullen and lethargic fifth-year boys in mind, twice as big as him and four times louder, reflected how curious it was that with so much talk of peace lately he so frequently had an impulse to thump someone very hard, and this was such an occasion. He reminded himself that Sam had brought, as well as the obligatory bottle of plonk, one also of gin: 'Not for public consumption, old mate, stash it away somewhere.' It was good to keep in touch with old friends. Even successful ones.

And so many new ones! The outlandish couple from up the road had arrived, with half a dozen others who happened to be at their house, along with bottles and a record just brought from New York called 'Hair'. Others came, who may have been colleagues of Peter, or fellow-campaigners, or mums and husbands from the playgroup; it was impossible to tell in the dim light for they were all so glamorous – men in fancy waistcoats and flared jeans, granny specs and beads, women in tiny skirts (like Renée, hers all sparkly, hair astonishingly quadrupled in bulk) or long dresses in brilliant patterns; oh, and here some young men in unbuttoned scarlet jackets with gold epaulettes, girls in transparent tops and drifting skirts. How pretty they all looked!

Imagine us, thought Rose, quickly tiddly on Spanish red and excitement, imagine us the hosts of such a gathering! But she did consider Peter quite the most desirable of the men, though he was quite plain in checked shirt and faded corduroys. Terry was the only man in a suit, and that wasn't for long as he discarded jacket and tie and prepared to have a good time. 'He's brought his own beer,' Alma confided. 'He can't stomach wine. It was me made him get all dressed up, he said all along that it wouldn't be formal.'

Indeed it was not. On the cushions lay a couple who were something to do with economics peaceably sharing a joint, soon passed amongst peaceable others, and there was a good deal of amorous mingling inspired by T. Jones and E. Humperdinck. Rose went all swoony to 'It's Not Unusual' and went and hugged Peter's back as he discoursed on the respective merits of Dusty Springfield and Marianne Faithfull.

Renée told her story to almost everyone, missing out Alma and Terry who might not have been appreciative, and was well received, especially by a post-graduate sociologist who found here living confirmation of his credo that everything was the fault of the system.

Terry got involved with some teachers and put them to rights about this idea of making schools comprehensive. 'Take our Gary,' he invited. 'Thick as two short planks. Give him equal opportunities till you're blue in the face and he'll still never make anything but a hod-carrier.' Alma punched him but not very hard and went off to Twist with a Germanist. Terry moved on to put the outlandish party (meeting stiff competition tonight) in the picture about modern art. 'That Picasso – what's it all supposed to be when it's at home? You arty types, encouraging all this rubbish and the minute your mates get into power trampling all over it like them Red Guards. Look at them sculptures with holes all over 'em. My dad didn't leave a leg behind at Anzio for the likes of that to get all over the public parks. So think on: there's plenty more like me. Come the revolution . . . !'

He was having a cracking good time. Bumping into Peter he said, 'Haven't enjoyed meself so much for years. You can tell 'em any amount of rubbish and so long as you speak a bit broad they'll swallow the lot. You couldn't get away with that in The Carpenters. And, by heck, there's plenty here need telling. Who's that daft sod in the necklace?' And off he went to instruct Sam in what the common man expected of commercial television.

Rose drifted around offering little sticks with cheese and pineapple, hearing snippets about macrobiotic food (which sounded nasty) and the Maharishi, sexual ambiguity and the film of *Ulysses* (which would save anyone the trouble of reading it, she thought cheerfully), and the campaign to legalise cannabis: 'Look at that – can anyone see any harm there?' And indeed the group on the cushions lolled most unthreateningly; whereas Terry by now was hugging everyone he could reach and looking ready to punch anyone who did not wish to be embraced. Fortunately they all did. Ailsa was unsteady, but she was never notably erect anyway, and there were plenty of men available to support her. She was blessedly oblivious of Sam, who had penned a foreign-looking girl into a corner and was engaged in heavily meaningful social intercourse.

At some point young Patrick made an entrance, too late for most of the food, Rose was delighted to observe. He wriggled through the crowd trying to cadge a drink and a cigarette. The sociologist gave him both and invited the story of his young life. He got a story, anyway. Later, this seeker after truth sought out Rose to thank her for a rewarding evening. 'In my work,' he explained, 'you don't often manage to meet real people.'

Alma took on the peace group. 'Don't talk so wet,' she advised them. 'Change human nature, that's all you're asking. Just try changing that one for a kick-off' (Terry was now recommending National Service to the young elegants in red coats) 'or that little bugger. Look at him, up all hours and his mam on the scrounge morning till night. You've no chance . . . They're daft as brushes, that lot,' she informed Rose. 'Talk about education! If that's what it does for you then thank God I'm ignorant. Here, you, our Terry, home. Come on, shift.'

Seeing them out, Rose found Ben and Amy sitting on the stairs side by side like a Victorian painting representing reproach. 'The loo keeps going.' She hitched them up one on each hip and was going upstairs when Ailsa came to her.

'Rose, let me stay. I can't go back with him.'

'There's only the bunk beds. You can have the bottom one, if Amy will settle in her old cot.'

'That'll do, anything will do. Just let me stay.'

Just as she had got Ailsa tucked up with a hot-water bottle, a small bearded man accosted her on the landing and put his arms around her. 'Let me go to bed with you. You're so cuddly. Why are there only thin women now?'

'Go away, I'm happily married.'

'One man one woman? Goodness me, how quaint.'

Downstairs it was now a matter of shaking bottles to see what was left. Dregs were not enough to vitalise Rose, however, who had had a long day. She did try for a while, animatedly asking, 'What's anomie?' but no one took any notice. She was about to follow the example of Renée and Patrick, also now disregarded, and go to bed, when there was a stumble in the hall, cold air swishing in, and a loud male voice enquiring jovially, 'Have I got the right house? The homestead of the Steads?'

Oh, not another of Sam's friends. They did tend to —

Then she noticed Peter, who had snapped alert like a stag scenting man.

It was Gerald!

He appeared in the doorway, a fine entrance, holding on to the frame at either side. Drunk, without doubt, and totally at ease. Noble, even. And, oh, benevolent.

'Rose? Rose! Dear girl. Mustn't leave the front door open, naughty; haven't you heard that the big city is full of wicked people? Where's little brother? You have some friends in, how delightful.' In the harsher light from the hall the garish clothes looked tawdry. 'And Beth, where are you hiding her? We'll see about that later. You see, I had an intuition this would be the right time to call. I do hope you haven't run out of the cup that cheers, as is apt to happen at these student affairs.'

Peter came forward, almost gently. 'Gerald. What brings you here? You're tired.'

'Not tired. Drunk. What else is there to do? Do you have such a thing as a chair?' He was swaying. 'Ah. So kind.' The Put-U-Up was hastily vacated for him and space made as his limp became apparent. Yet it was not the spectre at the feast; more as if a healthy bracing gust of country air had come to refresh a corrupt assembly. Or so Rose thought.

'I'll get you a drink.' There was only the gin, hidden under the sink. 'Or would you prefer coffee? A sandwich?'

Peter asked again, 'How do you come to be here?'

'The answer direct: by taxi. The answer indirect: I am playing the truant.'

People, once disturbed, were moving; it was after all very late. Had anyone known that Peter had a brother? And such a Colonel Blimp, with his leather-patched tweeds. But handsome, very.

He had been in a hospital in Harrogate specialising in treatment for rheumatism and arthritis. 'Three days, me and the old biddies. Mostly old, not all. It strikes, as they say, at random. Those whom the gods love . . . I thought, Leeds isn't far, I'll have an evening off. Stopped once or twice on the way, accommodating taxi driver. I am impressed with your domain. It has a charm all its own.' Bare boards and empty glasses, shabby old curtains and a strange gathering of weirdos. 'Oh, I left a note for the nursing staff, not to distress them: "Truanting. Back in the morning." They say one shouldn't drink whilst on medication, but really . . . How do you do?'

Sam was hovering, assured, apparently, of a recognition of like kind – which was unlikely, considering one thing or another. Peter shuddered to think of political talk – he had had enough. The foreign girl, abandoned, went off in a huff. Rose introduced them and whispered to Peter, 'I'll go and change our bed for him. We can manage down here, can't we? Then I can do a bit of tidying up by morning.'

'No,' he said fiercely. 'We'll tidy up when we feel like it. It makes no difference, his being here.' But it did.

She furtively did some of the washing-up while waiting for the coffee to percolate, and made some cheese sandwiches. She wasn't putting on a show for Gerald, perish the thought; only the house wasn't usually in such a mess and she very much didn't want him to get a wrong impression. Though probably he already had.

It was Rose he wanted to talk to, though Sam stayed on, insisting that he had plenty of beds and it would be more sensible if Gerald came back with him for the night. 'I've got the car, and I'm due in early at the studios. I could run you to the station and you could get a cab at the other end. They won't even know you've been away. Rose, go and tell Ailsa, would you?'

'No. She's tired, she's asleep.'

Gerald was amenable. 'I was quite prepared to doss down, knowing I'm in liberated territory – but thank you. The old back doesn't take kindly to roughing it, I'm afraid.' As if they would have asked him to sleep on the floor! He swallowed some gin with no great relish, then some more. As Rose set down the tray beside him he caught her wrist. 'Come and talk to me.'

Trapped, she sat down, noticing sticky ring marks on the mantelshelf and a spill of wine on the rug, cigarette stubs stamped out on the floor, used plates in a corner. 'How is Sheila? And Caroline?'

'No, no, no, no. I want to talk to *you*. Has she gone?'

'Who?'

'Beth. Has she gone? Not like her to leave a party early.'

'Beth hasn't been here, Gerald. She's still in America.'

'That's what I knew you'd say.' He still had her wrist, though he leaned back, confirmed in a suspicion but not surprised. 'That's what I knew you'd say. You're a loyal friend.'

'Gerald, you're not ill are you?'

'And concerned. You are a kind little person. And trusting, very. More gin?' Only then did he let go of her. 'Thank you. You won't join me? No, you know when you've had enough. I've had far more than enough, but then I haven't got babies to get up for in the morning, have I? You said she'd lost another. Any more, since then?'

'I don't — '

'Oh, all your friends have gone. Such decorative company. I am sure you have extremely interesting friends, animated conversations discussing the meaning of life. You attract the out-of-the-ordinary, wouldn't you say? I scare them away. All but that one time; but she used to say she was scared. Can you imagine that? Kind old Gerald, everybody's elder brother . . . But I'm very conventional. Too English. That's what the trouble was. Yes, that's the trouble: incapable of adapting.'

He began to cry.

Oh God! And Peter had taken Sam off to the kitchen.

'Gerald. Oh, poor Gerald . . .'

'No babies . . .' (She thought that was it.)

'But Caroline — '

'There won't be any more. No.'

What to say? No words for this terrible – frightening – despair.

She moved nearer and put an arm round his shoulders. She couldn't love Gerald, even as a brother, and didn't know why; perhaps it was her guilt, her unwitting complicity with Beth, but she wanted so much to comfort . . .

He thrust her off with a violent lurch of his upper body, and at the same time laughed mightily. 'So!' A great indrawn breath through tight nostrils, and the smile. 'So. And how are things with you? How is your friend Beth?'

'I haven't heard for a while. I send on all the news.' Not quite all.

'To lose one baby may be regarded as a misfortune; to lose two looks like carelessness. Was it? An accident?' Under the smile, a hard gaze that wasn't seeing her. 'Ah, she's a character, your friend Beth. Not careless, though. I don't think so. I don't think things happen to her that she does not wish to happen. This, I have experienced. I speak as a victim. Is that the word? She mesmerised me: I was caught. Oh, willingly, willingly.' He went into memory. Then back: 'Was she always like that?'

'She lost another baby?'

'She didn't tell you? Then it can't have been very important. Yes. Mine. Ours. Horse-riding, six months gone. Just like some character in a book; you'd know it, student of literature as you are. We must discuss this one day: to what extent does life reflect fiction. What kind of books did she read?'

'She used to prefer the cinema.'

'Ah yes. Action not words. Yes. As I was saying, she was warned not to go but she insisted. Actually she didn't look big, perhaps he didn't know her condition. Not that Wesley much resembled Lydgate's cousin – he was something of an aristocrat, was he not? This was an American. Finesse, style, is not largely in evidence over there. But that suited her, the peasant streak. The same kind of coarse vigour. Makes us English men look effete. Excitement, yes. She loved all that. She flowered, as she never did with me. And they adored her, thought she was the English rose personified. Demure. Did you ever see that aspect of her? No, I hadn't, before. Very far from it. But then she is a source of amazement. She'll go far, my wife. America suits her.'

'It does seem so,' Rose agreed sadly.

'You think I'm mad.'

'Oh, Gerald, no! I'm still trying to take it in — '

The roar of laughter was enough to bring Peter in, alarmed — so it didn't sound humorous to him either. 'Rose thinks I'm crazy, Peter. Tell her, I'm only drunk. That's all. Go to bed now, little Rose. Haven't been so drunk since May Ball.' It took Sam too, to get him up. He paused a moment after the effort, arms round their shoulders. 'Look at your little wife, brother: all concern. She's all heart. Don't be silly, child. Feeling never did any good. Ah, who's this? My friend with the spare beds. So kind.'

They steadied him out and down the steps, and it looked as if he was conferring an honour on them. He stopped again on the path. 'Back to the biddies in the morning. I shall be a model patient.' And by the gate. 'Mother and Caroline fine. All fine. Good night, good night. May flights of angels sing thee to thy Beth.'

Rose woke at ten thirty, the latest for years, turning herself against Peter's back with sweet familiarity — then leaping out of bed with the certainty that Ben and Amy, if not chattering by dawn, must surely have perished in the night.

But no: they were 'clearing up'. They had a bowl of bubbly water on the floor of the kitchen and had no doubt had valuable learning experiences with glasses and bottles; also a minor flood.

They all surveyed the scene.

'Er, we was helping,' said Ben experimentally.

Two pairs of eyes then turned to Rose. It was tacitly understood that the situation was not conducive to a harmonious breakfast-time. Rose's lips were very tight indeed, so that she should not explode into giggles.

'Go and bother Daddy,' she said meanly; and set to work.

Ailsa could at least be told that Sam had not departed with the pretty girl. 'They must sort it out between themselves.' Suddenly cross, she threw a chipped glass into the bin.

And had it really happened, that Gerald had been there?

After Ailsa, small and apologetic, had gone, the four of them sat down to a combined breakfast and lunch. The doorbell rang. Peter sighed, and went. A weighty dark-browed man stood above him. 'I've come for me wife.'

'You'll find her upstairs,' Peter replied with great charm. 'Right at the top.'

It appeared that the absence of resistance was neither familiar nor welcome. 'They told me at the hostel she was here.'

'That's right. Would you like to go up?'

Patrick senior moved suspiciously past him into the hall. 'I'm just out.'

'Congratulations.'

'I was at me brother's yesterday. Little celebration.'

'That's nice.'

'His wife's bogged off again.'

'Oh dear.'

'Ay.' He growled a bit and Peter thought of his bacon and eggs. 'So we're having his house.'

'That is good news.'

'Uh? For who?'

'For you all. So you can be together again.'

'Ah, family man yourself, are you?'

'Oh yes, one wife, two children, all correct.'

'Ah. Been behaving, has she?'

'Perfectly. A very quiet life.'

'Ah.'

This might have gone on, but Patrick junior clattered to the rescue. 'Dad! Have you got owt for us? Mam's in bed, she's got a 'angover. Are you going to belt her?'

The two gentlemen made their way up to sort out this troublesome female and Peter passed on the good news. The family beamed at each other and at the toast and at the home-made marmalade, and Ben and Amy beamed with bells on to make up for their little mistake earlier. Bumpings came from above, which they hoped denoted packing rather than grievous bodily harm. It was utterly self-indulgent, to sit on with more coffee while the children did things with Lego, feeling all glad and golden like a cornflakes advertisement, when they could have been doing some worrying, about Renée – Ailsa – Gerald. It was delicious.

A man of action, once more, Patrick senior had his loved ones out in no time, not forgetting the sofa-bed. This was removed with the aid of Our Mick, who had been waiting outside in a van ready to provide muscle in any contingency.

Renée was more animated than they had ever seen her. 'We're off then.'

'Good luck.'

'Told you he'd fix us up with a proper house. He's a good provider, my Pat. A proper house.'

Emancipated, Rose and Peter whooped upstairs – and then down again, deciding to postpone stocktaking for there were distinct gaps; then zoomed round the kitchen and sitting room, Ben on Peter's shoulders, Amy on Rose's back. 'We'll have a holiday.'

So despite the rain they took a ball into the park and chased and kicked ineptly in wellies, and came back and toasted crumpets before the children went into a hot bath. Peter lit a fire in the big room and brought down the television, and lo! there was Laurel and Hardy, the fire burning, and all was well. How lucky they were. Amy said, 'Isn't Ailsa funny? She never giddles.' Poor Ailsa.

When the children were in bed they settled to talk, with what remained of the gin. 'It must be months since we did this. I've hardly seen you.'

'It hasn't felt like home.'

'We'll have to think carefully before having anyone in again.'

'A bit of an interval, anyway.'

'Peter, tell me about Gerald.'

'Was he bothering you?'

Yes, she was very bothered. But time was needed before she would know just how. Meanwhile, loyalty was needed to one who had surely revealed more than he had meant to. 'No, not really. I was very sad for him.'

'Gerald will always be all right.'

She didn't want to think of her husband as insensitive. A change of topic. 'I've been thinking. Ben and Amy won't be sharing a room much longer. We could put them upstairs, and the nursery could be a guest room. And the little kitchen up at the top, that would be nice when they're teenagers, they could make their own coffee.'

'And keep their friends out of our way.'

'And about this room — '

'About the basement — '

'Go on.'

'No, you.'

The doorbell rang. It was Ailsa. 'I've left him, Rose. Can I come back?'

'I blame the times,' said Rose vigorously. 'She's a fifties person – Victorian, even – she should have had an ordinary old-fashioned marriage. She should have married Merry; he'd have taken care of her, instead of taking up with Sam and getting dragged into this do-your-own-thing scene. You have to be very selfish to enjoy that. Ailsa isn't, she'd rather take care of others. She'll go to pieces.'

Peter, rather tired of the subject, was impatient. 'She's a grown woman, not a child playing at being grown-up, and for better or worse she's living now. What do you expect to happen?'

Nothing good, thought Rose.

Ailsa slept most of the days, perhaps a recovery, and very occasionally went out (Rose had to check herself from asking where; she was not her mother), and eventually brought home one David, a silky-bearded young man with a guitar which he played very quietly and much better than Peter. He looked like many others, though more beautiful than most. Considering that Jesus Christ ranked low in the top ten inspirational figures of the time, superseded by J. Lennon, B. Zimmerman, Malcolm X and a number of Krishnas and Maharishis as He was, it was curious how many, with or without beards according to genetic capacity, went around like the light of the world – the long silk hair, the calm accepting gaze. Acceptance was the required attitude.

Perhaps this would be a calming influence on Ailsa, who suffered dangerously from disappointments. Liberated from hope, she might grow stronger.

David had travelled much and had acquired wisdom. Encountered on the stairs, he would talk about his life and learning most generously. This was most kind, to waste his time on a mere housewife when he could have been getting on with his poems. As Rose washed the bathroom floor or peeled potatoes he explained to her why the nuclear family was intrinsically harmful, conditioning its younger members to expect fulfilment through a single exclusive relationship. His own parents had damaged him severely and it was only through insight that he had been able to heal himself. Love should be universal, spreading its rays indiscriminately.

Rose took the hint and moved the Oxfam collecting tin on to the hall table instead of keeping it in the kitchen for small change; but David didn't believe in money, which was an artificial construct designed to maintain barriers. It was lucky that Ailsa could pay for their food.

One evening, late as usual, Peter came up from the basement where he had been working on a coffee table for Ted's wife. 'Long may she continue as leader of interior décor in Harley Garth. There was some talk of fitted wardrobes next.'

Rose put the cover on her sewing machine. 'I'll make some tea. It's cold down there. You shouldn't be working so many hours when you've done a full day at school.'

'I don't mind. It's one way of building up a decent collection of tools. There are some new attachments you can get for a power drill that — '

David came in. 'Have you any aspirin? Ailsa's a bit odd, it might be a migraine. I've got to go out, unfortunately.'

Peter offered him tea, which Rose would not have done. 'I want to know what's been happening to Ailsa. She's looking like death lately.'

David was calm, naturally. 'We are not here to be each other's keepers. Ailsa makes her own choices. I refuse to dominate.' He may have been unperturbed by Rose's sudden anger; nevertheless he declined tea. He smiled, without reproach, though: it was just a housewife acting true to type. He called from the foot of the stairs: 'Ailsa. Are you coming?' He did not call very loudly, and there was no response. Perhaps he had his own reasons for going. He picked up his guitar, and departed.

Ailsa was very ill. The doctor couldn't get any sense from her, but he'd seen this before. 'My guess is a bad LSD trip. What's the matter with these young people? It makes me furious. I've enough folk ill who don't wish to be, without these idiots sending themselves to hell and back – if they're lucky. If you can afford a good nursing home for her, that would be best. Her mind will come and go, maybe for months. I might be wrong, of course. To look at her, you'd take her for nought but a child. But she should be under supervision.'

Sam was aghast. He wept to see what was left of his wife. They couldn't blame him – or at least not more than they blamed themselves.

While she was in hospital the telephone bill came. One hundred and eighty three pounds. Ten times more than usual. David had friends in California.

Goodbye to Peter's plan to buy good tools. He had to turn down an invitation to make fitted bedroom furniture for Ted's wife because he couldn't afford the outlay on material and was too proud to ask for an advance.

Nor could they go to Stoners Court for Easter, as Rose had hoped.

They quarrelled about this. Peter refused to worry about Gerald's condition and how Sheila was coping. 'She's managed before.'

The last thing they needed was to have doubts about each other at such a low time; but each thought the other unfeeling.

IV

Cushioning the Blows

1970

My dear Beth,

Welcome to the fold! It's not too easy to imagine you weaving and spinning and growing herbs and vegetables, but you are after all a female Proteus and I shouldn't be so amazed. Your Bob does sound very – what's the word? – sensible sounds dull (more appropriate to me and I do get fed up with it and long for lace nightdresses and painted fingernails just to show people) – no: down-to-earth, would that be it? By now you'll know for sure if you are pregnant. I hope so, Beth. They – children – they're just so lovely and cuddly and honest and funny, and there's no way of saying that that doesn't sound soppy but I don't care, it's such fun you'll wonder what you ever did to deserve such delight (after the broken nights are over, anyway).

Now that Ben is at school and Amy at playgroup I am making a few pounds of my own – heady, after having to ask for every penny. I work at it like a job, regular hours. I'm making cushions – nice bit of symbolism there. First I did all shapes and sizes for us, and then one friend and another said, oh, make some for us, and a woman I know slightly from up the road, who knows everybody, got me a sort of contract with a friend who has a shop. Enterprise, huh?

Peter too has been getting lots of jobs and has a proper workshop in the basement. School is murder so it's just as well he can get some satisfaction. The boys won't work – why should they when they can have their pick of jobs the moment they leave? Some who left last summer came back to see him – and they're earning more than he is! Ouch. There's a crying shortage of teachers, not surprising, so I might go back in a couple of years.

We haven't seen Gerald for a long time but Sheila says his condition varies considerably, which is in a way good news because it means he does have some better times. Still no children, poor them.

Merry is a terrific success on television and the children love him. Ailsa and Sam are getting on better, though he's away a lot. Oh, and our friend Jethro, the one who went to the States, he's dropped out – or, rather, *in* to what you've just left, and keeps sending us cards advising us to make love not war. We do our best but he still keeps telling us. In his spare time from carrying banners he plays with computers. Is that funny or not?

'I think they'll settle now,' Rose sighed, 'though if Amy's throat's no better by morning I'll have to ring the health centre, if I dare. Oh, for dear old Dr Mackenzie, going along whenever you needed to, waiting in the dining room, always some old lady to tell everyone when it was their turn, *Country Life* and *Popular Gardening* to look at and his grandchildren's trikes cluttering the hall. Now it's one of Alma's fire stations.'

'Fire stations? What on earth are you talking about?'

'These new places. I told you. Make an appointment to be ill three weeks in advance, rows of chairs bolted together, no magazines because of germs and a loudspeaker calling names you can't make out. And a two-hour wait, very likely.'

'Yes, you told me.'

'Have you much more to do?'

'I told you. These new schemes for reorganisation.'

Rose turned her knitting. 'Ouch, my back. We could do with an armchair in here. Can't you find an old rocking chair somewhere? Well, at least it's handy for the kettle.'

'We agreed, the workshop first. But if you're going to go on about the sitting room — '

'I'm sorry, I know our priorities. It's not as though we do much sitting, anyway.'

Peter pressed a hand over his eyes, dragging his face. 'I'm run ragged. The tough lads are outdoing each other to prove how they'll show all the swots, when we amalgamate next year. One shaved off all his hair.'

'Deliberately to make oneself look hideous.' Rose pondered. 'I wonder why that is so menacing?'

'He's been suspended, thank God. But now he's a hero when he was a nobody.'

'What a reception the grammar school boys are going to have.'

'We tell ourselves it'll only be bad the first year.'

Trying not to worry about Ben, who wasn't tall, she said, 'The sooner you're out of it the better, love. Once the workshop is properly equipped — '

'*Once*. Huh. Mortgage, food, gas bill. Two weeks of month left over after every pay cheque . . .'

'I do my best! Prices are . . . Look, what if I pay this gas bill out of the cushion money?'

'Could you, just this once? If we can only start one month without being in the red, we might stay on top.'

Now she wouldn't be able to buy any material to make more cushions. Oh, well, the playgroup jumble sale would be coming up soon. How did people manage without jumble sales? Did they have them in America?

Peter frowned over his papers. He was putting in hours of work in the hope that when the schools were made comprehensive he might be appointed to co-ordinate non-academic subjects, while all the time suspecting that the grammar school staff would get the plum jobs. And he hadn't time to develop his own work. Several people had admired the old brown-painted dresser he had bought, stripped, restored. She looked across at it now with pride. It would be easy to sell – but definitely no. But how to find time or money to buy more old furniture to make good? Caught in a trap.

She kissed his bent head as she got up to make tea. He put up a hand to her. They'd manage.

Was Amy crying? She went up. The child was feverish, the room cold. Rose put another blanket over her. Ben, on the top bunk, moved jerkily in his sleep and gabbled, 'No car bobby woo, Ben doesn't want bobby woo, no no.'

'Sssh, pet.' She stroked the dream away. 'No, no car bobby woo, not tonight. Bobby woo all gone away.' School was a strain for him, though he went eagerly; like Peter, he went into every experience intensely. Dark, skinny, beautiful. And Amy quite different, plump and fair, curly and practical. Mysteries.

She found it disturbing now, not to know their ancestry. Only one grandparent known, out of four. It awed her to imagine the unbroken chain of predecessors who had culminated in this boy, this girl. One death, one missed encounter, through thousands and thousands of years, and the children would be other than they were. In time they too would be curious. She wished they had family photographs going back, that she would be able to say, 'Your Aunt Emily had a wonderful eye for colour, it's no surprise you're good at painting,' or 'Your great-grandfather died young of liver trouble, you'll always have to be careful about drinking.' Living was so perilous – she clasped her hands to see their snuggled smallness – every possible guidance was needed. If lost, what was the point of all the suffering and learning that had gone before?

At ten Peter closed his files and stretched, groaning. He wanted to talk himself down, worry aloud, grumble, air his schemes and theories. (They used to laugh, talking over the day.) Rose knew all about all of it, she'd heard it all many times. She wanted to discuss how much of the self was built-in, relentlessly itself despite damage or discouragement from without, and how much, fragile, was utterly dependent on experience, for fulfilment or harm. Lately her own sense of identity was less secure, even though she presented to the world a cheerful capability; and she wondered how much of what Peter was now was an artefact constructed to convince himself that he was living as he should, doing what he believed in. Knowing neither parent, rejecting Sheila (this is how Rose saw it) he had seemed to build himself in line with an adopted pattern of ideas, going against goodness knew what natural forces, with the risk of goodness knew what damaging contortion.

But he was tired and she did not think it fair to challenge him. His days were not his own as hers, for all her servitude, were. She must put aside eagerness, like an untimely impulse for lust, and wind down the evening, calm and domestic, to lull him.

'I had a stroke of luck today,' she said brightly, 'with this wool for your pullover.' For herself and the children she bought jumble sale garments, washed and unravelled and remade them; never for him. 'You know I was afraid of running out? You're deceptive: bigger than you look across the chest and shoulders. I didn't think I'd be able to match the wool. But not only did they have the same dye number still in stock, but there was twopence an ounce off, end-of-range!'

'Oh, Rose, Rose.' He rested his head in his hands, elbows on the table.

'What is it?'

'Listen to yourself, knitting wool and dye numbers.'

'What about it?'

'What's happened to you? God, we never imagined living this kind of life. I'm going to bed.'

The knitting fell, along with hot tears. The injustice! When her mind was fizzing with ideas she wanted to test out on him, when she yearned often in the days and the lonely evenings for the delights of talk they used to have, heady with enthusiasm and certainties, but holding herself back for his sake, thinking, Perhaps on Friday – if he's not too tired – if he hasn't got a meeting – if he doesn't go out with Terry . . . Earlier she had been planning: when they did have an evening to themselves she would shamelessly buy a bottle of wine out of the family allowance, and they could laugh and indulge and she could ask him, her best friend, 'Where do you think the self comes from?'

Sheila, no doubt, would say, 'Whatever gave you the idea that anything would be fair?'

Peter lay awake a long time until she came to bed and then, remorseful, enfolded her. She would never know how often he dreamed of leaving her. She was his other half, his centre, his stability – and there were times when unsheltered liberty beckoned like a peri. Absurd, of no substance, like the regret for youth when possibilities seemed wide. She would never know how little as well as much he loved their children because they came between them and their own purposes, the trusting miracles, nuisances, the drain of their years.

What might he not have done without her, without them?

Women (he thought) could never feel like this.

Sam called in on his way back to the studios. He looked rather too smart, and either very worried or very impatient. 'Rose, I wish you'd go and see Ailsa. I can't make sense of her.'

'What's the matter?'

'She's such a mess. I think she's having a nervous break-down or something and she refuses to see a doctor.'

'Sam, I'm not the right person. Whenever she sees me it reminds her that she can't have a baby.'

'There's no one else.'

'She needs to get away for a while. The house is so cut off — '

'I've suggested that. But she won't go on her own, and I've got at least two weeks filming in Belfast. And don't say take her there, please.'

'Don't *you* start implying that all my native wit has run away with the washing-up water.'

'Rose, lovey, pet, make me a nice cup of tea and be cosy. I've a T and D meeting at twelve and I can't go all frazzled. If you knew what bliss it is to be somewhere clean.' Mollified, Rose put out home-made biscuits. 'Oh, your dresser! That is divine. Marcia would go berserk for it. Friend of mine, colleague, she's just bought a cottage in the Dales and is crazy for old stuff.'

'Peter could do one for her,' Rose said quickly. 'He's got the workshop organised now, he's going to do up old furniture.' Perhaps Marcia would like patchwork cushions too?

'I'll keep you to that. Tell him, get one as close to that as possible, make an equally good job of it, and he can name his price. Money's about the one thing that isn't a problem. You're all so snug here, you've no idea how lucky you are.'

'What about work?'

'God, that's what keeps me sane. Suits me down to the ground. You always said I was a bit of a phoney. I can ponce around to my heart's content and they think I'm the bees knees. I also happen to be very good at my job. Love it. My scene. Just as you were born to queen it in a cosy kitchen with dozens of chubby infants, and Peter was made to do good works.'

'That puts me squarely in my place.'

'Don't be huffy. It's solid gold.'

'Are you having a serious affair?'

'Rose, you know me, I've always screwed around. But if you're latching on to the Marcia bit, then yes, it's more than that.'

'And you wonder why Ailsa is going to pieces?'

'Jesus, Rose, she's my wife. Would I be here if I didn't care? More than she does, I can tell you. She's given me sweet FA for years. I've tried everything. She has no interest in what I do, in or out of bed; she never was much for that, and since the baby – ' He snapped a ginger fairling in half and studied the two pieces. 'And she's so beautiful still. I never met a women to come near her. Gentle. I worship her, Rose, and she's disintegrating before my eyes. What did I do?'

'Screwed around, perhaps?' But it wasn't just that. 'People are what they are. I'm coming more and more to see that it doesn't much matter what happens or doesn't happen. She's always been – fragile.' Despite a kindly home, with two known parents.

'Do what you can, will you? I'll get my secretary to let you know where I can be contacted.' He took pleasure in sounding important, even at this moment; and, oddly, she found it endearing.

When she rang, Ailsa said, 'I'm fine, Rose. I like it here. I don't want anyone.'

'I'm coming anyway, to see for myself. About seven.'

Sam had bought a house in a prosperous suburb where it was taken for granted that there were cars. Buses did not intrude along the quiet avenue. Having changed buses in town, with a twenty-minute wait, Rose now had almost a mile to walk from the nearest stop.

There were no lights on in the house and no answer to her ring. Fearful, she tried the door. It was unlocked. 'Ailsa?'

'Hello,' came the voice of a little girl.

A glimmer of light came from under the lounge door. Ailsa was there, at first invisible on the big sofa, watching television in the dark with the sound off.

'Ailsa!' Relief. 'It's Rose.'

'Hello, Rose.'

'You shouldn't leave the door unlocked, love. Anyone could come in.'

'Oh, no, nobody comes. I leave it open so they could if they wanted to, but they don't.'

'Burglars — '

'They can have the things, I don't want them. Have you seen this programme? It's very good, I saw it before.'

Disconcerted, Rose sat down. On the screen a man was moving a golden bow and arrow about while people expressed great excitement. Ailsa was totally absorbed. 'He gets very close in the end,' she whispered. 'Look.'

The arrow shot into a target and quivered near the centre, the voiceless audience was ecstatic. 'That was good, wasn't it? He's one of the best.'

'Can I put a light on?'

'If you like. I like it like this.'

Ailsa was huddled under a dirty quilt. On the fur rug by the grubby pink sofa were used cups, an open tin with a fork stuck in it. Dead plants drooped grey and withered.

'Ailsa, have you been ill?'

'I was ill, before. Now I'm fine.'

'You can't be. This is terrible. You shouldn't be living like this.'

'I like it like this. I don't dither any more. I made a decision.'

'What decision?'

'To opt out. I got that from Sam, he's very good on special phrases. Optopt optopt o-u-t. I have made my option choice: out. It's very peaceful.' Her long hair was greasy and uncombed, her nails, creepily long, begrimed.

'Well, you can jolly well opt in to a bath. Is there plenty of hot water?'

'Oh, lots and lots. Every modern convenience. My husband is a very successful man, he sees I have everything I could possibly want.'

'Come on. Up.' She was dreadfully thin.

Ailsa stood uncertainly, clutching the quilt. 'Do I have to?'

'Yes.'

'Can I bring my quilt?'

'Yes. But tomorrow it goes in the washing machine. It's all right, you can stay in bed till it's dry.'

'Just for a little while?'

'Yes. I'll take it to the launderette, our machine isn't big enough. Can you bath yourself? What about your hair?'

Ailsa's shrunken face did not alter from blankness, but tears welled out. 'I can't, Rose! I can't manage!'

'All right, don't worry. Take my hand. Up we go.'

Soaping and sponging, scrubbing at hands and feet and elbows and neck, Rose put her mind to detesting Sam. How long had she been like this?

'I made a discovery, Rose. Eating isn't necessary. At all. You can if you like, if there are things you like to eat. Otherwise, it doesn't matter in the very least.' Brightly she looked out from a new white face and held out an arm obediently. 'But you do have to drink. That is very important.'

'What do you drink?' Was this the explanation?

'Tea. I drink tea all the time. I like tea. It's very nourishing too, full of vitamins and proteins and all the goodies.'

'No it isn't. It's very refreshing but there's no goodness in it at all. Now kneel up so I can do your hair.'

'Can I have my quilt?'

'Not yet. Bend over. That's right.' There was a hand shower at the end of the bath. 'Put your hair over.'

'No, I'm cold, I'm cold. Where's my quilt?' She had just realised her nakedness. 'Rose, help, give me my quilt — '

'It'll get wet. Here, put this towel round you and I'll run some more hot. Mind your knees.' It was harder than shampooing wriggling children, this inert unco-operativeness. Ailsa crouched over, the big towel half dry, half soaked, hair dangling into the dirty water. But in the end it was done. 'Now. Where are your clothes?'

'Not clothes, nightie. I'm going to sleep now.'

There was a warm nightdress in the unused bedroom sterile with white and gilt furnishings. Bundled again in the quilt, Ailsa went happily down the stairs. 'Off to sleep now, good night, sweet dreams.' She cuddled into the sofa. 'I like it here. Beds are too big.'

She couldn't be left.

'Ailsa, have you any money?'

'Oh, lots and lots. My husband is very — '

'Where is it?'

'In the bank. Lots. I can buy anything I like, he told me.'

'No, in the house. Is there any money in the house?'

'Oh, yes, in my purse. He put it there. He's very good to me.'

'Where is it?'

'On the mantelshelf. You have it, I don't want any. Ben and Amy can have it.'

There was fifty pounds or more. Rose had never held so much. She took out five pounds and sat by Ailsa, surprised there wasn't a childish thumb in the mouth. 'Now listen. I'm going to ring for a taxi and you're going to stay with us. Rose and Peter's house, remember? Back to your old rooms.'

Ailsa sat up excitedly. 'Your house? Oh, lovely!'

'Where can I find a suitcase?'

The taxi was some time in coming. 'These bleeding posh houses, Rowans and Larches and Summerfields, too infra dig to have such a thing as a number on the gatepost. I've been up and down best part of twenty minutes. It'll cost you.'

Then there was the matter of detaching Ailsa from the television, which now showed women dancers in swaying puff-ball skirts and rigid puff-ball hair, and gliding men in tails moving glibly. 'Come on now, off we go. I'm going to turn the electricity off.'

'Did you see Merry?'

'What? Where?' The notion of Merry in tails was hysterical.

'He was on the television.'

'When?' His series was off at the moment.

'Last week. Month. Didn't you see him?' she pleaded. 'He was with all the children.' Tears spilled again.

'Yes, I saw him. Now come on, love, it's late.'

Home in the warm kitchen, Ailsa drank three cups of tea and ate two plates of tomorrow's stew, and then was sick.

Steered up the many stairs she paused and said, 'Sofa.'

For a second Rose thought madly of hauling up the one from the sitting room, and then with the simple decisiveness of exhaustion said firmly, 'Bed. There's a hot-water bottle. In you get.'

Tucked up, scarcely making any shape under the covers, Ailsa murmured, 'You'll tell Merry I was good, won't you? I love Merry. He has brown children too. I like brown children.'

Rose went to breathe deep of the sturdy warm scent of Ben and Amy. All she wanted now was for Peter to say, 'You did the right thing.' But he was already asleep, and did not turn towards her when she slipped in beside him.

In March the teachers were awarded a pay rise of one hundred and twenty pounds a year. Peter arranged an advance from the bank against the back pay and at the start of the Easter holidays bought another old dresser to do up for Marcia. Rose spent a whole ten pounds on more fabric for cushions, but put it aside. She enjoyed having Peter working at home, and helped strip off old paint and ran errands for this or that grade of glass-paper and went up and down with coffee for him. The children helped. In their way. Sam took Ailsa to Rome, and that was another freedom. They could be pleased with her progress: the doctor said flatly that she would be better with them than in hospital: 'She needs a strong dose of normality, not a bunch of loonies.'

The house next door came up for sale: three thousand two hundred and fifty pounds. As soon as Sam saw the sign he said to Peter, 'Buy it for me. I've thought about this in vague terms but next door to you is providential. A flat for Ailsa, and decent tenants for company, to give her an interest. You'd like that, wouldn't you, darling?' Their house had been put on the market and most of the contents into storage.

Ailsa laughed, but not dissenting. 'Me a landlady?'

'I'll see to the business part, don't worry. And I won't do a Rachman, never fear.' The going rate was four pounds a week for a flat, two guineas for a bed-sitter. 'The income will pay off the mortgage. It's an investment. Property's rising in value, you know.'

'Even round here?'

'Everywhere.' Even theirs? 'I'd like you to do it up, Peter. You've had the experience by now, even if this place isn't finished – and I can trust you. See what needs doing to make it into four flats, and do it. Charge the going rate. And don't stint. We want a good standard, nothing botched up.'

It was as Sam said providential: the long summer holiday giving time to work, all the equipment they lacked when they began, extra money to be earned, and a safe place for Ailsa. A step towards leaving teaching. Working for wages was no way into the future.

Ailsa was excited, or pretended to be, but one evening she came down to consult them on a moral point. 'It's about making money out of other people. That's being a capitalist, isn't it? We used to say that was wrong, didn't we? That we should just share whatever we had.'

Peter looked back at the sweet convictions of less compli cated times, while Rose rushed in. 'Ailsa dear. You could say we've been doing that, couldn't you? Taking rent from you, and Sam when he's here. Does that make us wicked capitalists?'

'You?'

'And there are all these stories about students not being able to find anywhere to live, or paying high rents for sordid little rooms with the cistern not working half the time, and ten shillings in the meter to get a hot bath. So why shouldn't they pay the same to you for somewhere really nice?'

'Yes, that makes it feel better. Is that what you think, Peter?'

He said, getting up, 'It makes perfect sense. Nothing to worry about.' Though he didn't imagine students would be able to afford flats of the standard Sam wanted.

In the workshop, sanding down a rather fine overmantel he had found on a rubbish heap, he wondered how far they had moved from their original visions.

For here he was, prepared to make a profit out of friends. He would do a good job for Sam, would not exploit him, but he would make some money. If Marcia expressed interest in the overmantel he would ask as much as she might pay elsewhere, though it had cost him nothing but sweat – because he had a wife and children who needed shoes. (Why did shoes always come to mind? Because Rose couldn't make them?)

Seven years, since they came here, meaning to offer shelter. Money had scarcely entered their heads.

Naturally the children had made the greatest change. One salary instead of two, four mouths instead of two. But he didn't want Rose anywhere but at home; he wanted to come in to good cooking, bright faces, not to a worn working woman trying to do too much, and none of it well.

The need for money, though, was only a part of his confusion.

For only a short while, it now seemed, had he been quite certain of what he was, what he wanted: during the years at university, and after, before Ben. Now, he didn't know. Rose was uncomplicated, born to be a mother. Himself . . . where had independence brought him? From country to city, from big house to another big house, from dignity (yes, there had been that) to drudgery, from the hopes of a new age to the age-old sanding down of years. Well, he was past thirty now, past youthful optimism. This too had always happened.

But what, of what he was hating, was of this time only? Not the ordinary sour moments in the life of a school-master:

Sunday nights with, yes, still the quake of apprehension; bus duty and the smell of the boys' toilets, the bank account empty many days before the next pay cheque, mince yet again, the telephone bill . . . Foul language on young lips. Now, *that* hadn't always been so, surely? Nor the reek and pressure of traffic, litter, concrete shopping malls, strikes and vandalism. Nor the victims of these times: babies in Vietnam (perhaps before, but never so inexorably *known*), Hendrix and Joplin, self-sacrificed to excited madness. Gone the flower children, come the randomly focussed ferocity of demonstrations. Gone the clean future, come the ethos of grab, and devil take the hindmost.

So was he no more than a dupe of history, when he had imagined he could help to shape it?

Or, merely, corrupted by the innocent claims of family?

He had felt great virtue in rejecting his inheritance. Now he feared he had done a great wrong to his children. He was Sheila's legal son, and he had said, contemptuously, 'Let Gerald have it all.'

How much simpler it was for women, the defining of role, identity. Rose put on forms 'wife and mother', despising the indignity of 'housewife'; 'husband and father', however, was not sufficient. Then, Sheila. Of all the people he had ever known, she alone could never have had a day in her life when she wondered, what am I? What do *I* want? Because she was born to a place, perhaps, as well as a position? And, he admitted, because she had had no choice. They used to think that choice was the prize of the age.

In the early days away from home he had relished anonymity, the chance to do anything, form his own identity. Oh, perhaps by some measures there was a kind of success. He had become an effective teacher, a good workman. But not only in his own mind was he a failure. Gerald would certainly see it so.

How simple it must have been in the past, to know from the beginning, without question from oneself or others, that one had a label: worker, gentleman, farmer, Christian, historian. Now, nothing was fixed.

He should be glad of this. He had wanted freedom from the past.

He had avoided history, especially his own, because it

required too much by way of understanding. The problem of
faith got everywhere.

He was aware of cowardice. Rose was a bad influence on
him. He had, for a time, avoided suffering from guilt, which
was damaging, wasteful. A woman's ailment.

The conversion of 192 was both like and unlike the summer
seven years ago when Rose and Peter had begun on 194. In
two ways it was better and easier: for one thing, there was
money to do it properly; and towards the end of August Sam
took three weeks' leave and came to work alongside Peter
while the women went back and forth with drinks and food
and the spoils of massive shopping excursions. If there was a
snag it was Mr Gress, a sitting tenant who refused to move.
'I know my rights,' he stated. 'Put me in one of them tower
blocks? No, thank you very much. Do what you like, set
Alsatian dogs on me, bring in the heavy mob, I'm ready for
you.' It was possibly a disappointment to him when they
simply worked round him and his small bed-sitting room and
smiled at him on chance encounters. Ailsa, of course, took his
side. She wanted her tenants to be happy. Mr Gress became
her slave.

It was a hot dry summer; and they were older. Peter, the
acknowledged expert, forgot to be edgy because of Sam's
greater success, and Sam found that Peter was not such a prig
as he had thought.

For the first time Rose saw that the houses were actually
rather elegant. They had bought their house as a shelter in
which lives could go on, not as a building with its own dignity.
Sentiment for things, the concept of pride in ownership, had
been alien to their ideas. Now she was grateful that they had
not had to divide rooms, as was happening next door in order
to make more kitchens and bathrooms. She looked with new
appreciation at their place.

On the last night of Sam's leave she made a special dinner
for them all. How well it was all going!

It was a time for comparisons, recollections. Tract-like
cards with surrealistic designs still came intermittently from
Jethro, who was heavily into ecology and against pollution.
'That's original,' said Sam. They tried to imagine him with
long hair and a beard, for no doubt barber's scissors were an

insult to nature. 'Sandals, of course.' It would hurt his toes a lot, if he was still bumping into things.

'I think it's sweet,' Rose pronounced not too soberly. 'You don't expect mathematicians to have soul.'

They asked Sam if there was any news of Merry, which was pretty pointless since they worked in quite different areas of television, and in any case he was to be seen weekly on a children's programme, looking much the same. Nearly the same. That was why they asked.

Ben and Amy adored him. 'It's Mister Merry!' He always popped out of somewhere unexpected – out of a pie, through a solid-looking wall, down from the sky – just as the girl presenter was demonstrating how to make something; and he always got it wrong, how to blow bubbles or build a castle or shape a dragon out of Plasticine. He was so wounded when it turned out wrong, his trust in the natural order shaken. But it came right in the end, and then he would sing. He was both the ideal uncle and a child himself. People of all ages smiled when he was on. This was how life ought to be: fun, funny, happy after bouncing back. Universities had Mister Merry fan clubs whose members wore rumpled curly wigs and dungarees with patches on the knees (short men were in demand), and the highest in the land were reputed to stop work when he was on.

Even Sam acknowledged his pull. 'The little man coming out on top. Universal wish-fulfilment.'

'But what about him? Is he happy? Is he married?'

'He's supposed to be a bit of a goer. Long-legged dancing girls. Don't know if it's true, they say that about everybody. But there's not much doubt about the old . . .' He moved his forearm up and down, the hand curved.

Rose gasped – and then recalled how innocently, how comically he had got drunk as a student, and how there had always been someone to lend him a bed or take him home. She hoped there still was.

And naturally, Beth was mentioned. Rose told Ailsa at least some of the news whenever she had a letter, but Ailsa's memory was not good. She heard now about the smallholding in Oregon and the goats and vegetables and unusual poultry with mild amazement. 'I wonder how she keeps her nails nice?' she pondered.

This stopped the conversation. From time to time – though rarely of late; since the buying of 192, in fact – there had come glimpses of Ailsa's otherness. Sometimes these were funny, charming, bringing out protective affection. Now, although no eye signals were exchanged, the three were touched with alarm. But it passed quickly. All was as well as it could be.

So as they sat round the commodious table, aching, pleased with each other and themselves, Rose glanced with satisfaction from face to face under the low-hanging light – and was jarred into an alert second look at Ailsa. Lovely as a madonna, her suffering was painful to see. Ailsa knew she was in part destroyed. But it was to Sam that Rose's heart went out. Terrible, the power of a woman to reproach by mute suffering, terrible the accusation of a pale and controlled face beloved and unloving. He did not deserve this, she thought; none of them did. It nullified all their efforts, saying as it did, 'I am hurt beyond all possibility of aid. Do not imagine that anything you could ever do would be enough to heal me.'

It was cruel. Ailsa clung to her misery, cultivated it, sat it beside her to be a skeleton at a feast of friendship. Pat and Sheila had had losses and borne up with defiance, hadn't they? Then Rose accused herself of a failure of compassion. How could any of them know what it was to be trapped frozen in the bleak endless night of despair?

Then Ailsa responded to some remark of Peter's with such a sweet smile that they all glowed as though a hoped-for but not expected gift had been vouchsafed. They poured more wine and took more chicken, and all was good.

But Rose had learned a lesson to apply to herself. For how long had she been miserable, making it apparent in some way Peter was letting her down? How stoically – or obliviously – had he borne the silent accusation? Neither he nor Sam was a martyr; but they should not be made responsible for the happiness of their women. The women must to a large exent cultivate their own.

As always when she made discoveries, Rose referred her finding, in her mind, to Sheila.

She saw that it was up to her.

Unlike Sheila she did not have to manage on her own. The

hardest years were surely past, of too little money and the solipsistic demands of small children. Now, she and Peter could be more equal partners – as Ailsa could never be to Sam.

From now on she would not resent. She would act.

V

A Flying Visit

1972

My dear Beth,

Obviously my last few letters didn't reach you. I put it down to the postal strikes, till I saw how many times you've moved. Even for you, two marriages/liaisons in two years is going it a bit – and as for twins! Nothing by halves, that's my old friend Beth. Jacob and Martha, lovely. And it *is* good, isn't it?

Don't know why I still think of you as purposeful and us as continually bodging up as best we can. It's the state of the nation, perhaps – strikes and complaints, muddle and mess. I've been going to evening classes, Social Psychology, fascinating. Did you know that the self is under threat every single time we're with others? Wow. That rocked me. But the alternative would leave much to be desired . . .

We had a party a while ago and oh! it was dreary. No colours! Almost all the women in trouser suits, drab, and all the conversation about what is wrong. (Everyone has answers but me.) Whatever happened to fun?

But we had a mysterious phone call from Gerald and are going to Stoners Court next week, hurray, and there I always feel I'll find an answer without even having to worry it out. (Then we come back here and it's puzzlement again. There's an image that haunts me, don't know if you saw the picture: a young girl in Belfast, tied to a lamp-post, her hair hacked off and tar poured over her. She'd gone out with an English soldier . . .) You were right, though. I can't picture you as châtelaine there; you did know best even if it was necessary to be cruel at the time. Caroline calmly gets on with breeding (horses, that is).

As for you, I conjure you up, stirring and chanting spells. Do you actually make a living from your herbs and potions?

Gerald had rung – unusually – and said, 'What about coming up for a few days? Sheila's taken off, we can do with a hand.'

It was what Rose wanted, to be needed there. She started sorting out clothes at once, even before Peter got home; there was no question as to whether they should go, but many questions as to the why. Sheila, taking off?

Peter had no answers: but she saw he didn't need them; she

had seen the instant light in his face when she said they were going up, unmistakable, before it was darkened and she knew it was at the immediate thought of Gerald. 'He wanted us to come,' she emphasised. 'He asked us.'

By chance there was a one-day strike called for the Friday. 'We'll go on Thursday evening.'

'Shouldn't you be going to a union meeting instead?'

'I should, but I'm not.'

Here was a change. They did not discuss it. 'I'll bring in some tea. Merry's on.'

After his programme – Ben and Amy sat absorbed on the floor, leaning forward, eager to miss no opportunity to laugh, or sigh with unanxious concern – he appeared again on the local news, opening a home for seriously handicapped children. Everyone there was laughing too, civic dignitaries, nurses, the little ones in wheelchairs. Then he had turned straight to camera and said plainly, 'We still need more money. That's what makes it all possible. Go on giving.'

Ben was thoughtful over supper. 'Mummy, can't those children run?'

'No, dear.'

'Why?'

'Some of them were born like that.'

'And we were born that we could run about?'

'Thank God, yes.'

'Oh. I think they'd like to, when they get better.'

'Perhaps they will one day, some of them.'

He pondered. 'But they can still see the funny side, can't they?'

'Yes, they can still laugh.'

And there was Merry on the doorstep, just the same almost, beaming, though dark beneath the eyes, with a large bottle under each arm. 'Is this wheer Sir and Lady Stead lives? Run up, there's a good lass, and see if t'missus can spare a cup o' tea. That's if t'mester's out o' t'road, I'm a randy little bugger for cuddly women.'

'Oh, it's you! Come in, come in, and give me a hug.'

The children kept looking from him to the television set in some doubt (Amy whispered, 'He's too big!'), and bedtime was of course somewhat delayed while they climbed all over him in their pyjamas and touched his hair and asked what had happened to that big black dog that simply *wouldn't* come back, and why it didn't hurt when he jumped off the roof when the big fat witch was after him for not tying his shoe-laces . . . But finally there was that exquisite grown-up quiet and the opening of bottles. Ah, no. That had been earlier, was in fact at once upon his arrival, a glass or two as he played with the children, another as he sat in on the ritual of teeth-cleaning and tucking-in . . . so that by the time Rose had made Spanish omelettes and Peter had been to the off-licence and back, one empty bottle stood already by the back door and the other was jointly broached.

As Sam had, he said, 'It's good to find some people the same, in the same place. London is . . . well, different.'

'What do you do all the time? Is it all work?'

'Three days a week writing, rehearsing, recording. Then charity stuff. There are one or two homes I go to a lot. Not the ones that get on the news.'

'What sort of homes?'

He drank, didn't want to say; laughed. 'Monstrous little buggers. Big heads, no arms, no eyes. Enough to make you hurry your two away lest they should believe in the devil. Horrible little creatures, no wonder even their own mums can't bear to look at them. I tell the staff, you should have drowned that one at birth. Who's going to love that?'

'You, I suppose,' Rose said.

'Well, you have to laugh. All part of the divine comedy, no doubt. Thank the Good Lord for this, eh?' He raised his glass. 'Heavenly consolation.'

'You used to drink bitter,' Peter recalled.

'Ay, them were t'days. But have you tried London bitter? That's one reason. Also it makes you pee too much, excuse me, Rose. Furthermore, what's the point of being loaded with gold if you don't expand your tastes? And finally, beer makes me fat and spirits give me a hangover and the eyes show it on the box. Ergo the grape. I rest my case. Listen, is there plenty left? Where's the nearest offie?'

There was most of a litre, and the one Peter had brought, but that wouldn't suffice. Peter insisted on going out again – 'You're the guest' – but he had to take some of the notes Merry thrust at him. 'Champagne. See if they've any champagne. You two are worth celebrating.'

When he had gone Merry asked, 'How's the princess?'

Was it fortunate or not, that she was away? 'She was quite ill a while back. Some sort of nervous — '

'A dark night of the soul, yes?'

'Something like that. She stayed here – the house Sam bought wasn't right for her – and then they bought next door; it's in flats, with a lovely one for her. Sam's away most of the time.'

'Next door.'

'But she's not here now.'

'Ah.'

'It's all right, she's been much better. Her mother had an operation, not serious. Ailsa's gone with her to Filey for a week.'

'And she's better now, is she?'

How to put it clearly? 'There'll always be a gap. Because of not having a child. And, er, they wouldn't let her adopt, because of . . .'

'Frail health.'

'Yes. But she's coming to terms with it. I mean, everyone has disappointments. Peter's mother is a case in point — '

'She would have made a lovely mother.' Mothers needed to be tough, thought Rose, offering hostages to fortune, but she said nothing. 'Funny, isn't it? If I'd been a few inches taller she might have fallen for me. Might.'

She thought, no: there was a compulsion towards unhappiness in Ailsa which would always have obliged her towards wrong choices – but this insight came from wine and was not to be trusted. He didn't wait. 'Well, that's my secret sorrow that everyone knows about, that's my excuse for being a randy little lush. I think you're right – though she hadn't spoken – 'we are what we are', we've just got so flaming clever and analytical that we look for excuses for being so gormless.' Another deep swallow – and the lights went out.

'A power cut.'

They lit candles, so that when Peter came in again they all had to say how much it was like old times. Merry had a theory. 'It's my belief that practically everybody in London is mad, most people really, except for the ones who work at the homes. No, I tell a lie. There's one make-up girl and two canteen ladies at Television Centre who are certifiably sane.

132

Oh, and Morecambe and Wise. All the rest of them down there are barmy. I'll tell you what baffles me, it really gets my goat. It's the number of them that don't seem sure what sex they are. You'd think it was clear enough, wouldn't you? Given the natural equipment? Peter, have you ever had any doubt over whether you want to go to bed with a bloke or a woman? Exactly. We'll finish this, then we'll open the fizz. I put it down to over-stimulation: they do it so much they get bored and start looking for variations on the theme, and I tell you flatly in the sanctity of these hallowed walls that I do not think it is very *nice*. Because – fill up, fill up – it all comes down to thrills. Not people, thrills. Saps the moral fibre, makes it all me, me, me. Another good reason for this. It isn't half effective in stopping you. Playing about, I mean. You get so you can't, see. I used to. Good fun if all parties agreeable, beats clog-dancing any day of the week. For a bit. Then it gets silly. Better without it, I concluded. The best, or nothing at all. Open that champagne, Peter. Sad, really, and me only a slip of a lad.

'The toast! Be upstanding, lady and gentleman. Long life and happiness to my old mates Pose and Re – Rose and Peter Steadfast and the babes and the fortress. I should write you a song.'

'Good health, Merry.'

'Health and happiness, Merry dear.'

Their legs were quite wobbly as they sat down again. They competed to raise urgent issues with him, not least education, a matter of disappointment, and then apologised. 'Why do we keep coming back to that?'

'Because it's about everything. Lives, values. The future. This Little Red School Book.' For the only time, they saw him angry. 'It's not fair, stealing away childhood, loading kids with knowledge they're not ready for. And that slimy get-out: give them the information and let them make up their own minds. How can they? You've only got to look at the mess grown-ups make with sex and drugs' – they thought of Ailsa – 'and they expect little kids to do better? Cruel, cruel.'

But what underlay it all, they vaguely but surely grasped, was this question of what to do and where to be. Which was curious, seeing that it was not a question capable of answer, nor one they had themselves aired for a long time. They used

Merry as intermediary. 'We're going up to Stoners Court soon, you see,' Rose explained. Merry nodded, awaiting elucidation. It was the wrong time of night and the wrong end of the bottle for that. It was somehow to do with Renée but that wasn't the right example, was it? And the proper one just wouldn't come to mind; and they got confused, knowing that they were failing in some mysterious way no matter how hard they tried, and there wasn't any real alternative, Gerald being the landowner by law let alone by way of compensation – oh, there was unfairness, Merry – not to mention Sheila still alone and the courage (this from Rose), but the point was (Peter), the big worry was that if a person couldn't do much to help, or so it seemed day by day, what was the use? Or maybe he had made a great error of judgment long ago and was paying for it – which was proper, no one was trying to get away with anything . . . well, there was this constant sense of guilt. The correct word had been arrived at.

Heads bent – a confessional – Rose and Peter awaited wisdom.

'And being in the wrong place,' Peter added, very low, but Rose heard. She pretended she hadn't, but took his hand all the same.

Merry might or might not have followed all this. 'It's handing on the torch,' he assured them. 'It doesn't matter how or where you do it or for how many, as long as you do.' And they all knew, at the time, precisely what the torch was, lambent, precious, revealing wonders, lighting truths; and how fragile was the hold: a stumble, and the dark would swallow all. They all rejoiced, humbly, to be torch-bearers, and resolved to be worthy . . . Then Rose began to wonder who was not a torch-bearer, and found herself in the middle of a passionate defence of ordinariness (which had not been attacked) and the many decencies to be found in daily life, like Auntie May in the pub that time, and a bus driver who only that day had got down from his cab to see an old man across the road. 'You see what I mean?' Peter, who had heard the story earlier, was momentarily asleep, but Merry nodded a good deal and saw exactly what she meant. 'I mean, even Beth . . .'

'How is Beth? Didn't she go astray?'

'No, no, no. I mean, yes, I suppose . . . but what I was

going to say is, she could be very kind. Once . . .' But it had gone.

Two in the morning saw them falling about at hilarious stories of behind-the-scenes and gossip about well-known figures. Such a pity they couldn't remember any next day. At three Rose was inspired to cook bacon and eggs and Merry regretted there was no more champagne to make Bucks Fizz, but they made do with tea.

As the birds woke they went to bed, Merry in the one made up for Ailsa who still in the occasional *crise de nerfs* came to stay, but they didn't tell him that.

Even before the children stirred, a driver called to take him to Manchester. They said goodbye with much affection and thumping heads in the clean morning and Rose said from a blank mind, 'We'll never see him again,' and Peter very properly told her off for being over dramatic.

Ben and Amy were not surprised that he had gone. They had not expected to see Mister Merry in the morning.

Rose went up later to straighten the sheets and told herself that it wasn't worth changing them after only a couple of hours' use. Ailsa could jolly well sleep in them as they were. She was disappointed in Ailsa; unfairly.

Loss, she thought, can do terrible things to people. The loss of love. Many times she wondered about Gerald's broken confidences. And now Merry. The removal of love could make some strong – look at Sheila. And Pat? Others, in one way or another, it broke.

Pat, too, was packing. 'Frank's not too good,' she explained on the telephone. 'Heart. He's a silly devil, can't resist a good time.' She sounded happier than Rose had ever known her. 'And we're fairly busy, generally speaking. So we're off to Spain for a couple of weeks; we thought of looking round for a villa, or an apartment. He has some friends out there who are quite settled. Of course we'd only use it now and then. You could take the family, Rose. About time you had a bit of fun.'

'That would be wonderful!'

'I'll let you know if we find somewhere. I'm sorry we shan't be able to see you, we're flying from Manchester tonight. Listen, I'll put a few quid in the post. Buy the children a present from us.'

'Thanks, Mum, I will.'

Rose turned to Peter. 'She's happy!'

'Good.'

'Oh, I'm so glad! I never thought she would be. And easy to talk to!'

'Great.'

It was: it was a breakthrough, and a release. All her life Rose had felt that it was her fault, her mother's hardness. Now she was free – and they were going to Stoners Court. She sang as she got them all ready, with sleeping bags in the back of the car for Ben and Amy, for it would be dark long before they got there.

They had not travelled up at night before. Once the light went, clinging in red flashes to spaces between the hills, it was out of time, no sensation of movement, rather of being moved, kindly, from one life to another; of being given an interval in which to prepare like actors for a major transition, with no anxiety but an almost religious erasing of all that was other, irrelevant. The wide country gave them room, and silence.

At the familiar, but hushed, swish of the tyres on the courtyard gravel, the children stirred but were not disturbed, as though they knew their parts were not yet. Caroline met them, Gerald waved from the drawing room, and they carried the sleepy bundles up to bed and left them snuggled, happy to be here, too drowsy to do more than smile at pleasures in the morning.

Supper was ready, a casserole. The four of them ate slowly, quietly, with talk only of ordinary matters, wound down for a country night. The travellers could not but yawn, deliciously replete.

Gerald looked well. He was on a new treatment that was very promising, though they knew by now not to build up too many hopes. He took Caroline's hand across the corner of the table as they spoke of it.

It was strange not to see Sheila there. It made them feel young, Rose thought; but on good behaviour, shouldering adult responsibility in harmony, all vestiges of childish strife smoothed away. Even Peter did not rise with edge to a query about the teachers' action: 'It's a long job,' he said mildly. 'Time it was sorted out.'

'And meanwhile,' smiled Gerald, 'you can forget it all. Relax. Get some air.'

'Oh, it is *lovely* to be here!'

'You look better already, Rose.'

'Better? Don't I look well at home? I thought I was one of those boring women who always look the picture of health.'

'Better here,' Gerald repeated.

Caroline made tea: 'You don't mind? We prefer it at night.'

'Can I help?'

'No. Tomorrow, perhaps. I have to be there for the farrier.'

'Doesn't have to be,' Gerald said with a wink, '*wants* to be.'

Peter asked about the horses and while Caroline answered with enthusiasm Gerald said, 'I keep wondering about the end cottage, you know.'

'What about it?' Rose's heart stupidly lifted.

'Whether it could be put in order. It's been empty since George died. Terrible waste. Whether it would be big enough for a family. They only had Hugh. But there is a loft that might be – Oh, thank you, darling.' It was a little while before Caroline went to let out the dogs and Peter went to the door for a last breath of air. 'Sheila isn't getting any younger, of course. And with only Hugh, and contract labour . . . Ah well.' Gerald sighed comfortably, smiled with warmth. 'Time for bed, I think.'

Rose was too excited to sleep, for all of ten minutes, listening to the stillness, feeling the old house around them all. Home.

When she woke Peter's half of the bed was empty and cold; he had long been up, to help with the milking. Oh dear, she would never do for a farmer's wife, sleeping late. It was well after seven, later than she slept at home.

Ben and Amy were already out, playing with the dogs in pyjama tops and trousers in the light rain. She was able to redeem herself by making breakfast, queen of the kitchen in answer to a note from Caroline saying where bacon was to be found. She spoiled a few slices of bread before mastering the knack of making toast on the Aga, toast like no other, just caught crisp on the outside, soft in the middle. She fed the children and then Peter, but Gerald was not an early riser. The others went off to see to a fence that needed mending, and she waited, wondering what she might do towards lunch.

Pulling on one of Sheila's macs by the back door she went to inspect the vegetable patch, pulled some milk thistle, decided it was too soon to cut curly kale lest it should spoil by evening, and was about to start dusting in the drawing room when George's widow, now living in the village, appeared, evidently not best pleased to have her routine spoiled. Rose offered tea.

'We have our coffee at eleven. We like to break the back of the work first,' she was told, and the Hoover was busily switched on.

It was disconcerting to feel like an inexperienced visitor. But ironing came to the rescue. There was always heaps of clean washing in the scullery. Purposeful and virtuous, Rose began on the heap of sheets and shirts and towels and was soon so restored that when Emmy in passing observed, 'We don't iron the towels, just fold them,' she was able to say tranquilly, 'But I've time to do them at the moment.'

When she had finished, knowing her limitations, she left the tidy pile for someone else to put away. The last thing she wanted was to seem intrusive, proprietorial: she knew her place.

She had expected confidences from Gerald, after last night's hints; but he had an appointment with his bank manager in Hexham. 'Oh. Can I drive you in, then?'

'I can still drive, thank you.' He was irritable in the mornings, cursing the slowness of his limbs. Then he changed his mind. 'Yes, why not? Five minutes.'

Gladly she ran out to the field edge to call out to Peter where she was going, flew back for a coat, wishing she had good tweeds, however shabby, and fine leather walking shoes. Alas, the Oxfam shops in Leeds were not rich in such items. Perhaps there would be a find in Hexham.

She had the sense not to fuss as Gerald climbed laboriously into the Land Rover, nor to talk other than to ask for directions. But after some miles she was able to say, 'Why did Sheila "take off"? She is all right? Where has she gone?'

'She has to go now and again.'

'Where?'

'To the coast, usually. When it's stormy. When the sea is wild, that's what she likes.'

'Oh yes, I can understand that.' She had thought Sheila never took holidays. 'Does she go with a friend?'

'A friend? No, she just takes off.'

'To be alone?'

'Christ, Rose, she *is* alone, isn't she?'

She was obviously being very dense, but she was more concerned to understand Sheila, whom she greatly loved, than to fear Gerald's impatience.

'Why does she go, Gerald?'

'To work off the rage, of course.' He understood, spoke naturally; it was a natural thing to do. 'What else would you expect? Left at the T junction. Well, perhaps "rage" is putting it a bit strongly. For Sheila.'

There was nowhere to park near the bank, so she dropped him off and promised to be there in half an hour exactly. She left the Land Rover in a side street and walked around the lovely abbey and through the pretty market, keeping an eye on the clock but otherwise passive, letting the place and the sounds and people go through her. There was pain and shame. She was very stupid. Tranquillity, she saw, was hard-won, not a gift of nature. The process of resignation was continuous; a struggle.

On the way back Gerald was jovial. 'Good news from the bank manager?' she enquired politely.

'Mmm? Oh, good enough. I'm just waiting for us to get into the Common Market, then it'll be all right.'

'Do you think we'll all benefit, then?'

'All? I shouldn't think so. Now, Rose, tell me all. How are things with you and Peter in the big city?'

'We love the house, of course. You didn't see it at its best.' Useless to try to convey how lovely it could be. 'There's still a lot to do of course; it could take years and years. But I might be going back to teaching before long, now Amy's at school too.'

'God. You don't want to, surely? I can't think of anything more horrible.'

'Well.' She had been giving it some thought. 'I could get a job, I think. The school-leaving age is going up so if all the secondary school kids are staying another year there's sure to be a need. Not that I want to teach big ones; to be honest, I find them a bit scary.'

'Why do it, then? I thought you were happy being the little domestic.'

'To help out, Gerald. Wives do work, you know. It's different here. I know Caroline and Sheila both work, but not for wages. With us it's not the same. Peter doesn't earn that much though he works very hard. It's not fair that all the burden should fall on him.'

'Very noble.'

'No, it isn't noble at all, it's common sense. It's the way we are. We're partners.' She was cross and did not try to hide it.

There was a pause; but on this point she did not care if she had offended him. He patronised Peter and this was wrong. She was marshalling her case to demonstrate once and for all that Peter was not the starry-eyed impetuous wrong-headed younger brother – but Gerald spoke.

'You have a happy marriage,' he said.

'Yes, we do.' This given not defiantly, though, but gently, responding to a sadness in his tone.

'You're lucky. I often wonder what it's like. My wife was not the loyal kind, as you well know.'

'Caroline is of all people — '

'Beth I'm talking about.'

'But Caroline is — '

'Oh, Caroline's a good scout.' As one might say with dismissive affection of an old chair, 'Oh, it's comfortable, I suppose.'

Rose braced herself for blame, or questions about Beth's progress. She did not want to mention the twins. But something else came.

'It quite surprised me when Peter married. He was always such a romantic. Off with the old on with the new. Always a new ideal girl, once he found the previous one was merely human. He's changed, has he? Quite settled now?'

'Yes!'

'Mmmm. But then – to judge by your liberated circle – attitudes towards infidelity are different nowadays, aren't they? One understands that blind eyes are turned – or even that there is open discussion. Open marriages are the in thing, is that the jargon? No one takes such trivia seriously, am I right?'

'Well, we jolly well would. There may be some who — '

'Oh dear. Sorry I raised the subject.'

'No, it's . . .' This visit had begun so differently that Rose had thought her previous uncertainties about Gerald were of her own making. Now, she was lost again. Surely he hadn't spoken as if there were something he knew that she didn't – or something he thought she knew that she didn't? About *Peter*?

For the rest of the way he talked about the strikes, the IRA bombing, the rise in unemployment, and the fourteen-year-old English boy jailed in Turkey for carrying hashish. What did she think of this, of all these happenings? She was in a better position to judge than he was, isolated in the country, remote from public events.

'Gerald,' she told him finally, 'we're just about as far from Turkey or Aldershot as you are, and we both have access to radio and the newspapers. How does that make me an authority?'

He liked that. 'Ha! Touché, little sister.'

'There you are, then.'

'But you're more in touch with the changes, you must admit. One had only to look at your friends. We couldn't assemble such a company up here.'

'Oh, clothes . . .' But she remembered Ailsa's experiences, and had to stop. But to stop him going on she tried to make light-hearted a story of Ailsa and one of her tenants. 'She's very soft-hearted, you see. In fact, if you are talking of being out of the world . . . So naturally she has this tendency to fill her house with lame ducks — '

'I thought that was what you intended to do?'

'Us?'

'I'm sure you used to speak about having a houseful of, what was it, like-minded friends?'

Rose knew herself to be a fool but not a complete fool. This, however mild and brotherly the voice, was naked insult. She changed gear with unnecessary abruptness, for they were home, and turned into the drive, drawing up too sharply near the back door.

As she got out and called for Ben and Amy her heart rebuked her. It took him so long to get down. She was selfish and hard, touchy. There was nothing she could do to help.

He spent the afternoon in his office dealing with paperwork and telephone calls. Caroline gave in easily to Rose's offer to cook dinner. 'I'm not much of a housewife,' she agreed. 'Shall I take the children with me? They can help clean the tack.'

This was a good suggestion and well received. Rose prepared a joint of beef and potatoes and curly kale and carrots and found in the cool-room enough sound apples to make a charlotte, knowing she was taking over this three times as long as Sheila would have needed. But it was lovely when Peter came in, redolent of clean sweat, for a cup of tea before milking. They sat – she ready to move at once if anyone might suggest she was taking too much for granted – on the silver old bench in the yard, and didn't talk much. But Peter, aching and weary and pleased with his work, was at peace as she had rarely seen him.

After dinner – 'This is quite excellent, Rose. You should give Caroline lessons' (which, though she smiled politely, Caroline did not like, nor Rose) – Gerald proposed coffee – 'No, I know you prefer it; we'll have tea as usual, it's what Caroline likes' – in the drawing room. 'It doesn't get used enough. We're too often ready for bed once we've eaten. Either that, or there are things to be seen to. It needs a family, that's what it is.'

Caroline insisted on seeing to the dishes. Not comfortably, Rose and Peter accompanied Gerald, who was obviously tired in body, to the big room. It did look unused in the grey evening, and he did not suggest lights. Peter asked about his policy on bull calves, but there was no answer. The good glow of work done and full bellies thinned to discomfort.

Presently Rose said, 'I was thinking, if it's fine in the morning, I could dig over the vegetable garden, get out the spouts stumps and so on. It's not too late to put on some manure before seeding, is it? Shall I get some from outside the dairy, or, this would be better I think, go over with Caroline and get some good horse manure? Does she keep any bagged up or shall I take some sacks?'

'Mmm? Oh, we have a man to see to all that.'

Sheila had never said so. Rose had been slapped down, and knew it.

When Caroline came in with a tray and put on lamps there was some attempt at conversation which didn't take life. 'Amy has delightful manners. They both have.'

'Thank you. We do hope so.'

Rose asked when Sheila was due back. 'On Sunday, I expect. She's rarely away for more than two or three days. She likes the sea air occasionally. And this is a fairly quiet time, apart from the routine.'

'No. She goes to get rid of the rage,' Gerald muttered, or so Rose thought.

Soon he was jovial again, the host. 'You were telling me, Rose, about your friend next door. You have so many friends, I think you must spend a great deal of time on them. Keeping in touch, all that.'

Simultaneously Rose said, 'Oh, Ailsa – ' and Peter said, 'Ailsa?' and the risk of questions about Beth was past. Trying for animation Rose said, 'I was about to tell Gerald about Ailsa and her tenants. Well, that awful boy, do you remember, last winter? We have a friend next door, Caroline, who has flats to let. She will keep taking in lame ducks.'

'That was to be expected,' Peter commented.

'It was when we had a few friends in for supper, not a party. But there were several cars outside and when someone wanted to go – what was her name, Peter, that woman from the art department at your place?'

'Phyllis Tild.' This was becoming far from jokey: he had spent much time with Phyllis Tild last year working out a new scheme for integrated arts and craft subjects.

'Yes. A very thin woman. Anyway, she couldn't get the car out because there was a van in the way. None of us thought anything of it and it soon went. But when poor Ailsa went back, she found her stereo gone, and her cheque book and — '

'And practically everything portable,' Peter broke in impatiently. 'Well, she was asking for trouble.'

Rose had made a mistake in trying to produce an after-dinner story. Indeed it had not been amusing, and nor was it coming out as evidence that in a way they were after all closer to some harsh realities than Gerald and Caroline, as that morning she might have conceded.

'So what was it all about?' Gerald enquired with good-humoured eagerness. 'Is this a common event in Park Terrace?'

'No, it was this boy she had taken in. He'd been on drugs, you see, but he was coming off them and he came to the church, and she took him in . . .'

'And that was how he repaid her,' Peter concluded grimly.

There was a silence. Caroline said eventually, 'She must be very kind', but by now they had all virtually forgotten what the topic had been, and soon they made their separate ways to bed.

In the morning Peter again got up early, but was back in the bedroom within five minutes. 'What is it? Did you forget something?' Rose was already up.

'Hugh's cousin was there. He said Gerald had rung him yesterday to ask if he'd come in regularly.'

'But Gerald knew you were here to help!'

'Exactly.'

Gerald knew.

They went back that afternoon, to the children's dismay. 'Oh, won't you stay? Mother will probably be back soon after lunch tomorrow, she'll be sorry not to have seen you.' Gerald was all amiability; but one could never tell with these unpredictable townsfolk, always on the fidget.

'Give her our love.'

He came out to see them off, proffering invitations for other visits. Ben and Amy waved woefully till they rounded the curve of the drive, and the jolly uncle waved back.

What had all that been for? Rose wondered all the way home.

Peter did not speak, except to reprimand the crotchety children.

It was pouring with rain when they got back, tired and cross, and there was no milk in. And a possibility had gone. Very clearly they were not wanted at Stoners Court.

Days later, when they had recovered their good humour with each other, Peter asked 'Did Gerald talk to you about – did he hint that I might have – or you — '

'Had an affair?' This had been on Rose's mind.

'Yes.'

'Yes, he did. Only in passing, but . . .'

'Exactly.'

They looked at each other over the washing-up. Ready to laugh, but not yet able to.

'Have you?' It was Peter who asked.

'Don't be silly.'

'I thought not.'

'For goodness sake.'

'It hadn't entered my head. Till . . .'

'All right then. Have you?' There had been many meetings that went on till after she had gone to bed.

'No.'

'I didn't really think so.'

'I'd still murder you.'

'So would I.'

'But he would think things like that, wouldn't he? Despite Caroline.'

'Because of Beth? That was years ago – what? – seven?'

'Nine. When we first began.'

'That's no excuse for taking it out on other people.'

No excuse, perhaps; perhaps a reason. Already Rose was reverting to disbelief. She must have misinterpreted much of what had been said. No one, most especially one brought up by Sheila, was that unbalanced. Peter, however, believed in the evidence of his senses.

They planned a holiday, their first proper one, camping in Brittany. Rose brought out all her old school books and spent weeks bringing back her French. It proved not to be possible, in that unsettled angry year.

'Well, we shan't need to borrow the tent now.' Peter was grim. He had needed a change.

'Couldn't we go to Scotland instead?'

'And find there was a strike of whisky distillers? No, we'll stay at home. We couldn't have afforded it anyway, not if the car is to have a thorough overhaul, and God knows it needs one. Terry thought we were barmy to think of driving it that far anyway.'

Rose could have wept. 'What shall we tell Ben and Amy?'

'Tell them we're living in a country that's gone crazy, where to add to the general jollity the dockers have gone on strike at the beginning of the summer holidays. They might as well get used to the facts of life early.'

They wouldn't mind so very much; they didn't understand 'abroad'.

'That's that, then.' He would be happy enough having time for his carpentry. It was she who was most disappointed. 'Pass me Ben's jeans.' Another amusing contrast patch.

145

Peter flicked idly – was it idly? – through the evening paper.
'Remember those back-to-backs we looked at? When we
thought we'd just have a small place?'

'Just the two of us and one distant day a nursery. Yes. We
should never have changed our minds.' She had spent the
afternoon washing down the paintwork on the stairs.

'Remember what they were asking for them?'

'Very well. Four hundred and fifty pounds. It seemed a
fortune. Still is.'

'Know what they're going for now? Six hundred and
ninety-five pounds!'

'Amazing.'

'What does Ailsa charge for her flats, do you know?'

'The agency sees to all that. Mr Gress pays about thirty
bob.'

'Say on average two pounds fifty for a decent bed-sitter . . .'

'What is all this about? Are you going to send me and the
children home to mother and sub-let?'

'What?' He was busily making notes. 'Yes, that's it. Just a
minute.'

Rose stitched away, observing what a length of denim she
now had to gather over her hand in order to get to the knee.
Surely only weeks ago they had been mere toddlers . . . Ben
was still skinny. Tough as wire. Amy all cuddles. And
stubborn. She couldn't always be tickled out of a temper any
more. But enjoyable children. They didn't ask for much. Nor
did she. Usually.

'Peter?'

'Mmmm?'

'I think we should do some serious talking.'

'Yes?'

'About not going on like this.'

'That's what I was going to say.'

'It's all got pointless, hasn't it? Nothing but scrimp and
grind. I don't mind being hard-up, but — '

'But what for? That's it exactly. So I was thinking — '

'And before the children get to the exam stage — '

'What? Listen, it's feasible. Here's another. Modernised
through-terrace, one thousand three hundred and fifty
pounds. Deposit one hundred and thirty-five pounds. Say two
pound a week mortgage. Say six bed-sits at two pounds, that's

twelve coming in even if only in term-time. Enough to pay off a bank loan to do it up. Yes, it's possible.'

He leaned back and looked at her, and she knew this was not a fresh idea.

'You're serious.'

'I'm serious about being more in control of our own lives. I'm up to here with being – yes – helpless. Strikes, prices all over the place, working harder and harder for less and less. I want to work harder and have something to show for it. And this is a way.'

It wasn't the way she had had in mind. 'There's another way. To get out of town altogether.' She no longer thought of the end cottage at Stoners Court; but there were other places.

'Is that what you want?' Guarded.

'Peter, you won't let yourself know how much you miss the country. If we had some land . . .'

He went and fetched the cigarettes, which they kept in another room, not too easy to reach for. 'Perhaps later. Don't you think?'

When it wouldn't seem so much like giving up. She had expected this. So much for that idea. 'What were you going to suggest?'

'I don't think you'll like this one. We could let this house and move to a small one, cheaper to run. Not so tiring for you, either.'

She was aghast. 'Our house? Let our house?'

'It's a question of considering all the poss — '

'But we need it! I want a room of my own, a study, the way you have your workshop. That only leaves one spare room, for people coming to stay. We need all of it!'

'It's all right, I wasn't serious.' But she felt let-down that it had even entered his mind. 'Rose, don't be upset. It's a measure of how desperate I've been getting.'

'Oh, I know. It's like treading on water.'

'But I don't want you going out to work if it's only going to keep us where we were.'

She rethreaded her needle and, sick at heart but also with a tremor of excitement, went on to her second-best proposal. 'We never meant for you to be sole breadwinner. You've had eight years of it.'

'You did a year, while I did PGCE.'

'So it's about my turn again. If you're serious about doing up a house, you haven't time, not just at weekends and holidays.' There was a shortage of craft teachers. 'What if you were to teach part-time, to leave yourself free?'

'This begins to look like fate,' he said slowly. 'I'd never given that a thought. But there's someone on the staff whose wife wants to do a couple of days a week. She does jewellery. Metalwork isn't my forte, as you know. Suppose I put it to the head . . .'

Rose was scared. Could she cope? And invigorated. 'I'm not doing all the housework at weekends, that's flat.'

'We could do it together.' As they used to. Making a future together, instead of plodding miserably through the drab present.

Property owners, though. He used to describe Gerald as an old Tory. Now they were planning to make money out of property (if the bank would give them a loan).

They each caught the other's rueful expression. 'Who are we trying to justify ourselves to?'

'Ourselves. It is rather a change, after all.'

'The world has changed. We have to as well.'

'Otherwise we'd be like Ailsa's old hippie.'

'Still doing his own thing, courtesy of social security.' Still with a beard and long hair, though thin on top, moving gently and aimlessly through the days – a figure, perhaps, of integrity.

But he had no responsibilities. They had children.

The only pity was that the change had come about because of disillusion, not new ideals.

Perhaps the old ones had been illusions.

VI

Alterations

1974

My dear Beth,

Thank you for the suggestion about sunflower seed oil and also cider vinegar. I managed to find a herbal shop that sells them and sent some up for Gerald. He is virtually confined to a wheelchair now. We hope to go up as soon as it can be managed for Peter to make one or two alterations that might help – to the house, that is.

Changes here too. I'm applying for a job! Not with little children but teenagers – more openings in that age range. I'm looking forward to it. We thought of it ages ago but with one thing and another . . .

We thought we were back to square one a while ago when Frank – my mother's husband – died suddenly. Heart, like my father, but in Frank's case from a surfeit of good living. Pat says that at least she knows they had a heck of a good time these last years. She came to us very shaken and looking old and we quite thought it would be permanent. But she got restless and went back to the pub (found us very dull, and so we are). I can't but admire her, starting all over again at the age of fifty-three.

And now I too might be the main breadwinner while Peter gets his own business going. That used to be the dirtiest of words, business. I frequently remind myself of the good Caleb Garth . . .

'I got it!'

'What was it like?' Peter was worried. Maybrook was notorious – or famous; a huge spread of blocks and units planned in response to the comprehensive ideal. All that high spending and commitment could do was there seen to be done. The head was nationally known for his progressive opinions, his key staff much in evidence on courses, proselytising busily, distinguished by strange hair and hortatory badges, contemptuous of tradition in all its forms, not least uniform, subject divisions, rules and good manners.

'Well, I liked Jerrard Pickles.' It is natural to like those who like you. When he informed her over coffee that he valued commitment over qualifications or even experience, she was able ardently to respond, 'Oh, yes, I do want to *do* something!' It was time she did more to help the world along than take in Renée and collect for Oxfam and try to cultivate positive attitudes. She was wholly *en rapport* with his plans for the young people (never rcferred to as children) based on the development of individual capacities and autonomy. 'I always thought,' she said eagerly, 'what a waste it was for older ch – young people – to be taught so differently from the infants. I mean, they should still be excited by *discoveries*, not just sit there and be *told* . . .'

This had been well received. 'You're the kind of person we want at Maybrook. Not academics bound to arbitrary subject disciplines.'

'Ah yes. I, er, was going to ask about discipline.'

He smiled. 'It's a question of relationship. Mutual trust. If they sense negative expectations they will play up to them. If they are respected they will co-operate.'

Risking suspicion of authoritarianism, she pressed further. Some of the young people she had seen in the corridors had appeared less than approachable. 'But just supposing there are, you know, there is the odd one, young person, that one simply can't get a good relationship with?' Especially when they were so very big, with very big voices.

'We do have a unit for exceptionally disturbed youngsters. You may have noticed it: the block used as a youth club at night. But our aim is integration. We don't encourage exclusion.' This rang a bell with Rose. 'A positive approach is central. You'll find the flexible curriculum is helpful here. You won't find senior staff dictating to you: you are trusted to find your own way through to your groups.'

It was heady stuff to find oneself so empowered, after years as a mere wife and mother.

'In other words,' Peter commented, 'you'll be on your own.'

'Oh, no, there'll be plenty of people to ask.' Though it had been disconcerting that the head of English was out on a course and most of the department on a fourth-year trip to Blackpool. It was policy to enrich the young people's experience through getting out and about. One very young man to whom she had been directed flicked ungraciously through several tatty files. Rose saw she had made a mistake in buying a neat grey skirt and black court shoes for the interview: she would have done better to arrive in the old jersey and jeans she wore for housework. This bearded personage sported purple flared trousers and a massive belt buckle surely featuring the act of sexual congress. 'No, I can't tell you who you'll be having. It depends whether Julie wants to keep her fifths and whether Clark decided to integrate with Myra's lot. It's no good looking to me for cut-and-dried decisions. We come in the day before term starts and busk it out together.'

'I won't be able to do much preparation,' she admitted to Peter, 'if I don't know what groups I'll be having. Still, there's all the summer yet. I can do some general reading. Get in the frame of mind.'

The wealth of resources had been staggering. Shown the stockrooms by, amazingly, a woman actually in twin-set and a Munrospun skirt (the relief!) she gloated over stack after stack of glossy anthologies, plays, stories, exercises, many of them brand-new. At Peter's school they were hard put to it to assemble sufficient textbooks for two to share. Here, the most accessible resources, though, were boxes of dog-eared work-sheets, typed or handwritten. She pulled one out.

LETTERS

Choose a topic.
1. You suspect your friend's girl/boy-friend has VD. Write him/her a letter saying what you think should be done.
2. (Girls only.) You think you may be pregnant. Write to a) your doctor, b) your mother (or female guardian) c) your local abortion service.
3. Write to your MP protesting about nuclear arms.
4. You have a black friend who is been [sic] hassled by the police. Write to your local paper about it.

Rose went for a short walk.

Most of the classrooms were bare but for graffiti on walls and desks; two had posters and plants. But then came a rumble and roar denoting the end of break and the irruption of vigorous bodies. She fled back to the stockroom. One after another poetry collection, with titles like *War, Troubling Times, Outsiders,* proved to be full of unstructured items by

writers she had never heard of, liberally illustrated with black
and white pictures of Chicago slums or grimy old people in
wet cobbled alleys. One she seized on gladly, called *Living
Today* (she was beginning to feel her own youth had been a
long time ago, and in another country), invited debate on bad
housing, racial conflict, sexual problems in adolescence, and
starvation. Where was love? Joy? Beauty? Nature? And was
humour considered to be bad for them?

When she came across a set of *Cider with Rosie* she sighed
with relief. (When, later, the head of English learned of her
choice he was sceptical. 'They don't take to it, it doesn't relate
to their experience. It was Patty Bell who insisted on buying
it. She didn't last.')

'Oh,' she told Peter, 'I think it will be very exciting. And it's
time I was shaken up a bit. You said yourself I was getting
dull.'

Alma's reaction was not encouraging. 'Blimey, you're never
going to that Maybrook, are you? Going to teach them all
how to be little revolutionaries, are you? They'll skin you
alive.'

Books were more reassuring (they generally were). Rose
repeated to herself the maxim of respect for persons. If only
she could manage not to detest any of them she'd get by. And
the twin-set lady had said most of the staff survived. She
would use the summer to put herself in the proper mental
condition. Silly to get nervous months in advance!

Three weeks before the end of term, however, Jerrard
Pickles rang to ask if she could start at once. 'Something of an
emergency in staffing,' he explained meagrely. 'I thought it
would be useful experience for you. Tomorrow? I'll arrange
for someone to call round with some information this
evening. No, in the History department.'

Help!

No. It was a wonderful opportunity to test the water.
Wonderful. And the extra money!

From half past four onwards she listened eagerly for the
bell, rehearsing her many questions, not least of which was
the reason for this sudden vacancy. Peter was suspicious; she
could have done with encouragement.

But when, just after six, she answered the door, it was only another vagrant on his way to the Salvation Army hostel. The third this week; they must mark the gatepost. She felt for ten pence in her purse. 'It's straight down the hill, turn left at the bottom. You can't miss it.'

A surprised, cultured voice said from within the beard, 'Aren't you Rose Stead? I brought you some stuff from Maybrook.'

Rose's jaw dropped, but she had the presence of mind to drop her purse also. By the time the coins were recaptured she had recovered command sufficiently to offer coffee and to take the plastic carrier bag with a smile of thanks. 'Have you only just finished?'

'Yes. I've been doing the hutches. I'm ravenous.'

He shambled after her. She reached the kitchen ahead of him in time to mime to Ben and Amy, No comments! – 'Tell Daddy there's someone here from school. My school, not his. It's strange, saying that. Have you been there long?'

'Since it opened. One of the pioneers. Good days. Hardly any kids.'

'Is it all right, working there? Have some shortbread.'

'Beaut. Yes, well. You'll like it OK if you're that sort of person and not if not. This home-made? Smashing.'

'What kind of person do you have to be?'

'Survivor,' he said succinctly, and licked his very dirty fingers. Rose did hope that he would not have occasion to shake his head; it seemed very likely that *things* would fall out.

Peter came in warily, having been apprised of Mummy's gentleman caller.

'Peter, this is . . . ?'

'Adrian Bastable, Rural Studies. Peter Stead? Aren't you on the committee of Bradley CP? No? Oh well, common enough name.' He stirred a lot of sugar into his coffee and sucked.

'What kind of set-up do you have in Rural Studies?' (So the stains on his once navy suit were animal droppings, not the result of sleeping rough.)

'Just me and the sheds. Goat, hens, guinea pigs, rats. We had a pig but it got taken. Christmas time.'

'A splendid idea,' Peter said heartily, 'for kids so far from the country.'

But Rose was after enlightenment. 'What if you can't control – what if anyone has discipline problems?'

'Me, I put them on mucking out. They learn to love it. If that doesn't work I tell them to bugger off and if that doesn't, slug 'em.'

'Don't you get slugged back?' Peter had known this to happen.

'Not much. I'm pretty big, see.' They did. 'Also they think I'm a weirdo, so that helps. Besides, they only do RS as an option and I've got a waiting list. Told the boss the Health and Safety regs didn't permit me to have more than ten at a time. It's English and Maths have it hard, they get the lot.'

'Oh dear. I'm doing English.'

'Thought it was History? This is history stuff.'

'Only till the end of term.'

'You'll have three weeks of the quiet life, then. Ma Jennings runs a very tight ship.'

'What about Will Pennant?'

'Ah. Different matter. Liberty Hall in the English block, do your own thing. Good union fellow. Look, make yourself a corner. Nobody'll care. Me, I used to be Physics. Huh! They don't want to know all that stuff, it's difficult. Set myself up in this lark. Do the same, get some drama going, why don't you? No marking, no exams, call it creative and the old man's happy. This *is* good.'

Peter ushered him out. He said, returning, 'Rose, that's not the place for you.'

Their thoughts had coincided, but Rose said brightly, 'Well. I'm only committed to stay till the end of autumn term.'

She was astonished and relieved to find in the bag the clearest possible schemes of work, cross-referenced to source books, complete with class lists and time-table, and a note signed S. Jennings offering telephone consultation, if needed between eight fifteen and eight thirty p.m.

Peter made love to her very considerately that night, as though she was going to have an operation in the morning.

She survived.

Maybrook broke up a week before the primary schools, which gave Rose the chance to go into something worrying.

Twice recently Ben had come home disguising upset as best he could, once with a bad bruise on his arm. Reluctantly he admitted he was being bullied by an older boy. Rose first tried reassurance. 'Different people have different ways, you see. It probably doesn't seem like bullying to him, perhaps he's stronger than he realises . . .' And perhaps it was as well that Ben learned to endure this kind of thing before he moved to the senior school. (The idea of a child of hers at Maybrook woke her shaking.) He was, perhaps, over-sensitive; this did, perhaps, invite aggression . . . He needed, perhaps, to find out how to stand up for himself.

He was nine years of age.

And perhaps he needed a mother who would stand up for him.

When he came in with a bloody nose and a deeply cut knee, she made excuses no longer.

At the gate next morning, he ran in ahead, disowning her. It was Amy who pointed out the persecutor, chasing a group of smaller children in a manner half playful but not sufficiently so. 'There's his Mummy.' A heavy black woman was bringing along two little girls.

Rose put the case to her. 'He may not mean to hurt, perhaps he doesn't know his own strength. But he's hurt my son several times.'

'Sure, I teach him to be tough. He going to have to be. He got to get by.'

'But Ben hadn't done him any harm.'

'Your boy white.'

'But there are at least as many coloured children in the school as white ones.'

'Good, so now you know what it like to be minority. Not so good, hey? You don't like it, take him some other school, all white boys.'

'How would you feel if your son was picked on by a bigger white boy?'

'He fight back. That's what he learning.'

'That's a hard way to bring up a child, to show that brute force is the only way.'

'Look, lady, we choose, right? You bring your boy up gentle, he get hurt. I don't choose that way. Ain't nobody going to pick on my boy.'

Rose gave in and went to see the head.

But that didn't make it any easier, long-term, to know what was best. Not for Ben or herself. Let alone the world at large.

We used not to have to be afraid, did we?

*   *   *

So
Merry laughs his last at all things ugly.
On the horizon hunger and fire
Jeers
And clouds of mushroom
(Magic mushrooms gone with the flowers)
(Ain't no magic any more.)

And
It was a good time that we had
(Didn't we?)
Even despite the bomb,
With big C still some years away
Given luck and wholemeal fags.

But
Enough is enough as
The Dutch disease said to the elm
And the elbow said to the thalidomide baby
And Picasso said to his jokes
And the IRA to the little boy at the Tower
'What do you need two legs for?
It's all in the cause.'

All in the name of freedom (somebody's).
Think I'll start a cause:
Who's for injustice and despair?
Roll up, roll up. For once in your life
Be on the winning side.

But then again
Who can break the habit of a . . .

This came in the morning post, just after it had been on the news that Mister Merry was dead. At first, just that he was lost at sea on an overnight Channel crossing.

Later reports from fellow-passengers showed that, though unsteady (they put it down to *mal de mer*), he had responded to children who had recognised him.

One eye-witness told of seeing him on deck, though the night was very dark and rough, apparently balancing on the rail at the stern. The witness had chuckled and looked forward to telling his grandchildren that even in real life Mister Merry tried to do tricks. Next thing, Merry was gone.

The witness looked all over for the camera crew. It was a risky stunt; but of course there would be a safety net just out of sight. There wasn't, though. Nothing but the churning wake.

It proved not to be possible to take on another house. Tax changes meant that they would have to pay back far more in interest than Peter had calculated. 'And God knows what other changes there might be if there has to be another election. We could find taxes on rents would leave us out of pocket. And if the law on tenancies is altered we could find it impossible to get people out, even if they weren't paying.'

But he had already made arrangements to teach only three days a week, his salary almost halved. There was no longer any talk of Rose working only till Christmas, or indeed for only a couple of years. It all looked bleak.

'Well,' she said, as cheerfully as could be managed, 'at least we're no worse off. Two incomes instead of one! And you've got four whole days a week to develop your own work.'

But doing what? There was less money about generally. Would anyone buy good old furniture when new stuff could be cheaper? And with the unemployment figures creeping up he might not be able to get back into full-time work, even if he had to admit defeat. He had cheated Rose. She had thought she would be helping out for a short time. It might be for years.

Sam, ebullient, at first rubbed salt into the wound with talk of success. 'Marcia,' he pronounced, 'is a wonder. I don't know what I did to deserve her.' Since Marcia for obvious reasons did not visit here, they could not pronounce, but were not especially eager to hear her praises. 'You know she went freelance? Once she'd mastered the technical side she could see it would be slowly slowly up the ladder. Not good enough.

159

She started a small business with a woman friend, supplying special props. Eighteen months on – all the major companies come to her! That's mostly the London end, of course. But she still' (he actually blushed) 'wants to spend time in the north, weekends, holidays, whenever there's not a rush on. So: what to do up here? She's not the kind to sit in the cottage and wait. Right: start a chain of shops! We thought of a restaurant at first, but too much of a tie. Guess what she's calling them? Samarkand.'

'Very, er, inviting. Yes.'

'Sam – Mar – Can. Get it?' They didn't. 'You're playing dumb to embarrass me.' They weren't. 'Sam – Marcia – Can. Samarkand!'

They burst out laughing. 'Oh Sam, you are sweet. Next, you'll be calling the cottage Mar-Sam, or Sam-Marc . . . Sorry.'

'Sammar Shanty.'

'Oh, shut up.' He was quite tickled, though. 'Now, that's what I wanted to talk to you about.'

'What are you going to sell in these shops? Pokerwork mottoes and tea-cosies shaped like thatched cottages?'

'No. All quality stuff. Boutique set-up, but a wide range. Accessories, jewellery – she's got friends who travel a lot. Exotica, nothing run-of-the-mill. In places where there's still money, Cheshire, Lake District. London's overrun, but there aren't many off-beat shops up here.'

'Sounds fun.'

'We want to do some furniture, Peter. Good stuff. Pine. On the lines of that dresser and over-mantel you did for her, and smaller things too: bedside cabinets, magazine racks, coffee tables. But it's got to be, what's the word, it's got to have the Samarkand style.'

'There's Habitat — '

'No, no. It's got to look old, that's what people want, or will do, the ones who've risen above the chain stores. It's the flight from the modern age; they want tradition. Solidity.'

'How can you have a traditional coffee table?'

'You are a miserable bugger sometimes. I'm asking you to do this for us. On a biggish scale. We'll need a decent mark-up, we're not in this for charity. But it could be a good thing for you.'

He was a friend. And he knew his freedom would be severely restricted if Ailsa hadn't found a safe niche next door to them.

'I can't help with a loan to get you started; I'm stretched to the limit getting premises, seeing to alterations. But if you can manage equipment, a workshop, I can pretty well guarantee a steady flow of orders. Marcia has a nose for what will go. It'll be a success.'

Peter, paterfamilias, tried caution – indeed, there was much to be worked out – but he was light with relief.

'It's what you've been wanting, isn't it, love?'

'Thanks, Sam.'

Later they had to explore the how. He spoke of the bank, but dreaded using the house as security. What if he were ill – died – went bankrupt? His family on the streets?

Rose was ahead of him. She had to raise a topic they had never discussed. She had to fortify herself with a visit to the sleeping children before she dared begin. It's their future we're considering, she told herself. There might not be another chance like this.

'About Gerald,' she said bravely.

As she had known he would, Peter moved angrily, resisting.

'You have to acknowledge it. You are, in law, brothers. He has the farm. That's all right, we have our lives. But we need some money for a while.'

'I don't want — '

'Yes, I know, you want to stand on your own feet, you want no part of the "privilege", it's unearned and all the rest of that nonsense I've been hearing all these years.' She found herself hot with anger. 'We can't afford the luxury of this noble independence. It was all very well when we were younger, we could go it alone. But now we're in a spot, with a way out ready for the taking. You know all this.'

'Rose, you know how I always — '

'I know you're proud. And at times I think you're plain bloody silly, as well as ungrateful.'

'I didn't ask Sheila to — '

'She *chose* to take you on. To give you a home and a good childhood. And what do you do? Reject, reject, think yourself above it all. There's something wrong with you, Peter.'

They were both taken aback. Uncomfortably, he said, 'I don't expect you to understand. Mainly because I don't, either. But can't you see, it would be – it would be going *on* taking. To ask, now . . . it would be — '

'Sometimes I think you don't know about love at all.'

Not trusting herself, afraid of going too far (for where had this bitter fury come from? Not only from the present situation. There was, hidden, a deep impatience too dangerous to face), she stopped short, went up to their bedroom.

She had thought him the most honest person she had ever known.

Che and the purple ceiling had long gone. So had the impedimenta of babies. Changes, changes.

She was willing to work. But, just this once, they could not do it on their own.

He would let them all down, because of pride.

When he came to bed, for the first time she turned away.

In the night he said, 'I'll ask Gerald.'

'Oh, love!' Warmly she embraced him; afraid, now, that she had been wrong, that there were things she didn't understand.

Next evening she asked Ailsa and Sam round for supper. Ailsa was very pleased indeed at the project, more pleased with her husband than they had ever seen. She looked at him, yes, with love. There would be no coldness tonight. But it was too late. She was almost an old woman, pale hair faded and styleless, her thin face, though at last free from strain, no longer alluring.

Loyalty remained. That was enough.

It was Sam who spoke first of Merry, and then they all did. Ailsa's grief was no more than theirs, which hurt Rose. It was insensitive not to have recognised love. And Sam concluded it. 'It made me realise – well, that it isn't very long. Even if we don't go young. It makes you want to achieve something that matters. Not just money.' He began to speak of a series of programmes he had had in mind for a long time, but had thought were beyond him. 'No point in saying more – and I'm not certain I've the clout to carry it through. But I'll work on it. I need to do this.'

Carrying on a torch.

Gerald telephoned to suggest they came up 'To talk about

this exciting new venture. Peter taking another new direction? I almost envy you, Rose. It must be exciting to share your life with an adventurer. Unlike stick-in-the-mud me. No wonder your friend Beth couldn't bear me for long. You young women like a challenge.' He laughed warmly.

It was impossible to live and cultivate mistrust. Rose said, 'Gerald, I thought you'd understand. It will be lovely to come up again. I miss it terribly, and it's not even as though it's my home. I suspect Peter does too, though he doesn't say so.'

There was a tiny silence. 'Friday, then? And he can give us the benefit of his advice about one or two alterations. Mother said she'd mentioned them to you.'

And there hadn't been time. But there was no reproach in Gerald's voice. She liked this about him, that he did not make complaints. Like Sheila, he just got on. 'Friday, about teatime. We'll look forward to it enormously.'

Some of Peter's reaction was shut back, but he spoke in a businesslike manner about the building work. 'They'll need ramps,' he said, 'and a downstairs bathroom sooner or later. I can do that.'

So he would not be going merely as a supplicant.

He had found a workshop not far away, but was as yet unable to commit himself to the contract. After one or two calls from Sam, there had come a hiatus.

It was a curious time. In between.

They stopped on the journey to see Pat. What they wanted was to find she was managing on her own.

The pub was much altered. Part of the car park had been fenced off to make room for white plastic tables and chairs, and sun umbrellas advertising lager. Inside, work not yet completed, the small room had been knocked through to join the main bar, the old tables and benches done away with. Despite the presence of upholsterers busy with wine-coloured Dralon, the place was busy at two in the afternoon. The children sniffed rapturously. 'Chips!' Almost none of the former customers were to be seen; instead, business men in suits, pretty typists and couples in holiday clothes were drinking lager or gin and eating scampi and beefburgers. With chips.

Pat was very much in command, directing a couple of girls

and a barman, collecting used plates and chatting pleasantly. There was no raucous laughter now. Background music of an indeterminate but soothing kind was treacling on.

'Well, what a surprise! You've caught us at a busy time. How you two have grown! Go into the kitchen and tell Mabel what you want.' They went happily. 'You'll have to take it in the back room, my little den. I'm having an extension built for families but it won't be ready till next spring.'

In the back room, evidently not much used for sitting, where crates of beer were stacked and boxes of crisps, they ate chicken legs and chips with garnish and drank fizzy orange and waited for Pat to have a free minute. Presently she came in and sank gratefully into a low chair. 'I'm making some changes, as you see! The brewery are very supportive. I want to catch the holiday trade, and business lunches. Frank never made enough of the position.'

'Where do the locals go now?'

'Oh, The Partridge, Coach and Horses, I don't know. There's not much to be made out of old men making a single pint last out.'

'And you're not finding it too much for you? There must be a lot of worry.'

'You should have seen it a few weeks ago! Builders' rubble everywhere, plastic sheets all round the bar – chaos. But we got through. The builders like pub jobs, they've been as helpful as possible. Another few weeks and we'll have the official re-opening, big shots from the brewery, publicity . . . Not that I need it, I've trade enough already. But I don't want the figures dropping after the tourist season.'

'I'm glad to see you've kept the hand pumps,' said Peter.

'Oh yes, I've had CAMRA on to me. But I knew: I said to Monty Wilson at The Feathers years ago, you'll lose in the end if you go over to pressure pumps. I was thinking of having folk nights in the winter, but I'm told they're not big spenders. Disco nights might be better.'

'You've a flair for business, Mum.'

'Yes, I have. Amazing what you find out about yourself, isn't it? I thought I was done for when Frank died, but I was glad to get back to work. His brother's staying on, he's no head for figures but he's a good cellarman. But there was no future in staying a spit-and-sawdust, especially when that computer factory opened, and I saw how the holiday traffic was growing. Those kind of people expect a bit of comfort. Have you seen the Ladies? Touch of luxury – they remember that. And how are you?'

She heard out the news. Before going up for her afternoon rest she gave the children a pound each and a bag of crisps. As Peter saw them into the car Pat said to Rose, 'You must be mad, going back into school-teaching. What sort of husband is he, letting you? Teenagers these days . . . Your father wouldn't have dreamed of letting me do that kind of work.'

The irony of this could hardly be shared with Peter. Rose was indignant on his behalf – and glad to hear her father reinstated as a model of what a proper man ought to be.

Amy said, 'I think I'll have a pub when I'm old. It must be nice talking to everybody and making them laugh and having gold hair.'

Pat was thinner, harder, but she was not going to be a burden.

It was early evening as they approached Stoners Court. Ben sat up ever more alert. 'I'm going to live in spaces.'

There was no sound of pumps from the milking parlour, no fresh green dung smell. All was quiet until the dogs barked as they drew up in the courtyard. Then Sheila appeared, looking just the same. 'My dears, how lovely to see you all! How was your journey? My goodness, Ben, you're up to my shoulder! Amy, how pretty your hair is. Rose dear. Peter. We're in need of your expert advice. And here's Caroline.' Rose felt like a pudding beside the tall fair girl.

'How nice that you could come. I hope the journey wasn't too tiring?'

Ben and Amy were off with the dogs.

'We'll leave the bags here. You must come round and say hello to Gerald. He's enjoying the last of the sun.'

Round the corner of the house (Rose touched the warm old stone) on the terrace in a wheelchair was a heavy middle-aged man. There was just a moment before he smiled and became Gerald again. Perhaps he had been in a waking dream; something not agreeable.

'Ah! The Yorkshire cavalry to the rescue! Forgive me for not getting up, Rose.' They laughed, of course – except Caroline. 'Rose, you look well. Peter.'

'How are you, Gerald?' Rose took his hand. He kept it. 'As you see.'

Impossible to say, 'You look fine, otherwise `. . .'

Sheila said 'I'll bring sherry out here, unless you want to wash first.'

'I'll help,' Rose offered quickly.

The big dark kitchen smelled of roasting lamb. 'Is there no chance at all that he'll get better?'

'We try everything. The doctors are in disagreement: some say arthritis, some a trauma following the original fall. But who knows? Some modifications downstairs will help. Come along. Let's enjoy the evening light.'

It was another world. Even the heartbeats slowed. The wide lawn and rose beds below the terrace, the orchard beyond masking the rise of hills. The very birds seemed more leisurely. Rose felt that everything important that had ever happened to her and ever would, was here. Absurd.

'Observe the lawn, Peter! I have one of those excellent toys to sit on, to mow it. It gives one a great feeling of power.'

'It's never been so well cared for, that I can remember.'

'That is true. What I can do, I do. To the point of fanaticism.'

'You manage everything, dear. Of course it was a pity to break up the milking herd, after all the years of careful buying and breeding. But dairying takes a lot of time,' Sheila added.

'I'm all for arable,' Gerald said. 'Much of the work can go out to contract. Then there are the grants from the EEC for ploughing up pasture. All I have to do is sit in the office and mastermind the operation and watch the bank balance grow. Best thing the country ever did, from my point of view, going into Europe.'

Rose was still waiting for the duty-free wine and travel without passports.

'Just like the war,' Sheila said, 'all the ploughing. Ironic to think that the first thing we wanted to do afterwards was build up the livestock and put everything back.'

Caroline's manners were beyond reproach, but there was a distance. Peter said, as they unpacked and changed, 'She's had a pretty limited experience. Never lived anywhere but round here, apart from school. She can only function in her own sphere.' But Rose felt that Caroline viewed them as intruders; further, that she alone was always aware of Peter's origins.

About these she wondered more as they sat at dinner. Gerald was explaining to Ben that hedges had to come down to allow the combine harvesters twenty feet of turning room. It must have been the cast of light over the table that revealed a most astonishing likeness. She blinked – turned away – looked again. Surely everyone must notice? Ben could have been Gerald's son.

She flushed hot, and then shivered. The only actual thought was, We do belong here, after all, but Sheila was asking about her new job. 'I do admire you. Is it true what one hears about young people in the towns? Will you be able to have any help in the house?'

'But you've always worked. I mean, especially in the war, women did, didn't they? And thought nothing of managing a family as well.'

'Ah, but I had no choice, you see. That made life so much simpler. You have made a decision. That is hard, I think – and options, is it? that children have to choose at such an early stage? A terrible responsibility.'

Talk turned to what Peter proposed to do here. 'I've given it some thought, though I'll have to check measurements and so on. The old tack room adjoins the office, doesn't it? So it's a matter of knocking a door through. A sliding one might be easiest to manage. That would give you a loo, shower too, and hand-basin. The water supply is there already but you'll need an independent heater. Float the floor with cement. Pity to lose the cobbles but they're not safe. Lay polythene as a damp-course first. Then tiles. Vinyl is easiest to clean, and there are non-slip ones.' He became nervous. 'What do you think?'

Gerald smiled. 'I'm impressed. We hadn't got much further, in our impractical way, than wondering if we could make access to the outside john – but that wouldn't be very satisfactory, with the men using it. Not that we shall have so many. Derek will have to go.' Sheila's face was impassive. 'Now, let's give some thought to sleeping downstairs. There's the small sitting room across the passage, that's hardly used. Just a dust-collector for Caroline's rosettes, isn't it, darling?

But there's a step in the way. Come and look.' He raised himself by stages to his sticks. 'Sit down, Caroline. I've got little brother to help me now.'

Sheila said, to distract, 'You know, Rose, I hadn't imagined that Peter would turn out to be so practical. He was always the thinker.'

Rose rushed in to say what wonders he had done in Ailsa's house, but Caroline, collecting the plates, was speaking. 'It all sounds very sensible. I'll ring Mathers in the morning to see how soon they could start.'

'Oh – but Peter was intending to do it himself!' Caroline, who must have gathered this from earlier conversation, looked surprised. 'He wants to. He really does.' She turned to Sheila.

'Yes. I can see that Peter wants to do it.'

Later Sheila said, 'You have to understand that Caroline is – not exactly possessive. But when there are no children . . . As it is, his disability has brought them very close.'

Over the next days there was much activity and no strain. Sheila, of course, was back. Rose was confirmed in her belief that what had passed on the last visit was an aberration. If women had off-times, why should not a man in near-constant pain?

She had never seen him, now, so euphoric. 'Poor Peter sweats away, mixing concrete and humping drain-pipes while I sit around like the grand seigneur giving unneeded advice. I'd quite forgotten the pleasures of having a younger brother here to boss about.'

Peter's face was so begrimed that it was not possible to decipher his expression.

Rose did a lot of weeding, but her efforts to find common ground with Caroline were not successful. Every afternoon Caroline went to her uncle's farm to exercise his hunters and tend her own brood mares. On these topics Rose had nothing of intelligence to offer. Amy was longing to learn to ride but there was not a suitable mount, so she and Ben followed Hugh about and explored and collected the eggs and minnows and played with the dogs. Ben had been somewhat put out to find that he could not help Daddy. He had been told quietly that Uncle Gerald found children tiring.

The conversions were going to take longer than a week.

Sheila suggested they all stay till it was done; but no. For herself, for Ben and Amy, Rose would love to have stayed but she sensed there was more to be lost than gained by imposing themselves, despite the unstrained purposeful atmosphere. It was hard to remove the children, though. 'Another time,' she promised. When Caroline was staying with her old school-friend in Harrogate, perhaps.

What she had missed most was time alone with Sheila. She wanted to talk about 'the rage'. Of this, naturally, there was not the least evidence.

The night before she took the children home, leaving Peter to get on with the work, Sheila excused herself quite early. Sometimes she did look tired, but in the mornings was as fresh and strong as ever.

Gerald poured whisky. 'An interim celebration, shall we say? To work in progress. And to the various new undertakings.'

Peter shot Rose a swift look, a warning: don't mention the loan. He hadn't. The embarrassment now was that when he did it would seem as though he was asking for a reward for his labours; as though he had worked only in order to earn a favour. She only hoped it would be easier to approach the matter man-to-man once she was out of the way, in the spirit of pure business. If not, the Samarkand scheme could fall through . . .

They weren't accustomed to whisky and sipped it down incautiously, preoccupied. It did make a glow in a night turned cold. Caroline, though, was unable to relax and join them. She said more than once as ten passed and eleven came near, 'Gerald. Isn't it time for bed?' He smiled, shook his head. 'When I have company for once? I must make the most of it.' Caroline sat on. Peter was all but asleep, stretched out brown and strong. Rose loved him. This was how he should be all the time, tired and at ease from fresh air and sweating labour, not anxious and pale from the wrong kind of work. This was how it should be all the time . . .

Once again Caroline was up, whispering. 'No! Go to bed, woman. You'd make me helpless before I have to be. You've no need to stay. Leave me to talk with Peter and Rose.' The joviality had quite gone.

Caroline went.

Rose stirred uneasily. This was not home. She looked across at Gerald who was regarding herself and Peter, side by side on one of the squashed old sofas. 'The inheritors, eh?'

She must have misheard, in her drowsiness. The words had been shaped rather than uttered. Perhaps, even, it was her own guilty half-thoughts, not Gerald at all. 'What? Oh, Gerald, I'm nearly asleep. Did you say something?'

Peter sat up.

'No, no, another drink. You've earned it, Peter. And little Rose with her epic battle against the groundsel. Yes. Pour. I can't reach.'

Nothing to be done but refill his glass, ignore theirs. 'And you! I insist. Didn't you know it's bad form to refuse your host? Especially one who is – incapacitated.'

'I'm pretty whacked, Gerald, if you'll excuse me — '

'No, Peter. You have health on your side, you will recover. Sit. Down. Drink.' His lips smiled, not his eyes.

Weakly Rose poured a little into each of their glasses. She was in that state of almost total bodily tiredness and arbitrary mental alertness. Not balanced. Nor, she could tell, was Peter. Gerald, however, was totally in command.

They sat like victims, or petitioners.

Gerald drank deep. 'Put the bottle by me, Rose. You're poor drinkers, you two. But then whisky isn't cheap.'

'No,' said Rose with wavering dignity. 'We don't have much experience with drinking. Although' – politeness or a feeble attempt at showing they did not live always drably, stintingly – 'we did have an amazing evening with our friend Merry a while ago — '

'Yet another friend. My. A wealthy one?'

'Well, yes, I suppose — '

'And how are you going to finance this new venture?'

Silence fell like a stone. There could not have been a worse time. Guilty, they sat stupidly.

'Surely you've thought about it? I know nothing about business, it goes without saying. You might say I've been fortunate, that all this has fallen into my lap. You think that, no doubt? You who have worked for what you have. Workers of the world unite and all that.'

There was a trapped nudge from Peter, a warning. But Rose must defend him. 'There's no shame in that. We're not ashamed. And, and, you needn't be, Gerald, it's not your fault you were born first, or, or . . .'

'Rose, don't.'

'No, I don't like anything not open.'

'Bravo! What I would have expected of you!'

'No, Gerald, Peter, let's say . . . I mean, yes, we do need some money. But only as a buniss – business arrangement.'

Peter got up angrily and alas not as steadily as he would have wished. 'This isn't the right time. We should go to bed.'

'No. Talk. Say it.' Gerald made to lean forward, was caught by pain, froze white and summoned himself to overcome it: 'Say it.' His voice was a hiss and there was hate in his eyes which must, oh surely, surely, have been for what crippled him. 'Say you need money.'

The silence this time stretched and then sagged. Rose felt herself almost swooning – and was suddenly braced by Peter's voice somewhere above her saying quietly and firmly, 'Yes we do need money. But not from you, Gerald. We can manage.'

As though this had not been heard or was not worth hearing Gerald said, 'You shan't have the farm. Tell her.'

'We know that, Rose kn — '

'Tell *her*. My wife.' They looked in amazement at him. He shouted with laughter, triumphant. 'Tell Beth.'

The room was cold and the night seemed to have gone on for years. Rose looked up, certain the children had shuddered in their beds.

Gerald's tone was now teasing, reproachful. He subsided back into his chair, heavy and powerful and Rose wondered desperately how they would ever get him out of it and to his bed. 'Oh, Rose, Rose. "I don't like anything not open." What a little dissembler you are, for all your wide eyes. Like attracts like, they say. You and your *friends*. You and your sex-crazy political *friends*. You – *peasantry*.'

Drained, satisfied as after making love, he sank deeper, eyes closed, lips now tender.

Shaking, disbelieving, Rose turned to Peter who stood hard and unknown, looking at his brother.

'Fetch a rug. Cover him.'

She tucked him in with light touches, pitying, no longer fearful. 'Poor Gerald.'

171

In bed they lay not touching.

From shock or exhaustion, Peter was fast asleep.

Conscientiously, back in Leeds, she took the children swimming, on picnics, and in the evenings cleared and decorated the little room – eleven years ago it had been their first makeshift kitchen! – for her study. Ailsa came to supper and told her seriously, 'It's all right about Merry. He's all right.' She was becoming very mystical, more so than adherence to the Church of England might have led one to expect.

She and Alma took a tribe of assorted children to an awful Walt Disney film and afterwards put them all in the big room and revived themselves in the kitchen with tea.

'We're off out, Rose. Me and Terry, we've had enough, let somebody else have the house. It's nice enough, bit on the small side but a lovely bathroom. No, we've decided, we're going for one of them terrace houses, Grafton Terrace. Housing Association's doing them up, putting in all your mod cons but you've still got a bit of character. It's the kids round our way. Me mam's giving up the shop too. Paint spray on the windows, break-ins, little 'uns thieving. Same with us, they just run wild. See, you never used to get that. Any kid stepped out of line, then any grown-up'd give them a clip on the ear, tell their mam or dad and that was an end of it, and a good belt at home to follow. Now, well. They don't seem to have no parents.'

'Won't you miss your garden?'

'Oh, I'll still have that. Not so much but at least you can call it your own. Down on the estate they don't believe in fences, see; least, the council didn't, then they don't have to live there. No, I'll have me little patch and nice thick walls an' all. Mind, I wouldn't look at it if it was nearer to where all them Pakistanis are moving in. No disrespect, there's good and bad and it's white kids causing the trouble round me mam's. But some of them Pakis – there's scores of kids running wild all hours, and rubbish everywhere. Live and let live I say but not next to me, thank you very much. Then again, it's Pakis taking over from me mam; they was in with an offer soon as word got about, and credit where it's due they'll be open all hours and get an off-licence into the bargain. Good luck to them, I say. Now what's this about you having a study? Quite the intellectual. Let's have a look. Is that where you're going to do all your book-learning?'

'Well, marking and preparation mostly. It'll be odd for a while, with Peter not working full-time. And we don't know whether the furniture business will go ahead.'

'He's never dropped you in the muck, has he? Not your Peter!'

'No! It's just that . . . we don't quite know where we're going, at the moment.'

It was a long ten days.

When Peter came back he was altered. Waiting for him at the station Rose felt it was her fault that he had to come back to crowds and diesel fumes, him with the scent of the country still on him.

He was changed.

He was free.

She kept glancing at him as they went through the family meal, special play time with the children, bath and stories and bed. He did not look at her; but it wasn't a rejection – almost, a lover's secrecy, as one might say, 'Wait till we're alone.'

When they were, she had lit a fire in the sitting room. This was now gradually drawing furniture into itself, an unplanned accumulation from junk shops and jumble sales, even a chiffonier and china cabinet in dark complicated wood that Alma's mother had been glad to be rid of when she went into her modern house. At first she didn't switch on any of the lamps, but then the dark corners reminded her of the drawing room at Stoners Court that night.

Peter came down, already in dressing gown and pyjamas. 'But you never wear pyjamas!'

'They're some old ones of Gerald's. It gets cold up there, sleeping alone.'

'Are you tired out?'

'Tired, yes.'

'And pleased? Did you get it all done?'

'All but the painting. They'll get Mathers in to put the finishing touches.'

'Wasn't that disappointing? Didn't you want to see it through?'

'I did. I did what I planned to do.'

'So what happened?'

He sighed comfortably. 'It's good to be home. Come here.' She sat on the floor at his knee. 'Have you managed all right? Done anything nice?'

'I told you on the phone. Nothing very special. How was Gerald?'

Slowly he said, 'He's my brother. He's unhappy and in pain. We talked about what was to be done and not much else.'

'But? And?'

'Rose, I've spent a lot of time – wasted a lot of time – not knowing what I felt about – about Sheila. And Gerald. The place.'

'I know. And now you do?'

'Not much that could be put into words.'

'You've changed, though.'

'For better for worse we're going ahead with this furniture.'

'Oh good!' She had worried that he would be afraid, would hedge about with ifs and buts and the risks, and somehow slip back into his 'safe' job. 'I'd have hit you if you'd changed your mind about that.'

'No. I don't like your having to work — '

'Don't be silly.'

'But if that's the way to get going, then all right. Not for long, though.'

'Not unless I like it too much. I might turn into a career woman!'

'Hmm.'

'So are you going to see the bank manager? Because I was thinking, even if we have to put up the house as security, I'll have regular income. So there's virtually no danger of putting the house at risk — '

'Bank manager? Oh no, that won't be necessary. Gerald's putting up the money.'

'Gerald? But, that last time, he was . . .'

'He'd had too much to drink. Crazy things go on in people's minds when they're in pain. He was telling me: he actually had a notion, early on, that there was some kind of plot between you and Beth and me, to get him away to the States so I could have the farm!'

This was too funny for words. Rose laughed, relieved. 'Oh my goodness! He told you that?'

'Yes. He thought it was ridiculous too. He was explaining how he'd never known anyone like Beth, he was bowled over by her, really crazy about her, and then when she left him – without any explanation – and in a foreign country, remember, he almost went out of his mind trying to work out what was behind it.'

'I'm quite sure nothing was! Beth is – impulsive. That's all.'

'Well, you've known her longer than he has. It was the coincidence of you and me coming together, you see.'

'And he offered to lend the money? How much? When do we have to pay it back?'

'He was very insistent that it should be interest-free, Rose. We've only to add on any cost-of-living rises over the three years.'

'Three years. Will we manage that?'

He was obviously feeling very optimistic. 'Easy! We'll have to go carefully, of course — '

'No more of this riotous living, holidays abroad, new cars and three-piece suites, you mean?'

'Ha! You know what I mean.'

'Let's work it out.' She went for paper and pencil. 'I'll be earning . . . and you'll still have your three days a week at school . . .'

'Until the business builds up enough — '

'Then you can finish altogether. Now let's see . . .'

Figures weren't much help: too many factors were incalculable. Of their own stamina, however, they were in no doubt.

Going upstairs, excited and happy, she asked, 'And will Sheila be all right?'

'Sheila is the strongest person I've ever known.'

Rose thought so too.

Poor Gerald. Harbouring such notions! And at last, after all these years, he and Peter had been able to talk it out, as brothers, and laugh about it! She must now put aside any memory of those looks of his that had so frightened her.

On the first day of term Rose felt she had stepped on to a roller-coaster and would, at Christmas, be flung off it sick and empty. It did not help that there was no sense of anyone's being in entire control of the machinery. Without Adrian she would have gone under.

Peter dried her tears and made her take a grip on herself. 'Stop feeling responsible for it all.'

'The trouble is, I thought I was going there to teach. You know, actually to go into a classroom and help them get better at English. But it's all social work!'

'You're not qualified for that, so forget it. Do the job you're paid to do. It might be an idea if more of the staff did the same.'

The saving grace was that she did like most of the kids. Young people. Some – not as many as first appeared – were unpleasant, foul-mouthed and defiant. Most were prepared to give her a go; some were fun. Her own group was impressed with the bright posters and plants she brought in. 'They'll get nicked, Miss. But we'll duff anybody we catch. Got any kids, 'ave you? Think you'll stick it?'

What disconcerted her most was the sheer bad manners – not just of the Bay City Rollers fans who clumped around on platform shoes, tartan scarves tied to their wrists, letting doors slam back in her face – but of many of the staff. Meeting one day with her head of department, a rare event, she consulted him. 'Manners? You mean deference.'

'No, I don't. I mean ordinary consideration, like holding a door open for anyone carrying a stack of books, and not shoving.'

'We want our kids to be independent, not stuffed with empty formalities. Middle-class conventions. Irrelevant.'

Peter, told of this, was vehement, far more upset than her carefully light account warranted. 'I don't want any part of it any more. We were mistaken, Rose. All of us. We let loose a danger.' At the time it had been thrilling, casting off barren restrictions.

The young ones now were the inheritors of the least valuable manifestations of that glorious freedom: rights, but not responsibilities. Freedom of speech without regard to content. Goodbye to ordinary decencies as well as stale conventions.

These were the beneficiaries?

Venus, a pretty black girl, latched on to Rose. 'She does that with new staff,' someone told Rose. 'She's one of our stars.' Venus was beginning her third year in the sixth form. Sometimes she sat in with Rose's younger groups. 'I'll do you some essays,' she offered. 'That was a good one you gave them, finding out about their ancestors. I'll do one.'

Departmental policy was against setting homework. 'They'll never do it,' Will Pennant said impatiently. 'Why look for confrontations you can avoid?'

Joan, the twin-set lady, said, 'Take no notice. He's too bone idle to do any marking, that's why. When he does take a class they do oral work all the time.'

Venus produced twelve sides of neat writing entitled 'My People'. Delighted, Rose settled in her study to read it. 'My mother walk with bow head because she alway think of work and the childern, but my father he look up and around and say (this is no pardise, I go home now to the son) and leave us all to be in new countery without farther . . .'

It was superb, and worrying. 'She thinks she's going to university.'

Joan cast a perceptive look at the work. 'You have to bear in mind that Venus could barely write her name when she came here.'

That was a tribute to the school, then. 'But she's heading for a terrible disappointment. Is it fair to let her go on aiming at the wrong target?'

'She'll realise: she sits in on some A-level Lit classes. Or do you feel up to telling her?'

A star, yes. But wasn't Venus being used to assure Maybrook that what they were doing was altogether right, instead of only partially?

It was not – yet, anyway – for Rose to undertake the cruel task. She continued to encourage Venus, invited her home to tea, spent lunchtimes trying to improve her English but with the aim of writing for herself. She told Peter fearfully, 'The day may come when she feels she's been conned.'

Term went on inexorably, with break duties and dinner duty, workmen in and room changes, substitutions for absent colleagues, invasions by ex-pupils, year meetings and department meetings and union meetings (one and a half cheers for democracy, that took up so much time), insolent large pupils and pathetic small ones, the nit nurse and the health visitor and the police, outbreaks of violence or obscenity running through like viruses, idyllic times with half the class away, crises over bullying or heartbreaks or absconding mothers, and *noise* – clattering of feet, scraping of chairs, shrilling of girls and baying of lads, crackle and buzz from Tannoys giving incomprehensible messages, crash and jangle in the canteen . . .

'No, I love it,' Rose told Alma one Saturday morning. 'It's not nearly so bad once you get used to it.'

At Christmas, burning with guilt and a streaming cold, she tottered off the roller-coaster and determined to make the holiday a real festival for Ben and Amy who, neglected and abandoned by their mother, were showing so far no signs of neuroses.

For the day itself they invited Adrian and, perforce, his peculiar girl-friend. ('She doesn't cook,' he said mournfully.) 'I don't know how I'd have got through some days if I hadn't been able to take refuge in his sheds,' Rose told Peter. 'He really is a very kind man.'

'Is he going to have a bath?' Ben wanted to know. 'Shall we give him some smelly bath-salts?'

'Is he going to wear those stinky clothes?' Amy echoed. 'Shall we give him a Father Christmas outfit?'

'He'd make a very good Father Christmas,' Rose told them firmly, after the giggles.

'I bet his girl-friend's skinny and has awful thin long hair,' Ben pronounced.

'Why should she be?'

'Because big fat men have skinny girl-friends.'

'How do you know?' (Kids these days!)

'Because Mr Lawrence at our school is fat and he and Miss Puddenson . . .' The two of them snorted.

'She's never called Miss Puddenson! Here, talking of puddings, have a stir and make a wish.'

While Amy stood on a chair and used both plump arms to move round the big spoon in the aromatic mixture Ben explained. 'No, she *says* she's called Miss Pillotson — '

'And she tweaks your ear if you giddle — '

'*Giggle*, dumbo. But we call her Puddenson because she's so bony.'

'That's stupid, that's a fat name.'

'Well if she marries Mr Lawrence *he* can be called Mr Puddenson.'

'Then they could have lots of little dumplings!'

Sam invited himself and Ailsa. 'You couldn't turn us away. Imagine – Ailsa at church three times a day and me sitting about ignoring the pitiful cries of all the unwanted lodgers. Or else she'll be asking them all in. Loonies, to a man. I don't know where she gets them from. Have pity on an old mate. Marcia's off to the Caribbean.'

In the event only Mr Gress was without alternative arrangements, so they had him too.

The predominance of adults called for some changes in the usual Stead pattern. Stockings at the end of the bed ready for early wakening were *de rigueur*, as was the ceremonial unwrapping of presents after breakfast had been cleared away and the turkey and pudding duly started on their long ordeal by heat. But dinner was to be at three, not one. 'That way, with any luck they'll be ready to go home and sleep by about six,' Peter hoped. 'Then we can have the rest of the evening to ourselves.'

Rose had sophisticated ideas about a light supper, to which she hoped Alma and Terry might be able to come; but by Christmas Eve she was hoping they'd all go soon as the pudding was eaten so she could sleep till New Year.

It all worked out all right, though. They all went with Ailsa – even Sam – to the morning service, and then the children, by request, had baked beans and mince pies to enable them to survive till the big meal. Peter thought a glass of wine should be sampled as Rose did last-minute things very capably, while Ben and Amy explored the possibilities of Fischer-Technik and a xylophone respectively, 'In the sitting room!'

'That's all I need, to get tiddly even before we start.'

'Best thing to do. Enjoy! You might be the only one who does.'

'Whose side are you on?'

'Yours, of course. I know which side my mortgage is buttered.'

'Next year we'll join Jehovah's Witnesses and not have a Christmas.'

'Give me a cuddle.'

They yawned simultaneously and the doorbell rang.

'I'll go,' called Ben-and-Amy, who could be heard doing

their charming-children bit in the hall. Rose reluctantly unsnuggled herself from Peter's armpit.

In were ushered Adrian, resplendent in a massive sweater with reindeers across front and back; and a very skinny girl with fiery red hair like horse-hair bursting out of an old sofa. 'Told you so,' whispered Ben from behind her back; but Amy, queen of the social occasion, was graciously complimenting Adrian on his jersey.

'Er, yes. My auntie,' he explained, blushing. 'Er, this is Elsa.'

Elsa distributed brief bony handshakes, and requested the toilet.

'She gets bad periods,' Adrian explained.

'Ah.'

Sam and Ailsa arrived to share the load. Sam could talk to anyone about anything, and Ailsa was always interested in gynaecological topics though they did make her dangerously wistful around the eyes. Mr Gress had on his best suit, tight, but retained the bicycle clips that were a feature of his dress. 'They keep out the draught.' Mr Gress was a storeman at a motor factors, and even off-duty sported a battery of ball-point pens in his breast pocket. He had come to keep an eye on Ailsa, whose guardian he was. He didn't think much of Sam. Adrian and Elsa, however, were no more than might be expected from a household where the kitchen chairs didn't match and whose owners displayed a regrettable tendency to catch each other's eyes and then turn away trying to look sober. Ben had a lot of questions to put about cars, especially E-type Jaguars, but unfortunately Mr Gress knew only about the parts. Elsa, however, told him a great deal about the kind of people who ran E-type Jaguars, and it was all bad because they were capitalists and the enemy of the people.

Ben heard her out with interest, then blinked and turned to Sam. 'Are you one, then?'

Luckily Sam's Jaguar was of a different breed.

Rose called gaily, 'We're just about ready, I think! Peter, will you carve?' Peter did not like carving, though perfectly prepared to do his part. But Mr Gress was an expert carver and took over. He made a very neat job of it, and was good enough to explain every stage of the process. He stopped frequently to re-sharpen the knife, which he said was very important if the slices were to be cut thinly. They were cut very thinly indeed. The ladies were given delicate amounts of white breast meat and the children and gentlemen slices from the legs. 'This way you get plenty over,' Mr Gress pointed out unnecessarily. 'This'll last you into the New Year if you're sensible with it.'

Sensible was the last thing Rose and Peter wanted to be. Serving the vegetables, they managed privately to authorise the children to come back into the kitchen later and help themselves, much more fun than being polite. Unfortunately Elsa was taken with a fit of, they thought, nostalgia, halfway through the main course and fled weeping from the room. Adrian, gobbling rapidly, took a roast potato for sustenance and chivalrously went to find her. 'She's a vegetarian really,' he told them from the door. 'It's probably an attack of conscience.'

Those remaining talked among themselves.

When they returned Adrian's face on seeing that the table had been cleared of the main course was touching in the extreme. Rose vowed she would smuggle a packet of leftovers to him.

Coffee and port saw a rapprochement between Mr Gress and Sam who had exchanged dissimilar views on the respective merits of chestnut stuffing versus thyme and parsley. Mr Gress had resigned himself to there being no Yorkshire pudding but could not forbear expressing his firm opinion that a dinner could hardly be called a roast dinner without one. Rose's special mince pies were, however, approved. Even Elsa overlooked the likely presence of animal fats and ate four and Adrian looked fully restored over his fifth.

It looked as if Peter's wish would be fulfilled except that early retirement to sleep was likely to be here in the sitting room. There was a limit to the desirability of togetherness. But though he fidgetted through the mandatory game of Monopoly while weaker vessels snoozed, Morecambe and Wise crowned the day and there was for once no protest from the children when Rose called 'Bed, you two.'

Ben took up his battered old rat-bear as if doing him a favour, ready to tell them all, 'He couldn't sleep without me, poor thing' and Amy forgot to make a big exit for she was all but walking in her sleep.

'Nice day, Mum.'

181

'Love you too.'

'I'll see to the brats,' Sam offered. 'I've got to take a leak anyway.'

They went, idly debating whether leeks were to be found or facilitated in kitchen or bathroom. The children adored Sam, were indifferent to Ailsa, how unfair.

Bossily deciding that James Bond would be over-stimulating, Rose put on a record of Chopin Nocturnes, hint hint, and passed the box of liqueur chocolates that Sam had brought. This led to a difficulty when Elsa strongly rejected one that Adrian had in sentimental fashion unwrapped for her. She was perfectly capable of seeing to her own, thank you very much. There was a coda about women not being dolls but no one was taking much notice by now. It became very important to her to get the silver paper off without tearing it but this was tricky and tears ensued. Adrian bravely put his arms around this sharp offended little person and buried her frailty against his manly and now re-spotted chest. 'Undoing things always disturbs her,' he told them all gravely. 'We think it goes back to when she was bothered by a flasher at the age of twelve. Once I came in and she'd been struggling with a banana skin for seventeen minutes. It's worse when she's pre-menstrual.'

Elsa, re-animated, was ready to tell them all about this but Mr Gress deciding that enough bounds of common decency had been transgressed for one day, and a holy one at that, stood determinedly to take his leave, his bullet-head shining with indignation and crème de cacao. Ailsa obediently got up too and Sam, descending after a short bout of carol-singing, promised to follow soon. Adrian fielded a look from Elsa who was feeling rejected and departed with warm thanks and a pocket full of Christmas cake.

Sam wanted to talk about Marcia but Rose and Peter did not. 'Not on Christmas Day, Sam. After all, Ailsa is one of my oldest friends.'

'Point taken. Fair point.' Cheerfully enough he drank one more glass with them and took his leave, though he didn't want to go. 'All right to call round tomorrow? One or two things to discuss, about the shops. Keep you in the picture.'

'Fine,' said Peter. 'I'll be in the workshop anyway.' He'd have had enough of festivity by then.

On their own, they sighed and stretched. 'We'll just see the fire go down a bit, shall we?'

'Pass me a tangerine.'

'That was all right, wasn't it?'

'Went very well, considering.'

'Pity Alma and Terry didn't make it. I didn't think they would. All the family rounds to do.'

'"You don't half know some funny people."'

'She's right, we do.'

'Come here. Time for the ultimate luxury.'

Love in front of a coal fire. A happy interval.

VII

The Granny Flat

1976–7

My dear Beth,

School starts tomorrow, oh terrors (life out of my control again), and I'm remembering as usual all the things I promised myself to do and didn't, including writing to you.

But oh! what a summer! Day following day, week after week, of sun! The change has been astonishing, people slower and happier, shorts and skimpy dresses, sitting outside pubs till after dark, eating outside, taking to it like natives, and yet an all-in-it-together kind of amaze: can this really be happening to us? As if we'd all won the pools.

Worrying for farmers, though – the drought – a blow for Gerald, having put so much land down to cereal and expecting a very poor harvest. (No, he's no better, alas.)

Even Peter has been persuaded to take off the occasional afternoon and – Sorry, telephone —

Cont February 1977
It speaks for itself, doesn't it, the long gap? Work, work and more work.

'She looked *dead*, Peter,' Rose had reported, 'with all those tubes and drips. It was awful, and I thought, she has had a hard life and never complained, and we did nothing to help, hardly even took an interest. The sister said they're getting more women with ulcers now.'

'Should we have her here for a while? Is that what you want? Would she come?'

'Please. I think she would, now. There's no one else.'

Amy, who at this stage wanted to be a nurse, was eager to tiptoe about with cologne-soaked handkerchiefs and daffodils. She soon found that a function better appreciated was nipping out for *Cosmopolitan, Over 21, Spare Rib* and Marlboro cigarettes. 'If I've got to be a granny I'm going to be a selfish one,' Pat declared feebly. 'Everybody running round after me.' But she was for a time too frail even to hold the heavy magazines. Peter rented a large colour television and set it at the end of her bed. 'Bristol Cream, that's what you can get me.' She wasn't supposed to drink, or eat anything but pallid foods, but, Lord, there had to be some pleasure in life. Then on bad days she would give up, turn away, refuse food and medicine. 'What's the point? I'm past it. I look seventy. Why should I care if the relief manager is fiddling the books? I'm sick of trying.'

Rose, torn between two guilts, took a week off from work. Then Ailsa undertook to call in.

Pat liked her, and even more enjoyed despising her. 'Look at her! Every advantage, she had, and look at her now. No husband to speak of, and a house full of strangers. Call that a life? She looks as old as me.' Slowly slowly vigour reasserted itself. 'I'm not ending up like that.' She picked up the magazines and Alma came to do her hair for her. They had a good talk about Clairol versus Sta-Blonde. That did her more good than anything.

Rose was keeping an eye on a house further up which had just changed hands. Music was often to be heard, chamber music, sometimes just a piano, or a flute and cello. She would love to know people who made music like that: it seemed to offer a wise and soothing and implicitly damning perspective on her own hurries and anxieties. It was some weeks before she was lucky. As she was passing from a hasty dash to buy bread, a short tired man was turning in at the gate. But what to say? Feeling foolish, Rose called 'Excuse me!'

He looked around. 'Yes? You are calling me?'

'Yes. We live there, at number 194. My name is Rose Stead. I just wanted to say, er, hello.'

'Mrs Stead. Yes, we should know our neighbours. I am Rolf Eisner, Dr Eisner.'

'How do you do.' He bowed slightly. 'Do you think you will like it here? Have you a family? Would you like to call round one evening?'

Gravely he dealt with each question in turn – the scientific mind. 'Yes, we like it here. We have been in Washington some years and at first could find only a flat. So we are pleased to have all our things around us again. I have a wife, unfortunately not in good health, and a daughter. We do not go out, I am afraid.'

'I am sorry. But I have a daughter, eleven, and a son of

twelve. I wonder if they would have much in common? Does your daughter have friends locally?'

'Rebecca is thirteen. A solitary child, for better or worse. She studies hard and practises her instruments. And she likes to spend as much time as possible with her mother. I'm sure you understand.'

'Yes, of course.' She had been given the brush-off, but he had not made her feel silly. 'May I just say, then, that if you need help of any kind – or information – well, there we are.'

'Mrs Stead, come in for a moment. Have you time? I would like to present you to my wife.'

She hadn't really time, but that didn't matter.

Her first thought on seeing Mrs Eisner was 'Oh! She is going to die and we shall not be able to be friends.' Her second was that Mrs Eisner knew exactly what had gone through her mind.

She sat in a high wing chair with her feet on a low stool, warmly and prettily wrapped, a fragile remnant of beauty as blonde, or silver, as her husband was dark. They were introduced, and liked each other.

'Rebecca,' called the mother.

Never far away, one felt, the girl came in: dark too, but tall, polite, an old-fashioned girl.

'We would love you to come to our house, Rebecca, if you'd like to. My son and daughter are about your age.'

'Thank you. Perhaps one day – in the holidays . . .' Her eyes were on her mother's thin face.

'Yes, you must make new friends,' said Mrs Eisner lightly. 'We've been too tied up with ourselves. Being abroad,' she explained to Rose. 'It can make a family curiously insular; we must break the habit.'

'I'm so pleased to meet you all at last. I've heard the music and wondered about you.'

'It's very pleasant here. I like to see people go by, to look at the park.'

All this time Rolf Eisner stood by, protective. Rose was aware that she must not tire the sick woman.

'Yes, we like it here. When there's time, that is, just to look. No time to stand and stare, you know. Life gets ridiculously busy.'

'Oh, I have time. Will you have some tea?'

'Oh dear, I'm afraid I must go and feed my tribe.' She told them briefly about her mother, her job.

'We mustn't encroach on your time.'

'No, no, I didn't mean – I mean, I would love to come another day, if that's possible.'

'On Sunday? Good. We shall look forward to it.'

Ushered out, she felt she had done the right thing in not staying; also, that she would be welcomed back.

She told Peter eagerly about them, but not Pat. The family was obviously self-sufficient, and, though she wished heartily to find companionship and purpose for her mother, Pat could not be imagined as the tenderest of sick visitors, not for someone seriously ill.

It was worrying, lest she sink into apathy. Pat made a habit of sleeping late, of going into town for coffee most mornings, resting after lunch, so there were only a couple of hours before the family was home. But it was an empty life for someone used to busy days. 'What about joining a club?'

'Rose, I'm fifty-five not seventy.'

'A class of some kind?'

'Later, perhaps. I might take up an interest.' She alternated between over-animation, spending money, trying different hairstyles, dressing Amy up, and lethargy.

'I expect it's delayed shock, you know,' Rose said to Peter, 'as well as being so ill. It never quite came home to her before that she's on her own again.'

Peter would have found sympathy easier if his sleep had not been disturbed by late-night television from overhead. 'Shouldn't she have a holiday?'

'It would remind her of Frank, to go to Spain so soon. An agency sees to the lettings – the flat might not be free.'

'Well, I don't know what to do with her.'

He was going through a bad time having given up teaching to go it alone and was unable to share it with Rose; partly from pride, partly because she didn't have time to listen. So it seemed to him. He thought she was doing too much, in some cases making hardship where there need be none. Even Pat had said to her, 'Why not get someone in to do the cleaning? You make weekends a misery, rushing round.'

It was a question of principle. 'Why should I pay some other woman to do menial chores for me?'

'Why not?'

'No. It's up to me to cope.' Sheila always had.

It was also up to her, apparently, to do the washing and ironing, shopping and cooking, to run the children to ballet class and riding classes, Scouts and music lessons, to call on Pat at least three times a day and of course to put in hours every night and much of the weekend on school work. Making love had become a Saturday night obligation, another item on the list.

He missed her. Where was his woman? There was under the same roof, in his very bed, a capable housekeeper, nurse, mother, professional educator But not his Rose.

At night she was so exhausted she either fell asleep at once or lay awake pretending not to be. So did he. They lay side by side but separate.

To her it was the greatest comfort in the world that he was there. Even if they had almost no time on their own it meant everything to her to lie next to him. Her mother's loss made her fear the loneliness of the body. He was the one person she could count on not to make demands; the one who understood what it cost her to get from day to day.

He did not. He felt left out. Everything, everyone, came before him.

He worked even later, sometimes not even coming home for meals; Ben would run round to the workshop with a covered dish, a thermos flask.

He should, he reminded himself joylessly, be glad there was plenty of work. But the demands were for more of the same: this coffee table, that magazine rack, storage unit, bedside cabinet. All decent stuff. But every week much the same. And though the cost of timber rose he was held to a price. He had to buy wood of lower quality than he would have liked, spend less time on perfection of finish.

It was a living – and gladly done, if there was a loving wife to come home to, to talk over other possibilities with. But no. Rose was not the only one tied to a roller-coaster that swooped her through the weeks, but she had no time to regret it. Peter did, as he sawed and jointed and sanded and sealed.

The stay at Stoners Court had, he thought, released him from uncertainties. There had been a brief return to the lightness with which as a youth he had shrugged off the land, the work he denied that he loved. He was still sure his future was not there – Gerald had made that totally plain – but a longing he could well have done without had infiltrated his very bones as remorselessly as Gerald's arthritis.

Rose found time to go to the Eisners on Sunday. Rebecca brought in a tray and then excused herself; Dr Eisner was elsewhere.

Once the door was closed upon them Mrs Eisner said, 'I haven't long to live. I hope you are not one to be embarrassed about this. So you are not to watch everything you say or we shall be uncomfortable together. I became afraid of meeting new people because of this. We all know it, we face it as a family. Don't be awkward, please.'

'Thank you. No, I don't think I shall be. I admire you all so much.'

'Oh, you would be the same, I think. It is nonsense to pretend. We are more familiar with death, our families, perhaps that helps. But now we need talk no more of this. You said you have a son and a daughter?'

'Yes. We were lucky to have one of each, and so close in age.'

'We would have liked a son, of course. But this stupid illness began. I often say to Rolf, we should have taken more care to meet earlier! He went from Germany so long ago, when he was very young. Here he was in England all those terrible years, when I was still a child. And here it was that we met at last, I on holiday to see your swinging London, he already deep in his researches – you know he is in cancer research, an irony – me a school-teacher who knew nothing. That was our famous year, 1962.'

'That's when we met too! And I'm a teacher as well!'

'There. Rolf knew I would like you. So rosy and wholesome, he said, a real English woman. Though more of the country than the town, I would have thought.'

Rose blushed.

'This is one advantage of my situation, that I can say anything. Why not? Time is too precious to waste.'

The opportunity did not arise for another private word with her. No sooner had they drunk tea and eaten small cakes than Rolf came in. He welcomed Rose but it was evident that his wife was tired. 'Next Sunday? It is good of you to spare the time, when you have such a busy life.'

'The pleasure is truly all mine.'

Please let her live. She had so much to learn from these people.

Pat insisted on going back to the pub for the Whitsun holiday. 'You young ones have your own lives to lead. Who can be bothered with an old woman?'

Rose drove her back. 'No, I shan't tell them I'm coming. You don't understand about staff, you have to keep them on their toes. I shall just appear and then I'll know what they've really been up to.'

'It was awful,' Rose reported later to Peter. 'You could tell she wasn't wanted. A lot of the old regulars had come back and, seeing it through her eyes, they did look out of place on those velvet benches. There weren't so many of the business men and the staff weren't paying much attention to them. They were the only ones who were glad to see her.'

The longest serving barmaid had told Rose straight, 'I shan't like working for a woman again. Say what you like, it's not natural. It's all been going very nicely without her; no offence, but that's a fact.'

Mercifully Pat had been oblivious to antagonism. She was full of purpose and ready to get the place going as she intended. 'There now, Rose, you've done your best and I'm grateful. But as you see, I have my own life.'

On the return journey Rose found she had taken the road leading on to Stoners Court. Turning, she set course for home.

Rebecca came to supper while her mother was in hospital for a few days. Her control and her manners were superb, and Rose suppressed as coarse an impulse to put her arms round the girl and weep with her.

Amy, curious, somewhat awed, did her best with questions about horses and ballet classes, but she and Rebecca had little in common. Amy said afterwards, 'She's a bit po-faced, isn't she?'

But Ben was captivated. He was torn between wanting to sit at the feet of this tragic beauty – already a young woman – and an impulse to show off, make an impression. Knowing she was much involved in music he fetched his recorder and, not wisely, displayed his prowess, which was not great. Rebecca listened solemnly, and thanked him. He showed her the cottage piano, masterfully adjusted the stool for her height, and invited her to play. When, shyly, she did, her skills were a revelation. They did manage to converse on school subjects – Rebecca was at an independent school – and they did find common ground in a love of Latin and loathing of peripheral subjects like Civics and Social Studies; but age came between them. Rebecca was taller than Ben by half a head. But she smiled rather specially at him as she went – and then he rushed out after her to escort her up the road. 'You get all sorts round here,' he warned her. 'You better be careful. I think you'd better ring me when you're going out after dark any time.'

She never did go out in the evenings; but Ben was in love.

'I'm going to be a doctor,' he announced later that evening. It was the first he had known about this, let alone the rest of them. Rose was very sharp with Amy when she teased him. The boy was so like Peter, but already with an unconscious authority. It was very likely indeed that he would not suffer from second thoughts.

Mrs Eisner, home again, was frighteningly weak. When her husband let Rose in it was obvious that he would have preferred no visitors. 'Please, a few moments only. She asked to see you but . . .' There was not much time left, and he was jealous of it for Rebecca and himself.

Rose sat slowly by the bed. Mrs Eisner was almost not there, so little of her substance was left. She smiled faintly, made a tiny gesture of her weightless hand as if to say, 'I know you're here, and thank you,' and presently willed up enough strength to open her eyes. 'You came.'

'I am so sorry.' Rose's chest was suffocated with tears, but before such force how could she be the one to give way?

'Please, if you will,' came a thin voice, already far away, 'from time to time, see Rebecca . . .'

Rose touched her cold hand with her warm one. 'Yes, of course,' and went.

The weeks crawled, raced by, and Mrs Eisner was dead. Rebecca went to relations in Manchester; Dr Eisner worked.

Rose worked, Peter worked. But there was a telephone call from Pat in May to say the flat in Spain was unexpectedly free in late August: would they like to go? 'You were good to me when I was ill, and God knows you don't seem to get a lot of fun.'

'We won't tell Ben and Amy till it's absolutely certain,' Rose advised. But oh! – could it be possible? Sun, different smells and sights, different food, rhythms, days . . . Her whole weary body sighed at the very prospect . . .

There was a crisis at Maybrook: a full inspection brought about by pressure from some parents and governors. Rose became, she wasn't sure how, a focus of antagonism from some colleagues who considered she had been indiscreet at a PTA meeting, encouraging suspicions that all was not well. Indeed she had not lied when asked, as a comparative new-comer, whether she was entirely satisfied with the balance of priorities. Although she had, conscious of a glare from Will Pennant, tried to accuse herself rather than the school – 'Of course, I'm old-fashioned' – she had done herself harm. She had not put the parents in their places.

'Whose side are you on?' demanded one of the badge-brigade next morning.

Stung, she now wished she had spoken out more boldly. 'On the kids'.'

Nevertheless, she did not sleep well. Amy noticed. 'Mum, you go back to bed. I'll stay at home and make a fuss of you.'

'Thank you, love. But it's all right.'

She had allowed her job to grow like a predatory inexorable yeast, pushing itself into every corner of her life, pushing aside almost everything and everyone else. This must be controlled.

It was the Eisners she kept thinking of. The muddles at Maybrook seemed petty. But what could she do, what could ever be done, for the bereft girl?

And how interesting, what could be discovered about oneself. By nature Rose had always been the first to smile, make pleasant greetings, placate. Now, at work, she was hard against the hardness she met. Not only did she not care about the antagonism she strongly sensed, but was strengthened by it.

But why death should be visited upon the good, she was no

nearer to comprehending. She consulted Ailsa. 'Remember,' she said urgently, 'how we were brought up to believe that if we did our best then life would treat us fairly. It isn't so, is it?'

Ailsa's faith made her impregnable. 'It's not for us to understand.'

There was too much to do in the last weeks of term to concentrate on anything but getting by. If there was action behind the scenes she neither knew nor cared.

One evening she made it to the health centre with a minute to spare, to find the doctor about to go. Had she an appointment? Oh, well then . . . Pointedly examining his watch he sent for her file and flicked through it, pausing now and again. 'Well, Mrs Stead, and what can I do for you?'

You mean, apart from take me away from all this?

They had not met before. Her heart had already sunk. She tried to describe migraine, abdominal cramps – but what was the good? His mind was made up. She had once, she remembered, been given tranquillising tablets (though she had taken only one, disliking the effect) when Ben had mastitis and she was frantic with worry and lack of sleep. Condemned: a neurotic woman.

He took her pulse and gave her a penetrating glance.

Teacher. Say no more. Psychosomatic: anything to escape from the classroom.

He scribbled a prescription. 'Take a week off, get into the fresh air, spoil yourself. You have a husband? Get him to spoil you. Here's something for the headaches, something to help you unwind.' A professionally encouraging smile, at the notes, not her. 'If there's no improvement in a couple of weeks, come and see me again.'

She didn't tell Peter. He would have been angry that she wasn't looking after herself. And he was much occupied with a new undertaking that there had been no opportunity to discuss with her. He did notice that she was pale, and poured her a whisky after the inevitable marking had been done. She was drained, fatigued to the limit, brain-numbed by the accumulated demands of the day, of nearly three years of Maybrook days.

She forced herself to bed, haggard for sleep. It didn't come. Oh, she yearned for it – Take me! – willing a gradual fall . . . but tensions crept inexorably through her limbs, throttling, tightening – and an involuntary jerk of release – and again . . . again . . .

Time hurtled her through the days, hauled her through the evenings and threw her aside, spent, at night, when there should have been, used to be, when she and Peter talked properly, a firm sense of having stayed it long enough to plant new seeds, let a Thought-Fox emerge . . .

How old am I? Thirty-six. How old must I be before time and I are in harmony, not enemies (for we all know who is the loser), before I am in connection with my own self?

On the last day Venus gave her a large bottle of scent and a card showing a fluffy kitten with tears in its eyes. 'To my friend Mrs Stead.' Venus was going on a pre-nursing course and was happy. There were other cards and presents, and she bought a box of biscuits for all those who dropped in to the stockroom she had made her den. She awarded herself the luxury of a good cry in the bath that night, and moaned in ecstasy at the prospect of freedom.

Rolf Eisner called to say that he was taking Rebecca to Israel for the summer. 'Why can't she come here?' Ben cried. 'We could take her up to Stoners Court; she'd like it there, Grandma would look after her.' And added, manly and dispassionate, 'She shouldn't be with old people all the time. She doesn't know how to have fun.'

But it was settled. 'We shall look forward to seeing you in the fall.' Oh, so would Rose look forward to it. She was in need of their grievous wisdom.

What she got, in August, was Pat.

'You look like death warmed over,' Alma accused. 'What have you been up to? Go and get us a table, I'll fetch the coffee. Let's have a cream cake, my treat.'

Rose looked automatically at her watch, and sighed with relief that it was not there for she made a point of not wearing it in the school holidays. Indeed there was no great rush, with Ben and Amy away at Stoners Court. They had insisted on going by train, on their own. 'We're not babies!' It was just that she had promised to get this paint back in time to undercoat the doors that evening . . .

'Here, get this down you. Was that your mam I saw you with last week? She looked almost as bad as you do.

What's the matter with your family, can't you let up for five minutes?'

Rose told her how Pat had become ill again and, worse, that the brewery had decided that the pub was too much for a woman on her own. 'It's rotten, after she put so much into it. It was all her idea, doing the place up, expanding – but she underestimated how the locals would take it. There's been a lot of bad feeling with the staff too. I think that was what made her ill again.'

'So is she back here for good?'

'I don't know. She's broke at the moment, though there'll probably be a fair bit once the tenancy's sorted out. She had to sell the flat in Spain.' The holiday was off. 'She'll be with us for a while, anyway.'

'Doesn't it hit you sometimes, the way years go by and *you're* getting on, not just them? I've been touching up Terry's hair; he'd kill me if he knew I'd said, though I says to him, I've no complaints in any other quarter. Well, you've got to keep their spirits up, haven't you, not to mention other parts. Me gran popped her clogs a month back, you know, shows you how long since I've seen you. No it was lovely, honest, what a way to go. Me Uncle Jack had passed on not long before and it was coming up to his birthday as would have been; oh she did feel it, he was always her favourite on account of never marrying though not a poofter by any means, lady friend at Wakefield, holidays in Scarborough twice a year, very respectable really. Anyway we all thought, poor old bat, can't leave her moping, so me and me mam got up a bit of a party down the club, neighbours and aunties and all, booked the concert room and laid on the sausage rolls and vol-au-vents. It was a real good do, not overloud but cheerful.'

'With dancing? Oh, you do have fun, Alma.'

'Of course with dancing. Now, she never touched a drop in her life, Gran, not to be wondered at when you think what it did to her old man and him going off sudden leaving her with five little 'uns at twenty-seven years of age. But they put on "Climb Every Mountain" and that set her off. Uncle Jack's favourite. Oh, bugger it, we thought, just when she was letting herself go a bit. So me Auntie Winnie said sod this, and gave her a rum and black, do you the world of good, Mam, she said, soothe that nasty tickle in your throat. She took to it like a babe to the breast, supped it off like cherryade. So then she had another and another and though me mam was a bit dubious we said oh, let her enjoy herself. And off she went! Just fell asleep. That was the beauty of it, died before she started to feel the effect and worry about letting herself down. The way I look at it is, the Lord looked down and he thought, poor old cow, she hasn't had a lot to laugh about, we'll just lift her off at this good moment. I call that proper Christian.'

They ate the eclairs with relish and Rose made up her mind that the painting could wait, they'd go out for once – yes, even if it did mean leaving Pat on her own. This perhaps was not very Christian. 'Oh Alma, you are a tonic.'

Before joining Peter, Rose called in at home to unload the shopping and make a call to see how Ben and Amy were. Ben must have been near the telephone.

'Mum? Thought it would be you. We're fine, everybody says send their love, Amy's showing off again. I've been on the tractor, Aunt Caroline's mare's due to foal, we're going there later to see — '

'And you're not being a nuisance?'

'Course not. We're *helping*. And we've got gypsies. Hey listen, Mum.' His lips were close to the mouth-piece, excited and secret. 'We're on the trail of a mystery.'

'Gosh. What?'

'It's the case of the missing trees — '

'Missing what?'

But Ben wasn't there; Caroline, untypically, came on. 'Rose, how nice to hear from you. How is work on the new house? No, they're not the least trouble. Amy has appointed herself dogsbody to Gerald, and Ben's hardly ever in. And you're both well? So glad. Sheila asked me to say, if you've much work on, to leave the children here till almost term-time. No, we enjoy having them. My regards to Peter. Oh. Gerald sends his love, he looks forward to seeing you when you come up for them. Stay a night or two if you can. Goodbye.'

Missing trees? And Caroline so talkative? It sounded almost as though she was cutting Ben off. Strange. Perhaps Peter would make something of it.

They were on their own! It had just sunk in. She hurried round, having called up a message to Pat.

'I've brought coffee. Shall we get a Special Fried Rice later?'

'Good idea.' He was struggling to re-hang the back door. 'Just steady this, can you?'

His sweat smelled wonderful to her. It was wonderful to be working together again. 'It won't be long, will it, till we're on our own again? Say six years. We won't be exactly past it.'

He grunted. 'That's got it.' Swung the door to and fro, was pleased – and locked it. 'Past what?'

She giggled. 'You know.'

'This.'

They weren't past it. They gasped and clung. 'It's better than ever.'

The house wasn't for them: it was to repair, redecorate, and sell. To make money. But there was for them something erotic about an empty house smelling of paint. For the rest of the time the children were away, as it rained outside or the sun blazed in, he would set down hammer and chisel and come and raise her cotton skirt and drive straight in, or she would come up behind him as he worked and put her hands round to find him already hard. In this way they had a re-creation after all.

Peter truly could not spare the time to collect the children. Despite their protests that they could manage perfectly all right on the train Rose was uneasy and would go up for them. It would be a brief stay, literally overnight, for on the way she would spend some hours in York with Pat. The holiday was all but gone and she had neglected her mother.

Pat had occupied herself in making changes to the top rooms, buying bits and pieces, making it more like home. She had not felt neglected in the least but she saw that her dutiful daughter needed to feel virtuous so she agreed with every sign of enthusiasm to the proposed trip. 'Have they got a Habitat there? And isn't there a Laura Ashley? I'm not going to be able to live with these curtains.'

'Yes, I think so. And we'll have lunch somewhere very nice.'

In that loveliest of cities Pat looked at shops. She found

Rose poor company. 'You don't seem to know how to enjoy yourself.' Rose looked at the golden buildings whenever they emerged, hot and burdened, on to the streets. She carried the parcels and made an effort. What was there to be apprehensive about?

On the unfamiliar route she got lost more than once. When, weary and cross with herself she finally drew up in the courtyard, everyone had been long in bed but Sheila, waiting for her with soup.

'My dear.' She looked older once the warm smile faded. 'How is everything?'

'We jog along. And with you? How is Peter getting along with the house?'

'It's coming on well. We've enjoyed doing it. Thanks to you. They haven't been a nuisance?'

'Anything but. It's done us all good, having them here.'

It was the wrong time for it, but Rose burst out, 'What's all this about trees?'

'Ah.' Sheila made tea. 'It's – a project Gerald had in mind. We – Caroline and I – rather held it up, for various reasons. We didn't think it necessary to tell Gerald. No mystery!' She smiled brightly – but she wasn't happy. No, this wasn't – if ever – the time to talk.

Rose made haste over her supper. 'How is Gerald?'

'Frankly, not well.' Always anxious to save others from anxiety, she added, 'Nothing we can't cope with. Tell me about your colleagues at the school. Ben had us in stitches describing one called – Adrian, is it? And his friend.'

They both knew it was a deliberate change of subject, and both retired gratefully to sleep.

The plan was for an early start, to disturb the household and the morning routine as little as possible; and in truth Ben was ready to go, that was apparent despite his great affection for his grandmother and the dogs. Children should grow up with animals, Rose sighed to herself, more than accommodating guinea pigs and hamsters. Already their childhood was nearly over; they had surely grown inches in four weeks.

It was Caroline's shopping day – she shopped for her uncle too – and the unusual talkativeness on the telephone was not repeated. She and the children parted as mild friends of similar age: no display, no speeches. 'See you again!'

And over breakfast it was not possible to talk with Sheila; neither was it appropriate. For the first time there, Rose felt excluded. Sadly she loaded the car, made thanks for the warm brown eggs and the roses. 'Oh, the rosemary cutting! It's a lovely bush now. Oh Sheila, I wish you could see it. I wish you could come to us for a while. You look tired, you need a change.'

The worn warm strong hands gripped hers for a moment, the shrewd eyes acknowledged sadness fleetingly. 'One day perhaps. Dear Rose. Give my love to Peter.'

Unexpectedly at this hour, Gerald appeared at the back door. 'Rose.. A word with you before you go.' It was a command. The children fidgetted in the back seat.

This was it, whatever she had been fearing. 'About the loan. I'm buying some land and I'm a bit overstretched. Could you ask Peter? No great hurry. A couple of weeks. I'm sure he'll be able to arrange something. We hear he's into property now, wise man. No trouble with squatters or that kind of thing? One hears such stories.'

She swallowed hard. 'No, nothing like that. I'll tell Peter, we'll manage somehow.'

'Excellent. I knew I could count on you! Bon voyage, little sister. My regards to the man of property!'

'Caroline's going to teach me show-jumping,' Amy announced as they set off. 'I've been over the low bars already.'

'And what is this mystery you started to tell me about?'

Ben wasn't as elated as he had been on the phone. 'Oh that.'

'Well, what is it? Did you say trees, missing trees?'

'Oh, I don't suppose it's anything.'

Amy took it up. 'I expect Ben imagined it. He's been moony about Rebecca.'

'I did not!' After a brief scuffle: 'Uncle Gerald specially asked me to see how the conifers were coming on. I looked and looked and there aren't any. Simple as that.'

'You can't have looked in the right place then.'

'They'd be a bit hard to miss, wouldn't they? Down by the river, where the copse was.'

'He must have meant another copse.'

'What do you know? You didn't come and search, you were

never out of the house hardly unless you were at Caroline's uncle's. Greasing up.'

'What a disgusting phrase,' Rose intervened. 'But I still don't understand, about the trees.'

Ben sighed. Mothers! 'The copse by the river, down where it bends.'

'Where we found the wood anemones?'

'Yes, that one. Well, it was supposed to have been cut down — '

'Cut down?'

'And replanted with conifers. That's pine trees, isn't it? A crop, Uncle Gerald says, a cash crop He's gone mad on money. You know where the wet patch was with the marsh marigolds?'

'King-cups,' Amy inserted.

'He's had it drained. Planted rape. That's another cash crop.' He elbowed Amy to stop the sniggers. 'And anyway, there aren't any conifers. That's all.'

'And had the real trees been cut down?'

'They're still there.'

'It's part of the plot,' Amy said angrily. 'They're all conspiring against him.'

'Now *you*'re on about mysteries,' said Rose more lightly than she felt.

'They're all ganging up on Uncle Gerald. I think it's rotten.'

'What do you mean?'

'They try to make a joke of it but I don't think it's funny. "Say the plantation is coming on well," Grandma said. Hiding things from him, just because he's helpless.'

'If Grandma said that there must be a very good reason. So let's hear no more about plots'. Which was, of course, all she did want to hear about.

'It isn't just the trees either,' Amy persisted. 'I heard Grandma talking to Hugh about some hedges, saying, "Don't take them out", and then she saw me and started on about the silos. They've got two enormous silos, for the grain. Uncle Gerald is *very* successful, and they don't seem proud one bit.'

She added after a moment's reflection, 'They only do it where he can't see, away from the roads.' And, deciding to risk it: 'That's why I say plots.'

It was hard to refute. Rose didn't greatly care for Caroline; but she was glad that Sheila had her and Hugh; that she was not conducting this strange defiance on her own.

'What about the gypsies, then?' Ben asked. 'They're not plots, because Uncle Gerald asked them there himself.'

'*Asked* them? Gypsies? Where?'

'In the field down by the railway line. They look like gypsies but not the old-fashioned sort; in big vans and trucks. Dirty, with masses of dogs and little children that swear. They say —'

'Never mind what they say.'.

'They're *hippies*,' Amy said scornfully.

'But Gerald loathes other people's dogs on his land!'

'He doesn't hate these, he asked them to stay.'

Stranger by the minute.

'They were on the news, we saw them before we went up there. You and Dad saw it, and you gave each other a sort of look and didn't say anything even though they looked very awful.'

'The ones round Stonehenge?'

'Yes, and the farmers didn't want them. Well, Uncle Gerald thought it was very sad not being wanted and he asked them to stay.'

'I'm bewildered. How could he talk to them?'

'He told me,' Amy said importantly. 'He rang up a local radio station and complained about haroldment.'

'Harassment, dummy.'

'And offered space for any that wanted to come. He said he admired their – principates?'

'Principles?'

'Yes, and some people understood that and so they all came to Stoners Court.'

'All! There's only about twenty and there were thousands and thousands on the television.'

'Anyway they're there. He goes and talks to them at night. He takes the Land Rover down.'

'He takes whisky down.'

'And you shouldn't be looking like that because your friend is one, so there.'

'How do you know I'm "looking like that"?' Rose laughed. It was lovely to have them back, despite the curious news.

'I know your back.'

'And what friend?' She merely passed the time of day with Ailsa's ageing relict, and mostly he didn't even notice.

'Bess.'

'Beth, dummy.'

'If you call me that one more time — '

'Hush now. Shall we stop in Richmond for a break?'

Beth! But that was years ago, when she had been in that phase! Oh, how she wanted to be with Peter and talk about it all and try to make some sense of it. And to know the children were safe home.

And they were glad to be back, rediscovering treasures – though Amy was rather off-hand with the guinea pigs. They were a bit small after horses, after all. Ben went along to inspect the job his father had been making of the house and they returned together, family again.

But Ben came down, after bedtime, while Peter soaked in the bath. 'Nice to be back, Mum.'

'It's super to have you back.' He was too big for cuddles, alas, standing by the sitting room door looking so like Peter; not a bit like Gerald – how had she ever imagined that? 'Wasn't it so happy there this time?'

'It was good at first. But — '

'What, love?'

'Oh, it's Amy. You know what she's like.'

'In what way?'

'You know, wanting to have a fuss made of her. Being *cute*.'

'I can't see Grandma standing for that.'

'For Uncle Gerald. She makes me sick. Overdoing it. He loved it, you wouldn't think he was grown-up at all. "My little friend, my hand-maiden, my pretty bird." *Yuk*. I told her, he's going to think you're sucking up to him because he's rich and hasn't any heirs.'

'Ben!'

'She told me to mind my own business. It *is* my business. I don't want him thinking we – ingratitate?'

'Ingratiate?'

'Yes, that, just because we're hard up. It makes our family look like creeps.'

Yet there was more.

'Is that the only reason you didn't like it? Probably she only meant to be helpful, you know she wants to be a nurse . . .'

'Nurse? Oh no, she doesn't. She's got grander ideas than that.'

'So what is it, really?'

He picked at a hangnail, and muttered . . .

'What, love? I didn't catch that.'

'Nothing.'

'Ben!'

'Oh, I don't know.' He edged round the door – but then paused and looked his mother clearly in the eyes. Accusing? If he didn't understand, she ought to? 'It wasn't right, though.' And went.

As if this wasn't disturbing enough she now had to tell Peter about the loan.

It was not the surprise she had imagined. It would be difficult but not desperate. 'We've already paid half, from the Samarkand earnings. If this house sells quickly there'll be no problem.'

'But he said within a couple of weeks.'

'Lord. Well, the only thing is a bridging loan from the bank. It'll cost us interest, but that can't be helped.'

It was their own fault if it was awkward: perhaps they should have paid off before instead of buying this house. But it seemed the way to make a step forward.

'Well, it won't be the end of the world then.' There was no point in telling him how cold Gerald's manner had been; the facts were enough.

Pat came in, full of herself. She had been back to York to exchange some of yesterday's purchases. Yesterday! Could it be less than twenty-four hours since she had arrived at Stoners Court?

'Oh, I did have a lovely time.' Better than yesterday, evidently. 'Americans are such good company.' She told how they had met over coffee, Herbert and Lorraine and Gus and she, how they spent the day together sightseeing – 'You never told me, Rose, how many sights there are in York' – and ended with a slap-up dinner, and how she was going to stay with them in Pittsburgh once the pub business was settled. 'Oh, I'm whacked. Haven't had such a laugh in months.' She gathered up her parcels and was going – 'Oh! You'll never guess what! They know Beth!'

'They what?' What a day of revelations!

'Not personally, of course. But I just happened to mention this rash on my hands, worry, the doctor said, and Lorraine told me about this amazing treatment her sister had used, and blow me if it didn't turn out to be Liz Conway!'

'Who's that?'

'Beth! That was her name, surely you remember, she just changed the first bit. It all came out because they'd seen her on television talking about the traditional English herbal methods she'd learned about as a girl – I didn't know that, you don't tell me much – anyway, she's getting very big over there. You didn't even tell me she was in business, Rose.'

'It was only in a small way, making herbal cosmetics — '

'Well, it's not small now. Oh, it's nationwide. She's doing very well for herself, your friend Beth. Yes, out of the three of you . . . when I look at poor Ailsa . . .' And when she looked at her own disappointing daughter, no doubt . . .

As a girl Beth had known as much about herbs as about astrophysics.

And now: Beth a success, Gerald encouraging hippies. Time, or natural expectations, had slipped askew.

Trying to sleep, Rose grieved. No one meant to harm you, Gerald.

But she remembered him telling her how Beth had laughed, as she rode off and lost the baby: 'Oh, this is *fun!*'

VIII

Mis-Match

1980–1

My dear Beth,

Thank you for the brochures, and I quite understand you don't have much time to write. Aren't your children *American*! – marvellous advertisements for the Liz Conway regime, so natural and open and full of *sun*. And the centres so much more fun than health farms, with painting and dance and music-making – brilliant. How about expanding into Europe? Goodness, we can do with refreshing after the drab irritable seventies.

I wonder if you find, with your two, that they go in and out of focus, one moment your own known and loved children, the next strange new creatures, and you wonder where did *you* spring from? Ben – fifteen, imagine! – is as tall as Peter already, serious and occasionally quite zany; Amy bonnier in build. (My word for it but I'm sure it's only puppy fat. She blames me for it, has these scary bouts of refusing food, won't touch meat . . .)

Do you know what I regret? Not having brought them up to a religion. It needn't be like Ailsa's, all altar flowers and pew-polishing and meetings – though it has kept her sane – but a framework.

We thought we could make earth a heavenly place. And look at it.

'You know, I think we're doing it all wrong.'

'You've just discovered that, have you?' said Peter sourly.

'I was thinking about Merry. Do you remember, the last time he was here and we talked about passing on the light? We thought it could all be done with love. Now' – she paused before the admission – 'now I think we were wrong.' No response. She repeated 'Wrong. Do you know what we left out? Challenge.'

'Hmmm. One of these lads on Job Creation. Careless little sod. Broke the stained glass in a door I had for stripping. Sheer damned carelessness. If he was due for a challenge he got one, plus a telephone call to the organiser to say why.'

'Oh Peter, he might not get another chance!'

'So what's all this about challenge? You start by sounding

like Mrs Thatcher and then back down when somebody isn't up to it. They think the world owes them a living. He's the fourth I've had to send away.'

'But they do want jobs — '

'Maybe. But they don't want to work.'

This was not going the way Rose had anticipated. It was becoming very important to her to try to see what had gone wrong and why, but there was no longer a marriage of minds; they did not know each other as before.

'We're tired,' she said, propitiating, 'we'd better stop.'

'That's part of the same syndrome: start something, and when the going gets uncomfortable, turn away. Is that what kids pick up in school since I left? They get it from somewhere.' Rose gasped. 'And have you seen Amy's bedroom recently? A slum. She gets no pocket-money till it's cleaned up. And I'll thank you to tell Pat not to go behind my back, paying for riding lessons, when I've said she has to earn the money by helping you in the house.'

'But, Peter, we're not exactly hard up now. And I didn't know you'd said that.'

'No. Anything that doesn't get written up on the kitchen calendar doesn't register, it seems.' She was winded like a tossed rider, kicked in the middle. But there was more. 'It stuck in my mind, what Rolf Eisner said once. Leopold Mozart, wasn't it? "We owe it to our children to equip them to earn their own bread." Rather more realistic than all this "We only want you to be happy" bit.'

Her own faith in happiness sometimes took a knock.

'What do you want to do?' He didn't speak of it, but she was sure he was coming to hate the city.

'Oh, don't start your positive reinforcement therapy on me, I'm not one of your pet loonies. I'm in a filthy mood, that's all. Even the mantelshelf is thick with dust.'

He used not to care about dust, as long as they could talk. 'There's no point in having a thorough clean till the men have finished in the bathroom. And that's why I haven't been on to Amy.' At once she saw this was not a safe topic. It had been her idea to have contractors in to refit the bathroom and put in a shower. It was alien to their custom, to have outsiders in for money. Quickly she added, 'Shouldn't we leave all this to another time?'

'Such as? You've a parents' night tomorrow, year meeting on Wednesday, Thursday take Amy to opticians, Friday supermarket. All on the calendar. The only means of communication in the household.'

'Look, I can put up with being the butt for whatever's wrong, but only if it leads to a sorting-out. Please, Peter.' She should have been angry, cleansed by anger, burning out the sourness. But she was too tired. It was not the right time. Was it ever? Even love-making had become institutionalised: on Sundays before the week took over, on Wednesday from desperation. No time for what came naturally.

Next evening there wasn't time to go home before the first appointments. She went out at four to buy a sandwich, made coffee and retreated to her stockroom to sort out some books.

Bob Cohen came looking for her. 'About the conservatory.'

'Oh yes!' This was going to be a job Peter would really enjoy. 'Which design did she like best? I thought the pagoda was the prettiest.'

Bob looked awkward. 'The fact is, Rose, she's changed her mind, Betty's mother. She's going to move south after all. So it's all off.'

Peter had spent many evenings working out different designs and costing them. It was on the strength of this that she had persuaded him to let the bathroom be done at last. ('You detest plumbing, and you'd love to build a conservatory.')

'Oh dear. Well, it can't be helped.'

'Tell him we're sorry.'

She felt responsible.

The evening was about par for the course. She got away not long after ten.

During the time she managed to convince Mrs Fox that six O-levels were enough for Susie to cope with; assured Mr Parry that Modern Dance would not expose Jane to salacious exhibitionism; discovered that Derek's recent truancies were because he was anxious about his baby sister's leukaemia, that the death of his grandfather had upset Kevin, that Paul's dog had been run over when he was three and this made him nervous of traffic, and that Marty's mum was going in as a voluntary patient again. She defended the kitchen staff against accusations of not providing a cholesterol-free diet and the head of year against charges of sex-discrimination because Julie had not been able to get a place on the course for motor-cycle maintenance. She explained the procedure for transferring a child to another school, went through Petulia's English books and suggested for the nth time that ten minutes of reading to an interested mother would be more use than all the remedial help school could provide; promised to consult with the Maths department about Ricky's trouble with fractions ('I durstn't talk to Mr Hayes, he's that severe, but you have a little word with 'im love'), extolled the merits of 16+ to three suspicious fathers; and put up, she hoped, a convincing case for letting Valentine drop Physics if a nervous breakdown was to be averted. She had less success in indicating that though Selina was enjoying CSE Mode 3 English, a transfer next year to A-level Lit was rather too big a leap. She regretted that she could not assist Mr Paliensky with his VAT forms and pointed out the Maths staff. She sympathised with Mrs Carr over Elfrida's attempts to straighten her hair and advised engraving Black Is Beautiful on the bathroom mirror; warned Ms Moot that whether or not Lavender was a sensitive soul she would be suspended next time she threw a dart at anyone; and rejoiced (though not whole-heartedly) with Mrs Smith over the healthy progress of Kerry's pregnancy. 'No, of course fourteen won't be too old to pick up the threads when she comes back.' She was accused of interfering with tradition when she tried to make Mr Chadabastra see that his daughter had the potential for university and the prospect of an early arranged marriage was driving her to despair. With Mrs Montego she aimed to plant the seed of understanding that a career in surgery would not necessarily follow from CSEs in woodwork, metalwork, and community studies.

In the background was the racket of small children fed up with waiting around. How splendid that they were brought at all, that some parents cared enough to turn out on a cold dark night. She hoped no one would tell Darren that his father was noticeably drunk.

Perhaps, towards the end, she had become over-forceful in putting it to Mrs Wall that Sandra might not get so many migraines if she was forbidden to watch TV till it closed down every night, and to Mrs Berrin that a succession of uncles-in-residence was exposing Dorita to considerable danger.

Mrs Slipser, as usual, waited till last, comfy in the nice warm building, and then settled down to a nice chat. So much had she to confide that Rose was again defeated in her main purpose, which was to observe delicately that a bath twice a week might improve Quenna's rating in the popularity stakes no end. Mrs Slipser loved coming to the school. Teachers – some of them – were polite, and listened to her as no one else but the family doctor and the social worker did. This isolation was perhaps surprising in a lady who had borne seventeen young, but Mr Slipser, irresponsible to the end, had passed on some years ago, and although many of the offspring still lived at home, and several of their seed were now the small bundles of Mrs Slipser's days and nights, you couldn't, as she put it to Rose, rightly get what you might call a conversation with any of them. 'And I look forward to a night out here, it's quite a home from home with so many of them being at the school from the beginning.' Maybrook was unlikely to suffer from falling rolls as long as the Slipsers continued on form. There were nine of them here now, and six others had passed through previously (if 'passing' was not too inactive a word.) So Rose listened to accounts of what their Hermione and Gareth were up to since they left, and how the detention centre had done wonders with Alfred, and to the progress of our Lisa's twins and our Ellaline's youngest, him with the twisted foot, poor little mite; but when it got to what her-next-door had said to her-at-number-27 Rose put her books together and bade a tactful goodnight.

'Please God, let the car start first time.' She was saturated in weariness: the Ripper, if concealed behind the huts, would have had an easy target. All the other cars had gone.

And there was Mrs Slipser standing patient and trustful at the deserted bus stop. Rose drew up.

Mrs Slipser was no navigator, suffering as she did from the family confusion between right and left, and Rose did not help by diverging from the bus route, so it was twenty minutes, quartering the estate, before the street was found, and then Mrs Slipser sat on, sheltered from the cold and blissfully free from demands. 'Oooh, I could sit here all night,' she sighed, and then made a confidence. Do you ever feel,' she enquired, 'that you'd like to run away from it all? Sometimes I look at them old people's little bungalows, and I think, Oh, won't it be lovely?'

The next meeting Rose did not get to. As she passed the office at the end of the afternoon she was called in for a message. 'It came a while back but we couldn't find you. Elsie, would it be? Something about water, and would you ring back.'

Ailsa was upset and apologetic. 'I wouldn't have bothered you at work, but I couldn't get Peter anywhere and – well, it's not so very bad really, I put a rolled-up rug at the basement window so not much has actually got in, but Rose, it's been seeping out of your front door since early afternoon.'

She got back just as Peter did; also upon the scene arrived the plumber. 'Ooh, bloody 'ell. That must've sprung just after I left. I thought it were a poor compression joint so I thought, I'll just pick up a few fittings on me way to see about your bath, promised delivery today without fail or I'd never 'ave took the old one out, you can't rely on nobody these days — '

'Get that bloody stop-cock turned off and then clear off yourself,' shouted Peter in a rage. 'The bill for compensation will come after you.'

They surveyed the damage. The worst was to the hall ceiling: plaster sodden and loose. The carpet was saturated. The lampshade hung rotted, askew.

'We are insured,' Rose offered nervously.

'That's the last time we let anyone in to work here.' But he subsided, fed-up. She was glad his reaction was no worse. After last night she was afraid.

She gave in unscrupulously to Amy's suggestion that she and Ben should go and scrounge supper off Alma. 'They're having Chinese tonight, Gary said.'

'All right. Explain the situation, and if there isn't enough food you can jolly well make do with bread and cheese. And, Ben, you're to stick with Amy. Yes I know it's not far, but you take her every single step of the way there and back. Home by ten at the latest.'

While she mopped, wrung out, squeezed, dried, they metamorphosed from school-children into glamorous young things. Lucky them.

At the slam of the door she called to Peter, 'We are going out for a steak and a bottle of wine.'

'Right. Sod it all.'

Pat came back from her day at Oxfam. 'What a mess! I never liked the look of that plumber. The best thing you two can do is go out and forget it. I'll have a bath at Ailsa's, and then I've got a date.'

The place they had once liked was now 'Pizz-Burg', loud with primary colours and top twenty. They backed away. 'There's that one near the university.'

Oh yes, this was better, an assemblage of odd tables and chairs, paintings on white walls, some discreet café jazz. 'Lovely.'

Peter ordered a carafe of house red and steak. He knew that Rose would go through the entire menu, look at what was on other customers' plates, and then settle for steak. This she did. Then she told him about the conservatory.

He was very disappointed and pretended not to be.

'Tell me about the houses.'

'When I've eaten. I didn't get any lunch.'

Not her fault. She tried to entertain him with tales of Mrs Slipser, but they wouldn't come out funny. They weren't funny. Doing his part, he asked if she had seen much of Elsa and Adrian. No: Elsa had been to a retreat at Christmas, and was said to be considering Buddhism, or it might be astrology. Adrian kept more and more hidden with his animals. 'Oh, there was a woman he took up with. You'd have to guess *the* most unlikely liaison for Adrian. You'll never guess. Doesn't he remind you of Jethro, by the way? It struck me recently.'

'Yes. No use with his hands. Who's he taken up with?'

'A Conservative lady *d'un certain âge*! She breeds a special kind of goat, and Adrian wanted a goat so he went to consult her and it was instant rapport, romps in the paddock and veterinary manuals with the unpolluted yogurt. They had lots in common, you see. Loneliness, mainly.'

'What happened?'

'Her daughter came up from Hove and accused him of exploiting Mummy. She was afraid it would turn legitimate and she'd lose the property. She brought up her fiancé-the-accountant to make Mummy see sense. Poor Mummy was intimidated and started noticing the spots. On Adrian's clothes, I mean. It was sad. He was going to retire and go into goats in a big way.'

Peter laughed, the steaks came and some of the ice-floes began drifting down-river. 'Let's have some more wine.'

Headaches in the morning . . . Oh, so what? Only a different kind of headache.

She told him how strange it was, of late, to find herself in the mainstream at work and not shouldered aside. 'The other day I happened to look round the staff room, thinking of something else, and do you know what? Ties! On the men! No Zapata moustaches, no badges to speak of, no wild hair.' The pioneers of Maybrook had moved on to higher things – or aged. 'The talk is all of mortgage rates.' There was a senior job coming up. 'One or two people have said I'd have a good chance.'

'Do you want it?'

The very thought weighed her down. 'I should hate it. Paperwork and lists and meetings and trying to get hold of people.'

'Then don't apply.'

Which took her to the main point. 'Do you think – could we manage – do you need my help, on this next job?' Impossible to say to a man who had been brought up by Sheila that she was tired to the very marrow of her bones and thought she would die if she went on like this much longer. Sheila had gone on. Mrs Slipser had gone on.

He said, 'I think you should give up work.'

Oh! Oh, how she loved this man, who understood.

But he only automatically returned the excited pressure of her hand. He told her about the houses. 'Four of them. They've been empty for yonks. You know that little cul-de-sac near Terry's garage? Apparently they belonged to some old fellow who went gaga, and there's only one relation, in Canada, not interested. The council made a compulsory purchase order ages ago when everything was going to be pulled down and a vast council estate put up — '

'Including us. We were going to be torn down, don't you remember?'

'And now they're putting various such places up for tender.'

'And how do you know what to offer?'

'The main reason I didn't say much about it was that there was no guidance as to what might be in line. It was a shot in the dark.'

'And you made one? It was accepted? Lord, do you mean we own a whole row of houses?'

'Virtually, yes.'

'Then what are we doing here? I want to see!'

With the last house, they had had to sell at a loss, and take out a bank loan to pay Gerald back. It had taken all this time, solid work for Samarkand and all the odd jobs that came along, to get on their feet again. Without Rose's earnings they would have gone under.

But she had to ask, 'Where did the money come from?'

'The whole of the last cheque from Marcia. And I borrowed five thousand pounds from Terry. I haven't been open with you, Rose.'

'No, you haven't,' she mused. Had she been so hard to talk to?

'But it truly was that I didn't have the foggiest idea what they'd go for.'

'You shouldn't do that again, though.'

'I won't.'

It was the measure of how apart their lives had become. Now this must be the chance to bring them together again, work together as partners. That was what they were good at, doing up old places. She would finish with teaching and work with him – oh! – her throat constricted with delight. No more foul language on the lips of children, no more nights of marking; instead, the rhythms of painting, swish of paste brush on wallpaper; back to where they began.

'They're not in bad shape, all things considered; structurally sound. The big question is, money to do them up.'

Hope sank.

'You've had enough of the Samarkand stuff, haven't you?'

He didn't think she'd noticed. 'There are lots of firms doing pine now, it wouldn't be letting them down.'

'So you'd give that up, and I'd go on working.'

'For a year at most. I promise you, Rose. The trouble is, we'll need that security. Then once we've got some capital we can think seriously about what we really want to do.'

She knew already. But then again, she had thought that

even when times to talk were rare, they still understood each other. If this was not so, then their long-term aims might also have diverged. She no longer knew him completely, or knew what was best.

'I'd like some more wine.'

He was alarmed. He didn't know how she was reacting to his news. He thought he knew her inside out.

They had more wine and although Peter told her this and that about the houses and what it must surely lead to – freedom to decide for themselves what they would do – he was by no means sure it was going in. By the end of the meal she was asleep in her chair. Embarrassed, he called for the bill. 'She gets very tired,' he said to the waitress, who looked at Rose with some concern.

'Yes, I am very tired,' Rose enunciated with care, 'and also very emotional but it is not because I have drunk too much wine. We've lost our way, you see. All right, I'm coming. I have to tell this nice young lady . . . You have a boyfriend, no doubt? I have to warn you: don't let life get in between you. Yes.' She repeated this to herself as Peter got her into her coat and put a scarf round her neck and gloves in her hands. 'It happened to us, didn't it? Going against nature. That was what we were trying to do, you know, we thought we could make people happier and we didn't. Isn't that it?'

'Yes, dear, that's about it. Goodnight. I'm sorry about — '

'Oh, don't!' cried the waitress. 'She's tired out.'

'Oh I am, I am,' said Rose, and waved a deeply felt goodbye. It was only because the chairs were so light that one or two fell over as her coat brushed them in passing. 'Goodnight. Remember . . .'

But they were already in the street which was at first wonderfully beautiful as only city streets can be with lights streaked on the rain-wet paving; and suddenly appallingly steep and could not be climbed, no matter how she tried.

It was half past eleven when she woke next morning. Oh no!

At the ping of the telephone being lifted Pat appeared. 'You can put that back,' she said. 'Peter rang in first thing to say you were ill.'

'But I must — '

'Don't be so silly. Do you think the place will fall down

without you? Go and have a – Oh, no bath. Well, go and wash and I'll bring you a cup of tea.'

The bathroom was forlorn, the old shabby comfort gone, the envisaged luxury unfulfilled. Why didn't we leave well alone? Why did I make us spend all that money?

Miserable woman.

Then something altered, instantly, permanently. An overdose of guilt? Whatever the cause, it braced Rose. Why *not* spend money? They had worked very hard and gone without much. Why *not* enjoy?

Pat came in with a tray and was taken aback. 'What are you doing?'

Rose had half the contents of her wardrobe on the bed. 'I'm looking for something pretty to wear.' Too many sensible jerseys and skirts, plain blouses. They would have to go. 'I shall have a sort-out, you can take heaps to Oxfam.' Ah. Here was a full, printed velvet skirt, a cheese-cloth shirt. 'These will do.'

Pat perched on the edge, interested. 'Well, aren't you the one. You're supposed to be resting.'

'A change is as good. I'm going shopping.'

'Ooh! Day off work suffering from exhaustion, and off you go gadding.'

'Yes, I mustn't be seen. I'll go to York. I'll go on the train.'

'Peter's coming in at lunchtime to see how you are.'

If only he would come with her! But he wouldn't; and she discovered she didn't want him to. 'Tell him I'm fine. I'll be back about six.'

Truanting. It was marvellous. She had a lovely time. She bought a Laura Ashley dress, dark brown with a tiny white flower in the print, and tights to match. Then she went to Dorothy Perkins and bought a whole new set of underwear, including a black suspender belt and lacy stockings. For Peter she chose a soft dark sweater that seemed to her very sexy. For Pat and Ben and Amy she got nothing but some very expensive chocolates. She had tea at Betty's and flicked through *Spare Rib* whilst awaiting tea and toasted tea-cakes. The magazine she found dull so she purchased *Woman's Realm* for the journey back. This was very good indeed. The lady who wrote about children should be canonised. She read the gardening column twice, and marked three new recipes to try: Indian. At the station she bought four bunches of red tulips for the hall table and violets for the bedroom. Then she queued happily for a taxi.

The family was impressed. Amy heated a steak and kidney pie in a tin. Ben lit a fire in the sitting room and brought a footstool for her in front of the sofa. Pat made coffee and quite approved of the dress.

The new underwear, displayed in situ, was not quite the hit of the evening. Peter fell on the bed laughing. 'I'm not too fat, am I?' But, low as the shaded lights were, the long mirror revealed a plump lady who did look rather . . . She fell down and giggled too.

'You look better without all that stuff.' He made her feel quite lovely enough.

Afterwards he said, 'You've got it back.'

'What?'

'Knowing what to do.'

Yes. For the time being, anyway. She must try very hard indeed not to lose it again. They both relied on her.

When Sheila rang, Rose was unaccountably apprehensive. The call was short: 'I wonder Rose, could you take some cuttings of the rosemary? I thinks it's not too late. Try several, so that at least one takes. Then perhaps, next time you come up — '

'What happened to yours? Was it the frost?'

'No, a little accident, a – friend of Gerald's, with a mowing machine. I have to go, dear. Keep well.'

'I'll bring them up in the spring – ' But the line was dead.

Whatever was the matter, there was little they could do about it: their place was not there. But she could give something back, the rosemary. She had been in this tiny way a custodian.

When Pat announced her engagement the least they could do was put on a party for her. 'It doesn't matter whether you like him or not,' Rose told the family firmly, 'it's not our business.' It was not a well-aspected match, she felt it herself, but Pat was almost sixty and capable of making her own choices. Besides which they did not want her in the granny flat for ever.

Newly ash-blonde, Pat was busily radiant. 'We must invite Mrs Dawnton. I can't wait to see her face. All this time she's been crowing about her boyfriend' (Mrs Dawnton was sixty-two) 'but she's never got a ring out of him.'

The lucky man was, or was known as, Major Heath. Robert – never Bob. He and Pat had been keeping company for some months, ever since he offered his services at the Oxfam shop in Cross Trees where Pat did three days a week. Her one other friend from there was a lively divorcée with whom she had attended a singles club and gone on holidays.

'They're like a couple of silly teenagers,' Ben had said in disgust. 'All they're interested in is picking up men.' Pat had been heard to refer to their escorts as 'the boys'.

Amy thought her grandmother was terrific. 'She knows how to get some fun out of life.'

A friend of hers was planning to read Psychology at university, and Amy had borrowed some books. She had advice to offer her mother. 'It's to do with the fit between personality and social niche,' she explained. 'If this is satisfactory the personality is strengthened. Like Alma, for instance, she's completely at one with her social setting. No wonder she's confident. You dither. Not like Rebecca. I bet she's never had a doubt in her life, nothing but music and swotting. I don't know what Ben sees in her.'

'They talk.'

'People like that, they're sure of what they are.'

It was a disappointment to Rose that Amy and Rebecca didn't like each other more. Of the two, she sometimes preferred Rebecca, who did not make judgments.

Amy followed her mother out to the washing-line, on spring bank holiday, absently pinching the lemon-scented geranium leaves. 'Now, if there's a mis-match' (she consulted her textbook) 'there's trouble. What I'm saying, Mother, is that if the fit between personality and lifestyle is unsatisfactory, there are bound to be disturbances.'

Rose shook out a pair of jeans with unnecessary force in the gusty mild air and jammed pegs on the waistband.

'Are you listening, Mother? I'm trying to help.'

'Thank you very much. I had no idea I was such an interesting specimen.' Snap went another peg on to a flimsy bra.

'Well, not in terms of uniqueness. It's quite common in women of your age. Dissatisfied without knowing why. Most mums are like that. Ailsa, now, she's got it together.'

Aware of a number of disturbances proliferating beneath her Sainsbury's apron, Rose was at that moment in no doubt about one cause of dissatisfaction, and was occupied with a vision of upending her daughter and giving her a good smacked bottom. She said merely, 'Oh, I've given it some thought, never you fear. And come to one or two conclusions.' Such as, that the sooner teenagers left home the better.

Politely she declined the offer of a self-administered personality test to enable her to discover the most appropriate sphere for future activities, nor did she invite suggestions, being quite sure that some humble sort of social work would be in line, preferably with elderly folk of limited intellect.

She fetched the watering can and sprinkled in some Phostrogen to feed the sweet peas. Amy did not approve of this. Another of her interests was conservation, or it may have been ecology. In any event, Mother was doing it all wrong again. 'You need good honest manure, not stuff out of packets,' she said severely. 'You should be nourishing the earth, not just feeding the plants.'

There was a lot in this. 'Oh, I should love loads and loads of manure,' Rose agreed.

'If we lived in the country there'd be plenty.'

'True. But look at nasturtiums. They flower best in poor soil. If the soil is too rich they go all to leaf.'

'Yes, and look at all the nasty debris they leave behind, yards and yards of tendrils and – *and* last year they were covered in black fly. Ugh.' Even Amy's love for living creatures had limits. But now she turned to self-assessment. 'I suppose we're a classic case of middle-class neglect,' she brooded, nibbling on peanuts (organically grown) pulled from a Benetton pocket. 'A working mother preoccupied with other people's children. Dad giving up a secure income to do his own thing. Always the fear that we'd end up broke. Homeless, even. And stifled by conventional expectations.'

'Such as decent manners.'

'And we never had proper holidays abroad like other families.' Only school trips to France and Germany and Italy, where Rose and Peter had never been. 'Just staying at Grandma's.'

'We couldn't afford big holidays, with so much to do on the house.'

'Exactly! Why couldn't we have an ordinary semi like everybody else, and some money to spare? Why did you want a great white elephant like this?'

'Just now you were accusing us of being *too* conventional.'

'Oh, it's impossible to have a reasoned discussion with you, you always slide out of it.'

'Out of what?'

'There you go again, trying to pin me down. It's nothing but repression.'

Rose laughed at the time – but later she checked with Ben. 'Would you say you had an unhappy childhood?'

'Mum. I've got homework to do.'

'You can give me five minutes. And you can dry these dishes at the same time.'

With good enough grace he complied. 'Unhappy? No, it was all right.'

'Amy's been telling me we did it all wrong.'

'Oh, Amy. Everybody's wrong but her. I wish she'd grow up.'

'I wish she and Rebecca got along better.'

A quick blush came and went in his downy cheeks. 'Rebecca hasn't got time to suffer fools gladly.'

She did hope Rebecca wasn't a prig, only purposeful. Mercifully Ben was very good at Maths and was able to give her the benefit of his guidance – his patient guidance – in exchange for her adored company.

'So you've no complaints?'

'Well, I'll tell you one thing. I'm not going to waste half my life not knowing what I want to do with it. Not a complaint, mind. Just a comment.'

'What do you mean?'

'Oh, come on, Mum. Like Dad, trying to fit himself into square holes all the time. Even now he doesn't know himself. The only times I ever remember seeing him really happy was when he was working at Stoners Court, when he thought nobody was noticing.'

Ben had loved to be with his father.

'Look at him, cutting himself off from his background.

That's part of being a sixties person, I suppose, no stability. But it's pathetic, a man of his age still wondering – you too – what you'll do when the houses are finished and you can choose. We hear enough about it. Well, Amy and I'll be gone soon.'

'Oh, Ben.'

'Don't go weepy on me, it's not meant to be unkind. But we know where we're going, Rebecca and I. We don't mean to waste time.'

Rose hadn't come over all weepy: she was thinking. There was truth in parts of what they both had said.

She should have known by now that you don't ask leading questions of adolescents if you're going to be selective about the answers you get.

The Major ('In the Army Training Corps, I bet,' judged Peter) had requested a barbecue. A managing man with a wide range of contacts, he had organised the loan of grills and fitments and the delivery of steaks at cost price. He did not think it wise or necessary to pay more than cost price for anything. 'It's a matter of who you know,' he confided to Peter, man-to-man. 'Now, if your lady-wife can manage a few baked potatoes and one or two trimmings, you can leave the rest to me.' He was hearty in manner, stylish in appearance, and inexplicably untrustworthy.

Rose spent the Saturday seeing to one or two trimmings, such as crockery and cutlery and glasses and tables and garden chairs and mowing the grass and putting cushions on the steps and buying rolls and sausages and wine and beer and pickled onions and making sauces and fruit salad and folding red paper napkins. Pat was having her hair done, as befitted the bride-to-be, and so, less predictably, was Amy.

When she came in with the sides of her hair shaved off, and a scarlet quiff down the centre of her scalp, Rose gasped and retched. It was not fun; it was hideous. To think how we nurtured that perfect little body, and now this disfigurement! 'Pat dyes her hair!'

'That's to enhance nature, not to go against it!'

Had Amy not had the grace to weep, Rose would have hated her. The poor silly girl. First she hid, then at a hasty tea appeared defiant. Ben said in disgust, 'Oh, for God's sake.'

One could see Rebecca would not approve. The child re-emerged in hurt eyes when the father's revulsion was inexpressible except by turning away.

Oh, these generations, sighed Rose, and wished for the time when they would be free from the young and the old.

As the main purpose of the event was for Pat to have a good time, they were able afterwards to feel that it had been a success: perhaps in no other way, but Pat certainly enjoyed herself. She had, after all, waited a long time for the starring role. The first wedding must have been a drab wartime thing, hardly conducted, because of the shaming child, in a blaze of glamour; the second, less than formal. But tonight she was the queen.

Amy had cause to be grateful to her: Pat greeted the new hairstyle with whoops of delight not unmingled with malice at the knowledge of Rose's distress. The girl was presented to all the elders as 'My wayward darling', and made the most of this return to favour by being her most endearing. Having thus established rapport with the younger generation, Pat was then able to reminisce about her own youthful impetuosity in a way she had previously done only in the safe company of Rose's broad-minded friends. 'I made my mistakes,' she sighed. 'Romantic to a fault. I was a single parent. A victim of those terrible war years.' She clung to the Major's manly arm and her audience obediently conjured up memories of *Brief Encounter* and impulsive acts of sacrificial love.

The Oxfam ladies were left to their own devices after this, perhaps to have an opportunity to reflect on their own shortcomings compared with this vibrant woman who had borne a child out of wedlock and bravely carried on alone in a hostile world before making not one but two ecstatically happy marriages and who was still sufficiently vital to get another man, and a man of position to boot. How did she do it?

Ailsa provided an ear for their speculations, looking almost as old as they and rather less dynamic. Perhaps youth had been a burden to her, Rose thought sadly, with all those expectations of love and happy-ever-after; perhaps she was a natural spinster come into her own now with a quiet routine and little treats occasionally like sugar in Ovaltine. Mr Gress stood by her all evening.

'Show them over the house, dear,' Pat called to her in passing. 'I know Rose won't mind. They've made a wonderful job of it, years of work – and the new bathroom is sheer luxury. How I shall miss all this space when we're tucked up together in Robert's little box.' Robert had a modern flat in a smart area, but they planned to spend time in Spain where another apartment was to be bought.

This left the garden to the young, who didn't quite know what to do with it. Alma's Gary found a can of Carling Black Label and hung around looking patient and weary, as though in the uncertain intervals between undercover work for MI6 it was obligatory to try to behave like an ordinary human being. Ben brought him a dish of crisps and chatted for a while, but though they got along well enough there wasn't a great deal to say – and in any case he had a mission in life of his own. 'There's this girl up the road, she doesn't get out much. She's in the sixth form at the High.' (An older woman, wow!) 'I try to see she gets a break now and then.'

Amy had brought along her psychological friend, who was interested in senility this week, to provide solidarity in the Rare Hair movement, which in Xanthe's case took the form of dozens of tiny plaits threaded with beads and feathers and little ribbons going in all directions. It was a source of grievance to both girls that they were not black, for which, naturally, they blamed their so-called liberated mothers.

The two girls, with Gary hard put to it to maintain his stance of stoical exhaustion, speculated on the true nature of the sixties and concluded that not only had it been vastly over-described – how could it possibly have been exciting when you looked at the people who had been part of it, like parents and Paul McCartney – but it had also been a total waste of time when women so obviously hadn't learned a single thing about breaking the mould of custom. Gary perked up on hearing that it was incumbent on girls to make a proper job of it this time; then subsided when it became clear that sex was very low indeed in the list of priorities, way below the rights of animals and scarcely above the abolition of Barclays Bank. He made a punk girl very welcome as she passed along the back street, giving the impression that this was his pad and Rose merely the housekeeper. It didn't do him any good. The girls drew her into a full and frank discussion about housing benefits.

Ben did not fare much better. When he triumphantly produced Rebecca, rescued from a bout with the *Nun's Priest's Tale* and looking like every mother's dream daughter in a pretty dress, with her long smooth hair, she soon began comparing UCCA applications with Amy's friend.

The occasion did not seem likely to gell, but two great levellers were found: one, food, which smelled marvellous and went down very well after a technical hitch to do with the quality-of-charcoal-nowadays; and, two, the Beatles. This last was Peter's contribution. By eleven everyone was dancing. This was nice for the Oxfam ladies, for a partner was not essential for the twist, and for the neglected young men.

Alma, after helping Rose in with the dishes, leaned with her over the steps looking down on the scene. 'They look good for another twenty years, bless their little elastic stockings,' she said approvingly. 'Tell you what strikes me, Rose. Do you realise that when they've gone we'll be next in line for the popping of clogs? Fair makes you shiver. Not that they'll go without a fight. Wonder if we'll be that tough?'

Rose thought they would. Why, they hadn't even started yet.

'I was thinking of you the other night. I was trying on this new dress size twelve same as what I've had all these years, and I'd all on to get into it. I thought, hey up, I'm catching up with Rose. Not that you've changed a lot. But Terry – well, I like a man to have a bit of a belly, shows he's well looked after – but then there's your Peter, thin as a lath and you a right good cook. Course, Terry does more bevvying than what Peter's got time for. But it makes you wonder, doesn't it? Was we meant to be what we become, all along? Try as you might, is it all laid out for you? Here's me, thickening up like me Mam – but of course in your case you don't know both sides, do you? I'm coming to the conclusion it's in you from the start and there's not a lot you can do. It's in the stars, or these genetics. What do you think, Rose? You're the scholar.'

'I don't know. I'll tell you if ever I see old friends again after a long time. People that were in the house – Jethro, you never met him. Or Beth, that I was at school with . . .'

But what about Gerald? Cruel stars, that had fated his crippling disease. She was ashamed ever to have felt sorry for herself.

The evening was crowned with a rejuvenating touch of drama when a police car drove slowly down the back and stopped, and two awkward young coppers said there had been a complaint that the noise was keeping an old lady's dog awake. Quite elated after a tolerant debate about the rights of the citizen, the guests severally departed, feeling quite naughty. The Major was very gracious about it.

Thank goodness that was over.

But Rose had an unforeseen confidence yet to come. Elevated by success and, perhaps, in love, Pat stopped her outside the bathroom. 'You can guess why I was drawn to Robert, I expect,' she murmured demurely.

'Er.' Apart from his being of suitable sex and age, oh, and presentable, Rose had no inspiration.

'He reminds me of your father.' Pat looked deep into her daughter's eyes, as one might say, 'I did it for you.'

Her father? He had been a small man, unassertive, scholarly rather than — The look prompted: Think again.

Her *father*!

For the first time in many years – since the children were small and she had sought for connections – Rose wondered, who had he been?

'Of course, he was air force, not army. But the military bearing . . .'

She stammered, 'But – I always thought that he was American!'

Pat was indignant, as though a meaningful offering had been turned away. 'Do you think I would have gone with a foreigner? He was a *gentleman*!' and, stiff-backed, took herself up to the granny flat.

No, Rose did not want more responsibility at work. She was keeping herself free, for a change. A small one came when, in the autumn, Rolf Eisner had a term's sabbatical in Washington. He wanted Rebecca to come – 'An experience for her' – but she was working for A-levels. It was agreed that she should come and stay for the ten weeks and Ben would escort her home every evening to check on the house and wait reading while she did her piano practice. He took on a Saturday job at a supermarket 'to save up' – though he didn't say for what.

Rebecca was appreciative and self-effacing. It is becoming a house for friends all over again, thought Rose, pleased. She was careful never to press Rebecca for confidences – not for worlds would she imply willingness to 'be a mother' to her. What impertinence that would be. So they were courteous and rather formal with each other; and there was fondness on both sides.

One act of defiance made (the hair was growing again, curly like a child's) Amy was going through a quiet phase. She had made a habit of spending evenings at her friend's house – doing homework, of course – but on one occasion she had not waited for Rose to collect her, set off home on her own, and been terrified by footsteps behind her. The Ripper was still not caught; girls and women did not walk alone. After that she stayed in, and at weekends did voluntary work for the RSPCA. 'No, I don't want a dog of my own,' she cried. 'It would be cruel, keeping it shut up all day. You need space to keep a dog, and someone home all day!' The accusation was implicit.

Peter was working on the remaining three houses simultaneously rather than one by one. 'It's more efficient, to get all the rewiring done, then the plastering . . .' By the October half term they might be at the stage when Rose would help with the papering and painting – but in the event they went to Stoners Court instead.

In one of her irregular telephone calls in answer to Rose's monthly letters, Sheila said that Gerald was rather hurt that Peter hadn't come to him for a loan. 'He's doing well now, out of the cereal crops.'

'Never again,' muttered Peter, out of hearing.

'How is he?'

'Much the same.' There had been a tiny pause, no more.

'And Caroline?' Rose was bothered about a lack of vigour in Sheila's voice.

'She spends more and more time with her brood mares.' Again the interval. 'Gerald has his friend, you see, to fetch and carry. It frees Caroline for the horses.'

'But you, you sound tired.'

'Oh, nothing important.' The voice brightened. 'And we're to have changes. I'm moving to the end cottage as soon as it can be put in order.'

'Oh! Who's doing the work?' Surely Peter . . . She looked to make sure he had heard.

'Probably not before the spring,' Sheila continued. 'I'm looking forward to it.'

'Have you been ill?'

'A little scare about my heart – but it was nothing, the doctors were completely reassuring, there's truly no need for concern. Just a matter of easing off a little.'

But there was something wrong – not least this mystery about Gerald's 'friend'.

'We ought to go up.'

It would be tiring for Sheila if they were all to go; but there was no problem. Amy vehemently declined: 'I want to put in the whole week at the dogs' home, they're short-staffed.' Why had she shuddered? And Ben and Rebecca were going to combine swotting for mocks with some walks in the Dales. This was Ben's suggestion: it was his opinion that Rebecca didn't get enough fresh air.

'You'll be all right on your own?'

'*Mum*!'

'Mum, we're not *kids*.'

Ailsa would keep an eye on them.

It was a great treat to be driving off on their own on a sharp clear day, but there were worries – and when they arrived they found there was indeed much that needed to be worried about.

Gerald met them in the yard, swerving his electric chair round in a wild arc and coming to a stop nose to nose with the car.

'Da dah! The cavalry galloping up from Yorkshire to the rescue!' he called sardonically. He was heavier, dissipated, his energies gone wild. "Off you go, legs. I have little sister to do my bidding now.' They just glimpsed a small figure taking off round the corner; the distinct impression was that their arrival had been awaited.

'My legs,' Gerald explained. 'My clown, my pet monkey. I told him to make himself scarce for a few days. How long are you staying? How *are* you?'

Rose bent, however reluctantly, to kiss his cheek, and smelled whisky. It was three in the afternoon.

'And you, Gerald?'

'Me? Fine. Never better. Don't I look in the pink? Peter.'

'All going well, Gerald?'

'Superbly. A farmer need never go out of his office nowadays, you know. It's simply a matter of organising the contractors and raking in the subsidies. Oh, this is the place to make money now. How is your newest undertaking? You should have called me in, I have capital to spare.'

'We're managing all right, thank you. Where's Sheila?'

'I don't know. Gardening, perhaps.'

Sheila came round the corner from the terrace pushing a wheelbarrow. 'My dears!'

She was very slightly breathless.

'Here, let me take that. Where do you want it?'

'On the compost heap, please. I've been cutting back the herbaceous stuff. Such a lot to see to at this time of year. Come along in and we'll have some tea.'

'I'll do it, you sit down.'

'I'm not an invalid, Rose dear, you mustn't get that idea. But we'll sit and talk for a little while. Gerald, you'll have some tea?'

'No, no tea. I've been waiting for Peter to have a look at the cottage. Once again, the building expert. Will it need re-roofing? That's the first question.' He was setting off through the yard.

'We'll take a look now,' Peter said. 'Though I'll need to get up there to have a proper look. I'll change later and take the ladders round.'

'I brought the rosemary cuttings,' Rose said. 'Three have taken very well. You must tell me where you want them.'

Sheila was obviously glad to sit down. 'They do look sturdy. Well done. I've missed the old bush.' It had leaned over the courtyard from the corner of the vegetable garden. 'One in the old place, definitely. I'll keep one to plant at the cottage And the other . . .'

'There's no hurry to decide,' Rose made the tea and gave news of the young ones to let Sheila recover. She was not an invalid, that was true; but she had lost her vitality.

It was noticeable, too, how the house was deteriorating.

Nothing much had been done by way of redecoration in all the years Rose had been coming there – fifteen years! – but now it was not comfortably shabby but distinctly neglected. And yet Gerald was making money.

Sheila missed nothing. 'It is all getting rather run down,' she agreed. 'We keep thinking, perhaps next year . . . But Gerald hates having outsiders about the place and somehow the years go by . . . His rooms downstairs are just the thing, though. Peter was wise to make provision for a bedroom too, when he did the alterations. He has it very snug, everything to hand.'

'Good.' There was no longer any talk of improvement in his condition. 'Tell me, are you happy about the cottage?' It was hard to think of Sheila anywhere but here.

'I am. We've talked of it long enough. Now it's time to make a move. There isn't so much for me to do here now all the livestock is gone – yes, even the calf-rearing unit, and there didn't seem much point in a dozen hens – though I may indulge myself with a few bantams when I move down, if Gerald will agree to my fencing off a bit of the paddock.'

They would phone Ben, Peter said when he came in as it grew dark. He would need more than two days to work out a complete plan for the cottage, and he would have to go to Hexham and perhaps further afield to ensure the right materials were available. 'A fireplace, for example. That old iron one is rusted out, and too poky. You'll have to come with me, Mother, to choose one. And will you want fitted wardrobes in the bedrooms? There's just room for a shower in the box room – that is where you'll have the bathroom, isn't it? And what about a downstairs loo?'

This was going to be a job he would love: giving something back to her. Sheila was excited, now that plans were in hand. She looked ten years younger than when they had arrived.

Gerald kept to his room after dinner, and Rose went to and fro with *The Times*, slippers, a thermos of coffee, beef sandwiches: 'Stocking up for the long night, you see. That's where Jacko is useful, he doesn't mind when he sleeps. But you, of course, keep regular hours. I'm sorry I sent him away now. Though he won't have gone far. He knows when he's well off, my Jacko.'

'Who is he?'

'My monkey.'

'No, I mean — '

'Yes, yes, where did he come from, what does he do, what were the colour of his grandmother's eyes? I don't know. He came here a while back. He was the only one who stayed. The rest of them . . . Tchah.' He all but spat. It must have been the hippies he was talking of. But that was all he would say.

'I do want to get to bed fairly early, if you don't mind. I'd like to go with Peter and Sheila in the morning, to help choose curtaining and so on. If we measure up first, and find the fabric Sheila likes, I could make them for her — '

'That won't be necessary, we can afford to have them made. Since she's set on moving.'

'She is tired, Gerald.'

'Everyone goes, I quite understand. I'm used to it. Good night.'

'Have you got everything you — '

'Good night. You'll sleep well, I'm sure.' He gave her the old charming smile; but it didn't come out open.

There were two possibilities as far as Peter was concerned: he could leave the houses in Leeds for a month or so and get on with the cottage before the harsh weather set in; or finish them and come back in the early spring. The three of them discussed this on the way back from a joyous day discovering good builders' merchants, suppliers of traditional fireplaces, fabric shops, carpet shops, tiles, electrical goods, yards where old paving stones might be found . . .

Caroline had prepared a meal and listened with her usual reserve to the animated talk. She, unlike Sheila, had not changed in the least: she was preserved, a school-girl still; she was untouched. Once again Gerald kept to himself; but quite late, as they were all yawning, he wheeled in. 'I must catch up on what you've been up to. Have you drawn up some plans, Peter?'

'Pretty rough, so far. They wouldn't mean much to anyone else, but I can explain what we have in mind.' Peter drew a chair alongside him and pointed out the details.

'No, no, that'll do, that's clear enough. I'm sure Mathers will be able to work it all out.'

Everything died.

'Mathers?' Peter's voice was flat.

'That was the idea, wasn't it? Of course we respect your expertise, Peter, and it's been very good of you to give us the benefit of your advice. But when it comes to the actual work – I think these things are better kept on a purely business basis. It doesn't do to mix private, er, relationships with business. Don't you agree?'

They had been set up. Deliberately, had been given a role only to have it removed.

Caroline silently brought Gerald coffee; Sheila, old again, bade them goodnight. Her back was straight as she left the room, but for the first time it was clear that it cost her effort.

They went back in the morning, after Rose planted the rosemary cuttings. That was all they had been able to give.

Peter broke the silence between them. 'Did you tell him where the houses are?'

The houses? Oh, their houses. 'Come to think of it, he did ask, the first night. Yes, I did.' She looked at him in alarm.

So they were half prepared for what they found. Each had been broken into. Water pipes were wrenched away from the walls, basins cracked. It had been quiet work; no one had been disturbed. It would take weeks, and money, to put all back to rights.

It was a hard winter and cost them dearly. Peter, drowning in anger and distress, thought again and again of the land, of the harm which he had not been able to stop. Rose tried to stop this – he was making himself ill. 'There was never any chance of your having the farm, you said so yourself. He was older — '

'And I left. I didn't have to go. If I'd been there — '

'I don't know about the legal side of it, but the fact is, it wasn't yours. He'd have made it impossible for you if you'd stayed.'

'Perhaps.'

Sheila telephoned more often than usual, telling of progress on the cottage. She was saying that she was sorry for her weakness. The truth was that there had been nothing she could do.

IX

Damaged Goods

1982–3

My dear Beth,

Oh, isn't there always an irony? The very year you move to New York, two thousand miles less far away, and I am free (finished teaching!!!) – Laker Airlines go bust. Heigho.

The children are all but gone. Ben is coming to A-levels and is planning to do medicine after a year on a kibbutz, and Amy is at college – and my mother is happily settled. Suddenly it's *our* lives again; and apart from serious intentions to become reborn as Rose (i.e. not wife, mother, daughter, teacher et al) we've still no definite plans, though we are thinking in terms of a small country place with workshops where Peter can go back to furniture making.

As for you, this shilly-shallying (does it seem to you very English? Is that what's kept us back?) must be incomprehensible. You're practially an international name! Is it true that you might be expanding into Europe? We might meet at last!

Meanwhile . . .

Rose had yearned for change, and got it.

All at once she could call her days her own: no bells, no time-tables. Freedom.

This proved to be full of dangers. She had time to reflect and was not well pleased with her findings. Herself she saw to be well-intentioned and stupid, Peter as becoming preoccupied with his work from which she was now excluded. She had proposed doing the paperwork, but he had found a capable woman who did not want to relinquish the payment.

She was, in short, on her own.

Of course there was plenty she wanted to do. The city was rich in theatres and concert halls, there was an intriguing range of courses on offer – oh, what might she not learn!

And it happened to women, that they were left alone, widowed. She had no desire to be, if Peter died, his relict merely. Had she not read with ardour about the achievements of women? Had Sheila not been her inspiration?

What was different was that Rose now had choice, and it cast a large responsibility on her for which she was not in condition. This was a matter of shame.

Still domestic duties claimed her and these she came to resent where she had imagined glorying in the house, filling it with friends, entertaining, making it a lovelier – comfortable now, even – place for talk. But their circle of friends had shrunk while they had been so busy.

Old ideas could not be revivified. What was needed was a new start. It might have to be almost complete.

She braced herself, brought back to mind her terror, when she thought Peter had left her so long ago, at the prospect of a tidy room of her own with no demands, no interruptions of what she wanted to do. It scared her still, and drew her: there was something to prove.

Meanwhile she tried: did some preliminary reading for the Open University (couldn't feel comfortable, reading in the afternoon), sewed, wondered if she could still draw (she couldn't), joined a record library. But the only occupation she did not feel guilty about was cooking. The slave mentality is not easily shed.

She wanted to be late getting dinner on the table, not from spite but because she had been engrossed elsewhere, then to arrive slightly flushed with excitement, abstracted but bursting with discoveries to share, so that those waiting were not resentful but glad to see her so alive, anticipating good food and good talk and later good love. But they were all busy and did not need her.

The trouble is, thought Rose sadly, I was born apologetic.

She bought Mozart's Requiem mass, shut herself in the sitting room and played it, rapt. When Peter came in she did not leap up to give him the choice. They heard it through. She should have been cleansed; but her own inner muddle wriggled, interfering. At the end, Peter sighed, and smiled across at her. 'That was — '

'Don't say a word! I know I usually leave it to you to choose; you always choose. Whenever we've had an hour to ourselves in here you've always put on what you wanted, all our old stuff, Dylan and — '

'I thought that was what you liked.'

'It isn't! It hasn't been for a long long time. I want to fin out what *I* like, before you die. I don't want to be left empty with no choice of *mine*, always putting myself second — '

'Nobody made you.'

He knew at once that he should have taken her hand, and said what was also true: 'How absurd, that all these years we have been thinking we were pleasing the other, and yet neither of us was content.' But she should not have implied that it was his fault.

'I'm going away.'

'Yes, you need a change.'

'For a year.'

'*What*?'

Both their hearts staggered momentarily.

'Yes. On my own.'

'Where?'

'I don't know yet.'

She had gone too far too quickly; but she wouldn't give way. What would make it clear? – to herself as well as to him. 'You said to me once that I'd lost – what was it? – spontaneity. That there was a time when I knew instinctively what was right. And then I lost it.'

Who hadn't? he thought. Life got busy; but there was not time for the long view. 'Yes?'

'Yes, but . . . But I mean to do something about it. On my own.' Other women were strong alone. 'I'm not going to be . . . eaten away.'

He tightened his lips, very angry. She had the luxury of choice. A man did not have this; he had to work to the end.

Now she was frightened, knowing exactly what was in his mind. It had come out selfish, when it should have sounded worthy of respect. She came over and sat on the floor by him, putting her cheek against his work-hard hand. 'I didn't mean that.' But there was no answering pressure. 'Listen, why don't we go away? Just for a few days? Then perhaps we can see straight.'

After a silence that flooded her with fear (she wanted him *and* her self, not one or the other) he said neutrally, 'All right.'

'Honestly? Where? When? How long?' (Was this what she really wanted, then, just to be with him, with nothing in the way? This must be considered. Later.)

'What about London?'

Alma said, 'Ooh, you'll have a great time. Posh hotel, telly in your bedroom, make your own tea or coffee. Pity they don't give you proper milk – mind, we had some champagne, no stinting. Terry said, Let's have a right good mucky weekend, and so we did. But foreigners! You had to wonder if you was still in the same country; we think we've a fair old mix up here, but there, you could walk the length of Oxford Street and not hear English spoke. And money! I made Terry come with me to that Harrods; I didn't let on but I was thinking, Blimey, will they let us in? But yes, you could go where you wanted. Course he doesn't like shops at the best of times, and the prices, well they make you see why some's for the revolution. I stood by one of the perfume counters and gawped, watching this woman, an Arab of some sort, and she spent, wait for it, seven hundred quid. On scent! Without batting an eyelid! Doesn't seem right, does it, when you see about all the poverty in them countries? Oh, it was an education. Talk about broadening the mind, beats the Costa del Sol.

'But best of all was the museums. Anybody ever taught me'd drop dead to hear little Alma say that, but they're different again. Terry wanted to go to the Science Museum, and I nearly said, All right then, I'll meet you later, but you can't go off separate on a dirty weekend, can you? Well, it was a revelation. You can touch things, did you know that? And the V and A, you could spend three months and not see half. Them little porcelain figures! We must've looked like school-kids, just gawping. Mind, you *look* better when you're older, don't you? I always said school comes at the wrong time. Child labour, that's what you ought to have, say ten to twenty, then have your kids and get an education after. And what's nice is there's cafés, so you can have a sit down and a fag and go for a wee and off again. Well, this'll give you the measure: we was late back to see the Cup Final on telly. So then we had a bit of a session, and then I nearly killed him, me hair was all over, and then we went to the theatre. Dennis Waterman! Don't you love him on *Minder*? It was a musical about newspapers in the twenties; oh, it was great, I clapped till me hands stung. And then we hadn't finished, we went out to dinner! Italian. I was dead proud of Terry, the way he di the ordering, but they wasn't a bit stuck up, the waiters, they kept giving me the eye, and he got a bit ratty, you know, so you know they're possessive – and oh! it was the best day and night I ever had. Then on the Sunday — '

Rose went and booked.

They found they weren't much bothered about the children, but as it happened Ben was on a field trip, and Amy could stay with Ailsa.

They did not stint either. Albeit aware that this was not settling anything, was only an oasis (but what a needed one, they were parched for pleasure), a halt in a long journey, destination unknown, they gave themselves over and enjoyed. The markets, pictures, the river, bookshops, the diversity of strangers, food, the Festival Hall and walking back over Hungerford Bridge, sky, wandering, looking. Why didn't they do this more often?

And they liked each other.

Coming back, to the cleaner sharper air, they stood, arms round each other, under the canopy at the station waiting for a taxi. 'With any luck, we'll have the house to ourselves for a couple of hours.' They had come back earlier than necessary, on the Sunday afternoon, wanting to go over the house, take stock, consider: should they go, or stay?

'Park Terrace?' asked the taxi driver. 'Nice round there, isn't it?'

When had people stopped saying, 'Park Terrace? You don't live in that dump, do you?'

He pulled in rather far up the road, so difficult was it now to find space among a row of cars. 'This'll do,' said Peter, 'we can walk back a bit.' While he paid, Rose assembled on the pavement their cases and the bright carrier bags from the Body Shop and the National Gallery and Harrods Food Hall.

'Goodness, don't we look rich? Could you — '

'Good God.'

'What?'

Oh no. Oh how hideous.

They were outside the Eisners'. The lower windows were boarded over, the garden ravaged. Red spray paint on door and gateposts said 'Murderer!'

'Oh, dear Lord. What can we do? There must be something. Who could . . .'

'It must have happened yesterday, if there's been time to board the windows.'

Feeling responsible, they knocked, but there was no reply.

Just then they loathed the city.

Had Rolf been in, and Rebecca, when stones smashed through the glass into the civilised quiet, and the tidy garden was destroyed, the evil hiss of cans spat out the message of hate?

Contamination.

More wearily than before they went, they picked up their bags. 'It was just this house, was it?' They looked along the terrace. Just this one. Chosen.

Nor was the house to be just theirs for a little while. Heavy metal sounds thumped out, lights were on all over.

Sick, they set down the bags in the hall, switched off the lights in the sitting room where a large fire blazed away to emptiness, and retreated to the kitchen. They took in the spills on the floor, stack of bottles, the mess of glasses and paper cups, crushed lager cans and breakages. It was only when Peter went to the bathroom and the cistern flushed that the noise in Amy's room was abruptly switched off.

Ben came in, eyes blazing. 'What happened? Where's Rebecca?'

'We don't know, Ben.'

'Well, haven't you been? Haven't you tried to find out?'

'There was no answer — '

He dropped his rucksack, threw off his anorak and scarf and stood thinking. 'He'll have taken her to Manchester. Was anyone hurt, for God's sake? Was the house — '

'Dear, we don't know. It looks like just a – a demonstration of some kind.'

Savage with frustration he raced out, and was back in a moment. 'No one.'

'Darling, if they've gone away there's not much — '

'I'll find out. Where's the phone book? No, that won't do. Webster, Weber, Weber, that's it. What's directory enquiries?'

He was on the telephone a long time, trying wrong numbers, finally getting through. His voice changed; he was talking to Rebecca. Rose closed the door and gave him privacy. Amy had gone out – wisely. And Rose had started on the clearing-up. She wasn't being a martyr; she simply wanted it all back her way.

Ben came in and sat exhausted. 'She's with her cousins. She's all right.'

'And Rolf?'

'He's coming back tomorrow. Rebecca doesn't want to.'

This was his first adult pain. 'How long is she staying, did she say?'

'A while.'

'It's probably best, love. To get over the shock. Was she in when it happened?'

'Yes.'

'Oh, poor girl.'

'She wouldn't talk about it. I'm going over in the morning.'

Missing school – but yes, this was more important.

'Yes, you must. Now we'll have something to eat.'

He changed his mind and telephoned again, to see if there were trains that night, but then realised that to put him up might be awkward for the Webers. He was calmer now, and suddenly very tired. Yes, the weekend had been fine but the hostel uncomfortable, he hadn't had much sleep. He ate without noticing and went to his room. But he could rest now, ready for next day, now that he knew what he was going to do.

Peter had been out to check on the house he was currently working on. It was all right.

In the morning he and Ben went out early and Rose continued with the cleaning. Amy came into the kitchen and started polishing glasses.

'You should be getting ready for college.'

'I've no classes till eleven. In fact I thought I'd miss today and give you a hand. I'm sorry about the mess, Mum, but there's no harm — '

'I'm not interested in the mess or the party. I want to know what happened at Rolf Eisner's house.'

'Are you sure it's his house? We didn't know. Someone just said it was somebody who did experiments on animals.'

'Would it have made any difference if you'd known whose house it was? Would you have thought twice, any of you, if you'd remembered that he's a German Jew, a refugee who came here for safety, whose wife died of cancer? I'd really like to know. Is it easier if the victims are faceless?'

'You seem to be making an accusation, Mum. I told you, we just heard this — '

'Amy. Tell me.'

The girl chose indignation as the means of defence. 'It's all very well for you to come out with this stuff about refugees and cancer, but what about the animals? Defenceless little mice, and rats and even pigs, they can feel pain, they suffer the most horrible torments and *they* can't run away to another country! Some of these experiments are awful, you wouldn't want to know, I suppose, but we know, and — '

'He does cancer research. He tries to stop suffering.'

'I don't care, he works in that laboratory and some of the things that are done are horrible. Jason has a friend whose cousin worked in one of those places — '

'A friend whose cousin? One of those places? This is evidence? And on this you dare to condemn Rolf Eisner?'

'It's not only him. I didn't know about that, I told you. A lot of houses were done on Saturday night, it'll be in the papers and then perhaps everyone will realise that some of us *care*.'

'So you and your friends planned it. This group does this house, that group wil . . . Jesus wept. In cold blood you planned to attack the homes of hard-working — '

'The experiments are done in cold blood.'

'There are codes of practice — '

'Huh! You don't know, you don't want to know, all you're concerned about is houses, stone and wood and glass. Uncle Gerald understands. I'm talking about living creatures!'

'So is Rolf Eisner a living creature.'

'But he wasn't hurt, it was only the house, only *things*. Can't you see?'

Rose sat down, weak. 'A house *is* a life, Amy. A place to be safe. People put their lives into houses — '

'Property!' Amy's contempt was total now. 'You value property above the pain of dumb animals. That says it all, doesn't it?'

'Can't you imagine what it does to a person, to have the sanctuary of home violated? Especially someone who's known it all before.'

'I can't lose any sleep over a man who hurts helpless creatures. Sorry.'

A child who had never known war. She couldn't understand. They had grown up taking freedom for granted. Mea culpa, yet again?

'Go away, Amy. I don't trust myself. I want to work.'

All morning she scrubbed and wiped and brushed and scoured, trying to cleanse her mind of rage. She knew what it was to want to change the world. But not through violence. She feared infection with violence. Yet, upstairs, she broke off and went to Amy's room, to stand and look, not to pry. But all she could take in was a poster, for some band called Black Sabbath. It showed a baby. The baby had pointed teeth and horns and pointed red fingernails. Obscenity and perversion. She moved slowly over and pulled it down, then in the sitting room tore it into small pieces and set it alight and watched the ashes for a long time. It was grief she felt. Then she went to the bathroom and stood under the shower, the benison of hot water, and dressed completely in fresh clothes.

She knew Peter would be in soon. When he came she said, 'We must go and see Rolf.'

'Yes. We'll go now.'

Glaziers were at work. When they rang the bell there was presently a shuffling within, and after a moment a doubtful voice. 'Who is that?'

'Rose and Peter Stead.'

Chains were drawn and dropped, a key turned. The clever heavy face peered out, warily, a refugee's look, before it lightened to the warmth they knew. 'Come in, come in. You must excuse all this.' He shrugged. 'Reporters.'

He had been clearing up. In the sitting room a bin contained shards of glass, though specks glittered in the carpet. 'You must excuse the . . . I have only now begun. I took Rebecca away and have just returned. Please, sit down – oh, excuse — ' In an armchair was propped a water-colour, its frame broken. On a side table a vase lay, dead flowers falling, a sodden patch on the rug.

'This is terrible. Please let us help.'

'No, no. You are very kind, many friends have offered. But I like to do it myself – can you explain why? Partly of course so that my cleaning lady should not be upset, but also – can you explain?'

A kind of catharsis. Rose understood that.

Peter asked, 'Do the police know who did it?'

'Oh, the police. They have other matters, more serious . . . They were very good. Rebecca was on her own, you see. I was at the concert. Mahler. She wanted to finish an essay, my little swot.' He smiled. 'So of course she telephoned the police. They stayed with her till I came home. There was apparently a spate of these events. Some of my colleagues too . . . Some lovers of animals had "claimed responsibility". A curious phase, isn't it? Now I'm wandering. Sometimes I fear old age is not far way – and then I'm glad Rebecca has young friends. As for individuals, no, they don't know. And who would press charges? For what good?'

'How is Rebecca?'

'Oh. As you can imagine. She was afraid most of a break-in, after the stones. It was some time before she dared to move, to telephone for help. She hid there.' he nodded his head: the corner behind the grand piano. The raised lid was split, some of the wires buckled. Oh God. 'An interesting example of race memory. She said she felt as my mother, my sisters, in Germany. We even had a piano destroyed. But of course the situation is very different. This I tried to convince her of.'

Not wholly different, Peter muttered to himself. Not sufficiently different.

'And is she all right now?'

'Shaken . . . I took her to relations of my wife, in Manchester. Irma is very happy to spoil her, her own daughters being grown.'

'So naturally you want her to find it all back to normal.'

'At the moment, I am afraid, she does not want to come back. But in a few weeks, perhaps. The young are resilient.'

The first term of her degree course. Rebecca had chosen to study at Leeds so she could stay with her father.

'Now, some coffee? A glass of wine?'

They went home for tools and sacks and spent the afternoon tidying the garden, pruning back the broken shrubs, replanting, picking out glass, turning trampled earth. 'I suppose anyone passing thought it was a student prank.' Peter rubbed down and repainted the gate posts and the front door.

More harm would have been done to the growing things if

this had been spring or summer. With the autumn decay it was not so serious; not much that would not grow again. What was inside the house might not be so easily restored.

Rose spoke no more of her need for change, but she did not forget. Being a reasonable woman, she concluded that since Ben and Amy would soon have left, she could wait a year. Meanwhile, she pursued her Open University course with delight, and on a practical level undertook the complete refurbishment of their bedroom. It had evolved into some comfort over the years, but was shabby. To this she did not especially object; but the spreading presence of large teen-agers (Amy was toeing the line, but noisy) caused her to assert the supremacy of those who paid the mortgage by spending quite a deal of money on themselves. She took time over all this: first, the redecoration, then the making of new curtains and covers for bed and chairs. Was it a propitiation, for the betrayal she had in mind? Perhaps . . . but, first, the clear statement that this was where it had all begun.

In the family there was determined goodwill, though sometimes Amy's records, which strangely did not disturb Ben, blasted her and Peter out to the refuge of the local, where they were initiates of the snug.

Tonight Alma and Terry came in and for once did not separate, Terry to the dartboard and Alma on a circuit of friends. Silently they brought their drinks over and sat down.

'It's our Gary,' Alma said eventually.

'If he thinks he's coming back to our house after that,' Terry snapped, 'he's another think coming.'

'We'll he can't stay at me mam's for ever, she's only the one bedroom.'

'What's the matter?'

Terry groaned, and swung his torso back in disbelief. 'He's up for violence. At the match. Silly young sod, he's not even the nous to follow a real game like Rugby League, he has to get in with that gang of yobs down at United. And now look.'

'It was last night. Floodlit match against Manchester. Trouble started and he was in the thick. Next thing, they've got a copper on the floor.'

'It's that I can't understand,' Terry burst out. 'Putting the boot in. You get trouble, fair enough; we used to have a bit of a punch-up of a Saturday night, silly young buggers but that's lads for you. But fists, not boots. What the bloody hell's up with them? Call themselves men? He's no son of mine, I'll tell you that much, and I'll say the same in court if it comes to it. You've always been too soft with him, I've said it for years.'

Alma turned to Rose and Peter. 'Terry thinks if he'd been brought up tougher, like . . . But, you know, I used to take a lot of notice of you, when they was all little, being teachers and that. I mean, you never belted yours, did you?'

They walked home more sober than when they had come out.

In the dark time of the year a friend of Ben's died. It was in the evening paper: 'Seventeen-year-old has heart attack after solvent sniffing.'

Ben hadn't mentioned it. 'Oh, Ralph,' he said. 'Silly fool.'

'But this is tragic! Did you know he was doing this? Didn't any of you try to stop him?'

'Mum, it was his own stupid fault. He wasn't thick, he knew the risks.'

'But why?'

'Curiosity? I bet you tried pot, in the happy hippy days, didn't you? Well, then.'

'His poor parents.' The burden to carry to their graves: what had they done wrong?

'Sure, it's a damned waste. All the broken nights and bottom-wiping, trikes and teddy-bears, all for nix.'

'Ben, you sound callous.'

'What's the point in getting emotional? He bought it, that's all. And it's nothing to do with his parents, poor devils. It might just as well have been coming off a motor-bike. Parents have nothing to do with any of it.'

That should have been a comfort.

Ben made himself a doorstep peanut-butter sandwich to take up to his room. Rose called him back. 'Ben. Going into medicine . . . Are you doing it for the right reasons?'

'Absolutely, Mater. A steady income and a good chance of a bit on the side with all the pretty nurses. Even better if I don't make the grade and end up a dentist. Twice the money for half the hassle.'

'But you do care about, well, helping people?'

'Honestly, old duck, you sound seventeen sometimes. What could relieve the suffering world more than curing toothache? Listen, coming from a family like this I couldn't avoid having a social conscience even if I wanted to. Why else would I be trekking off to Israel in the summer?'

'Because you like Rebecca.'

'And that.'

'So you're not going to Stoners Court to help with the harvest?'

'One thing I've learned: you can't make much difference for the better without power. And that means money. I know you and Dad are doing all right now, but it's taken too long. There's no pleasing some mothers. Here am I, going prematurely grey swotting deep into the nights, to give you the chance to brag about my-son the-doctor, and all you can do is tremble in case I've no ideals. And there's my beloved sister, as much a rebel as any flower child could have wished for, and you won't be happy till she's straightened herself out. Cheer up, chuck, her heart's in the right place. It's just her brains that've slipped a bit. By the time you're a very old lady you'll probably be able to relax and stop feeling responsible for every sparrow that falls. You'll grow out of it.'

Ailsa was anxious about Sam. 'It's Marcia. She's got a new young man, she doesn't want him any more. It is rotten, after all these years. And he's been working so hard.'

Sam's programmes were called *The Unnoticed*. It had taken him five years to get the idea accepted and into production, for it did not correspond either to the favoured modes of despair or success. One had dealt with women burdened with responsibility for aged parents or terribly afflicted children, another about ordinary people in Northern Ireland getting along with life beside the fears and stresses. Six had been planned, taking all his skill and influence to get approval – but such had been the public and critical acclaim that another thirteen had been made and a further series was scheduled. He was busier than ever before, but on fleeting visits talked passionately of club entertainers who never made the big-time, of ancillary hospital workers, local councillors who did not seek publicity, charity workers who ran jumble sales and stood in the cold on flag days, volunteers who kept youth clubs going . . . 'There could be years of it, the source is inexhaustible!'

Ailsa was enormously proud.

In the spring Rose and Amy were having a blazing row about Arthur Scargill, who had tried to bring the miners out on strike without a ballot. They insisted on having one, and he lost.

'They deserve hundreds and hundreds of pounds a week, going down into a hole every day. How would you like it?'

'Very likely they do deserve more. But they must be their own best judges as to how far they'll go in demanding it.'

'They don't know their own power, they don't realise how much they could get!'

'Are you saying they're stupid? They voted. That's democracy.'

'Oh, democracy.'

There were times when Rose couldn't wait for her to go. She had had enough of this dangerous nonsense. But before she could throw out the familiar challenge of 'What would you have in its place, then?' Ben called from the front room 'Ailsa's coming up the path. She looks in a state.'

Sam had died of a heart attack in the changing room of a smart squash club in London.

After the first shock – she had kept saying, 'Why did nobody tell me? I could have been with him?' (but there had been no time, it happened in a moment) – she was calm. It worried Rose that she wasn't more upset. Surely there was danger, if grief did not take the natural course? But Ailsa had her religion.

'He achieved all he wanted to,' she said quietly a few weeks later. There had been a tribute to him on television, with excerpts from some of the best programmes. 'Do you remember that time when Merry was here? That's when he knew what he wanted to do. Gosh, do you realise they were both famous? Not that that matters. But it shows that people wanted what they did.' They had got her a video recorder so that she could watch the series time and again; but she didn't, often. She was without distress; and she had been alone for a long time.

Sam's death had shaken Rose and Peter more. He had been forty-two, Peter's age. Now two of their friends were dead,

Beth and Jethro halfway across the world, Ailsa in her own world. They should talk about their own lives. 'When I've finished this job,' Peter said, knowing Rose's thoughts.

He had reliable help now, doing conversions for a housing association. Rose was not needed.

Curiously, that summer, she slowed down, waiting. It had become apparent that striving did not necessarily lead to good outcomes, contrary to what they had always believed. She read a great deal, and gardened, did some decorating in the house, as if putting it in order.

And Amy had moved out. She had fallen in with a group of students, or ex-students, who had a vacancy in their rented house. She had renounced her college course in order to 'find where I'm at. And I'm going to be financially independent, so don't worry about me. You've done your best, but I've got to find my own way now.' Rose was deeply afraid that it was guilt which was driving her. She also knew there was nothing she could do about that, either.

'Independent?' Peter asked sourly. 'On social security? If you intend to stand on your own feet, clean offices, wash glasses in a pub, don't take handouts.'

But this did not accord with the ethos of the house, wittily known as Liberty Hall. Where she was at was a broken-down street some ten minutes' walk away, with milk bottles under hedges and a smell of drains and curry. On the one occasion that Rose visited – it was forbidden, but she had not seen her daughter for over a week and feared flu, or worse – she was admitted to a barish room well furnished with vertical and horizontal hair of assorted colours surmounting human young, clothed uniformly in dusty black ornamented with arrangements of metal studs. She was privileged to listen, in the middle of a fresh afternoon, to meandering talk of yin and yang and I Ching, of how X got busted and what the Soshe had said to Y, and of getting an old lorry from somewhere and joining the Convoy when the days drew out. They talked of peace and resembled perverted storm-troopers, without the muscle. Rose made an excuse and left. It was nothing to do with her. She loved her daughter and wished her peace and happiness; but she had not the least desire to placate, try to understand, gain acceptance.

I no longer wish to please, she realised. Perhaps the

feminist movement was right: all her life fear had been her ruler. 'If I'm not good enough they won't love me.'

No more. There had to be clarity, not muddling through.

Ben had got his B grades and would be off to Birmingham. He had sent cards; he knew where he was going.

Rose knew where she had to go before she and Peter could talk.

At a day's notice, she arrived at Stoners Court.

'I wanted to see you,' she told Sheila.

'My first guest in the cottage,' said Sheila, kissing her. 'Shall we sit outside? I'm very pleased with this little yard, so out of the draught.' She had shrunk, but was as straight as ever. She was in her sixties now, and had worked hard. Rose carried out the tea-tray, thankful that there had been no need to pass the big house. She had parked in the old farm yard, clean now without the animals, behind the great silos. Sheila followed with a basket of seed-heads and a packet of buff envelopes. 'I couldn't stop myself,' she confessed. 'Most of the plants from the main garden won't do here, there isn't the space. But all these years there's never been time to collect them, and now there is. Would you like to mark the envelopes for me? Perhaps you'd like to take some home.'

Rose printed carefully 'Russell Lupins' and Sheila cracked open the dry pods and shook the seeds into the envelope; then 'Iceland Poppies, dwarf'. The walls of the yard were steeped in warmth from the lowering sun, and thrift grew in cracks between the paving stones.

'The rosemary has taken, you see!' Yes. It had been given a sheltered corner and was well established.

'For remembrance. You're happy here, aren't you?' Sheila had shed some part of a duty.

'It occurred to me the other night: I always liked small places. I loved our little flat in Durham near the cathedral when we were first married. But it's only now become possible. Polyanthus, giant mixed, please. I'm very fortunate to have lived long enough to enjoy this.'

'You waited all this time to do what you wanted.'

Sheila paused to watch a late bumble-bee stumbling round the asters. Then, 'Sorry. I forget what you said.'

'You've had about the hardest life of any woman I know. Except Mrs Slipser.'

'Aquilegia next. Hard? Hard work, yes. That doesn't make a hard life, does it?'

'I don't know.' Rose sighed, easily. She found, up here, that she knew very little. 'We've always worked hard too. But you had the war.'

'Thank God you never had that. Otherwise the whole six years would have been wasted. But there have been anxious times since. And all this awful worry of making choices. I was spared that.'

That was one way of looking at it.

They both knew there were important worries; Sheila asked no questions; Rose was full of questions. But just now they sat in the sun and breathed the intensified autumn air, saved the seeds and were slow and quiet together.

'Godetia. Oh, this is a lovely one, you must try it, Sybil Sherwood. Such a rich salmon pink, and the edges white – if it comes true.'

Rose said, 'It's a different kind of summer here.'

'How is that?'

'An older kind of summer.'

There was nothing old about the blue bright spark in Sheila's eye as she surveyed this daughter of hers, forbearing to point out that summer was gone. 'You're still young, Rose. You're not one to run away.'

Weariness knew no age group; but it wasn't that. 'We wondered if that was what we were thinking of doing, often and often.' Later would come the time to go into the present, find a conclusion. 'But I'm not young, Sheila dear; goodness, I could be a grandmother! And quite old enough to know we're coming to a change. You knew Peter and his hopes, didn't you? – a better world by Tuesday fortnight, or in a decade at the most. My friend Alma could have told him otherwise at the age of twelve. You must meet, you and Alma. You're alike.'

'You could bring her up for a few days.'

'She'd love that. But to go back, Sheila. We are running away. We've given up, I think, quite a while ago. Without noticing, except that . . . Yes. Except that we both became terribly tired. What kind of reason is that?'

'Pretty unanswerable. I should have thought. It does come.'

'But it should go again! It's as if we never had time to recover.'

'You've both worked very hard.'

'Yes, that's true. But for what? We've changed nothing. We've had a few people to stay and there's no telling if it helped. We've taught a lot of children between us, but I don't know whether we did better for them than anyone else would have done.' She did still get Christmas cards from Venus. This meant a great deal.

'What did you think you were setting out to do? Change the world?'

'Now that's like Alma again! She used to say all pacifists hoped for was to change human nature. Is that possible?'

Sheila considered. 'We don't have public hangings or fashionable jaunts to laugh at lunatic asylums.'

'True. So there is some progress?'

'Yes.' The answer was straight. 'Morning Glory. Now this is the most perfect blue, but tender. Oh, and you haven't a conservatory. Neither have I. I'm hoping to have a small greenhouse, though. Over by the far wall, do you think? Each flower lasts only a day, but worth it.'

'I could try them in the kitchen window, that gets the afternoon sun.'

'No, they want the morning sun.'

'The sitting room, then.' Two envelopes. 'Could you say . . . was there a time when you came to some point – not a decision exactly, but when you were quite, quite certain about, well — '

'Eccremocarpus. Now if this goes at all it will climb through anything. You might need to make several attempts but after that it will take care of itself. Quite exotic.' The deft strong hands worked carefully. 'It came when my husband died, and I knew without doubt that he had broken faith with me. So I felt I had lost him twice over. I also knew without doubt that I would be alone and that I would survive.'

'You make it sound easy,' said Rose humbly.

'Moments like that are easy because you don't make them happen, they just come. The pain – and the weakness – they come later. Not once but many times. But you've had the moment of certainty. The rest can be lived through. Ah, Alyssum, the lemon one. It behaves as though it's rampant, but it can do with preserving. I'm always afraid it will disappear one winter and not come back. Be careful, they're very fine.

'So,' she continued, 'is it that you feel you have failed at what you took on, or that you discovered it was the wrong challenge?'

There was no hurry to answer. Rose was given pause, which was what she had come for.

'Aquilegia.'

'Granny bonnets.'

They eased their positions and laughed, noting that the sun had turned the corner of the roof and they were now in shade, though the warmth lingered.

Unhurriedly Rose faced the point in the mauve shadow of the sheltered yard.

She reviewed the nineteen years that she and Peter had had, the house, the people who had been there, the work they had done. It was nothing to be ashamed of nor any great achievement, but it was coming to an end.

'It's more a question of moving on. Only we don't know where yet.' They had grown out of ideas. What was needed now was wisdom.

Caroline came over to invite them to dinner. 'Gerald wants to see you, you see.'

Sheila excused herself. 'I shall be staying with him next week remember, while you go to Cheltenham.'

'Yes,' said Caroline simply, 'it was Rose he wanted to see.'

Of course it was not possible to come up here and pretend Gerald did not exist. 'Yes, thank you. What time?'

Eight. So she had another two hours with Sheila, and she turned away from the evening's prospect back to what was important. 'Tell me about the war,' she said.

'We'll go inside now. The best of the day is over.'

When they sat before the wood fire, its flames almost invisible in the low gold that still came in at this side of the cottage, Sheila said, instead of answering, 'I have often wondered that neither of you ever asked about Peter's mother.'

'That's because I've always thought of you as his mother. And men can make themselves incurious. But I do know she was a landgirl, so you must have known her.'

'Working here, yes. She joined even before war was declared. For a lot of young women it was a chance to break away from a narrow life. We had three of them eventually.'

'So you were all women? The farm was run by women?'

'Except for George – you knew him, didn't you? Later there were the prisoners of war, too.'

'Did they mind, having to work on an English farm?'

'They were mostly from the land themselves. Italians, oh, and Ukrainians, displaced persons. Taddeus still lives in the village. Many of them didn't want to go back.'

And never could, now. How terrible, never to be able to go home.

Rose looked out at the harvest-coloured fallen flounces of a great beech tree. 'How comforting it is,' she said wistfully, 'not to have to draw curtains for privacy. Or lock cars or put wheelbarrows away in case they get stolen.'

'I thought you must have come for a special reason.'

'It's more a matter of trying to get the past straight, before we move on. That's what we neglected to do in the first place, and it led us to mistakes.'

After a moment, Sheila said, 'Come upstairs for a moment.'

In the small bedroom Rose was moved by the 1930s bedroom suite of bird's-eye maple, reminded that the young couple had never expected to come to Stoners Court, that they had started on their own quite different lives.

'On the dressing table. My husband, aged seven.' And, by it, a picture of Ben at the same age. They were all but identical. There could be no doubt. 'He was Peter's father.'

'A long time ago, I suddenly thought that was it.'

'She told me, the mother. I didn't believe her for a second, I thought she was in a panic, not surprisingly, and had made up a story that would enable her to stay. She said her parents would disown her. In any case my sympathies were with her, there was no question of turning her out.' She went into herself for a little while and Rose turned away from the pain that passed behind the habitual composure. Then she continued. 'When he died the bank passed on to me a letter he had left. It was true.'

'How did you bear it?'

Sheila shuddered. 'It's cold up here.'

When had she ever felt the cold? In the sitting room Rose said, 'I brought a bottle of malt whisky. Would you like one?'

'Yes. Thank you, Rose.' Steady again, she went on, 'It was completely out of character. You must always remember that he was just back from Dunkirk.'

Needing to be sure she understood, sensing that she would become the one person who would carry the whole truth, Rose asked, 'Were you living here permanently then?'

'In 1939 we were in Durham. James was a historian. He had a sense of urgency about his work – unfashionable then, the history of working people. He said once that if Stoners Court had been his, had he been the elder son, he would keep it intact, repair all the old cottages and barns that were already being let go, save all the tackle and machinery that tractors were replacing, keep the heavy horses and the old breeds of sheep and cattle . . . He foresaw so many of the changes. Perhaps that's what history does, if one understands? Shows what is likely to happen?

'But of course Jeremy – Gerald's father – was the heir, and exempt from service because of the farm. So when James was called up, it was agreed that I should come here for the duration.'

'Did you mind?' Bringing the maple bedroom suite . . .

'I was not sorry. My father farmed at Totley, you know, only three miles away. That was how we met.'

'But to say goodbye to your husband — '

'Yes. It was the same for many. We had four years. We knew war was coming. But I hadn't been able to give him a child.' They had been quite on their own.

'Peter and I used to think it was coming again. Especially at the time of the Cuban crisis. That was why we got married in such a rush. I hope you weren't hurt.'

'My dear, as if it matters. You've been a good wife to him.'

'And since then, you've always shared a house. No wonder you love this cottage.'

'True. But Lucy and I – Jeremy's wife – had been at school together. We got along very well. We shared the chores, she in the house, me outside, and looking after young Gerald.'

'And yet you ended up running the farm on your own.'

'It was September 1940. James had just gone back from embarkation leave. I was always thankful he had that time with his brother. Lucy's sister was taking her children to America, for safety, and there was a family party in Sussex to see them off. On the way back Lucy and Jeremy stayed the night in London. A massive air-raid. Hundreds were killed.'

'Including them.'

'Including them.'

'So that left you in charge, of the child and the farm.'

'James could have been released from the army, theoretically. But he felt he should not get out of it.'

'And you?'

Sheila smiled. 'Contrary to what your generation thinks, there has always been equality in good marriages. But I had no doubt at all that such a decision could only be made by the man. It was his life that was at risk; it was his perception that it had to be done.'

It made Rose ashamed of the many times she had felt sorry for herself.

Pursuing a different line, Sheila let her knitting fall into her lap. 'He came home just the one time more. It's not hard to understand, the desperate urgency to do everything *now*. No experience of home to be missed. He was at Dunkirk. This was his rest leave. Rest. He had seen friends killed. Terrible woundings . . . He must have known he would not have much longer. And he had no child . . . When he wept, I put it down to the war. Thank God, I did not know while he lived.'

But Rose choked, that she had been betrayed by the husband she wholly trusted.

'Poor Heather,' Sheila continued. 'Poor silly girl.'

'What became of her?'

'The other girls looked after her – they had the cottage next door – and she took care of domestic matters for them when she was too big to work outside. The delivery was quite straightforward. She made a quick recovery, but she couldn't feed the child. She wasn't interested in him. "I want to make something of my life!" she used to cry. I almost admired her. And from the start I wanted him. Even his name came from me. After a few weeks she said she needed a change of scene, and went to visit friends in Sheffield. And there was another air-raid.'

'She was killed too?' Peter had always assumed his mother had died in labour.

'So we thought, when she didn't return. I wrote to her parents – her father was a Methodist minister in Salford but they literally did not want to know. They declined to acknowledge the child's existence. Luckily there wasn't much red-tape to do with adoption in those days. Once death was presumed, it was only a formality for me to adopt him, with James's written agreement. He was in North Africa by then. That was where he died. It was the last time I heard from him. Except for that letter . . .' An agony long dismissed was reborn with pangs as sharp as ever. For a bleak freeze of time Rose saw her confined in it . . . and then Sheila sighed, as if a contraction had passed, and smiled. 'He was a very thoughtful baby. Many and many a time I'd find him staring at me, as though he was trying to work something out. Young Gerald found him very unexciting – but he'd started school by then and was full of his own adventures. I think he felt he was pushed out. He was old enough, at four, to know – but what does a child understand? More than we choose to think: that his own parents were dead, and that I was only a substitute. And then a new child.' She broke off; considered for a moment, and then said with unusual force: 'So you must never blame him. You must always remember that he lost the ones he loved most when he was very young. And later his wife. Do not ever judge him.'

Not sure if she understood, Rose nevertheless nodded solemnly in response to the power of Sheila's command.

'Caroline understands him very well. Poor Caroline. It hasn't been easy for her.' Then, briskly: 'But she is very strong, in her own way. She'll be all right.'

All right when? But the telephone rang. It was Peter. 'No, of course there's no problem,' he said irritably. 'I just thought I'd make sure you'd arrived safely. How's everyone? It's been pouring down here all day . . .'

She went back, blushing rather. 'I think he must be missing me.'

'He was very lucky to find you. You keep his feet on the ground. I used to fear he'd be unhappy all his life, wanting the impossible.'

'He does have a small demon that gnaws,' Rose acknowledged. Hesitantly she added, 'Here, much of what we worry about seems . . . irrelevant. But they do matter, don't they? Politics . . . Towerblock flats – cutting down rain forests – young people in trouble . . . And the way dissatisfaction is nurtured, and gratitude is seen as in some way demeaning. But it's bitty, unless we can work out some underlying principles. I know there are the Ten Commandments, but they don't answer all the new problems.'

'No? I'm very limited in my views. But is it possible to make very hard work out of simple matters? I heard a woman on the radio recently talking about marriage. She described it as a contract – let me see; yes: a contract that had to be constantly renegotiated. It sounded very exhausting. Aren't the vows enough?' They had been for her.

Lamely Rose said, 'You must think us great fools, the way we get agitated — '

'My dear girl, no! I admire you very much. I'm not very good with ideas, you see, and I find it hard to have decided opinions on complicated issues. For example – Amy would be appalled – fox-hunting seems to have some practical value, at least until a tidy way of controlling foxes is found, though I see all the objections, generally raised by city-dwellers who don't come across the slaughtered chickens . . . Cannibalism, even! I don't suppose the dead minded. I'm not very serious. Perhaps very clever people can say exactly why these things are entirely wrong, not just partially. I simply avoid standing in judgment as far as possible on matters I don't completely understand. And isn't it interesting – this may be obvious to you, but it's often intrigued me – that the word is *under*stand? Only from inside, from *under* an experience, is it possible to . . . Not the bird's-eye view, that is for God . . . you see, I can't express my notions. Now, you and Peter search for consistency, which is brave, because it's bound to lead to disappointment. Consistency isn't in nature, is it? Or only in the very long term.'

'No,' Rose agreed slowly. There was so much she wanted to ask, but this must not be passed over. 'But it's in civilisation, or should be. That's what it's for, isn't it? To try to improve on nature? Otherwise the sick would be left to die, the way animals reject the weak ones.'

'Indeed. As long as – and this must be difficult, in cities – one doesn't come to believe that nature has no part in what

makes people as they are, do what they do. But you're quite
right, it's important to keep trying for fairness.'

'But?'

'But . . . Not to hope for too much, too quickly?'

Reluctantly Rose prepared to go over to the big house.
Discoveries were here, with Sheila. And she was afraid of
Gerald.

But the evening lit the patient trees, the even grass, beyond
the ha-ha the modest sheep. Peace was natural too. And
inconsistency. One must not strive to be God. What a
nonsense it was to wear themselves down, troubled by what
they could not affect. Better to get on with what they could do
well; and, first, to find out what this was.

She had wondered of late whether she should go to a place
called Greenham Common, to demonstrate for peace. She
had come here instead. She had asked Sheila: 'What do you
think about these women? Can it help? Because, if so, I must
join them.'

The reply had been sad, but sure. 'I always think of this:
that if we had been prepared, during the thirties, Hitler would
not have dared. And my husband might be with me still.'

As Rose went, Sheila said, 'You'll find Gerald greatly
changed. Be prepared.'

Peter had agreed that it would do Rose good to get away for a
while. He had not been altogether sorry to have a break from
the strain of what he took to be reproach on her part: she was
restless, so it must be his fault. He had become accustomed to
a working wife, glad of him but not dependent; he was
impatient, now, to feel she wanted too much of him. The old
notion of their working together was agreeable, would one
day come about, of course, but not just now. He was too busy.
He had a good reputation, had built up a good team of
workers. And he was earning money, necessary to buy the
freedom she vaguely seemed to desire. He could not spare
time or attention for a demanding wife.

But now, at a late hour on Saturday night, he was aware of
the weight of emptiness. The house expanded with her
absence. He took a slow bath instead of a shower, idly
imagining bachelor indulgences. Pretty girls? Ha. He was a
middle-aged man, unused to charming; lean and strong, but

grey in the beard; set in his ways. Married. Oh, the effort –
and for what? Slender flesh, raw mind, small comfort. He
wanted only Rose. He wanted her now. Ridiculous, this
notion of needing time apart. What could possibly be settled
alone that could not better be decided together? What in the
world, he wondered with increasing panic, could be the better
for her absence?

He poured a whisky and went from room to room, seeing
what they had made. Flourishing plants everywhere; Lord, he
had promised to water them. To the kitchen for the silly
watering can. They looked deprived already. And the
cushions on the sofa, they looked just like stuffed pieces of
fabric, not like comfort, as they did when she was there. That
tiny picture of a curlew she had made him buy – it was very
beautiful. He had never seen it properly before. Her knitting
bag was gone, the corner of the sofa uninhabited.

Chutney and plum jam in the larder. She claimed it was a
waste of time to make it now the children were gone. But the
scent of spices and vinegar lingered even now; it would not be
autumn if he did not come home to that rich odour. He
straightened the line of mugs along the shelf; she hated it if
one hung the wrong way. And that was better, harmony
restored. She would not like the brown casserole to be
spoiled. Women's fussiness. No: it was a respect for made
objects, and for growing things.

The whisky was making him maudlin.

Through the night he kept waking with a start, fearing
accidents. What would he do without her? It was all *for* her –
whatever 'it' was.

Caroline said, in the kitchen, 'He's in the drawing room – go
through.'

'Can I do anything to help?'

'You could try to stop him drinking too much. You might
have some effect.' The tone was light, the boarding-school
voice uninflected.

'Oh. Well, I don't think I have much influence.'

'He talks a lot of you. And he responds to a change of
company. We don't see many fresh faces.'

What had happened to the years? 'I'm sorry we haven't
been more help, Caroline.'

'Oh no, we know you're very busy. How has Ben settled down?'

'Very well, I think. It's what he always wanted to do, and he's very independent.'

'And Amy?'

'She's – still deciding. Caroline, how would it be if I came for a week or two some time soon, so that you and Gerald could have a break?'

'Gerald won't go away.'

'But you?'

'I quite often do. I don't do any farm work now we have a good manager, and Sheila will always come in.'

A bellow from across the hall: 'Rose! Is that Rose?'

'You'd better go in. We'll eat in about twenty minutes.'

In the dusk it was hard at first to make anyone out in the big room. Rose felt she was being watched and shook herself crossly. 'Gerald. How are you?'

'Little sister. Come here. Have a drink.'

The wheelchair was beside the drinks table. The man she bent to kiss was old, and drunk; this she perceived before she saw. 'Gerald. You're sitting in the dark.'

'Oh, can't have that. Illumination!' He reached unsteadily and clicked on a lamp, knocking over glasses. 'Here is illumination for the dark corners of our souls: the clear-eyed one is here. Presto!'

While nervously she said something about the journey, Peter, Sheila, she didn't know what, she could not but stare, wanting not to see. The body huge now, shapeless under the knee-rug, hands tremulous, face sagged, eyes sunk.

'The wreck of the young master, eh?' he cried triumphantly. 'You can't fool me. Have a drink. Pour me a drink. Sit down – here – and offer solace, gaiety, bring news of the great world of events. Sing for your supper, little Rose. How is your friend Beth?'

'She's doing very well.' Rose gave herself a sherry, and poured a little more whisky into Gerald's glass.

'More, more. For Christ's sake don't listen to these women, give me a proper drink. One has to have some pleasure, Jesus. Here, give it here.' He slopped in more. 'I asked about your friend Beth.'

'She's doing very well with Liz Conway — '

'Beth, I said.'

'That's the name of her firm. The beauty products, the health holidays — '

'Yes, yes, yes, I remember. So what's she doing?' Drink in hand, he leaned back calm, the old charm re-emerging, the face lifting, losing years. 'Tell me all. Amuse me.'

'Er. The business is flourishing, it appears. She's starting in Europe soon. There was an item in the *Sunday Times* a few weeks ago.'

'Good, good. And?'

'I don't know about the twins, she hasn't mentioned them lately. But you know we only write every year or so. She may be coming to England next year to see about opening branches here.'

'Ah. Ah.'

'But it's not certain. You can never tell with Beth.'

'No, indeed. She laughed, you know.'

'Laughed? When?'

'When she rode off, for God's sake. When she killed the baby. "This is fun," she called over her shoulder. Good old Beth. Unpredictable, full of fun.'

'Yes, she was always doing the unexpected. But I haven't seen her, you know, for twenty years. She may have changed. We all do, don't we?' She was clutching her glass so rigidly it was impossible to lift it. What had gone so wrong? If Peter were here . . .

'No we don't,' he said harshly. 'You don't change. I don't. It's not in some of us to change.'

At a loss, Rose could think of nothing to say, and Gerald had gone into his own preoccupations as old men do. The grandfather clock in the hall tapped time impartially away with the slow inexorable measure of country clocks.

Caroline came in and picked up her glass. She was as it were encased in an invisible protective bubble: the atmosphere did not touch her. 'Ten minutes or so,' she said. 'How was the journey, Rose? I heard there were delays near Richmond.'

'Oh, there were, a good quarter of an hour there, and then just outside Totley there was some complication, lots of water board vans. But I never feel in a great rush, coming up here. Time is different once out of the city; we always feel we'll get here eventually so why fuss? It's quite different from driving to work in the mornings; I'm so relieved that's over, it starts you off tired. I'm so glad Peter doesn't have far to go. You know he's got some very good contracts now, all houses nearby; the council is actually putting money into bringing properties up to standard. It amazes us to think that when we moved there it was all due to come down, but that's one benefit of government cuts, there isn't the money to flatten a whole neighbourhood and start anew, it's more a policy of — '

Through the nervous gush Gerald said loudly, 'Ten minutes, did you say? Time for a pee.' He swung his chair round, facing Rose knee to knee. She was frozen.

'Could you move your chair, Rose?' Caroline asked.

'Oh! Oh I'm sorry, yes of course.' Some of the sherry spilled.

'Jacko knew when to get out of the way. But he's gone, of course,' Gerald muttered as he swung past her, across the rugs and down the ramp.

'Who's Jacko?'

'That was Gerald's compan — '

'My pet monkey!' he shouted back. 'The jester.'

Rose looked helplessly at Caroline.

'He stayed on, when the others went. The hippies. Ben and Amy were here.'

'Oh yes.' Gerald's pet hippy. 'Does he miss him very much?'

'I'm afraid so.' Caroline bent to pat the young spaniel which had been released into the room. 'I don't, though.'

Again there was nothing to say, though many questions surged.

Dinner, however, was easier. There was affection between them. Caroline, impartial as a nurse, cut his meat and placed fork and spoon to his hands, wiped up spills neutrally with kitchen paper, took no account of food that juddered down Gerald's waistcoat, ate well herself. The talk was of barley prices, local point-to-points, radio programmes, the new tractor driver. Taking little wine, Gerald seemed to become sober. They sat on round the table with coffee.

'And what are your plans, now you come to a change of life with the offspring fled? Take in students? Have more parties with your delightful friends? Delightful friends they have,' he said to his wife. 'It's a pity you haven't been there. Such enterprise and originality, compared with our dull lives.'

'Oh, this is anything but dull! It's the most lovely place on earth. To me,' Rose added stupidly.

'You feel at home here?'

'Oh yes, right from the beginning.'

'We like it, don't we, darling? Too large for us, of course. It needs grandchildren.'

There was no edge to his voice, so Rose was able to laugh and say, 'Caroline a grandmother? Impossible!' – meaning that she looked far too young – and realising, yes, it was.

But Caroline smiled slightly and said, 'If you'll excuse me, I must ring through before it gets too late.'

'She has another mare due to foal.'

'That must be wonderful to see.'

'Breeding is fascinating, seeing a good blood line develop. And so Ben has started his course. Has he arranged his farm experience yet?'

Puzzled, Rose said, 'He's reading medicine.'

'No no. He always intended to farm. Agricultural college.'

'Not Ben. Amy, perhaps? She loves animals. Is it Amy you're thinking of?'

'One of them.' She could only conclude some passing enthusiasm had been spoken of once when they were staying here. 'And you? You still keep up your study of the farming journals?'

She laughed uncertainly. 'Only when I'm here.'

'That's rather half-hearted, isn't it?' He smiled, teasing. 'And Peter, does he keep abreast of the latest developments? Never one to do anything by halves, my little brother.'

She was grateful that he acknowledged Peter as his brother, knowing the truth as he had done. 'He doesn't have much time for general reading. He works long hours.'

'Tell me again what he's doing.'

She described the conversions. 'It's upsetting, sometimes, to cut houses about, dividing rooms, spoiling the character. It would be much more satisfying simply to restore them. But there's such a need for flats — '

'Peter developing an interest in the past, well well. At one time he couldn't get away from it fast enough. I tried, once.

As you know. That wasn't a success either. She's in good health, you say?'

'As far as I know.'

'You must be very excited at the prospect of meeting again.'

'It can't fail to be interesting.'

'Such a loyal friend, all these years.'

'I like to keep in touch . . . Gerald, I hope you've never thought that I defend what she did. Hurting you so badly . . .'

From leaning over the table he thrust his body back, head back, lips pursed as though exaggeratedly judicious, considering a nice point of law. 'Hmmm.' From the same position he suddenly swerved his eyes to her. 'Hmmm.' She felt on trial, for more offences than her own. 'I wonder.' Almost with contempt he withdrew his attention and absently tore up the remains of a bread roll. 'It's about par for the course.'

'Sorry?'

'A golfing term, I believe. Typical, expected, average, representative, what you like.'

'Er – what is?'

'Betrayal, of course,' he said impatiently, suddenly bored. 'Oh, come and have a drink.' He wheeled away from the table.

Quickly Rose followed to help him manoeuvre through the doors.

'I can manage, for Christ's sake; I've been managing all this time, don't fuss. Come through.'

'I mustn't be late. Sheila goes to bed quite early and I don't want to disturb her — '

'Stay. Sheila can manage. Ha! Yes, we're both good managers. We've had to be. Here, Glendfiddich. Sit down. Surely you can spare an hour for the cripple?'

Caroline came in. 'She's having some trouble. They've sent for the vet, but I'd like to go over. You'll excuse me, Rose? Gerald, is there anything you need?'

'Good question. Short answer, yes. But I'm not likely to get it.'

Of this she took no notice; it had evidently been said before. 'I'll say goodnight, then, in case she has a long struggle.'

'I hope all goes well,' Rose called after her, wishing with all her heart that she would stay, or that Peter were here.

'Well now, Rose, tell me all about it.'

'About what?'

Whatever had been in his mind – again the slanted inquisitorial gaze – he changed it. 'Oh, anything. How do you find Sheila?'

'Very happy, I think. Pleased with the cottage. And it was about time she had less to do with the farm — '

'Yes, she went too. Par for the course. Oh, the farm. I was always in charge of that, still am, never fear. Make no mistake about that. She didn't care for Jacko.'

'Was he a good friend? You must miss him.'

'Friend?' He sounded incredulous. 'Oh Rose, Rose, how little you've learned. I thought it was country folk who were naïve. It suited him to stay. Until it didn't suit him, and then he went. That is what happens. He amused me. He had a fascinating life, Rose. Many fascinating lives. I've never come across such an inventive liar. It amused me to see if he'd run out of lies, but he didn't. A true professional.'

She was going to try to draw him out, seeing the nearest to real pleasure in his expression, but he cut across her. 'Worth his keep, for honesty. For being an honest liar. I found that so refreshing, by comparison. He was the only one who stayed. I gave them land, freedom, that's what they're supposed to want, isn't it? She would have enjoyed it when she came back, amongst her own kind.' He turned on Rose with hate. 'And now you tell me she's changed too? A business woman? You expect me to believe that?'

Bewildered, she stammered, 'Beth? You mean Beth? But it was years ago, Gerald, in the sixties, that she was involved with — '

'Heigho.' He sang 'Heigho, the wind and the rain,' and became reflective. He smiled at her with warmth. 'You think I'm mad.'

'No, Gerald. I often get the past mixed up and — '

'She won't come back. She wouldn't be interested in damaged goods. I bet her standards of – what do you call it? – production control? I bet her goods are meticulously inspected. Wild yes, careless no. That's why – I'm speaking in confidence here' – he leaned towards her – 'that's why I'm surprised the plan didn't work. Tell me, confidentially, aren't you? Just between the two of us, let us be honest together.'

'What plan, Gerald? I don't understand.'

'Oh, for God's sake.' He swivelled the chair savagely around. 'Don't treat me like a cretin for Christ's sake. To get the land, of course, the plan to get the land. Don't insult what intelligence I have left. It took me a long time to work it out but I did. I'm not altogether stupid. You were all in it.'

'In what? In *what*?'

He chuckled. 'It's like Jacko again, I can't help admiring . . . Oh dear, Rose, you've disappointed me. I did expect a modicum of honesty from you. Especially when you were so open earlier on, saying you've always wanted Stoners Court, getting the next generation trained up to take over. I thought: at last! Here's one of them prepared to admit it at last.'

'You're frightening me, Gerald. I don't know what this is.'

Patiently he explained, as to a stubborn and rather favoured pupil who really knows but is feigning denseness. 'That Beth would take me off so you and Peter could have Stoners Court. Sheila wanted it too. After all, he's more her son than I am. But, Rose, I have to warn you, for all your loyalty to your friend Beth, she is not to be trusted. That's what spoiled the whole thing in the first place. *Or*' – again the confidential whisper – '*or* perhaps you knew she'd leave me, but banked on me following her, keeping out of the way. Now tell me, just for curiosity's sake, tell me which it was? The rest is clear enough, but I've never been sure about that part.'

Rose found herself very angry. 'This is total nonsense. I hadn't even met Peter when you and Beth went to America. I didn't know she was going, I didn't know you, I didn't know Stoners Court existed. You must stop this fantasy before it does any more harm. Harm to *you*, Gerald.'

'Ah.' Slowly he rested back as if a certainty he would have preferred to do without had been confirmed. 'Hmmm.' Slowly he drank off half a tumbler of whisky and poured more, hand rock steady. 'I was afraid of that.'

'I have to go now. Will you be all right? Is there anything I can do?'

'Oh, sit down, don't be so fidgetty. You promised to entertain me. Tell me a story – yes, take over from Jacko, tell me another story!'

She was uneasy now about leaving him alone. His speech was slurring, he did not seem in command of the upper half of his body for all his deliberation. What if he were to fall out of the chair? Oh Lord, let Caroline not be long.

He lolled, all but asleep.

Gently she said, 'I wish you'd believe me, Gerald. No one has ever wanted to harm you.'

'No one has ever wanted me,' he said carefully. 'Listen, listen. This is the key. Are you listening? Sheila knows. She's the only one. But she left me too. They all do. My pare – parents went away. Then there was her. I called her Mother but I didn't mean it. But she knows how it is. He did it to her. You think she took it all in her stride but she didn't: she nearly died. Where was I? They didn't come back. But she was always there and I started to call her Mother. She liked that. We were very happy. And then she did the same, betrayed me, she took in that baby. That was the first time I knew no one wanted me. Are you listening? You're clever, you'll understand. I didn't. That's why it took me so long to work it all out. But it's clear now. Jacko helped me to see. But then. Then . . .' He seemed to fall into sleep; but he was falling forwards, she dared not just creep away. It was cold now, the fire was dying. Very quietly she lifted another log, set it on with care, and crouched down to watch as the grey surface ash was shifted to release the red heat beneath to kindle new wood.

The hiss and sparkle grew, the old clock sounded as wearily enduring as she felt. Then she was aware of change. But alarm was misplaced. Tears were streaming down Gerald's cheeks. She kneeled beside him.

'I didn't deserve this, did I?' His wrecked body.

'No, Gerald. It isn't fair. It was a cruel accident.'

'Accident. Not planned.'

'You must get some sleep now.'

'I'm going, I'm going. Listen . . .' She waited. He summoned strength. 'Listen. If this is all . . .' Bleakness defied the burning logs. 'Wait. Yes.' With deliberation he turned to her and spoke very clearly. 'I didn't ask for this.'

'No, Gerald.'

'*Listen*!' A snarling shout from tight lips; then the quiet. 'You can tell the others if you choose. I want it to be plainly understood: when I have power – and I do have power – then by Christ I use it. In control! Have you understood?'

'I think so –' But he was already off, across the room, down the ramp into his solitary den across the hall.

Trembling, she listened to the distant flush of the lavatory; crept closer to wait for the heavy fall into bed, the immediate snores. She drew up the fireguard, poked down the logs, turned off the lights, and let herself out.

It was late afternoon when she got back and Peter was waiting for her. He came out to the car and put both arms around her. 'Safe journey?'

'Do you know, I've no recollection of it. I was so busy thinking.'

'How are things up there? Is she happy with the cottage? What sort of job did Mathers make of it?'

'Well. Good enough. But there are all sorts of little things you'd want to change.'

He wanted details, of every window that stuck, where the plastering by the fireplace was rough, of the back door that wasn't the right type for the age of the building. She knew he was seething at not having been able to do this one important job for Sheila, his thanks. But he cut off the feeling as they came in.

She told him about Gerald.

'Is he dangerous?' There with the two women . . .

'Only to himself.'

'We haven't been much help, have we?'

'We have no power to change anything.'

'Not there, no.'

'Though you ought to go up soon.'

'I will.'

'People find their own ways.'

He looked at her. 'Have you found yours?'

'Not certainly. I'm making comparisons. I'm becoming less cluttered.'

'Yes, I know. I know what you mean.'

Now there was no rush, no need to force issues.

In bed he held her so tight it hurt; next morning she laughed over her bruises like an amazed young bride.

And younger women than she had been widowed because of the Falklands war. Of what account was her little fretting 'self' compared with that? Let it wait its natural turn.

X

Then Followed That
Beautiful Season

1984

June 1984

To: Liz Conway
Hilton Hotel
Amsterdam
Meet you 3:45 on 19th love Rose.

They knew each other at once, but it was Liz Conway who
came through the barrier at the station, with more traces of
Beth in the quirk of eyebrows and the buccaneer grin. 'Rose!
You look so English! So cosy! Promise me you'll never never
go on a Liz Conway course and lose it all, right? You are just
precisely the same. Have you got it all, seven pieces?' She
snapped her fingers at the porter – she had got a porter – who
seemed quite unperturbed at such treatment. Not every day
would he have dealings with a traveller like this, so totally of a
piece, with clothes and furbishments so *clean* that another
word needed inventing for the condition, so much more was it
than a simple absence of dirt. She gleamed. 'Are we going for
a cab, or — ?'
    'The car's in the yard. Golly, I hope it'll all go in.'
    'Jeez, it's fresher than London. Amsterdam was so breezy,
London just steamed. It used not to reek of diesel, did it? And
where have all the Londoners gone?'
    'Over here, the Escort. Look, if it won't all go in I can come
back for the rest, it's not far — '
    'We'll get a cab for the stuff. They won't hijack it, will
they?'
    'Certainly not,' promised Rose with pride. Did New York
drivers hijack luggage? 'It'll be perfectly safe.' To the
Yorkshire-Pakistani driver she said, 'Follow us if you can, but
if we get separated it's 194 Park Terrace.'
    'Do you have any summer at *all*?'
    Leeds was letting Rose down. But she could not forbear to
point out: 'Look at the buildings, they're all white or grey or
red now, aren't they? Not black any more. And some of the
dark satanic mills are museums.'

277

'Great. Rose, you look well. Contented living, right? You look as if not one single bad thing has happened to you in twenty years.'

Negotiating traffic, Rose said warmly, 'You look marvellous.' Which was true and not true. Beth looked as if a great deal had happened to her which had taken a lot of effort and money to stop from showing. She glowed, shone, was a living example of the benefits of the Liz Conway regime, lean and whippy with clear eyes and bright hair that had not heard of the law of gravity, so vigorously did it lift and enframe; teeth as even – and many – as a film star's; she seemed to have emerged like Venus complete, but from no sea-shell; rather, from a glossy gift package bearing the proud label '1980's Woman, American Brand'.

She was a charming guest, admiring the house – 'So old!' – while Rose described their dilemma. Should they, now that so much needed re-doing, and now that there was money to do it decently, should they go back to fundamentals and do a genuine job of restoration? Even if that meant looking critically at all their possessions, to be sure they harmonised? Or was that merely to create a living museum? They had little taste for that. But the house had some small importance in its own right. But then, they did yearn for space around them . . .

But she did not want to be a bore. To Beth, home was where she stayed between activities, no more. She found all this enchantingly studenty. 'All these postcard reproductions! We all used to have them, didn't we?' They covered the chimney breast in the kitchen, the study, the back of the hall.

'They just accumulated.' As had some rather nice prints she had bought from time to time, stuck up with Blu-Tack.

'Well, it's charming. I'm just so used to everything being done for effect, you know? It's refreshing to come to where no one gives that a single thought.'

Studenty? The pictures should be framed.

They had the house to themselves for the afternoon, and made tea. 'Amy might look in, she often does. But she doesn't approve of us.' Beth laughed. 'Or our food. She's a vegetarian.'

'Wise girl. There's one who doesn't need my book, huh?'

'Oh dear. Are you?'

'I take a little white meat, or fish. I'm not fanatic.'

Fortunately there was to be tarragon chicken for dinner. 'Now, tell me all, tell me, tell me, tell me *all*.'

In fact Rose spent most of the time listening, and there was much to hear, of travels, negotiations, the New York apartment and the cabin in Vermont and co-designing the Liz Conway Movement Collection and launching the European end in association with a hotel chain. 'People don't want just to lie on beaches any more, right? They work hard, so they want to rest up but also to go back feeling good and ready.'

'No wonder it's such a success. It's so simple.'

'All the best ideas are. I have the ideas – it must be the British in me! – and my partner has the organisational genius to implement them. That's Richard Dengerman, he used to be on keyboard in Black Tulip, way back.'

'Are you, er – ?'

'He's gay. Find me a man that isn't. For friendship, give me gay men.'

'Have you no women friends over there?'

Rose was cuddled in a corner of the big sofa, Beth cross-legged on the floor, straight-backed and perfectly relaxed. 'I guess not, not any more. Colleagues, sure, I employ women when I can. Hey, I'm avid to see Ailsa! You say she's much the same? Is it this God-awful climate acts as a preservative or what? But if you're asking about my sex-life, the person I see is Paul Milasky, Senator Paul Milasky. But nobody sleeps around any more.'

'How do you find the time to be involved with politics still?'

'Apart from fund-raising, I don't. But I shall try to get to one or two conventions this fall.'

'Neither Mondale nor Jackson looks likely from here, but I suppose we can't tell.'

'Paul,' said Beth with the smallest tilt of her head, 'is a Republican. We'll walk it, you can tell everybody. The Democrats are a spent force.'

Beth a Republican!

'OK, you can look like that. I've not forgotten the demos, the protests. But that's all been taken care of. I guess you're still nibbling at it here, right? Positive discrimination and all that stuff? Sure, I have black employees, they have to be good, that's all. But listen, welfare doesn't help; they're better off on welfare than working, the dumbos, white and black. It's no kindness. If they want to work they'll make it, if not, not. So don't let's waste time on stuff we worked through and moved on from.' Very slowly she circled her head on the long fleshless neck, smiling.

After a pause, Rose said, 'But isn't it strange, Beth, how much has altered? Never could we have imagined how it would all turn out.'

'No regrets,' Beth commanded. 'That's debilitating. That's what holds this country behind, too much looking back. Why be surprised by the present? It's here.'

'Yes . . . But don't you ever grieve over something lost? Hope? Young people don't seem to have it any more. They're harder. Oh, it was all vague and formless and didn't stand up to the test, but there was love in the air, wasn't there? Not hate. Merry! You can't have forgotten Merry! Do you know something amazing? Ben wrote, and, do you know what? There's a Mister Merry Society at the university! There are lots, apparently, all over, and they have conventions and they all wear curly wigs and dungarees with patches, and they sing his songs and look at his old programmes.'

'Yes, he was *muy simpatico*. A figure of those times. No wonder he didn't survive: he couldn't adapt. That's the name of the game, kid, adaptation.'

'But to think of the students still loving him! And all the money goes to children's charities.'

'That's not natural, kids being into nostalgia. They should be looking forward.'

'Perhaps they're scared.'

'Sure, who isn't? So what do you do? Give up, or go on?'

'You've adapted, Beth. You're completely a figure of these times. I bet your very skeleton is different.'

'I guess that's pretty much the same. But I did have my boobs done.'

'Ouch. Didn't it hurt?'

'That's not important.'

Rose giggled. 'Perhaps I should.'

'You just leave yourself alone, you hear me? You don't have to change. And I don't know why they had to go cleaning up all those buildings; I liked them grimy, I don't want England messed about.' Although she laughed, it was a child's indignation: leave it all as I remembered it.

'What would you like to do tomorrow?'

She got up lithely and stretched, a body without age, but harder than youth. 'You know what I'd like? Not to have to make one single decision. Right now I'd like to go for a run, just ten minutes, and then freshen up a little. I dreaded you wouldn't have a shower.'

'I'll get on with dinner, then.' Rose picked up the tea-tray. 'Oh, Beth, you haven't told me about the twins. Do they travel with you? I hope you've brought some photographs.'

Beth paused at the bottom of the stairs. 'Jacob's dead. An OD last year. Martha's planning to go into social work.' Her voice stayed level while the tray shuddered in Rose's hands. 'I'll be an hour, right?'

Jacob would have been fifteen.

Peter came in early, rather pleased. 'I've another place to do for the housing association. Another three or four months' work.'

'That's super. Unless you wanted a change?'

This was not the time to discuss long-term plans, though. They still went on in lurches, waiting.

A variety of electrical sounds accompanied Beth's freshening process: buzz, whine, hum, purr. Rose changed into her Laura Ashley dress, combed her hair, put on lipstick and pearl earrings. 'Understatement for you, my girl.' Cosy indeed. She consulted Peter as to the accuracy of this description and was not displeased with the response.

The sun hospitably came out to warm the kitchen and the food smelled good. Beth entered in what could only be called a leisure garment, top and pants all in one with soft drapes that fell as gracefully as only very expensive fabrics do, a creamy apricot, immaculate.

'So this is Peter! My, you have a look of Gerald. How are you? How is he?'

They told her he was not mobile. 'That's tough. And all from that one little fall? He wasn't a fighter – but that's tough. I hope he's got a good country wife to take care of him.'

There were gifts to be presented. For Rose, a 'robe' kimono style, brilliant flowers on black. For Peter a shiny box which he was afraid would contain after-shave; but it held a beautifully carved miniature totem pole. 'They do them in

Navajo. Rose said you liked working with wood. For the kids I was lost – I mean, are they anarchists or yuppies or what?' She had settled for sweat shirts declaring 'I Love Big Apple'.

'They'll love them. They're all lovely, Beth. You're very kind.'

Beth declined sherry and Peter offered to slip out for one of those ready-mixed cocktails. 'We should have, thought — '

'No, I'm fine.' She set beside her place a small container with some twenty or thirty pills in different shapes and colours, very pretty. 'Vitamins. I have them sent from Chicago.'

'But how on earth do you know what to take?'

'That comes after a thorough analysis.' She told them about it. And all this time Rose had supposed that if one ate decent food . . .

Peter thought that Beth did indeed look marvellous – but doubted if it was natural to look that healthy. You didn't see Masai *warriors* going around looking *that* healthy, even . . .

'Champagne!' Sainsbury's pink, recommended by the *Sunday Times*. 'Welcome, Beth.'

But she put a finger over her glass. 'I don't, thanks. If you've some orange juice? And every good thing, to you both.'

'We have another small celebration, as well as your being here. Peter's got another contract.'

He told her about it.

'But this is all wrong,' was Beth's verdict. 'At your age, still to be hustling for another quarter's work? You should have it made by now. Then, I guess you are British, amateur to the last.'

'Small is beautiful,' put in Rose loyally.

'Small is not beautiful, small is *small*. You should be aiming at . . . give me a minute to think. Just a little breast meat, Rose. Listen. I'll give you a job. We've all but finalised the purchase of our first centre in England. A country hotel in Buckinghamshire. Do it for me.'

'Do what?'

'It'll need total conversion – without losing character, we respect character. Bathrooms, kitchens, they'll need ripping out and starting fresh. Then, exercise halls, jacuzzis, saunas, beauty salons, indoor and outdoor games areas. The landscaping will need specialists. Say yes, you have yourself a *real* contract.'

'What makes you think I could handle a job on that scale? It would be more a matter of organising than actually getting stuck in and doing it.'

'Sure. You want to carry a hod the rest of your days? Grab yourself a hard hat and a clipboard. We have our own architects; what we don't have over here is anyone reliable to oversee the work and make sure we're not ripped off at every turn.'

He said, 'Would you pass the potatoes? Beth, you may be right: I'm too small to tackle it.'

She laughed, with a trace of impatience. 'Think twice. Money is good to have. I'm talking big money, and more to come as we grow.'

'Yes, we should talk it over. Thank you, we'll talk it over tonight.'

'You do that thing. Rose should have her say.'

The door bell rang. 'Amy. She'll have lost her key. I'll go.'

'You talk to him,' Beth advised Rose, who was still stunned. 'Chances! Don't pass them up. Do you want to live like this for ever?' Rose had never imagined a different style. 'There are more things in life.'

'We rather like it.'

'So, stay small. It's your life.'

Perhaps they were unimaginative, had not seen wider horizons, had settled without a fight for more-of-the-same . . . It registered that there were two male voices in the hall, Peter's loud with surprise, and the other familiar and yet not. Impossible!

'You're not going to believe this,' Peter announced. 'Come on in.'

And it was Jethro – and wasn't. It was another American. 'I *don't* believe it!' He was at once still gangly yet self-possessed, as if at some point he had come to terms: 'Yep, I'm clumsy. That's the way I am,' and stopped apologising for it. Neatly shorn hair, tweed jacket but nothing to do with country living, light coloured slacks, awkward hands and a large gold watch glinting beneath blue cuffs. Just as she thought, No, it can't be him, he hasn't broken anything yet, he tripped over Beth's soft leather bag. 'Jethro! Of all coincidences!'

'Rose, hi! You've not changed in the least degree! I guessed you'd still be here.'

'This is astonishing. The very day that – Beth, this is our old friend Jethro, who was here at the very beginning. I wrote to you about him, do you remember? He went to live quite near you at one time. My friend Beth. Liz Conway, I mean.'

'How are you?'

'I'm happy to meet you.'

'Sit down, sit down. The champagne's almost gone but there's food. White wine? A beer?'

'Orange juice, if you have it.' Jethro grabbed the chair before it fell right over and sat by Beth. 'Well, well, well. I knew I could rely on you two not to have moved on.'

'There have been one or two improvements. After all, it's been — '

'Sixty-four I went out in – no, sixty-three.'

'And are you back on holiday, or . . . ?'

'Maybe. Maybe. For now, I just decided to take a sabbatical, shake the pieces around and see how they fell out.'

He had been doing well in Silicon Valley, developing computerised speech, until his partner sold all Jethro's innovations to a rival company. 'And then came the scare about pollution in the water. Annamae upped and went with the kids.'

'You have children?'

'Annamae's, two boys two girls. We married four years back, but I guess the relationship wasn't enduring. There were inter-personal conflicts.'

So homeless Jethro had once more turned up at the house. They gave him food and camomile tea, left by Amy, and listened as he and Beth compared the courses of their lives and gave their views on the sad decline of Britain since they left; and wondered as Beth ceased to snap her fingers, and softened inside her soft clothes. Almost they expected him to take her to bed. But both declared themselves ready to retire soon after ten, after pitying glances at Peter's small cigar.

They put Jethro in Ben's room.

An early-morning jog was arranged. 'Seven? Right.'

The idle English settled for a chat.

'I'm gob-struck.'

'That's the only word for it.'

'Of all things! Coming right now!'

'Shouldn't we talk about Beth's suggestion?'

'I suppose so.'

'Well?'

'What do you think?'

'I think we ought to consider it. Don't you?'

'Definitely. Come and give me a cuddle. Smashing meal.'

'I'm glad someone enjoyed it. It wasn't exactly crawling with cholesterol, was it? Oh dear. Parmesan on the courgettes.'

'Butter on the potatoes.'

'Chicken cooked in olive oil.'

'That's good for you. Look at all those healthy Italians.'

'But was it virgin? I didn't check.'

'To think my digestive system has been in your careless hands all these years.'

'I bet our arteries are like the M62 on a Monday morning.'

'I feel fit enough.'

'Fit enough to become a dynamic young executive? You could have a personalised document case.'

'Honestly, Rose, can you see it? Where do you buy jacuzzis, anyway?'

'We could live in a caravan, on site. That would be fun. You could have one of those yellow hats. Helmets. Safety things.'

'Why didn't she ask you? Equality. You're a good organiser.'

'My jumble sale for Save the Children is still talked of at the church hall.'

The front door sounded. Amy. Quiet footsteps: she was in placatory mood. 'I saw your bedroom curtains weren't drawn or I wouldn't have bothered you. Have you got fifty pence for the gas meter? I've got five tens. Have you been having new potatoes?'

'Take the leftovers. Fifty pence in my purse.'

'Has your friend gone to bed? Posh luggage.'

'Yes. Another friend turned up too, from the olden days. He's gone to bed as well.'

'Poor old wrinklies. I was going to the disco at the Union, but I got landed with baby-sitting again. It's all right, Keith's staying till I get back.'

'That's more your child than hers. Wicked girl.'

'That may be truer than you know. I shouldn't be surprised if she pisses off – sorry, goes – any day now. She's got a new bloke.'

'Oh Amy, be careful.'

'I know what I'm doing, Mum. Shall I come and let you show me off tomorrow? I'll find a skirt somewhere – yes, and wash my hair. Though this magenta's quite subdued, don't you think? Have you any milk to spare?'

'Take a pint, and bring the bottle back. Clean. And then goodnight-sweet-dreams, we've something to talk over.'

They didn't, though. They washed up, and Peter went into more detail about the new conversion, and at the end Rose said, 'You don't even want to consider it, do you? Do you think she didn't mean it?'

'It was impulsive, to say the least. No doubt that's how they make decisions. Why not? No, the truth is, I can't believe she's real. If that world does exist, it's so apart from ours that — '

'You can't imagine functioning in it. I know. But we mustn't dismiss it. I'm serious, Peter.'

She could not bear that they should go on just the same for ever.

Yorkshire did Rose proud by providing a perfect morning, clear and soft with the promise of heat. While Peter was having breakfast there came the light patter of steps downstairs, the front door opened and shut, and from the front window could be seen the two guests jogging easily down the path and along the tree-lined avenues of the park. 'Their legs are so brown!' Each wore very short shorts.

Disconsolate, she went back to the kitchen. 'Brown bodies are better to look at, aren't they? I'll have to join a keep-fit class.'

'Do no such thing, I like you fat and lethargic. No, don't hit me. You're cuddly to hold and warm in winter and you've energy to spare. Stop that nonsense.'

Sniff sniff.

When he'd gone and the joggers hadn't returned she pottered into the back garden and pulled out a few groundsel and felt the lettuce for heart and gave the runner beans a good drink. Better put the kettle on: a cup of tea would surely be acceptable, even if scrambled eggs and bacon were *verboten*.

But no. 'Not before noon, thanks. I have my own lemon juice, if I could have a glass of hot water?' And, 'Not Indian. Do you have any more of the tisane?' They sipped standing up, Beth unarguably glowing rather than sweating, Jethro manfully beaded on forehead and upper lip, breathing slowly. It was almost a relief – from perfection – when he sat on the edge of the table (did he always have such strong legs? One wouldn't have imagined it) and knocked over a cup.

'It's all in the shoulders,' Beth diagnosed, 'the occasional lack of co-ordination. You're free enough in continuous movement, but there's subversive tension at work somewhere. I'll find it. Lie down and I'll give you a massage and find where the knot is. Upstairs, dumbo. We don't want to be in Rose's way.'

Rose found this and that to do until she realised she was waiting around below stairs for the important people to make their wishes known. She ought to make a foray and see if any of the local shops had any goats' cheese or Quark. Buy fish to replace the lamb marinating for dinner. She called up, between the grunts and 'Aaaaaah's!' (agony or ecstasy?) 'Back in ten minutes.'

Alma was in the fishmonger's. 'Honest to God, our Gary. He'll be the death of me; half past two he comes in this morning and due in court by ten; I told him sleep in if you want but when they put you away for not turning up I'll be first in the queue to cheer, stupid little bugger, and then he's got the nerve to say lend us a couple of quid for a taxi, Mam, I'm late. I said you can bleeding run like all them students, sweat off some of the bevvy, idle young sod, and then he gave us a smacking great kiss and says bake us a cake with a file in it, Mam. What can you do? So I just popped up to get a bit of fish for Terry's dinner, he likes fish fingers but I don't trust frozen stuff, and then I'm off down the court. They won't get round to him till this afternoon, I'll bet. I've sometimes wondered if that's what did for our Gary, all them chemicals; I know for a fact he never ate anything for his school dinners but beefburgers day in day out. But when all's said and done it's only for non-payment; they're not going to put him inside for that, are they? If they knew what a cow that little madam is they'd be paying him compensation for being such a mug. You've only to look at the baby to see she's the dead spit of Wayne Marshall; trust our Gary to get lumbered, *and* he thinks the world of her, little Donna. Her mam half lives at our house already, and expects maintenance on top. So how's your glamorous friend? Like something out of *Dallas*, isn't she? You're never giving her haddock, are you? I'd have thought a nice fillet of plaice. Still, you know your own business. See you at the pub Friday?'

Beth and Jethro were enjoying a special high fibre cereal that one of them had brought, and discussing the texture and weight of the stools produced by other brands. Rose made herself some excellent coffee and concentrated on relishing every tingle of caffeine. 'What would you like to do today?' If they wanted to go to a sports centre or Turkish bath she would spend the afternoon sitting on the back steps with V. S. Pritchett.

But no. Against all the odds, nostalgia was in.

'What was that park you took me to once, with the lake and ducks and all, and the rose garden and the Elizabethan mansion? I'm wild for antiques. Why not let's stroll and talk and — '

Jethro became very manly and self-effacing. 'You won't want me around, I guess. I'll just — '

'Ah, come on, you've some reminiscing to do too, right? Either that or you can just stroll on alongside and listen to the hen talk. Come on, come on, come on, let's *go!*'

It was a pleasure Rose had looked forward to, recalling this or that meeting or event that had been so important at the time. But she had not imagined it would be so exhausting. And this was not because she was talking much. She was called upon to listen, endorse, concur, correct, as both of them used her as an excuse to talk about themselves. By teatime (they had no lunch but apples) she felt like the wall of a squash court upon which an exceptionally vigorous game had been played out.

Reeling, home again, she made herself a pot of tea while mercifully, Beth retired to meditate, and Jethro went to do his breathing exercises. If she had had the strength she would have gone and bought a Mars bar. This remorseless energy was killing her.

Television saved the day. Beth, in another exquisite suit, this time the shade of periwinkle blended with cream, was in high delight. 'Oh, British television! It's so wonderful after all the crap we have.'

'I'm sorry we haven't a video or we could have shown you something really good. *Nicholas Nickleby*, for example, that was — '

'I saw that on Broadway!' they exclaimed simultaneously.

Thus came Rose's first clear conviction that there genuinely was a lot to be said for having money. She determined to have a serious word with Peter before it was too late.

The guests were well satisfied with an evening of situation comedy, the repeat of a play, and a discussion programme. The hosts, who could rarely watch for more than an hour without falling asleep, went to bed early, and Rose's intentions were lost in love-making. They were not surprised to be half-woken later by a rhythmic pounding from upstairs. They snorted, giggled, turned and slept, relieved of responsibility.

Next morning there was no sound from above till after nine. No early morning exercise, unless of the horizontal variety. Then a burst of flushing water, spray of shower, and Jethro singing 'American Pie', eventually crashing the door against the kitchen wall, to announce a necessary call at the bank and a car-hire firm. 'See you around, huh?'

'Well yes, quite possibly.'

Then Beth came in. Hair in a towelling turban, no make-up, in pyjamas. 'Rose, quick, give me a hug. I've hardly seen you. Is there any tea? Rose, the craziest thing: I want that man.' She looked at once younger, because defenceless, and older, for the same reason; altogether more likeable. 'This is nice. You know, I was so afraid we wouldn't like each other any more.'

'You, afraid? Good grief, I never met anyone more – *adequate*, equal to any — '

'You've got this whole earth mother bit – no, don't laugh. You're rock solid, you and Peter both. It's daunting.'

'We've been very lucky, we are lucky, good health, the children well, despite – oh God, Beth. I'm sorry.'

Beth gazed at her brown lean hands for a long time, attending to something inside with all care. Did her voice really become more English as she spoke? 'I knew it was here I'd have to face it. I've never cried. I know it happened but it's as though Jacob never was. It was a case history. Months of therapy I had, before and during and after: it all only existed in the presence of counsellors. Not my son, just another young addict; not me, just the classic single-parent-working-mother, all held at a distance by jargon. I needed that. That's why I dreaded seeing you, being back in England, able to see it whole. For what? Where's the profit in breaking down?'

Was she asking, or denying? 'Beth, we don't have to talk about it.'

'What happened I can tell you. Pot, OK, it's everywhere. But cocaine, no. That was one reason for moving east. Huh. I had money, we were ripe for a new start. Good school, expensive; even so I had to pull strings to get them in. Never believe class distinction is an English vice. I've seen more of it over there . . .

'All I blame myself for is naïveté – me! On visits, it all seemed just fine. Jacob was happy, had friends from excellent backgrounds – so call me a snob. I wanted that for them. Life's tough; if you can get influence, don't knock it. Martha was more worrying. She got in with some Bible-study group. Now her friends I did find scary; how can you embrace Christianity and make love so narrow? It was disapproval that gave them their kicks. After an hour of that it was a holiday to be with Jacob's crowd, they actually had fun! Once or twice I wondered if it was a bit frenetic. Easily dismissed: the contrast with Martha's crowd, or my being there. You know, when I'd done TV and stuff, maybe they showed off a little . . .

'All that set were shooting heroin. Jacob was the one that got unlucky.'

She drank some cooling tea but didn't like it. It didn't do to break carefully devised customs. She had too nearly weakened. She stood up.

'I'll tell you why I haven't cried and why I won't now. I've cut a nerve, Rose. And I'll tell you one last thing: I'm glad What good would it do to destroy myself as well?'

Rose had to ask, 'Why did you leave Gerald?'

Beth sat again. 'Over twenty years ago. Still, I can tell you he terrified me.'

'He idolised you! He still does, you know.'

'Yes? More fool him, what's past is past. So maybe it was being made into an idol that was scary. He wanted to possess me. Not only sex though, wow, I liked that fine. I've had plenty since, but for uninhibited passion there's been no one to come near that stiff-backed English country gent. Positively bacchanalian. Generations of repression bursting out? Great at first, I couldn't believe my luck. Hell, I was only twenty or so. I was bowled over.'

'When did it begin to go wrong?'

'When there were more people around than just us. Jealousy is what goes with that kind of love. He began to hurt me. He threatened to kill me. And he didn't like it over there.'

'Whose idea was it to go?'

'I don't know. We both . . . I guess I must have talked about wanting to – we all did, didn't we? And he . . . Yep. I remember. He has some thing about feeling imprisoned, didn't want to have to take on the weight of the past. New starts, all that – Hah!' She gave a sudden laugh. 'I just remembered. New blood, he said I was, good vigorous *peasant* blood! Carmen, he called me.' As suddenly, she shuddered. 'Something vampirish about it, don't you think? He wanted to feed off me. I couldn't take that.'

'He's – rather unbalanced now.'

'Crazy? It doesn't surprise me. How come Peter's so different?'

It wasn't worth going into. 'They're different people, that's all.'

An hour later Liz Conway was back. The meeting of minds would not occur. Amiably enough they patted small memories back and forth: 'Odorono! Friday night is Amami night! How could it take a whole evening to wash our hair? Lipstick in two shades, medium or dark . . . *Britannia and Eve*! What a title for a magazine, how could it ever have failed?'

'We were war babies. Products of change and instability.'

'So how come we're not bundles of neuroses?'

'Perhaps we are and don't know it.'

'*We* had the bomb.'

'And the cold war. And ration books.'

'Listen and I'll tell you another thing. It isn't to do with us, what the kids are. People make their own luck.' This led to more on welfare spending, and Jethro came in. Oh dear. Now the brief romance would end in exchanges of 'fascist' and 'woolly-minded liberal.'

But Jethro was ardent in support of Reagan.

He sipped rose-hip tea and Beth tenderly suggested he get lost for another half hour. 'We girls have talking to do.'

'Till noon, OK?'

'It's all fixed, then?'

'All fixed and raring to go. I'll have a look over the house, Rose, all right? After all, I was in on the pioneering days.'

'How could we forget?'

He could be heard going about the place, stumbling over stairs and creaking the boards where surely no creaks were normally to be known. More was recalled, about early loves and disappointments, each other's parents, about Ailsa and how they had all envied her, so beautiful and serene. Rose wanted to know about her young self. 'Was I always going to be – this?'

'You always sold yourself short.'

All that was important had been said. When Jethro, on the dot, returned, it was almost a relief. The encounter had taken up its allotted space in time, which turned out not to be long.

'I fixed that door-catch for you in the top back, Rose. It shuts now.'

'Well, thank you, Jethro. But we don't expect you to do odd jobs on your holiday.'

'Think nothing of it. I've got a stake in the place, after all.'

Was he thinking of staying indefinitely?

But that was not on the cards. That very afternoon he and Beth were driving down to Buckinghamshire to see the hotel. 'I could tell Peter wasn't interested,' Beth said, 'and rightly so. It wouldn't have been his scene. You hang on to what you've got here. But this man is just perfect. Organisational experience, practical ability, concern with historic buildings – and whole-hearted about the Liz Conway concept. And since I have only tomorrow free, it has to be now.'

'Oh, what about Ailsa? She's due back tonight.'

'There'll be other times, right? I'll be over often now the European end is taking off. Give her my best. Rose, it's been great.'

Promises were made of future visits; but it was over. It was Liz Conway who drove away in the hired estate car, augmented by a curiously confident Jethro. It was he who drove.

He had fixed the door all right: it wouldn't open at all now.

Ailsa, back from retreat, was not upset about missing Beth. 'There'll be other times. How was she?'

'I think,' said Rose thoughtfully, 'you'd have been sorry for her. But then you feel sorry for us too, don't you? Not having whatever it is you've got.'

'It's there, Rose. You'll find it when you're ready.'

Trying to work it out, as the kitchen filled with the scent of lamb, Rose used Peter as a sounding board. 'They're both calm. And controlled. They don't get into muddles. Not much bothers Ailsa any more. But the difference! Beth *works* at it. Oh, that's admirable. I'm a slob by comparison. But Ailsa . . . there's no striving. It's a calm that comes from some source she's tapped into. An eternal spring. No – ah, this is it – no *self* getting in the way all the time. I think she finds herself – everyone – mildly amusing, in a detached sort of way. As if human life is a prolonged childhood; but she knows that maturing is as inevitable as dusk or dawn. All the trying is commendable, but irrelevant . . .' Thoughtfully she studied the pattern of core and seeds inside a red pepper.

'Just as well she's got me to mend dripping taps and blown fuses, then.' Peter was shaken to realise the extent of his disappointment about the job Beth had offered and withdrawn. He would like to have had the choice.

When Amy came round he escaped to the pub.

'Sorry I didn't put in an appearance this morning, Mum. We were awake half the night with the baby. Have they gone? Had enough of slumming it? I can smell lamb. Is there any left?'

'Lamb is meat.'

'That's all right, it doesn't do to be inflexible. You should be pleased, you were always telling me that. Now you can say "I told you so "'

'Amy, I'd like a quiet couple of hours and that doesn't include a sparring match. You don't live here any more and I can do without being used as a punch bag when you do come.

Is this a social call or is there anything special?' She must have learned a few tricks from Beth's dynamism.

Amy sat down at the table. 'The social worker came to see Zena today. You know, the one with the baby. They want to take her into care, they say Zena can't cope. And it's true – but it is not to be endured, to think of her in a home, not belonging to *anyone*. Mum, I've said that I'll help, sort of co-parent, like the way elephant calves have aunties. But she wasn't over-impressed with me either. Typical bureaucrat. Since when has the colour of anybody's hair been a criterion for moral fitness? God knows how many babies are battered behind net curtains.'

'Yes, yes — '

'So, well. I had to say that you would, sort of, offer support. You're ideal – middle-aged, former school-teacher, property-owner – it went down very well. Just in a supervisory capacity, you wouldn't be expected to wash nappies, not actually to *do* anything.'

'I'm not sure I understand.'

Eagerly – this truly mattered to her – Amy enlarged. 'Just being around. Like if Zena had a proper mother. Well, they might want to insist you saw her every day. There'll be all sorts keeping tabs on us, health visitor, social worker . . . She said it would be different if there was a grandmother nearby, but Zena hasn't got one, she pissed off, sorry, went, years ago, and her Dad's got another woman and anyway they're in Liverpool . . . Actually I said we were cousins, so they'd think we were family . . .' Her voice tailed away. She looked young and painfully anxious. 'It doesn't sound very convincing, does it? Why should they believe I could help, and why should you get dragged in? Forget it, it's no concern of yours.'

Instead of, 'But we were thinking of moving away,' Rose said, 'Shush, love. Put the kettle on and let's try to see what might be done.'

Subdued, Amy made the tea and nibbled on the cold meat. There was one flare-up. 'Oh, and I didn't tell you it's black. Half-caste. Some grandchild, eh?'

'Will you stop talking so silly,' Rose sighed, 'and try to convince me you're even halfway suitable to take this on. And don't call it "it".'

Tears seeped through the black eye make-up. 'I daren'

love her too much if they're going to take it away. Zena's the same. She pretends not to care but I've seen her looking at her, sort of hopeless. She knows she can't cope on her own.'

Stupid, stupid girl. Hadn't they heard about the pill?

'She's called Cara, that's Italian for "dear". Oh, Mum, she's so tiny and perfect, creamy brown and curls already! She's a good little baby, she smiles if you do anything for her. We've got a sterilising unit for the bottles, and social services let you have a washing machine sometimes, because I don't think those disposable nappies are good for them — '

'And where's the father?'

'Oh, around. You mustn't think Zena's promiscuous, well, not now. No' – Amy's face went proud with respectability – 'He wanted to marry her.'

'Then why on earth — '

A cloud of shame. 'Mum, it's unbelievable. She said she couldn't marry a black man. Can you beat that? Good enough to screw – sorry, sleep with – but not to marry. Stupid little snob.'

Rose had to laugh, which was always dangerous with Amy. 'Oh, dear, oh dear. It would be hilarious if it wasn't so sad.'

'I know. And when you think of us two loony punks sterilising teats and examining dirty nappies!' She gave a shriek of laughter not far removed from pain. 'The poor little bastard has no chance. What about rashes? How would we know if it was serious? And temperatures? Dr Spock says one thing . . . Last night we were in floods. Cara was screaming and we were hunting through the books and she wouldn't stop, it was awful.'

'Colic, perhaps. If it's three months' colic you're in for some bad evenings . . .'

'Mum. Will you?'

'Never mind me. Amy, love, you're talking of twenty years of *your* lives. Why wouldn't adoption be best? Two loving parents, a safe home — '

'It's Zena's baby. She loves her.'

All you need is love? Sentimental attachment to a pretty doll? Or the sacrifice of youth and freedom to the inexorable demands of another life? Rose sighed again.

But the decision had been made.

'She consulted me from the start, you know,' Amy said proudly. 'We agreed that abortion is murder.'

So Amy was a person others went to for advice. 'That's all very fine and I'm sure it made you both feel noble,' Rose said with deliberate harshness, 'but now you've let her be born, the child is all that matters. What kind of life is she going to have? What is the father going to do to help?'

'He comes and sees her, he brought her a dear little dress, an angel-top. But he can't do much financially, he's on the dole because he has a full-time training programme for his weight-lifting; he could be an international champion, he's totally dedicated — '

'Oh, *stuff* his weight-training!' Amy was shocked. 'He's spawned a tiny human being – can't he take on the burden of that? What kind of man . . .' Rose sat down and tried to compose herself. 'At the very least he could do a bit of navvying or coal-heaving to provide for her. The dole indeed. The dole didn't conceive her.'

Patiently, and not patronising, Amy pointed out, 'It isn't easy to get work, you know. And in any case, it isn't Cara's fault.'

'No.' No, it wasn't. 'So let's get to practicalities. How can you contemplate bringing up a child in that dreadful house?'

'They'll give her a council flat. Zena only refused before because she didn't want to be on her own.'

'Right. Now, you. On the dole for ever? How long before you're desperate to live your own life? Sooner or later you're going to want an occupation, a place of your own, a man of your own. Far worse to abandon Cara and Zena when they've come to depend on you.'

'We've thought about that,' the girl said eagerly. 'With furniture and stuff, we'd have definite mine-and-yours, in case one of us wanted to move on. We'd get one of those Dyno things and put our names on so there'd be no arguing. And we're going to get work, even if it's only alternate nights in a pub. Job-sharing, you know. And go back to college, either taking turns or finding one with a crêche; we're not thick, we've worked it all out.'

'You've more sense than I thought. But I never even heard you speak of Zena before.'

'I didn't know her particularly, she was just around the house. I like her now, though, she's got guts. And – ' Amy looked down. 'I want to do something worthwhile. I've been pretty useless so far, haven't I? All the suffering there is, and I can't do much about any of it till I get money, or a training. But Cara's *here*.'

She looked like a little match-girl, going down the path, street fashion emulating the poor of other times: uneven long dark skirt, drab coat, socks wrinkling over little low black boots designed to look worn-down, designed with the uppers almost to the hard ground, soon really to let in the cold and the rain. In other times saints used to sleep on cold stone in order to identify with those who suffered.

Peter was very angry. 'These stupid girls! How far has equality got them? When it was up to the man to take precautions you didn't get all these illegitimate babies. And now, with the pill – look at them! It's enough to make you wonder if they're capable of taking responsibility.'

'They have to, all the same. They're not off weight-training, they're wiping up the sick.'

He could see Rose's age burdened, just when they were free to decide for themselves. They had waited too long; and now it was too late.

Later, as they sat without lamps in the gentle dusk, a rose in a vase shedding silently first one petal, then minutes later another, she told him that his mother might be alive. There was now legislation enabling adopted children to contact natural parents. 'Do you want that?'

A cluster of red petals fluttered down as he considered. In their early days it had been a bitter thrust with him, to find out one day who she had been, this woman – but then he had thought she had died at his birth; now he knew she had chosen to leave him. Now . . . some old woman, marked by who knew what experiences without him . . . There could be no re-cognition. They would not know each other.

He said slowly. 'I suppose you saw those photographs that Sheila keeps.'

'Yes.'

'Well then. If she knew, all this time, and still wanted me . . : No. I don't want to know the other one.'

Irrelevantly, perhaps, she was glad that she had not let it be known at Stoners Court that Beth was in the country. Too much knowing was not always for the good.

In September Rose was cutting hydrangeas in the front garden, the door ajar in case Cara cried. The girls were at college, sorting out which courses to register for – supposedly. But the old evasiveness was back in Amy: more likely she was rattling a plastic bucket in the shopping centre, crying for donations for the miners' hardship fund. They had seen her once, and been both touched and deeply annoyed. Next time she was round, Peter said, 'Don't get into issues you don't fully understand. And how do you know where the money is really going?'

As of old she flared up, attack the best form of defence. 'These are people fighting for their communities!'

They spoke together. 'They didn't have the chance to vote, Amy.'

It hurt terribly to be on the other side.

'They're being used. And so are you.'

It was like betrayal to pass the rattling buckets.

'Rose?'

At the gate was a strange young man, with a very smart pram. He was slightly plump, with a neat haircut and nice casual clothes hanging not quite comfortably. 'Yes? Good gracious – Adrian!'

'Just airing the daughter and heir.' He blushed, visibly, the beard being no more.

'Let me see!' Beneath a pretty pink quilt was a big ugly baby, unmistakably her father's daughter. 'How old is she? Where are you living now? How is Elsa?'

'Oh, er. Elsa and I split up, you know, nearly two years ago. Mutual consent. Well, you knew how it was. She's doing well, very well, she's an adviser now, for special education. She's developed a special interest in gifted children.'

'So?'

'Amanda.' He blushed again. Was there a whiff of after-shave? 'We met last year, at the Stop-the-Runway meeting. She has a house not far from the airport. And, er, we . . .'

'Fell in love. Adrian, I'm glad you're happy.'

He told her all about it, how impressed he was by

Amanda's genuine independence as a self-made insurance agent, own house, own car, holidays in Greece. 'But you can always tell, can't you, Rose, when someone is lonely, deep down? She's not physically little, about my build actually, but vulnerable, you know?' So, naturally, events had taken their course. 'But all above board. We wanted it that way. I took it hard, Rose, Elsa going for good.' She could imagine it. 'But it is wonderful, how it all works out for the best. Priscilla, for example. Amanda couldn't believe it, when she was on the way. And it can be quite dangerous, you know, a first baby at thirty-eight.' He was serious in his recollected concern. How he must have sat by weeping bedsides, bringing little drinks, being a tower of encouragement. 'But of course we think the world of her.' He glowed shyly at the pouchy cheeks and flat little nose. 'She's very advanced for her age.'

'And are you still at Maybrook?'

'I'm a house-husband. Yes, it's worked out wonderfully well. Amanda earns more than I ever could, so it was logical . . . It suits us ideally.'

'Your wife sounds a remarkable woman.'

'Oh, she is, she is. You'd get along like a house on fire, I'm sure, though we don't do a lot of socialising. The odd cheese and wine, you know.'

'So what brings you all the way down here?'

'To tell the truth, I walk down now and again, just for a wander, old times' sake. It takes an hour or so. More going back, because of the hill. Of course, Amanda needs the car, for her work.' That would explain the diminution of Adrian, in part. 'You get a bit fed up, walking round the same old streets. And it's very quiet up there, during the day.'

Cara began to whimper. 'Look, I have to go in now. Would you like a cup of tea? Slice of Dundee cake?'

A twinge of yearning crossed his kind puzzled face. 'I'd love to, but it's time I was getting back. Sometimes she's delayed, you can imagine how it is with clients, and then we eat later. I've got a microwave so it can be ready in minutes. But usually it's about four on a Wednesday, so — '

'Call in next time you're round, Adrian.'

The dear good man. Perhaps there were more of them about than might be thought.

A week later Amy arrived with her belongings. 'Can I stay for a bit?'

'What happened?'

Zena had a new man, who wanted to look after Cara. 'It's all right, we've known him for ages, he's a friend of Randy's actually, the father, and he kept saying he was really pissed off – fed up – with Randy for dodging his responsibilities; it's against all his principles. He's a Rasta you see, and he feels very strongly about children; you can tell principles mean a lot to him because he absolutely refuses to take social security.'

'What does he live on?'

'He's a very gifted artist, he sells quite a lot of pictures and — '

'And?'

'Oh, you don't understand. People get by.'

Better not ask.

'So Zena is happy, is she?'

'Oh, she is. She's not the type to make her own life. And you must admit it's better for Cara to have a black father or there'll be all that role confusion later, cultural identity. We talked it all out.'

So the decision was ideologically sound as well. But Amy was deeply hurt. She began courses in Art and Economics and Creative Writing, but her heart was not in it.

'Another set of chances blown,' raged Peter. 'She's bloody lucky to live in a country that sets it all up for her again and again, and all she can do is rant about restrictions and deprivation — '

'She doesn't do that much any more.'

But if they had tried to anticipate the next scenario, never would they have visualised a key prop in the form of the magazine called the *Lady*.

Coming across a copy by the telephone, Rose shrieked. 'I don't believe it!'

But it led to escape; possibly to Amy's destiny. She got a job through its small advertisements, a residential job at a refuge for retired horses and mistreated donkeys in the depths of Shropshire.

'It's what I've been searching for all this time. You don't need to worry about me any more.'

They drove her down in pouring rain, having trouble finding the place. 'Mother Harvard's? Straight down the lane till you get to the T junction, then go right and it's half a mile beyond the pig farm.'

'Please God,' prayed Rose, 'let the pig farmer be single, and lonely. And very kind. Preferably not hard up.'

They were silent on the way back, each knowing why. As the city lights appeared above the rise of the motorway, Peter said 'It's time we started looking, Rose.'

'Yes. Yes, we must.'

The house was too big now.

The trouble was they didn't know what they were looking for, except that it must have some land. Without much hope, with considerable apprehension, they leafed through estate agents' handouts. 'I'm sure we'll see a place sooner or later that simply calls out to us,' said Rose bravely.

They had been bowled over by the possible price the house might fetch. 'Of course it's not everybody's cup of tea,' the agent said, 'you might have to come down a bit if it doesn't shift. But plenty of families need a granny flat now the old dears are hanging on so long. Or of course a speculator, it would convert nicely into flats. No? Well, we'll have to hope for someone a bit off-beat. An American professor with a long contract, that's the kind of buyer you could do with. Er, don't mention about windscreen wipers getting bent. Mortgage paid off, is it? You'll be in for a tidy bit. I'll send you the info on Pateley Bridge, some lovely new developments out that way. You won't be wanting anywhere big, family all gone. Thought of a bungalow?'

After he had gone they avoided discussion.

And next came news of Gerald's death.

Sheila was washed smooth, unnaturally still, all marks of age gone from her face. 'He said to me "Let it stop", and so I did.'

Rose left tea beside her and signalled to Peter to come away.

Caroline, busy with arrangements, told briefly how it had come about. 'I was at Hexham, a committee meeting for the hunt ball. I stayed the night with the Whittakers. Sheila came over to spend the evening with Gerald. He didn't usually drink much when she was there. But he was agitated, so she gave him his sleeping pills, and then went to bed. He must have started drinking after that, and the combination – ' The telephone summoned her. Polite as a school-girl, she could be heard saying, 'Thank you, Belinda. Yes, on Thursday at two. I hope you'll both be able to come back here afterwards?'

'Can I see to dinner?' asked Rose. 'Or, will you need to make up beds, if anyone's staying overnight?'

'Emmy's seen to all that, thank you. You can give me a hand to pack up, if you like, after the funeral.'

'Surely you don't have to leave at once?' This was horrifying.

'I want to. I'm going to my uncle's. Then I'm with the horses. Peter, could you have a word with Andrew, the farm manager? At the Gate House. Explain that as far as we know there'll be no changes for a while.'

There was nothing for Rose to do. Presumably Caroline was going to sell. What would become of Sheila? To her she went again, feeling useless when she wanted to offer strength.

Sheila was just as they had left her. 'I must have fallen asleep,' she said, 'and wasted that good pot of tea.'

'Shall I make some more?'

'Would you pour me a whisky? There's some left, of that malt you brought me.' A year ago. 'I do feel astonishingly tired.'

'Of course you do. It's a shock. Everything's being seen to, you mustn't worry.'

Sheila wasn't worried. Although drained, she was at peace. She sipped, gazing into the fire, and took more, and some colour came back into her. 'He had come across an item in *The Times*. It excited him dreadfully. About the girl he had married – your friend.'

'What did it say?' He would never forgive her, for not telling him Beth was here. No: he could never forgive her, now.

'Her business, that it was expanding into England. He showed me the photograph. A very glamorous woman. Not at all Rose's type of person, I thought. Of course, I never met her. It was a long time ago. But his wasn't the kind of temperament that easily forgets. When important losses come so early, it's not easy, probably, to let go.'

You did, thought Rose. Or at least you managed not to let loss damage you. But she kept silent, because she was out of her depth, and at the same time afraid she knew more than she should.

'He had hoped for so long.' That Beth would return to him? Surely not. 'And when you told him, last year, that she might be coming, and then in the paper it reported that she had been and gone . . .'

'He didn't say he wanted to see her, did he?' Oh, if he had, if she'd have known it meant so much, perhaps she could have arranged . . . But Beth would do only what she chose to do.

'No one is suggesting it's your fault, my dear. And what good could it have done? She was, presumably, somewhat altered. He wanted to lay a ghost, I suppose. But I don't believe it would have cleared his mind. It would have been far too late. It was the fall that did the damage.'

'Oh, yes,' Rose agreed sadly. 'She was much changed.' And added, with a little more confidence, 'What did Caroline think about it?'

'Caroline,' said Sheila with a return of briskness, 'knew the terms. They had been engaged before Gerald went away, and when he came back she took him back. She doesn't suffer from illusions and she doesn't hope for the impossible. She has kept herself intact. When the sorrow comes, she'll know she could have done no more than she did.'

Intact. That was exactly the case.

'He could endure no more of living,' Sheila said plainly. 'It was a terrible thing to see his agony of body – he hid this when you were here; he had great pain – and then of mind. He would have hurt himself more if he could. Like a two-year-old, like he was at two, the temper tantrums, devastated by a fury he didn't understand and couldn't control. Never blame him,' she repeated fiercely, 'never.'

'How could I?'

'He wanted to be stopped. I nursed him to sleep. He was utterly exhausted.'

She had, of course, done it deliberately, the tablets and the drink together.

After a long time, during which Sheila seemed to sleep again, and then began to pull her usual self together, Rose asked – it had become the most urgent question: 'What kept you going, all these years?'

Sheila gave a little exhaling laugh, as one might say, 'What a silly question.'

'Anger.'

Anger? Against – the war? her unfaithful husband? childlessness?

But at once Sheila got up, stiffly. 'Or it may have been mere training. I'm no intellectual, Rose dear. If it matters, you must work it out for yourself. The main thing now is to keep going. Just a little longer.'

Peter felt inadequate. The farm manager, only there since Lady Day, wanted to know where he stood. 'All the plans to develop plantations on the higher ground – what's going to happen about that? The arable's been taken as far as it can go, there's nothing left that can be drained or ploughed. It's been taken too far, if you want my opinion. Prosperous, yes – I saw the harvest in – but there'll be a backlash very soon over the EEC reserves. And he's been piling on the nitrogen year after year, to judge by the records, the ones he let me see. It'll leave your land weakened. Credit where it's due, he saw it for himself, that's why he appointed me. I'm a woodsman. But it promised to be a battle royal as to what we put in, him all for your soft woods, cash crops, well and good up to a point if you don't mind ruining your landscape. Broad leaf takes longer, and of course him having no heir . . . He liked a battle, mind, but I don't see how I can do my job with only half the reins in my hands. And now what?'

'I'm not in a position to say.'

With marginally disguised contempt, the man said finally, 'Well, whoever's taking over's going to have a lot of serious thinking to do. The wife hasn't settled here. I might do well to start looking around.'

'We'll let you know as soon as — ' But the door was closed.

Peter walked, without noticing where, and found himself at the top of the track where he had always gone, the highest point near to the house. There had been a dead oak into which he had climbed. It had gone, of course. He looked round. He knew the land, the hollows and swells, despite the less-featured space between tidy fencing, the hedges gone.

The shape remained, as a skull does without the flesh. Ploughing was well advanced, acres of steady brown ribbing the stubble, singed in patches. The scattered old barns had been pulled down. Industrial-looking silos in the yards, massive concrete sheds for the machinery.

He turned away. By the river, the copse still; on the hills the woods still. The women had saved what they could, out of sight of the low road from which Gerald could survey his power. And the sheep? Thank God, yes.

And he had done nothing; had opted out. Had washed his hands of it, turned his back (the manager's glint had been fleeting but unmistakable) on Sheila who had kept going.

He leaned his arms along the top bar of the gate – metal gate which had been idiosyncratic wood – and let himself be ravaged by tearing sobs of regret.

Rose met him in the yard and saw. She took his arm and they stood with bowed heads, hearing the fantail pigeons, the blackbirds, smelling thyme. 'I'm sorry too.'

'Caroline asked if we would stay in the house tonight, in case there are telephone calls.'

'Yes, of course.' They hadn't unloaded the car yet, even. 'What about Sheila?'

'She wants to be on her own, but she'll come over during the evening.'

'At least we could take some of the business matters off her shoulders.'

'If she wants us to, yes. Where will she go?'

'I don't know.'

They were still letting her down.

In the big kitchen, cooking in unfamiliar pans, Rose said, 'It's important not to be ridiculous about this. There was never any question of our living here.'

'No.'

'And it's for Caroline to decide now. Obviously she'll do what she can for Sheila. As a sitting tenant she couldn't be moved by new owners.' Would she want to stay, with strangers? Impossible to imagine, strangers at Stoners Court . . . 'But I was thinking: we could look for somewhere that had a cottage for her. A house, and a bit of land, and a cottage. It wouldn't be impossible.'

'No. I thought that too. If she'd like that.'

They didn't know. It was one thing to have been there for Pat, a straightforward offer accepted while the need lasted and then shrugged off; no problem. But Pat didn't have deep roots; Pat was adaptable.

They ate in silence, fed the unsettled dogs, lit the fire in the drawing room, waiting for Sheila, and Rose said, 'I'm going in to see Gerald.'

He should have lain in state in the main bedroom, an old man respected, full of well-used years. It was the single bed, the orthopaedic bed, clinical despite the soft covers, laid flat to accommodate him, a young man now, handsome again, the sagging flesh gone in, the closed expression simply of absence. He was forty-eight. He had been young when they were, and had had hopes as they had; had staked much on love.

I'm sorry, Gerald.

Suddenly possessed by a fury that came from outside herself, she went quickly in to Peter, standing by the long window. 'Did you always hate him?'

'I thought he was wonderful. He could do so much that was beyond me. And, yes, hated him as well. He didn't want me here. He always made me aware of that.'

'Because he had lost his parents, he wanted Sheila at least all to himself!'

'Yes, I know.'

The anger went as quickly as it had come. We mustn't quarrel, she thought. We went wrong somewhere and there's no telling how, or how it will be cured. We set out to live differently and it hasn't done much good. Jethro, Renée, Ailsa, they'd have managed without us. Renée hated it, at our house. The others who have come and gone – anywhere would have done as well. We thought we could make a difference, and we haven't. One or two pupils, perhaps . . . And some decent places for people to live. It wasn't a lot to show for years of trying.

'If Sheila doesn't want to come with us, what shall we do?' They had talked of travelling, of seeing the world when the children were grown and they were free. 'Travel? Or do you want a smallholding?'

'I don't know.' He sounded defeated, and anger flinted in

her again. If he was done for, she was not; she would – would – 'No one takes the self-sufficiency bit seriously any more. Too many hopefuls have gone under.'

'What, then?'

Wearily he said, 'Rose, I don't know. Just thank the stars we have the luxury of choice. The house is worth money and I can still earn.'

Choice, the burden of the age. Or were they too feeble to see it as privilege?

The dogs leapt to the door as Sheila came in, and the telephone rang. 'I'll take it.' From the hall her voice, calm, capable. 'Thursday, yes. At St James's, of course.'

She came and sat in the wing chair and they joined her by the fire, prepared to put their proposal gently, to an old lady. Instead, she began at once.

'Now, if possible this should be settled so that Caroline knows exactly where she is – though she has her own life, it won't make so very much difference either way. But so much has been in a hiatus, for a long time. I'd like us to talk it over before the funeral, or, rather, to put it to you so you can discuss it together. Are you at all interested in 'taking over here, or would it be an interference with your plans?'

'Taking over? But we assumed the farm would be sold, since Caroline doesn't mean to stay.'

'No. Stoners Court belongs to me.'

'Not Gerald?'

'I let him understand it was his. In fact, my father bought it when Jeremy and Lucy were killed. The lawyers thought it would be better for young Gerald to have other assets; the farm was not doing well, and by the time he was of age, who knew what the situation might be? My father believed in this land, and also he wanted me to be secure if anything happened to James. The money went into trust for Gerald, so Caroline will be well taken care of financially. My brother never had any interest in farming; he hoped to paint. He had a great talent with water-colour.'

'Your brother?'

'Paul, yes. He was shot down during the Battle of Britain.'

Peter had not stirred, but she became strongly aware of the heat of blood in his arm next to hers. He said quietly, 'Yes.'

'Good,' said Sheila at once, as though the exchange had

been a mere formality, the outcome taken for granted. 'That's settled. We can go on from here.'

She opened her mouth as if to proceed to business, and then her face gave. For once Sheila, no more than they, could command what happened next. As if from her deepest depths broke out a groaning shuddering sigh – before the tears came. Peter knelt instantly before her, and she rested her forehead against his. 'Peter. My son.'

Their arms went around each other, and Rose left them to this homecoming.

It would have been wrong to make plans before the funeral. But next day Peter caught Rose's hand and told her: 'I wasn't right for this place on my own. But with you . . .'

Never had she been given a greater accolade.

Hundreds were at the funeral. Drunkard and recluse he may have been, but Gerald had had a place, was known. And country people are long used to eccentric squires.

Twenty or thirty came back to the house afterwards. Sheila had intended to call in a caterer, but Rose said no, she would like to make the food. She was happy as she worked. Amy and Ben came up and gave a hand with serving, both looking astonishingly tall, and clean, and composed: they looked like young people who have been well brought up.

The occasion was jolly, after the gravity of the church service. People were meeting who did not often see each other and there was much to talk about once respects had been paid. Caroline laughed with horsey friends, busy with reminders of events that she would now be free to attend. Sheila chatted here and there with old acquaintances, and it was not surprising to see she had an admirer who kept close by: Colonel Hall from the next village. 'He's been after her for just about all my life,' Caroline told Rose, who felt a most unfair resentment: Sheila was theirs, must be at the cottage!

It was all very amiable and it was necessary to find supper for the late-stayers. At midnight the family gathered in the kitchen, sighing, relieved. How fine Peter looked in his dark suit, white shirt, loosened black tie. The young master. Well, not quite.

Suddenly Rose gave way to tears. Amy made her a cup of tea, but she did not cry, nor Ben.

'Well, that's over.'

'Will somebody see Sheila back to the cottage?' Rose asked, blowing her nose.

'Mum, people don't need escorts in the country.'

'Colonel Hall will be there, fear not. He's dotty about her, it's sweet.'

'So let the grown-ups look after themselves.'

It did not go unappreciated that the term 'wrinklies' had been superseded. They were nice kids.

What had been said, about Gerald?

In a haze of sleepiness (different from town-tiredness) Rose recollected odd remarks, direct or overheard. 'A good business head . . . No feel for the land, no respecter of tradition . . . Blood will out: remember old Matthew Stead? Great-uncle, he must have been. Hard rider to hounds, broke both his legs, took to the bottle . . . Never the same after that time in America. America! Wrong influence on an impressionable fellow . . . Even as a boy, he was unsettled, not like young Peter, I'd have laid odds on him taking over . . . Always felt he was laughing at us – but it doesn't do to speak ill of the dead.'

She had not heard one single tribute to kindness done.

How dreadful to be dead, having left no memories of kindness. But 'Never blame him!' Sheila had said. No indeed.

The farm manager agreed to stay on till Lady Day. 'That'll give you the winter to think what you're going to do.' Ploughing would continue, and Hugh would see to the sheep. Conifer planting would not go ahead, broad-leaf planting would. It was necessary for Rose and Peter to go back to Leeds for him to come to arrangements with his workmen, finish contracted work, put the house up for sale.

Amy, and Ben, were quiet when this was discussed. So, after breakfast, there was a family conference.

'We haven't consulted you at all, about the move.'

'Fair enough. We've left home anyway, haven't we?'

'Can't expect you to ask permission.'

'It was hardly that. But — '

'It was your home, all your lives, wasn't it?'

Past tense. Rose, in a heart-stop moment of love for their house, knew that Amy was feeling the same.

There wasn't much to be said; the decision had been made. Still, it was a breaking-up more final than when each of them had gone their ways.

'It's all right, old love, don't look so stricken. This has been home too, all the holidays we've spent here. Let's face it, we'd rather think of you up here than tucked away in some geriatric bungalow.'

'Geriatric? Cheek!'

'Only a matter of time. We medics can see deterioration setting in, you know. Look at your hair! Look at Dad's beard! Speckled, already. No, my best prognostication is a mere thirty or forty years of work before you finally have to take to the chimney corner. Better make a start, hadn't you, instead of all this sitting around over second cups of coffee. You don't want to get accustomed to ways you'll never be able to indulge. Roll up the sleeves, old dears, get stuck in. That's what you're good at, isn't it?'

Amy asked quietly how soon they would be leaving Park Terrace. 'I'd like to come one more time.'

'Love, of course! It won't be this side of Christmas, that's for sure. Will it, Peter?'

'Not a chance. Too much to see to. Anyway, it's a bad time of year to be putting a house on the market, it might not go till spring.'

They would have a last Christmas there, then. Ben would bring Rebecca, and Dr Eisner might well join them; perhaps Pat and the Major, Terry and Alma. And Amy had blushed promisingly when the pig-farmer had been casually enquired about earlier.

Ben was driving Amy back. How strange it was to be waving them off from the yard with Sheila, instead of her saying goodbye to them all.

At the last minute Rose ran forward to halt them. 'Amy.' She wound down the window. 'I always remember what you said, about feeding the land, not just the plants.' They smiled at each other. 'That's all.'

'What was that about?'

She told him. 'She's quite right, of course.' They strolled round the corner and along the terrace. The morning was milky with mist. 'I've thought many a time that perhaps that was where we went wrong, somehow. I mean, if you take our pupils as the plants. All that effort to nourish them, treat them as having individual needs, thinking that was the way. And it could only go so far, couldn't it, if the soil was impoverished?'

'Or nourished only with junk food and the tabloids. Well, Rose, this isn't the first time we've seen the limits of what could be done.'

'It's a limited analogy anyway. We couldn't take up this soil, land, and shift it to Maybrook. Plants naturalise, revert to type . . .'

He'd stopped listening. 'Get some wellies, we must go for a walk.'

Solid old black wellies from the assortment at the back door. As Rose stoked the Aga and found a mac, she pursued her train of thought. They had said, in certain conversations, that Gerald had set his monkey on them: more than once he had caused them harm. But they were as much responsible, for silly hopes, misjudgments. And he as much as they had been swung – believing he had strength – on the tides of history, swayed perversely by notions owing something to politics and more to fashion; and it had all come about through passionate love. They had been lucky, he had not.

'Where are we going?'

'Up the hill. Come on.'

He took her hand and towed her, giggling, at a brisk pace. Not for years had he so pulsed with energy, laughing – in fact, not ever. Work on the house had brought laughter many times; but not like this. Before, it had gone against the grain and they had thought this was the natural order, that work was hard, needed effort. Indeed they were right; but this was different. Sweat and aches to come without doubt, but in a more rhythmic time-scale, with limits to what they could enforce. They must learn to pause, and listen.

Nevertheless, when they leaned, panting, against the gate, ideas bubbled up irresistibly.

'We could take people in.'

'Would they come?'

'Certainly they would.' The house had kept its self; people would be happy here.

'And more sheep. There's a French strain — '

'French!'

'Well, it'll need some thought.'

'We could run a snail farm.'

'I'd like to put some of the home fields back to meadow. Not just let it revert, it'd need management — '

'And no more – well, as little as possible – artificial fertiliser.'

'We'd need plenty of muck. I think beef would be best, there's no future in dairying and anyway there's talk of quotas so we wouldn't be eligible.'

'Sheila was disappointed when Gerald let the herd go.'

'There've always been changes, she knew that.'

'I'd like to do more with vegetables. And if we raise young bullocks — '

'With nurse cows — '

'So we'd have naturally grown meat and vegetables – and some free range hens — '

'Foxes. Still, go on.'

'Then as well as being able to offer guests good food, I bet we could build up a clientele among the best hotels and restaurants.'

'The house will need a lot of work.'

'We can do that.'

Nothing that they had learned had been wasted. The mist was very slowly clearing, distant bare trees emerging, and pale intense light coming down and across the valley.

'It will take money.' But they would have that, from the sale of the house.

'I was wondering about converting the old stables. You know, into a couple of cottages for holidays.'

'We'll have no one who would be a nuisance to Mother.'

'City people who want quiet, they're not going to be a nuisance. It would be lovely for the children.' They would have to be able to pay their way, though: only if, later, there was not the pressing need for money for repairs and improvements, then they might be able to offer hospitality to those who could not pay.

'Come on.'

'Now where?'

'Across the fields, to the copse.'

They squelched their way through the wet grass as happy

and careless as children. This was not play-time: Rose was impressed by the extent and clarity of Peter's plans for the farm and his knowledge of the difficulties. It was a joy to hear him talk, and at the same time she let develop some of the possibilities that came to her. Wasn't there an agency that kept records of houses that might be suitable for film locations? Weren't grants available for developing facilities for tourists? What about – in the long term – some of Liz Conway's ideas, holidays with a purpose?

Peter had moved on, in slower vein now as they climbed again towards the little wood. 'In years to come there's one thing I'd like to do. That scheme of my father's – did Sheila ever talk to you about it? To make a collection of old farm equipment, a country museum — '

'Old breeds of animals?'

'Possibly. Though as soon as you think of livestock you're thinking of more labour.'

'Students? City kids? Remember those you used to take out to the dales, that thought there'd be monkeys and lions?'

They let themselves indulge, knowing full well – for they had learned lessons and Peter was a man of business now – that the constraints of history would apply just as much now as when they began.

Work had been started on clearing the copse. Undergrowth had been cut and lay in heaps, side growths pruned out, some rotten trees felled. Young ones that had been making growth unseen now stood clear. As Rose gazed at mist-dewed cobwebs diamonded by the thin penetrating sun, Peter stood very still and closed his eyes, breathing deeply the smell of rotting leaves and cut wood. She turned to call him to see a minute spider like a dancer limbering up – and stopped her voice. He was a man in ecstasy. She smiled and closed her eyes too.

'That's another possibility,' he said on the way back via the thickened river.

'Furniture.'

'How did you know?'

'In the winter months, from our own timber.'

'There is that shed next to the wood store.'

'That could be a workshop, yes.'

'I'd like to make just one piece, that would stay here.'

'Yes.'

It was peace like after love-making. Awed, aware that difficulties were waiting, but strengthened by this affirmation. In the yard they faced each other briefly and nodded once, glad, before Peter went to see the manager – he would come up weekly until they were able to move – and Rose went to Sheila's cottage.

'I was just about to come over, dear. Look. You must have this. My brother painted it just before he was called up.'

It was a water-colour, done from the high point where they had just been. Smaller, irregular fields, hedges running untidily, barns and sheds run-down, hay-stacks, random trees. The weather was sunny.

'We can't put it back,' said Rose.

'Nor should you try to.'

'It was lovely, though.'

'Yes, but those times have gone. You should have it, however.'

'Thank you, Sheila.' She didn't need to say how much it meant.

'Coffee before you go?'

'May I get it? You look tired.'

'I am. It's been a long time.' She did not have to say what.

Rose brought the coffee to the sitting room where there was already a fire, and could not forbear: 'It's rotten, Sheila, oh, it's rotten being on your own all these years!'

'Yes, it was very hard at times. And to see you and Peter together has often reminded me of what I've missed.'

Sex especially? Sheila was still a lovely woman.

'There is a thing else. Very like love. With just as many fears. I'm not a woman for words, you know that. But it is – what one tries to grasp at . . . and cannot.'

No more than one could force happiness. 'But you have to keep on trying? Or being ready?'

'Yes. Even when it hurts. And only when you fail, suddenly it's here. The sweet agony of giving over.' That's what Sheila was at last able to do.

'That's how it's like making love, then.'

'Yes.'

'You'll be all right till we come?'

'Of course.'

She was, seemingly, almost asleep as Rose left. An earned rest.

'I think Amy will come back, don't you?'

'I wouldn't be surprised.'

'Perhaps not Ben.'

'Doctors are needed even in the country.'

Greedy to hope for too much. Meanwhile, there was a lot to be done.

The For Sale board went up almost as soon as they got back.

Alma came round hotfoot. 'Well, I can't say I'm surprised. Your Peter was always a fish out of water round here, though you fitted in all right. But you're more adaptable. Terry'll miss Peter – hey, I'll miss you! Can we come and stay? Get you, châtelaine of a big house; I can just see you with a bunch of keys hanging round your waist and skivvies doing your bidding, Peter in his tweed cap with them red dogs bouncing round him, red setters, quite the squire. Tell you what, I'll get one of them dairy-maid outfits, frilly skirts and a mob-cap, just see myself giving the teat to little lambs, hay-making and that. Terry can be your swine-herd. Well, mend your tractor, any road.'

'Silly devil,' Rose laughed. 'We'll be working as hard as ever.'

'Think I need telling? You're gluttons for it, you two. Then again, I couldn't tear myself away from our little Donna, oh she is a duck. Four months and sitting up already, has our Gary at her beck and call. She recognises me, gives such a chuckle, but Terry she worships. He'll spoil her rotten, which is more than I ever did with our Gary, say what he likes. Then, grandchildren's different, aren't they? You'll find out.'

'It might take a while.' There ought to be children at Stoners Court.

'Course, *she* wants to go back to work, misses the company. I can see me getting landed.' And she would love it.

Beginning the task of packing (what were they giving up?) Rose ignored a brief ring at the door. She had been surprised, when first at home in the day, how many callers there were.

No more the brush salesmen – ah, good patient brush salesmen, modest and giving good value, where were you now? – nor yet so many clean-cut identical young Mormons with their infant-school roll-up maps to show the ignorant how Jesus had found his way to the promised land of America. Still the gypsies from time to time, dark pregnant women with cigarettes burning and grubby fake-fur coats selling packets of needles and plastic clothes pegs. Quite often, well-dressed women in pairs looking like Avon ladies (never yet these, in Park Terrace) radiant in their certainty of salvation, talking contentedly about the end of the world. No more the shambling smelly tramps, old men down on their luck; only the alkies upending huge bottles of cider over in the park.

Whoever came she was disturbed, even while buying needles at dear prices or telling the Witnesses of Jehovah that she was Catholic, or busy. Come again, she cried as she closed them out. God help us when we are free from intrusion. We should always be reminded.

What kind of intrusions would remind them at Stoners Court?

Then at lunchtime, going down with a box of books, she found on the mat a hand-done invitation:

PARTY! PARTY!! PARTY!!!
Bonfire party at Number 202.
All friends and neighbours welcome!
Bring food or a bottle – or just yourselves.
Back garden from 8 onwards. Do come!

Peter said 'Uh, uh. It's been more peaceful round here lately. I hope they're not going in for late-night rave-ups, it isn't fair to the old people.' Rose made gingerbread and grated cheese for baked potatoes. She wanted to go. There had been a skip outside 202 for weeks, evidence of work going on. The yard at the back was being cleared of rubbish and tall weeds – even now from the kitchen window she could see three young men there setting up loudspeakers.

What would it matter to them if there were to be noisy parties? The For Sale board stood brazen in the front garden. There had been enquiries, but only from those who wanted to turn the house back into flats. But they would sell only to a family.

Sometimes it didn't seem real that they were going. What would they take with them? And could anywhere, even Stoners Court, ever be so much their own? There, they would have to bow modestly into a much tinier role in the house's history: there would be greater limits to the marks they could make.

Alma called in. 'Listen, we've been talking, me and Terry. We've been thinking about your house!'

'Honestly?'

'Honest. See, there's our Gary, and her and our little Donna, we're all on top of each other and they could be ages on the council list. And Terry doesn't want her brought up on no council estate. You know you had the top floor like a flat, when Pat was here? Well then!'

'The agent said about fifty thousand pounds,' Rose said tentatively.

'Fifty-two, I know, we rang them up. But we're not short, Terry's doing all right and I've not been as daft as I look with the little bits I've earned. If it comes to a push I could take in lodgers, like you used to do. Then again the size of the rooms . . . we'd have to get used to being perished in winter, compared with ours. But you can get them body-warmers, can't you? And kids ought to be brought up a bit hardy. Fancy our stuff in here! It'll be lost. But Terry always did want somewhere with a bit of history. When I think back to what a dump it was! You've done a lot. Hey, and just think: you could come and stay! Wouldn't that be a laugh? We won't be wanting any favours, mind, it'll be strictly business.'

It was a wonderful relief to know the house would be in good hands – and whose better?

Just after eight, the evening misty and appropriately chill, music started along the back lane and the first flames licked up from the bonfire. A rocket heralded the start. 'Peter, it's begun! Let's go, if only for a while.'

He could not have been so reluctant – he had bought a large box of fireworks..

Already the yard was quite crowded: skeins of slender

Pakistani children, elderly ladies well wrapped up, assorted youngish couples with cans of Special Brew. In charge of the display was a square young man who looked like a rock-climber. 'Hey that's great! Lizzie, here's some more fireworks.'

Lizzie came over from a trestle table on which were set parkin and treacle toffee, sausages and steaming pots of beans and soup. 'Oh, baked potatoes – and gingerbread, super! You're from 194, aren't you? We've seen you in the garden. It's been an inspiration to us, to see what you've made of your place. Isn't it rotten you're going, just as we've come? We decided to have a yard-warming, since the house is still a tip. Tom, this is Rose and Peter, from 194. They've been here yonks, Alec was telling me.' From a dark corner briefly emerged the old hippie to acknowledge his possession of a name.

Lizzie also looked as though she could climb mountains, and this indeed proved to be the case. 'What we'd really have loved,' she confided in an interval between dispensing hot dogs and apple juice, 'would have been a cottage in the Dales, but fat chance. The prices! But we were students here and after three years in London we thought Help! let's get back. A lot of the old mates are still around so we're going to sort of share. I love these old houses, don't you? Plenty of space.'

Alec went to get Ailsa, and Mr Gress followed to ensure that all was done with due decorum. A group of tall black youths hung around inside the gate ignoring their pretty girls. Some of the young men made forays and returned with more and more wood; the fire fell, and blazed up again; Tom kept the show of fireworks going. How lovely it was, all warmed together in the enclosed yard, songs of the sixties giving out their uncomplicated vitality, stars and showers of colour shooting and falling. The crotchety old man from the back came to complain and stayed to enjoy a good grumble with the old ladies, chomping parkin and being smoothed with Guinness. Primitive, it was, an ancient pleasure to watch the glow and flare, to be safe in the dark. Peter ran down to the Taj Mahal Emporium and came back with all the sparklers remaining in the shop and everyone waved the star sprays and inscribed their names in the air.

'Isn't it great?' cried Lizzie. 'Just look – that's what we love about it round here, the mix.'

And they were leaving it all.

'Do you think we could have a big bonfire up there? Would the village people like to come, do you think?' Rose whispered.

'They've managed without us for a fair number of centuries,' Peter said. But he squeezed her hand, understanding. They would think of something good to do.

Assistance was needed with the final display: six giant rockets, to be set off simultaneously. The men clustered giving advice, adjusting this stick and that bucket of earth. 'Stand back!' Excited, they all huddled away, jostling, smiling apologies, waiting – and at last the anxious ignition of blue touch-papers . . .

Up! Up, up, up and over the houses, bursting stars and flowers of gold and green, falling fire-sparks of red, sizzling phuts of silver snowflakes, the sky a regal panorama of momentary glory. 'Magic! Aaah! Oh look! Look!'

And still they watched, where it had been, all of them looking up.

A child asked, 'Is that the end?'

It was over, though the fire still glowed low and hot and many were set to stay, to see it out, too good to waste. Goodbyes were said, thanks, empty paper cups thrown on the embers, music turned down but not too far . . . It was over but not completely.

Peter and Rose went home hand in hand. 'Why did we never think of doing that?' Lizzie planned to make a herb garden; she must have a cutting from the rosemary bush. 'I hope you'll make this a tradition,' she had said wistfully to the girl.

'Oh, we will! We shall be here for ever!'

And they were giving up, turning their backs on the Renées, the mix. Only the trying was to be weighed in on the credit side. Ben was right, they were not going to a life of ease, by no means; and were starting again perhaps with marginally less chance to be effective, since nature operates in longer patterns. Well, this was salutary

Since the decision had been made Rose had been waiting for Peter to ask: 'Is it all right with you?

Would she be able to manage? Would she be sorry, miss the variety, the Taj Mahal open all hours, the neighbourhood? While they did not know the future there were all sorts of possibilities and they were not put to new tests. Now they knew. There was no longer any choice.

What would happen when it *snowed*?

Now she knew that he had not asked because he trusted her, and the love she had had for Stoners Court from the beginning. There was no question to be put.

She smelled smoke on his hair, and in the bedroom they noticed smudged faces and cleaned each other with wet fingertips, smiling, saying what fun it had been. And she had discovered, seeing him in the shadowy yard amongst all the faces, that she was still in love with him, this husband skinny and not very tall who had macheted a way to their front door, his face now lined with labour and anxieties. That steeled her. They had done it once together, they could do it again.

Reluctant to end the evening, they drew back the curtains and looked over the park, hearing shouts of laughter from among the bare trees.

In the garden the For Sale board had been uprooted for someone's bonfire, breaking off the young witch hazel. Now there would be no sweet scent in the house in January.

'But we'll be gone by then.'